Daggerspell

Daggerspell

KATHARINE KERR

GRAFTON BOOKS

A Division of the Collins Publishing Group

LONDON GLASGOW
TORONTO SYDNEY AUCKLAND

Grafton Books
A Division of the Collins Publishing Group
8 Grafton Street, London W1X 3LA

Published by Grafton Books 1987

British Library Cataloguing in Publication Data

Kerr, Katharine
Daggerspell.
I. Title
813'.54[F]   PS3561.E642

ISBN 0-246-13161-6
ISBN 0-246-13168-3 Pbk

Printed in Great Britain by
Billing & Sons Limited, Worcester

For my husband, Howard, who helped me even more than he can know. Without his support and loving loyalty, I never would have finished this book.

Acknowledgments

I owe many thanks to the following friends:

Barbara Jenkins in particular, who gave me a whole career in a box when she gave me my first fantasy role-playing game many Christmases past.

Alice Brahtin, my mother, who gave me moral support, constant encouragement, and best of all, an excellent typewriter.

Elizabeth Pomada, my agent, who took on an admittedly eccentric project and then actually sold it.

Greg Stafford, whose trust in my opinions about his writing helped me trust my opinions about my own.

Conrad Bulos, the fastest typewriter repairman in the West.

And especially, Jon Jacobsen, the best gaming buddy a girl ever had.

A Note on the Pronunciation
of Deverry Words

The language spoken in Deverry is a P-Celtic language. Although closely related to Welsh, Breton, and Cornish, it is by no means identical to any of these actual languages and should never be taken as such.

Vowels are divided by Deverry scribes into two classes: noble and common. Nobles have two pronunciations; commons, one.

A as in *father* when long; a shorter version of the same sound, as in *far,* when short.

O as in *bone* when long; as in *pot* when short.

W as the *oo* in *spook* when long; as in *roof* when short.

Y as the *i* in *machine* when long; as the *e* in *butter* when short.

E as in *pen.*

I as in *pin.*

U as in *pun.*

Vowels are generally long in stressed syllables; short in unstressed. Y is the primary exception to this rule. When it appears as the last letter of a word, it is always long, whether that syllable is stressed or not.

Diphthongs have one consistent pronunciation.

AE as the *a* in *mane.*

AI as in *aisle.*

AU as the *ow* in *how.*

EO as a combination of *eh* and *oh.*

EW as in Welsh, a combination of *eh* and *oo.*

IE as in *pier.*

OE as the *oy* in *boy.*

UI as the North Welsh *wy,* a combination of *oo* and *ee.*

Note that OI is never a diphthong, but is two distinct sounds, as in *carnoic* (KAR-noh-ik).

Consonants are as in English, with these exceptions:

C is always hard as in *cat*.

G is always hard as in *get*.

DD is the voiced *th* as in *thin* or *breathe*, but the voicing is considerably more pronounced than in English. It is opposed to TH, the unvoiced sound as in *the* or *breath*.

R is well and truly rolled.

RH is a voiceless R, approximately pronounced as if it were spelled *hr*.

DW, GW, and TW are single sounds, as in *Gwendolen* and *twit*.

Y is never a consonant.

I before a vowel at the beginning of a word is consonantal, as it is in the plural ending *-ion*.

Doubled consonants are both sounded clearly, unlike in English. Note that DD is considered a single consonant.

Accent is generally on the penultimate syllable, but compound words and place names are often an exception to this rule.

Following is a list of some of the more important names and words in the text, which should help the reader get a feel for the language.

Aberwyn   AHB-ehr-wuhn
Adoryc   a-DOR-yhk
Braedd   brayth (voiced *th)*
Brangwen   BRAHN-gwehn
Cadwallon   cad-WAHL-lon
Cannobaen   CAHN-noh-bayn
Cerrgonney   kairr-GON-nee
Cullyn   KUHL-luhn
Deverry   DEHV-ehr-ree
dweomer   DWEHOH-mer
Eldidd   EHL-dith (voiced *th)*
Gerraent   GAIR-raynt
Gilyan   gihl-LEE-an
Gweran   GWEHR-an
Lovyan   lov-EE-an
Lyssa   LEES-sah

Macyn MAHK-uhn
Maroic MAHR-oh-ihk
Nevyn NEH-vuhn
Rodda ROTH-ah (voiced *th)*
Rhodry HROH-dree
Rhys hrees
Wmmglaedd OOM-glayth (voiced *th;* the second *m* is silent here, an exception to the rule)
Ynydd EE-nuhth (voiced *th)*
Ysgerryn ees-GAIR-ruhn
Ysolla ee-SOHL-lah

A Note on Dating

Year One of the Deverry calender is the founding of the Holy City, approximately 76 C.E.

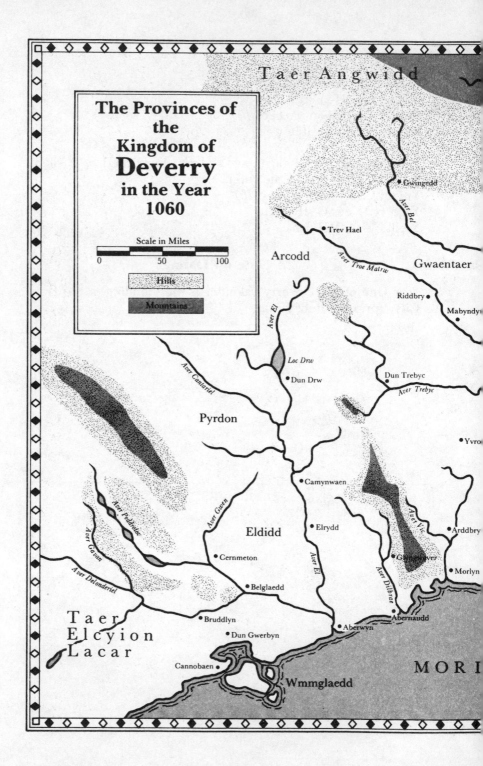

The Provinces of the Kingdom of **Deverry** in the Year **1060**

Scale in Miles

0   50   100

Hills

Mountains

Taer Angwidd

• Gwingedd

Aver Bel

• Trev Hael

Arcodd

Aver Troe Malrw

Gwaentaer

Riddbry •

Mabyndy

Aver El

Aver Cantariel

Loc Drw

• Dun Drw

• Dun Trebyc

Aver Trebyc

Pyrdon

• Yvro

• Camynwaen

Aver Gwen

Eldidd

• Elrydd

Aver Vic

• Arddbry

Aver Peddroloc

Aver Gwaun

• Cernmeton

Aver El

• Gwyngwyver

• Morlyn

Aver Delonderiel

• Belglaedd

Aver Dilbrae

Taer
Elcyion
Lacar

• Bruddlyn

• Dun Gwerbyn

• Aberwyn

Abernaudd

Cannobaen •

MORI

Wmmglaedd

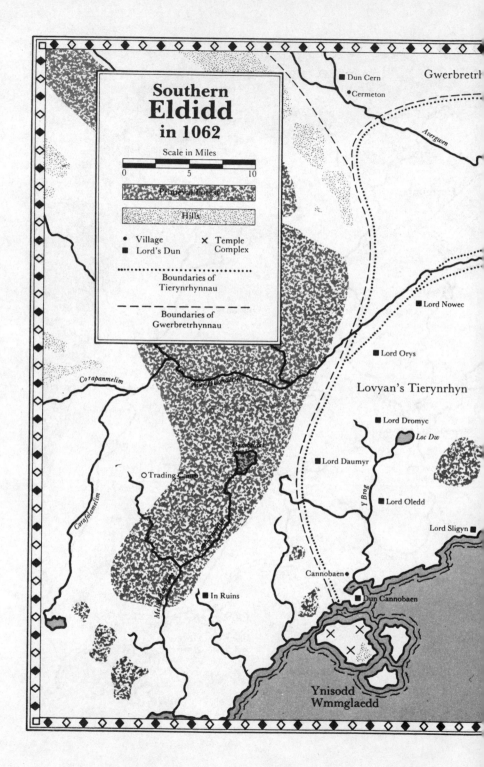

Southern
Eldidd
in 1062

Scale in Miles

0   5   10

Primeval Forest

Hills

- Village
- Lord's Dun
- ✕ Temple Complex

··········· Boundaries of Tierynrhynnau

— — — Boundaries of Gwerbretrhynnau

Dun Cern

Cermeton

Gwerbretrh

Avergwen

Corapanmelim

Avergwlannacht

Lord Nowec

Lord Orys

Lovyan's Tierynrhyn

Lord Dromyc

Loc Dw

Corafolamelim

Barodubal

Lord Daumyr

Y Brog

Lord Oledd

○ Trading Camp

Lord Sligyn

Melimachbil

Cannobaen

■ In Ruins

Dun Cannobaen

✕ ✕
✕

Ynisodd
Wmmglaedd

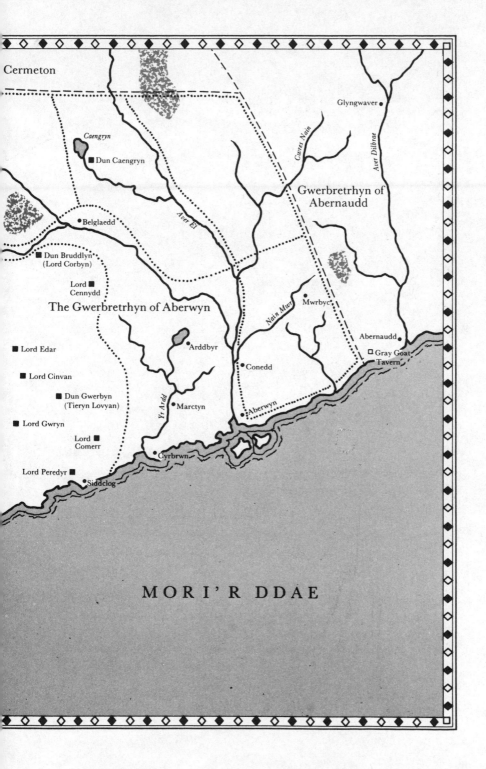

Cermeton

Caengryn

■ Dun Caengryn

Glyngwaver

Canct Nain

Aver Dilbrae

Gwerbretrhyn of
Abernaudd

Aver El

● Belglaedd

■ Dun Bruddlyn
(Lord Corbyn)

Lord ■
Cennydd

The Gwerbretrhyn of Aberwyn

Nain Maen

● Mwrbyc

■ Lord Edar

Arddbyr

Abernaudd

□ Gray Goat
Tavern

■ Lord Cinvan

● Conedd

Yr Ardd

■ Dun Gwerbyn
(Tieryn Lovyan)

● Marctyn

■ Lord Gwryn

Lord ■
Comerr

● Aberwyn

● Cyrbrwn

Lord Peredyr ■

● Siddclog

MORI'R DDAE

Prologue
in the Year 1045

Men see life going from a dark to a darkness. The gods see life as a death. . . .

The Secret Book of Cadwallon the Druid

In the hall of light, they reminded her of her destiny. There, all was light, a pulsing gold like the heart of a candle flame, filling eternity. The speakers were pillars of fire within the fiery light, and their words were sparks. They, the great Lords of Wyrd, had neither faces nor voices, because anything so human had long since been burned away by long dwelling in the halls of light. She had no face or voice either, because she was weak, a little flicker of pale flame. But she heard them speak to her of destiny, her grave task to be done, her long road to ride, her burden that she must lift willingly.

"Many deaths have led you to this turning," they said to her. "It is time to take your Wyrd in your hands. You belong to the dweomer in your very soul. Will you remember?"

In the hall of light, there are no lies.

"I'll try to remember," she said. "I'll do my best to remember the light."

She felt them grow amused in a gentle way.

"You will be helped to remember," they said. "Go now. It is time for you to die and enter the darkness."

When she began to kneel before them, to throw herself down before them, they rushed forward and forbade her. They knew that they were only servants of the one true light, paltry servants compared to the glory they served, the Light that shines beyond all the gods.

When she entered the gray misty land, she wept, longing for

the light. There, all was shifting fog, a thousand spirits and visions, and the speakers were like winds, tossing her with their
words. They wept with her at the bitter fall that she must make
into darkness. These spirits of wind had faces, and she realized
that she too now had a face, because they were all human and far
from the light. When they spoke to her of fleshly things, she
remembered lust, the ecstasy of flesh pressed against flesh.

"But remember the light," they whispered to her. "Cling to
the light and follow the dweomer."

The wind blew her down through the gray mist. All around
her she felt lust, snapping like lightning in a summer storm. All at
once, she remembered summer storms, rain on a fleshly face,
cool dampness in the air, warm fires and the taste of food in her
mouth. The memories netted her like a little bird and pulled her
down and down. She felt him, then, and his lust, a maleness that
once she had loved, felt him close to her, very close, like a fire.
His lust swept her down and down, round and round, like a dead
leaf caught in a tiny whirlpool at a river's edge. Then she remembered rivers, water sparkling under the sun. The light, she told
herself, remember the light you swore to serve. Suddenly she
was terrified: the task was very grave, she was very weak and
human. She wanted to break free and return to the Light, but it
was too late. The eddy of lust swept her round and round until
she felt herself grow heavy, thick, and palpable.

Then there was darkness, warm and gentle, a dreaming wa-
ter-darkness: the soft safe prison of the womb.

In those days, down on the Eldidd coast stretched wild
meadows, crisscrossed by tiny streams, where what farmers
there were pastured their cattle without bothering to lay claim to
the land. The meadows were a good place for an herbman to find
new stock, and old Nevyn went there frequently. He was a
shabby man, with a shock of white hair that always needed combing, and dirty brown clothes that always needed mending, but
there was something about the look in his ice-blue eyes that
commanded respect, even from the noble-born lords. Everyone
who met him remarked on his vigor, too, that even though his
face was as wrinkled as old leather and his hands dark with frog
spots, he strode around like a young prince. He traveled long
miles on horseback with a mule behind him, as he tended the ills

of the various poor folk in Eldidd province. A marvel he is, the farmers all said, a marvel and a half considering he must be near eighty. None knew the true marvel, that he was well over four hundred years old, and the greatest master of the dweomer that the kingdom had ever known.

That particular summer morning, Nevyn was out in the meadows to gather comfrey root, and the glove-finger white flowers danced on the skinny stems as he dug up the plants with a silver spade. The sun was so hot that he sat back on his heels for a bit of a rest and wiped his face on the old rag that passed for a handkerchief. It was then that he saw the omen. Out in the meadow, two larks broke cover with a heartbreaking beauty of song that was a battle cry. Two males swept up, circling and chasing each other. Yet even as they fought, the female who was their prize rose from the grass and flew indifferently away. With a cold clutch of dweomer knowledge, Nevyn knew that soon he would be watching two men fight over a woman that neither could rightfully have.

She had been reborn.

Somewhere in the kingdom, she was a new babe, lying in her exhausted mother's arms. Dimly he saw it in vision: the pretty young mother's face, bathed in sweat from the birth but smiling at the babe at her breast. When the Vision faded, he jumped to his feet in sheer excitement. The Lords of Wyrd had been kind. This time they were sending him a warning that somewhere she was waiting for him to bring her to the dweomer, somewhere in the vast expanse of the kingdom of Deverry. He could search and find her while she was still a child, before harsh circumstances made it impossible for him to untangle the snarl of their intertwined destinies. This time, perhaps, she would remember and listen to him. Perhaps. If he found her.

Cerrgonney, 1052

The young fool tells his master that he will suffer to gain the dweomer. Why is he a fool? Because the dweomer has already made him pay and pay and pay again before he even stood on its door-step. . . .

The Secret Book of Cadwallon the Druid

With a cold drizzling rain, the last of the twilight was closing in like gray steel. As she looked at the sky, Jill was frightened to be outside. She hurried to the woodpile and began to grab an untidy load of firewood. A gray gnome, all spindly legs and long nose, perched on a big log and picked at its teeth while it watched her. When she dropped a stick, it snatched it and refused to give it back.

"Beast!" Jill snapped. "Then keep it!"

At her anger, the gnome vanished with a puff of cold air. Half in tears, Jill hurried across the muddy yard to the round stone tavern, where cracks of cheerful light gleamed around wooden shutters. Clutching her firewood, she ran down the corridor to the chamber and slipped in, hesitating a moment at the door. The priestess in her long black robe was kneeling by Mama's bed. When she looked up, Jill saw the blue tattoo of the crescent moon that covered half her face.

"Put some wood on the fire now, child," the priestess said. "I need more light."

Jill picked out the thinnest pitchiest sticks and fed them carefully into the fire burning in the hearth. The flames sprang up, sending flares and shadows dancing round the room. Jill sat down on the straw-covered floor in a corner to watch the priestess. Mama lay very still, her face a deadly pale, running big drops of sweat from the fever. The priestess picked up a silver jar and helped Mama drink the herb water in it. Mama was coughing so hard that she couldn't keep the water down.

Jill grabbed her rag doll and held her tight. She wished that Heledd was real, and that she'd cry so Jill could be very brave and comfort her. The priestess set the silver jar down, wiped Mama's face, then began to pray, whispering the words in the ancient holy tongue that only priests and priestesses knew. Jill prayed, too, in her mind, begging the Holy Goddess of the Moon to let her mama stay alive.

Hesitantly Macyn came to the doorway and stood watching, his thick pudding face set in concern, his blunt hands twisting the hem of his heavy linen overshirt. Macyn owned this tavern, where Mama worked as a serving lass, and let her and Jill live in this chamber out of simple kindness to a woman with a bastard child to support. He reached up and rubbed the bald spot in the middle of his gray hair while he waited for the priestess to finish her prayer.

"How is she?" Macyn said.

The priestess looked at him, then pointedly at Jill.

"You can say it," Jill said. "I know she's going to die."

Jill wanted to cry, but she felt that she'd been turned to stone.

"She might as well know the truth," the priestess said. "Here, does she have a father?"

"Of a sort," Macyn said. "He's a silver dagger, you see, and he rides this way every now and then to give them what coin he can. It's been a good long while since the last time."

The priestess sighed in a hiss of irritation.

"I'll keep feeding the lass," Macyn went on. "Jill's always done a bit of work around the place, and ye gods, I wouldn't throw her out into the street to starve, anyway."

"Well and good, then." The priestess held out her hand to Jill. "How old are you, child?"

"Seven, your holiness."

"Well, now, that's very young, but you'll have to be brave, just like a warrior. Your father's a warrior, isn't he?"

"He is. A great warrior."

"Then you'll have to be as brave as he'd want you to be. Come say good-bye to your mama; then let Macyn take you out."

When Jill came to the bedside, Mama was awake, but her

eyes were red, swollen, and cloudy, as if she didn't really see her daughter standing there.

"Jill?" Mama was gasping for breath. "Mind what Macco tells you."

"I will. Promise."

Mama turned her head away and stared at the wall.

"Cullyn," she whispered.

Cullyn was Da's name. Jill wished he was there; she had never wished for anything so much in her life. Macyn picked Jill up, doll and all, and carried her from the chamber. As the door closed, Jill twisted around and caught a glimpse of the priestess praying over Mama again.

Since no one wanted to come to a tavern with fever in the back room, the big half-round of the alehouse was empty, the long wooden tables standing forlorn in the dim firelight. Macyn sat Jill down at a table near the fire, then went to get her something to eat. Just behind her was a stack of ale barrels, laced with particularly dark shadows. Jill was suddenly sure that Death was hiding behind them. She made herself turn around and look, because Da always said a warrior should look Death in the face, but she was glad when there was nothing there. Macyn brought her a plate of bread and honey and a wooden cup of milk. When Jill tried to eat, the food seemed to turn dry and sour in her mouth. With a sigh, Macyn rubbed his bald spot.

"Well now," he said. "Maybe your da will ride our way soon."

"I hope so."

Macyn had a long swallow of ale from his pewter tankard.

"Does your doll want a sip of milk?" he said.

"She doesn't. She's just rags."

Then they heard the priestess, chanting a long sobbing note, keening for the soul of the dead. Jill tried to make herself feel brave, then laid her head on the table and sobbed aloud.

They buried Mama out in the sacred oak grove behind the village. For a week, Jill went every morning to cry beside the grave until Macyn finally told her that visiting the grave was like pouring oil on a fire—she would never put her grief out by doing it. Since Mama had told her to mind what he said, Jill stopped going. Soon custom picked up again in the tavern, and she was busy enough to keep from thinking about Mama all the time.

Local people came in to gossip, farmers stopped by on market day, and every now and then merchants and peddlars paid to sleep on the floor for want of a proper inn in the village. Jill washed tankards, ran errands, and even served the ale when the tavern was crowded at night. Whenever a man from out of town came through, Jill would ask him if he'd ever heard of her father, Cullyn of Cerrmor, the silver dagger. No one ever had any news at all.

The village was in the northmost province of the kingdom of Deverry, the greatest kingdom in the whole world of Annwn—or so Jill had always been told. She knew that down to the south was the splendid city of Dun Deverry, where the High King lived in an enormous palace. Bobyr, however, where Jill had spent her whole life, had about fifty round houses, made of rough slabs of flint packed with earth to keep the wind out of the walls. On the side of a steep Cerrgonney hill, they clung to narrow twisted streets so that the village looked like a handful of boulders thrown among a stand of straggly pine trees. In the little valleys among the hills, farmers wrestled small fields out of the rocky land and walled their plots with the stones.

About a mile away was the dun, or fort, of Lord Melyn, to whom the village owed fealty. Jill had always been told that it was everyone's Wyrd to do what the noble-born said, because the gods had made them noble. The dun was certainly impressive enough to Jill's way of thinking to have had some divine aid behind it. It stood on the top of the highest hill, surrounded by both a ring of earthworks and a ramparted stone wall. A broch, a round tower of slabbed stone, rose in the middle and loomed over the other buildings inside the walls. From the top of the village, Jill could see the dun and Lord Melyn's blue banner flapping on the broch.

Much more rarely Jill saw Lord Melyn himself, who only occasionally rode into the village, usually to administer a judgment on someone who'd broken the law. When, on one particularly hot and airless day, Lord Melyn actually came into the tavern for some ale, it was an important event. Although the lord had thin gray hair, a florid face, and a paunch, he was an impressive man, standing ramrod straight and striding in like the warrior he was. With him were two young men from his warband, because a noble lord never went anywhere alone. Jill hastily ran her hands through her messy hair and made the lord a curtsey. Macyn came hurrying with his hands full of tankards; he set them down and made the lord a bow.

"Cursed hot day," Lord Melyn remarked, drinking thirstily.

"It is, my lord," Macyn said, somewhat awestruck that the lord would speak to him.

"Pretty child." Lord Melyn glanced at Jill. "Your granddaughter?"

"She's not, my lord," Macyn said. "But the child of the lass who used to work here for me."

"She died of a fever," one of the riders interrupted. "Cursed sad thing."

"Who's her father?" Lord Melyn said. "Or does anyone even know?"

"Oh, not a doubt in the world, my lord," the rider said with an unpleasant grin. "Cullyn of Cerrmor, and no man would have dared to trifle with his wench."

"True enough." Lord Melyn laughed under his breath. "So, lass, you've got a famous father, do you?"

"I do?" Jill said.

Lord Melyn laughed again.

"Well, no doubt a warrior's glory doesn't mean much to a little lass, but your da's the greatest swordsman in all Deverry, silver dagger or no." The lord reached into the leather pouch at his belt and brought out some coppers to pay Macyn, then handed Jill a silver piece. "Here, child, without a mother you'll need a bit of coin to get a new dress."

"My humble thanks, my lord." As she made him a curtsey, Jill realized that her dress was indeed awfully shabby. "May the gods bless you."

After the lord and his men left the tavern, Jill put her silver piece into a little wooden box in her chamber. At first, looking at it gleaming in the box made her feel like a rich lady herself; then all at once she realized that his lordship had just given her charity. Without that coin, she wouldn't be able to get a new dress, just as without Macyn's kindness, she would have nothing to eat and nowhere to sleep. The thought seemed to burn in her mind. Blindly she ran outside to the stand of trees behind the tavern and threw herself facedown onto the shady grass. When she called out to them, the Wildfolk came—her favorite gray gnome, a pair of warty blue fellows with long pointed teeth, and a sprite, who would have looked like a tiny beautiful woman if it weren't for her eyes, wide, slit like a cat's, and utterly mindless. Jill sat up to let the gray gnome climb into her lap.

"I wish you could talk," Jill said. "If something should happen to Macyn, could I come live in the woods with your folk?"

The gnome idly scratched his armpit while he considered.

"I mean, you could show me how to find things to eat," Jill went on. "And how to keep warm when it snows."

The gnome nodded in a way that seemed to mean yes, but it was always hard to tell what the Wildfolk meant. Jill was not even exactly sure what they were. Although they suddenly appeared and vanished at will, they felt real enough when you touched them, and they could pick up things and drink the milk that Jill set out for them at night. Thinking of living with them in the woods was as much frightening as it was comforting.

"Well, I hope nothing happens to Macco," Jill said. "But I worry."

The gnome nodded sympathetically and patted her arm with a skinny twisted hand. Since the other children in the village made fun of Jill for being a bastard, the Wildfolk were the only real friends she had.

"Jill?" Macyn was calling her from the tavern yard. "Time to come in and help cook dinner."

"I've got to go," Jill said to the Wildfolk. "I'll give you milk tonight."

They all laughed, dancing in a little circle around her feet, then vanishing without a trace. As Jill walked back, Macyn came to meet her.

"Who were you talking to out here?" he said.

"No one. Just talking."

"To the Wildfolk, I suppose?" Macyn was grinning, teasing her.

Jill merely shrugged. She'd learned very early that nobody believed her when she told them that she could see the Wildfolk.

"I've got a nice bit of pork for our dinner," Macyn said. "We'd best eat quickly, because on a hot night like this one, everyone's going to come for a bit of ale."

Macyn was exactly right. As soon as the sun went down, the room filled up with local people, men and women both, come to have a good gossip. No one in Bobyr had much real money; Macyn kept track of what everyone owed him on a wooden plank. When there were enough marks under someone's name, Macyn would get food or cloth or shoes from that person and start keeping track all over again. They did earn a few coppers that night from a wandering peddler, who had a big pack of fancy thread for embroidery, needles, and even some ribands from a big town to the west. When Jill served him, she asked, as usual, if he'd ever heard of Cullyn of Cerrmor.

"Heard of him?" the peddler said. "I just saw him, lass, about a fortnight ago."

Jill's heart started pounding.

"Where?" she said.

"Up in Gwingedd. There's something of a war up there, two lords and one of their cursed blood feuds, which is why, I don't mind telling you, I came down this southern way. But I was drinking in a tavern my last night there, and I see this lad with a silver dagger in his belt. That's Cullyn of Cerrmor, a lad says to me, and don't you ever cross him, neither." He shook his head dolefully. "Them silver daggers is all a bad lot."

"Now here! He's my da!"

"Oh, is he now? Well, what harsh Wyrd you've got for such a little lass—a silver dagger for a da."

Although Jill was furious, she knew that there was no use in arguing. Everyone despised silver daggers. Although most warriors lived in the dun of a noble lord and served him as part of his honor-sworn warband, silver daggers traveled around the kingdom and fought for any lord who had the coin to hire them. Sometimes when Da rode to see Jill and her mother, he would have lots of money to give them; at others, barely a copper, all depending on how much he could loot from a battlefield. Although Jill didn't understand why, she knew that once a man was a silver dagger, no one would ever let him be anything else. Cullyn had never had the chance to marry her mother and take her to live with him in a dun, the way honor-sworn warriors could do with their women.

That night Jill prayed to the Goddess of the Moon to keep her father safe in the Gwingedd war. Almost as an afterthought, she asked the Moon to let the war be over soon, so that Cullyn could come see her right away. Apparently, though, wars were under the jurisdiction of some other god, because it was two months before Jill had the dream. Every now and then, she would dream in a way that was exceptionally vivid and realistic. Those dreams always came true. Just like with the Wildfolk, she had learned early to keep her true dreams to herself. In this particular one, she saw Cullyn come riding into town.

Jill woke in a fever of excitement. Judging from the short shadows that everything had in the dream, Da would arrive around noon. All morning Jill worked as hard as she could to make the time pass faster. Finally, she ran to the front door of the tavern and stood there looking out. The sun was almost directly overhead when she saw Cullyn, leading a big chestnut warhorse up the narrow street. All at once Jill remembered that he didn't know about Mama. She dodged back inside fast.

"Macco! Da's coming! Who's going to tell him?"

"Oh by the hells!" Macyn ran for the door. "Wait here."

For a few miserable minutes Jill stayed inside, painfully aware that the men sitting at one table were looking at her with pity. The looks made her remember the terrible night when Mama died so much that she had to get away from them, and she ran out the door. Just down the street Macyn was talking to her father with a sympathetic hand on Cullyn's shoulder. Cullyn was staring at the ground, his face set and grim, saying not a word.

Cullyn of Cerrmor was well over six feet tall, warrior-straight and heavy-shouldered, with blond hair and ice-blue eyes. Down his left cheek ran an old scar, which made him look frightening even when he smiled. His plain linen shirt was filthy from the road, and so were his brigga, the loose woolen trousers that all Deverry men wore. On his heavy belt hung his one splendor—a sword in a gold-trimmed scabbard, a gift from a great lord—and his shame, the silver dagger in a tattered leather sheath. The silver pommel with its three little knobs gleamed, as if warning people against its owner. When Macyn finished talking, Cullyn laid his hand on his sword hilt, as if for comfort. Macyn took the horse's reins, and they walked up to the tavern.

Jill ran to Cullyn and threw herself into his arms. He picked her up, holding her tightly. He smelled of sweat and horses, the comforting familiar scent of her beloved da.

"My poor little lass!" Cullyn said. "By the hells, what a rotten father you've got!"

Jill was crying too hard to say anything. Cullyn carried her into the tavern and sat down with her in his lap at a table near the door. The men at the far table set down their tankards and looked at him with cold, hard eyes.

"You know what, Da?" Jill sniveled out. "The last thing Mama said was your name."

Cullyn tossed his head back and keened, a long, low howl of mourning. Hovering nearby, Macyn risked patting his shoulder.

"Here, lad," Macyn said. "Here, now."

Cullyn kept keening, one long moan after another, even though Macyn kept patting his shoulder and saying "here now" in a helpless voice. The other men walked over, and Jill hated their tight little smiles, as if they were taunting her da for his grief. All at once, Cullyn realized that they were there. He slipped Jill off his lap, and as he stood up, his sword leapt into his hand as if by dweomer.

"And why shouldn't I mourn her?" Cullyn yelled. "She was as decent a woman as the Queen herself, no matter what you pack of dogs thought of her. Is there anyone in this stinking village who wants to say otherwise to my face?"

The clot of men faded back, one cautious step at a time.

"None of you are even fit to be killed to pour blood on her grave," Cullyn said. "Admit it."

All the men muttered, "We aren't, truly." Cullyn took one step forward, the sword glittering in the sunlight from the door.

"Well and good," he said. "Go on, scum—get back to your drinking."

Instead, shoving each other to be the first out the door, the men fled the tavern. Cullyn sheathed the sword with a slap of the metal into leather. Macyn wiped sweat off his face.

"Well, Macco," Cullyn said. "You and the village can think as low of me as you want, but my Seryan deserved better than a dishonored piss-poor excuse for a man like me."

"Er ah well," Macyn said.

"And now you're all I've got left of her." Cullyn turned to Jill. "We've got a cursed strange road ahead of us, my sweet, but we'll manage."

"What?" Jill said. "Da, are you going to take me with you?"

"Cursed right. And today."

"Now here," Macyn broke in. "Hadn't you best wait and think this over? You're not yourself right now, and—"

"By all the ice in all the hells!" Cullyn spun around, his hand on his sword hilt. "I'm as much myself as I need to be!"

"Ah well." Macyn stepped back. "So you are."

"Get your clothes, Jill. We'll go see your mother's grave, and then we'll be on our way. I never want to see this stinking village again."

Pleased and terrified all at the same time, Jill ran to the chamber and began bundling the few things she owned up into a blanket. She could hear Macyn trying to talk to Cullyn and Cullyn snarling right back at him. She risked calling out softly to the Wildfolk. The gray gnome materialized in midair and floated to the straw-strewn floor.

"Da's taking me away," Jill whispered. "Do you want to come? If you do, you'd better follow us or get on his horse."

When the gnome vanished, Jill wondered if she'd ever see him again.

"Jill!" Cullyn yelled. "Stop talking to yourself and get out here!"

Jill grabbed her bundle and ran out of the tavern. Cullyn shoved her things into the bedroll tied behind his saddle, then lifted her up on top of it. When he mounted, Jill slipped her arms around his waist and rested her face against his broad back. His shirt was stained all over in a pattern of blurry rings, rust marks made by his sweating inside his chain mail. His shirts always looked like that.

"Well," Macyn said. "Farewell, Jill."

"Farewell." All at once she wanted to cry. "And my thanks for being so good to me."

Macyn waved, somewhat teary-eyed. Jill turned on her uneasy perch to wave back as they started downhill.

On the downhill side of the village stood the holy oaks, sacred to Bel, god of the sun and the king of all the gods. Scattered among them were the village burials. Although Seryan had no stone to mark her grave as the richer people did, Jill knew that she would never forget where it lay. As soon as she led her father there, Cullyn began to keen, throwing himself down full-length on it, as if he were trying to hold his beloved through the earth. Jill was terrified until at last, he fell silent and sat up.

"I brought your mama a present this trip," Cullyn said. "And by the gods, she's going to have it."

Cullyn pulled his silver dagger and cut out a piece of sod, then dug down like a badger to make a shallow hole. He took a gold bracelet out of his shirt and held it up for Jill to see: a thin rod of pure gold, twisted round and round to look like rope. He put it into the hole, smoothed the dirt down, then put the chunk of sod back.

"Farewell, my love," he whispered. "For all my wandering, I never loved a woman but you, and I pray to every god you believed me when I told you that." He stood up and wiped the dagger blade clean on the side of his brigga. "That's all the mourning you'll ever see me do, Jill, but remember how I loved your mother."

"I will, Da. Promise."

All afternoon, they rode down the east-running road, a narrow dirt track through the sharp-peaked hills and pine forests. Every now and then they passed fields where the grain stood green and young, and the farmers would turn to stare at the strange sight of a warrior with a child behind his saddle. Jill was soon stiff and sore on her uncomfortable perch, but Cullyn was so wrapped in a dark brooding that she was afraid to speak to him.

Just at twilight, they crossed a shallow river and reached the walled town of Averby. Cullyn dismounted and led the horse along narrow twisting streets while Jill clung to the saddle and looked around wide-eyed. She had never seen so many houses in her life—easily two hundred of them. At last they reached a shabby inn with a big stables out in back, where the innkeep greeted Cullyn by name and gave him a friendly slap on the shoulder. Jill was too tired to eat dinner. Cullyn carried her upstairs to a dusty wedge-shaped chamber and made her a bed out of his cloak on a straw mattress. She fell asleep before he'd blown the candle out.

When she woke, the room was full of sunlight, and Cullyn was gone. Jill sat up in panic, trying to remember why she was in this strange chamber with nothing but a pile of gear. It took her several minutes to remember that Da had come and taken her with him. It wasn't long before Cullyn came back, with a brass bowl of steaming water in one hand and a large chunk of bread in the other.

"Eat this, my sweet," he said.

Eagerly Jill started in on the bread, which was studded with nuts and currants. Cullyn set the bowl down, rummaged in his saddlebags for soap and a fragment of mirror, then knelt on the floor to shave. He always shaved with his silver dagger. As he took it out, Jill could see the device engraved on the blade, a striking falcon, which was Cullyn's mark, graved or stamped on everything he owned.

"That dagger's awfully sharp, Da," Jill said.

"It is." Cullyn began lathering his face. "It's not pure silver, you see, but some sort of alloy. It doesn't tarnish as easily as real silver, and it holds an edge better than any steel. Only a few silversmiths in the kingdom know the secret, and they won't tell anyone else."

"Why not?"

"And how should I know? A suspicious lot, the smiths who serve the silver dagger. I tell you, not just any exile or dishonored man can buy one of these blades. You have to find yourself another silver dagger and ride with him awhile—prove yourself, like—and then he'll pledge you to the band."

"Do you have to show him you can fight good?"

"Fight *well.*" Cullyn began to shave in neat, precise strokes. "That's somewhat of it, truly, but only a part. Here, silver daggers have an honor of our own. We're scum, all of us, but we don't steal or murder. The noble lords know we don't, and so they trust us enough to give us our hires. If a couple of the wrong kind of lads got into the band, gave us a bad name, like, well, then, we'd all starve."

Jill had a few more bites of bread.

"Da, why did you want to be a silver dagger?"

"Don't talk with your mouth full. I didn't want to. It was the only choice I had, that's all. I've never heard of a man being so big a fool as to join up just because he wanted to."

"I don't understand."

Cullyn considered, wiping the last bit of lather off his upper lip with the back of his hand.

"Well," he said at last. "No man joins the daggers if he has a chance at a decent life in a lord's dun. Sometimes men are fools, and we do things that mean no lord would let us ride in his warband ever again. When that happens, well, carrying the dagger is a cursed sight better than sweeping out a stable or suchlike. At least you get to fight for your hire, like a man."

"You never could have been a fool!"

Cullyn's lips twitched in a brief smile.

"I was, truly," he said. "A long time ago your old Da here was a rider in a warband in Cerrmor, and he got himself into a good bit of trouble. Never dishonor yourself, Jill. You listen to me. Dishonor sticks closer to you than blood on your hands. So my lord kicked me out, as he had every right to do, and there was nothing left for me but the long road."

"The what?"

"The long road. That's what silver daggers call our life."

"But Da, what did you do?"

Cullyn turned to look at her with eyes so cold that Jill was afraid he was going to slap her.

"When you're done eating," he said mildly. "We're going to the market fair and buy you some lad's clothes. Dresses aren't any good for riding and camping by the road."

And Jill realized that she would never have the courage to ask him that question again.

Cullyn was as good as his word about the new clothes. In fact, he bought her so many things, boots, brigga, shirts, a good wool cloak and a small ring brooch to clasp it with that Jill realized she'd never seen him with so much money before, real coins, all of them bright-minted silver. When she asked him about it, Cullyn told her that he'd captured a great lord's son on the field of battle, and that this money was the ransom the lord's family had to pay him to get their son back.

"That was honorable, Da," Jill said. "Not killing him, I mean, and then letting him go home."

"Honorable?" Cullyn smiled faintly. "I'll tell you, my sweet, it's every silver dagger's dream to capture a lord single-handedly. It's the coin you want, not the glory. And by the hells, many a poor lordling has made himself a rich lord doing the same thing."

Jill was honestly shocked. Taking someone prisoner for profit was one of those things that never got mentioned in the bard songs and the glorious tales of war. She was glad enough of the coin, however, especially when Cullyn bought her a pony, a slender gray that she named Gwindyc after the great hero of ancient times. When they returned to the inn, Cullyn took Jill up to their chamber, made her change her clothes, then unceremoniously cropped off her hair like a lad's with his silver dagger.

"That long hair's too messy for the road," he said. "Cursed if I'll spend my time combing it for you like a nursemaid."

Jill supposed that he was right, but when she looked at herself in the bit of mirror, she felt that she no longer really knew who she was. The feeling persisted when they went down to the tavern room of the inn for the noon meal. She felt that she should get up and help Blaer the innkeep serve, not sit there and eat stew with the other customers. Because it was market day, the tavern was crowded with merchants, who all wore checked brigga as a sign of their station. They looked Cullyn over with a shudder for the silver dagger in his belt and gave him as wide a berth as possible.

Jill was just finishing her stew when three young riders from a warband swaggered in and demanded ale. Jill knew they were a lord's riders because their shirts had embroidered blazons, running stags in this case, on the yokes. They stood right in the way near the door and kept Blaer so busy that when Cullyn wanted more ale, he had to get up and fetch it himself. As he was coming back with the full tankard, he had to pass the three riders. One of them stepped forward and deliberately jogged Cullyn's arm, making him spill the ale.

"Watch your step," the rider sneered. "Silver dagger."

Cullyn set the tankard down and turned to face him. Jill climbed up on the table so she could see. Grinning, the other two riders moved back to the wall to leave a clear space around Cullyn and their fellow.

"Are you looking for a fight?" Cullyn said.

"Just looking to make a lout of a silver dagger mind his manners," the rider said. "What's your name, scum?"

"Cullyn of Cerrmor. And what's it to you?"

The room went dead silent as every man in it turned to stare. The other two riders laid urgent hands on their friend's shoulders.

"Come along, Gruffidd," one of them said. "Just drink your cursed ale. You're a bit young to die."

"Get away," Gruffidd snarled. "Are you calling me a coward?"

"Calling you a fool," the rider said, glancing at Cullyn. "Here, our apologies."

"Don't you apologize for me," Gruffidd said. "I don't give a pig's fart if he's the Lord of Hell! Listen, silver dagger, not half of those tales about you can be true."

"Indeed?" Cullyn laid his hand on his sword hilt.

It seemed that the whole room gasped, even the walls. Jill clasped her hands over her mouth to keep from screaming. Frightened men moved back and away, leaving Cullyn and Gruffidd facing each other.

"Here!" Blaer yelped. "Not in my inn!"

Too late—Gruffidd drew his sword. With a sour smile, Cullyn drew his own, but he let the blade trail lazily in his hand with the point near the floor. The room was so quiet that Jill heard her heart pounding. Gruffidd moved and struck—the sword went flying out of his hand. Across the room men yelped and dodged as the sword fell clattering to the floor. Cullyn had his blade raised, but casually, as if he were only using it to point out something. There was a smear of blood on it. Cursing under his breath, Gruffidd clutched his right wrist with his left hand. Blood welled between his fingers.

"I call you all to witness that he struck first," Cullyn said mildly.

The room broke into excited whispers as Gruffidd's friends dragged him away. Blaer hurried after them, quite pale and carrying the rider's sword. Cullyn wiped the blood off his sword on his brigga leg, sheathed it, then picked up his tankard and came back to the table.

"Jill, get down!" he snapped. "Where's your courtesy?"

"I just wanted to see, Da," Jill said as she scrambled down. "That was splendid. I never even saw you move."

"Neither did he. Well, Jill, I'm going to drink this ale, and then we'll be packing up and getting on the road."

"I thought we were going to stay here tonight."

"We *were*."

All a-flutter, Blaer ran over to them.

"By the hells," Blaer said. "How often does this sort of thing happen to you?"

"Far too often," Cullyn said. "These young dogs would count it an honor to be the man who killed Cullyn of Cerrmor." He had a long swallow of ale. "So far all they've won for their trouble is a broken wrist, but by the hells, it wearies me."

"So it must." Blaer shuddered as if he were cold. "Well, lass, it's a strange life you're going to lead, riding with him. You'll make some man a cursed strange wife someday, too."

"I'll never marry a man who isn't as great a swordsman as my Da," Jill said. "So probably I'll never marry at all."

That afternoon they rode fast and steadily, finally stopping about an hour before sunset when Cullyn judged that they were far enough away from Gruffidd's warband. They found a farmer who let them camp in a corner of his pasture and who sold them oats for Cullyn's horse and the new pony. While Cullyn scrounged dead wood from the nearby forest for a fire, Jill put the horses on their tether ropes and staked them out. She had to stand on the head of the stakes and use her whole weight, but finally she forced them in. She was starting back to the camp when the gray gnome appeared, popping into reality in front of her and dancing up and down. With a laugh, Jill picked him up in her arms.

"You did follow me! That gladdens my heart."

The gnome gave her a gape-mouthed grin and put his arms around her neck. He felt dry, a little scaly to the touch, and smelled of freshly turned earth. Without thinking, Jill carried him back to camp and talked all the while about the things that had happened on the road. He listened solemnly, then suddenly twisted in her arms in alarm and pointed. Jill saw Cullyn, trotting back with a load of wood, and his eyes were narrow with exasperation. The gnome vanished.

"Jill, by the gods!" Cullyn snapped. "What cursed strange kind of game or suchlike were you playing? Talking to yourself and pretending to carry something, I mean."

"It was naught, Da. Just a game."

Cullyn dumped the wood onto the ground.

"I won't have it," he snapped. "It makes you look like a half-wit or suchlike, standing around talking to yourself. I'll buy you a doll if you want something to talk to that badly."

"I've got a doll, my thanks."

"Then why don't you talk to it?"

"I will, Da. Promise."

Cullyn set his hands on his hips and looked her over.

"And just what were you pretending?" he said. "More of that nonsense about the Wildfolk?"

Jill hung her head and began scrubbing at the grass with the toe of her boot. Cullyn slapped her across the face.

"I don't want to hear a word of it," he said. "No more of this babbling to yourself."

"I won't, Da. Promise." Jill bit her lip hard to keep back the tears.

"Oh here." Suddenly Cullyn knelt down in front of her and put his hands on her shoulders. "Forgive me the slap, my sweet. Your poor old father's all to pieces these days." He hesitated for a moment, looking honestly troubled. "Jill, listen to me. There's plenty of people in the kingdom who believe the Wildfolk are real enough. Do you know what else they believe? That anyone who can see them is a witch. Do you know what could happen to you if someone heard you talking to the Wildfolk? For all that you're but a little lass, there could be trouble over it. I don't want to have to cut my way through a crowd of peasants to keep you from being beaten to death."

Jill went cold all over and started shaking. Cullyn drew her into his arms and hugged her, but she felt like shoving him away and running wildly into the forest. But I do see them, she thought, does that make me a witch? She felt sick at the thought —was she going to turn into an old hag who had the evil eye and poisoned people with herbs? When she realized that she couldn't even share these fears with her father, she began to cry.

"Oh here, here," Cullyn said. "My apologies. Now don't think of it anymore, and we'll have a bit to eat. But now you know why you can't go babbling about Wildfolk where other people can hear you."

"I won't, Da. I truly truly promise."

In the middle of the night, Jill woke up to find the world turned to silver by moonlight. The gray gnome was hunkered down near her head as if he was keeping guard over her. Since Cullyn was snoring loudly, Jill risked whispering to him.

"You're my best and truest friend," she said. "But I don't want to be a witch."

The gnome shook his head in a vigorous no.

"Isn't it true? Do only witches see you?"

Again came the reassuring no. He patted her face gently,

then disappeared with a gust of wind that seemed to send the moonlight dancing. For a long time Jill lay awake, smiling to herself in profound relief. Yet she knew that her Da was right; from now on, she would have to be very careful.

The folk of Deverry have always been the restless sort. In the old days of the Dawntime they wandered thousands of miles before they settled the old kingdom, Devetia Riga, in the Homeland. The bards still tell many a tale of how they fled the encroaching Rhwmanes and sailed across a vast ocean under the leadership of King Bran to find the Western Isles. Then they rode all over the Isles, too, before King Bran saw the omen of the white sow that told him where to found the holy city of Dun Deverry. Even during Jill's time, there were still people who lived more on the roads than at home—merchants with caravans, peddlers with packs, tinkers, priests on pilgrimages, young men riding from one lord to another in the hopes of finding a place in a warband, and of course, silver daggers. After a few weeks of riding with her father, Jill realized that the lure of the road had caught her, too. There was always something new to see, someone new to meet; she wondered how she'd ever endured being confined to one small village.

Since Cullyn had plenty of coin, Jill was surprised when he began to look for another hire. As they rode aimlessly east through Cerrgonney, he was always asking for news of feuds and border wars.

"The summer's half gone," he told Jill one night at their campfire. "A silver dagger has to think about coin for the winter. Well, not that many of my cursed band do think, mind, but they don't have a daughter to worry about."

"True spoken, Da. Did you ever have to sleep out in the snow?"

"I didn't, because I could always ride back and winter with your mother." All at once, Cullyn turned melancholy, his face slack as if he were suddenly exhausted. "Ah ye gods, I only hope no word of this comes to her in the Otherlands. Her only child, riding the roads with a man like me!"

"Da, you're splendid, and this is splendid, too. When I grow up, I'll be a silver dagger like you."

"Listen to you. Lasses can't be warriors."

"Why not? They were, back in the Dawntime. Like Aiva. Have you heard those songs, Da? Lord Melyn's bard used to come to the tavern, and he'd sing for me sometimes. I always asked for the ones about Aiva. She was splendid. She was a Hawk woman, you see."

"Oh, I've heard the tales, but that was long ago. Things are different now."

"Why? That's not fair. Besides, there was Lady Gweniver, too, and she was only back in the Time of Troubles, not the Dawntime. These men insulted her honor, and she gets them for it." Jill laid her hand on her heart, just as the bard did. " 'Back they fall, and bright blood blooms, on helm and heart as the hells claim them.' I learned that bit by heart."

"If ever we ride back to Bobyr, I'm going to have a thing or two to say to Lord Melyn's bard. Ye gods, what have I sired?"

"Someone just like you. That's what Mama always said. She said I was stubborn just like you and every bit as nasty when I wanted to be."

Cullyn laughed, a muttered chuckle under his breath. It was the first time Jill had ever heard him laugh aloud in her life.

It was two days later that Cullyn got the news he wanted about a hire. They had stopped in the midst of a grove of oak trees for their noon meal, and they were eating bread and cheese when Jill heard the sound of two horses, trotting straight for them. Cullyn was up and standing with his sword drawn before the sound truly made sense to her. Jill scrambled up just as the horsemen came in sight, ducking and dodging under the branches. They were armed, wearing chainmail, and their swords were drawn.

"Hold and stand!" the leader called out.

As they rode into the clearing, Cullyn stepped smoothly between them and Jill. The men pulled up their horses, then suddenly smiled. The leader leaned over in his saddle.

"My apologies," he said. "I thought you were some of Lord Ynydd's men."

"Never even heard of him," Cullyn said. "What have we done, wandered into a feud?"

"Just that. We serve Tieryn Braedd, and these woods are his, by every god!"

"I'd never deny it. Does Lord Ynydd?"

"He does. Here, you're a silver dagger! Looking for a hire? There's only four of us against Ynydd's seven, you see."

"By the hells!" Cullyn tossed his head. "This must have been a bloody little affair."

"Well, not truly," the rider said regretfully. "You see, there was only five against seven to begin with. But truly, go speak with our lord. The dun's just two miles down this road. You can't miss it."

The rider spoke the truth about that, certainly. Out in the middle of cleared farmland was a low hill, ringed with the massive stone walls of the tieryn's dun. Behind them stood a broch that was at least four stories high, with a red and gray pennant flying proudly at the top. Yet as they rode up to it, Jill saw that the great iron-bound gates in the walls were only for show. A long time ago the walls had been slighted and breached, three gaps wide enough to drive a wagon through. Ivy grew over the rubble left lying around. Inside the walls, they found a muddy ward that had once sheltered many buildings, to judge from the circular foundations and the occasional piece of standing wall left amid the tall grass. Around to one side of the broch, the wall of the top story had been knocked away. Jill could see into little empty chambers.

"What did that, Da?"

"A catapult, no doubt."

The ward was silent and empty except for a flock of big white geese, poking for snails in the ivy-covered rubble. When Cullyn called out a halloo, a young boy with a dirty red and gray tabard over his shirt and brigga ran out of the broch.

"Who are you?" he said.

"Cullyn of Cerrmor. I want to speak with your lord."

"Well, Da's talking to him right now, but they won't mind if you just come in."

"Now here!" Cullyn said sternly. "You're supposed to bow to me and say: I'll see, good sir, but the great Tieryn Braedd may have important business afoot."

"But he doesn't. He never does anything unless he's fighting with Lord Ynydd, and he isn't today."

"Oh very well then. Lead on."

Tieryn Braedd's great hall had once been great indeed, a vast circular room encompassing the entire ground floor of the broch. At either side were two massive stone hearths, carved with bands of interlacement and lions. In between was easily enough room for two hundred men to have feasted there. Now, however, the far hearth was a kitchen, where a slatternly lass was standing at a battered table and chopping carrots and turnips while a joint of mutton roasted on a spit. By the nearer hearth were three tables and unsteady-looking benches. Two men were sitting and drinking at one of them: a man of solid years, with a soft black beard, and a tall pale lad of about seventeen with a long nose that reminded Jill of a rabbit. Since he was wearing plaid brigga and a shirt embroidered with lions, the lad had to be the tieryn. The young page skipped up to the table and tugged on the tieryn's sleeve.

"Your Grace? There's a silver dagger here named Cullyn of Cerrmor."

"Indeed?" Braedd rose from his chair. "Now, this is a handy thing. Come join me."

Without ceremony Braedd sat Jill and Cullyn down on a bench, sent the boy, Abryn, to fetch more ale all round, and introduced the older man as Glyn, his councillor. When the tieryn sat down again, his chair creaked alarmingly, but he ignored the sound.

"I met a pair of your men in the oak wood, Your Grace," Cullyn said. "They told me of your feud."

"Ah Ynydd, that bastard-born son of a slug." Braedd had a moody sip of ale. "Truly, I want to offer you a hire, but my treasury matches my dun walls." He glanced at Glyn. "Could we squeeze out something?"

"A horse, I suppose," Glyn said. "He could always sell it in town for the coin."

"True," Braedd said, grinning. "Or here, what about cabbages? I've got fields and fields of those. Here, silver dagger, think of all the uses cabbages have. You can let them rot, then throw them at enemies in the street, or if you're courting a wench, you can give her a bouquet of fresh ones, and that's something she'd never have seen before, or—"

"Your Grace?" Glyn said wearily.

"Well, truly, I ramble a bit." Braedd had another long swallow of ale. "But if you'll take a horse, and your maintenance, and maintenance for your page, of course?"

"I will," Cullyn said. "Done, Your Grace—I'm on. But this is my daughter, actually, not a page."

"So she is," Braedd said, leaning closer. "Do you honor your father, child?"

"More than any man in the world," Jill said. "Except the King, of course, but I've never even met him."

"Well spoken." Braedd belched profoundly. "What a pity that the pusboil Ynydd doesn't have the respect for the King that we see in this innocent little lass."

Cullyn turned to address his questions to Councillor Glyn.

"What's this feud about, good sir? The riders only told me that the woods were in dispute."

"Well, more or less." Glyn stroked his beard thoughtfully. "The feud goes back a long time, when Lord Ynydd's grandfather declared war on his grace's grandfather. In those days, they were fighting over who should be tieryn, and many other grave matters, but bit by bit, the thing's gotten itself settled. The woods, you see, lie on the border of the two demesnes. They're the last thing left to squabble over."

"So Ynydd thinks." Braedd slammed his hand onto the table. "A councillor from the High King himself judged the matter and awarded the claim to me."

"Now Your Grace," Glyn said soothingly. "Ynydd's only disputing part of the judgment. He's ceded you the trees."

"But the bastard!" Braedd snapped. "Insisting he has ancient and prior claim to swine rights."

"Swine rights?" Cullyn said.

"Swine rights," Glyn said. "In the fall, you see, the peasants take the swine into the woods to eat the acorns. Now, there's only enough acorns for one herd of swine—his or ours."

"And the withered testicle of a sterile donkey says it's his," Braedd broke in. "His men killed one of my riders when the lad turned Ynydd's hogs out of the woods last fall."

Cullyn sighed and had a very long swallow of ale.

"Da, I don't understand," Jill said. "You mean someone was killed over pig food?"

"It's the honor of the thing!" Braedd slammed his tankard on the table so hard that the ale jumped out and spilled. "Never will I let a man take what's rightfully mine! The honor of my warband calls out for vengeance! We'll fight to the last man."

"Pity we can't arm the swine," Cullyn said. "Everyone will fight for their own food."

"Now, splendid." Braedd gave him a delighted grin. "They shall have little helms, with their tusks for swords, and we shall teach them to trot at the sound of a horn."

"Your Grace?" Glyn said.

"Well, truly, I ramble again."

Glyn and Abryn, the councillor's son as it turned out, took Jill and Cullyn out to the last building standing in the ward, the barracks. As was usually the case, the warband slept directly above the stables. In the winter, the body heat from the horses helped keep the men warm, but now, on this warm summer day, the smell of horse was overwhelming. Glyn showed Cullyn a pair of unoccupied bunks, then lingered to watch as Cullyn began to stow away their gear.

"You know, silver dagger," Glyn said. "I don't mind admitting that it gladdens my heart to have a man of your experience joining the warband."

"My thanks," Cullyn said. "Have you served the tieryn long, good sir?"

"All his life. I served his father first, you see, and truly, he was a great man. He's the one who settled the war, and more by law than the sword. I fear me that Tieryn Braedd takes more after his grandfather." Glyn paused, turning to Abryn. "Now, Abryn, Jill is our guest, so be courteous to her and take her outside to play."

"That means you're going to say something interesting," Abryn said.

"Jill," Cullyn said. "Out."

Jill grabbed Abryn's arm and hustled him out of the barracks fast. They lingered by the stables and watched the geese waddling through the rubble.

"Do those geese bite?" Jill said.

"They do. Huh, I bet you're scared."

"Oh, do you now?"

"You're a lass. Lasses are always scared. You shouldn't be wearing those brigga, either."

"Oh, are we now? And my da gave me these brigga."

"Your da's a silver dagger, and they're all scum."

Jill hauled back and hit him in the face as hard as she could. Abryn shrieked and hit back, but she dodged and punched him on the ear. With a howl, he leapt for her and knocked her down, but she shoved her elbow into his stomach until he let go. They wrestled, kicking, punching, and writhing, until Jill heard Cullyn and Glyn yelling at them to stop. Suddenly Cullyn grabbed Jill by the shoulders and pulled her off the helpless Abryn.

"Now what's all this?" Cullyn snapped.

"He said silver daggers were all scum," Jill said. "So I hit him."

Abryn sat up sniveling and wiping his bloody nose. Cullyn gave Jill a broad grin, then hastily looked stern again.

"Now here, Abryn!" Glyn said, grabbing him. "That's a nasty way to treat a guest! If you don't learn courtesy, how can you serve a great lord someday?"

Berating him all the while, Glyn hauled Abryn off into the broch. Cullyn began brushing the dirt off Jill's clothes.

"By the asses of the gods, my sweet," he said. "How did you learn to fight like that?"

"Back in Bobyr, you know? All the children always called me a bastard, and they said you were scum, and so I'd hit them, and then I learned how to win."

"Well, so you did. Ye gods, you're Cullyn of Cerrmor's daughter, sure enough."

For the rest of the day, Jill and Abryn scrupulously avoided each other, but on the morrow morning Abryn came up to her. He looked at the ground near her feet and kicked at a lump of dirt with the toe of his clog.

"I'm sorry I said your da was scum," Abryn said. "And you can wear brigga if you want to."

"My thanks. And I'm sorry I made your nose bleed. I didn't mean to hit you that hard."

Abryn looked up with a smile.

"Want to play warrior?" he said. "I've got two wooden swords."

For the next couple of days, life went on quietly in Tieryn Braedd's dun. In the mornings, Cullyn and two of the riders went out to patrol the oak wood; in the afternoons, the tieryn and the other two riders rode out to relieve them. Jill helped Abryn with his tasks around the dun, which left them plenty of time to play at swords or with Abryn's leather ball. Jill's only problem was Abryn's mother, who was sure that Jill should be learning needlework instead of playing outside. Jill grew quite clever at avoiding her. At meals, the warband ate at one table in the great hall, while the tieryn and Glyn's family ate at another. Once the councillor retired to his chambers, however, Braedd would come drink with the riders. He always talked about the feud, which he knew year by year, events that had happened long before he was born down to the most recent insult.

Finally, after about a week of this pleasant routine, Braedd hurried over to the warband's table one evening with his pale eyes gleaming. He had news: one of the servants had been to the local village and had overheard gossip about Ynydd's plans.

"The baseborn pusboil!" Braedd said. "He's claiming that since the swine rights are his, he can send in his swine any time he likes, summer or fall. They say he's planning on sending a few pigs in under armed guard."

Except for Cullyn, the warband began cursing and slamming their tankards on the table.

"And I say he won't set one trotter in my woods," Braedd went on. "From now on, the full warband's going to ride on patrol."

The warband cheered.

"Your Grace?" Cullyn said. "If I may speak?"

"By all means," Braedd said. "I value your experience in the field highly."

"My thanks, Your Grace. Well, here, the woods are a bit long for only one patrol. The warband might be down at one end while Ynydd's making his entry at the other. We'd best split into two patrols and ride a crisscross route. We can use the page and a servant to send messages and suchlike."

"Well spoken," Braedd said. "We'll do just that, and take Abryn along with us."

"Can I go, Your Grace?" Jill burst out. "I've got my own pony."

"Jill, hush!" Cullyn snapped.

"Now there's a lass with her father's spirit," Braedd said with a grin. "You may come indeed."

Since Braedd was the tieryn and he the silver dagger, Cullyn could say nothing more, but he gave Jill a good slap later when he got her alone.

After two days of riding with the patrol, Jill was sorry she'd

pressed the issue, because it was very boring. With Cullyn and
two riders, she trotted up to one end of the wood, then turned
and trotted back to meet the tieryn and the rest of the warband
—back and forth, from dawn to dusk. Her one solace was that she
got to carry a beautiful silver horn slung over her shoulder on a
leather strap. Finally, on the third day, when they'd been out on
patrol no more than an hour, Jill heard a strange noise a good
ways from them on the edge of the woods. She slowed her pony
and fell back to listen: a clattering, grunting, snorfling sound.

"Da!" Jill called out. "I hear pigs and horses!"

The three men swung their horses around and rode back.

"So it is." Cullyn drew his sword with a flourish. "Ride for the
tieryn. We'll hold them off."

As she galloped, Jill blew her horn repeatedly. At last she
heard Abryn's horn close at hand. Tieryn Braedd burst out of the
trees to meet her.

"Your Grace!" Jill screamed. "They're here."

Then she turned her pony and raced back ahead of them,
because she didn't want to miss a single thing. As she burst out of
the forest, she could hear the swine clearly, grunting their way
along. There was a path crossing a wide green meadow, and
Cullyn and the others were sitting on their horses to block it.
Down across the meadow came a strange procession. At its head
was a lord who had to be Ynydd, carrying a green-blazoned
shield with a gold boss. Seven riders, also armed and ready, rode
behind him. At the rear was a herd of ten swine with two terrified
peasants poking the pigs with sticks to keep them moving. Tieryn
Braedd and his men galloped into position beside Cullyn and the
others. When Braedd drew his sword, the other men did the
same, screaming out insults to Lord Ynydd, whose men screamed
right back. Cullyn yelled at Jill and Abryn to stay out of the way,
then sat quietly on his horse, his sword resting on his saddle peak.

"Lord Ynydd's a swine himself," Abryn said. "Bringing all his
men just so he can outnumber us."

"He is, but we're not truly outnumbered. My da's worth at
least three men."

Slowly the procession came on. The swine kept breaking
ranks, grunting and complaining, forcing the men to wait while
the peasants rounded them up again. At last Lord Ynydd pulled
his horse up about ten feet in front of Tieryn Braedd. While the

two lords glared at each other, the swine milled around. Even
from her distance, Jill could smell the big gray boars, with a roach
of dark hair down their backs and shiny tusks curling out of their
snouts.

"So," Ynydd called out. "Would you block me from my law-
ful rights, Braedd?"

"These rights are not yours to take," Braedd said.

"They are. I will not be blocked this way and dishonored."

The swine grunted loudly, as if they were cheering him on.
Cullyn urged his horse up closer and bowed in his saddle to the
lords.

"Your Grace, my lord, both of you," Cullyn said. "Can't you
see what a pretty picture we make, with the swine to watch our
tournament?"

"Hold your tongue, silver dagger," Ynydd snapped. "I won't
be mocked by a dishonored man."

"I meant no mockery, my lord," Cullyn said. "If I may speak,
would you claim that you yourself have the right to ride into the
grove?"

Braedd grinned smugly at Ynydd's sullen silence.

"Tell me, my lord," Cullyn went on. "If these swine weren't
at stake, would you dishonor the High King's judgment on these
woods?"

"Never would I dishonor the High King," Ynydd said. "But
my swine—"

With a whoop, Cullyn kicked his horse to a gallop, dodged
around Ynydd and his men, and rode straight for the herd of
swine. Yelling a war cry at the top of his lungs, he swung around
with the flat of his sword. The swine and their tenders fled in
terror, pig and peasant alike grunting and yelling as they raced
across the meadow toward home. Both warbands were laughing
too hard at the sight to give chase, much less battle. Only Ynydd
was furious, yelling at his men to stop laughing and do something.
Finally Cullyn left the chase and jogged back.

"Good my lord?" Cullyn called out. "Your swine no longer
desire passage here."

Ynydd spurred his horse forward and swung at Cullyn. Cullyn parried, catching the blade on his own and leaning slightly to
one side. Ynydd tumbled out of his saddle and onto the ground.
In his warband, yells exploded. Chasing swine was one thing:

dishonoring their lord, quite another. The seven men swung their horses around and charged straight for Cullyn with Braedd's men in close pursuit. Jill clutched her saddle peak and screamed. Da was out there all alone. She saw Ynydd scrambling back onto his horse just as the warbands closed around them.

The horses were plunging and kicking; the men, swinging and cursing. Dust rose up as thick as smoke. The men were dodging and parrying more than they were honestly trying to strike. Jill wondered if any of them had ever been in battle before. The flash of blades, the horses rearing, men pushing and swinging and yelling—it began to look like a terrifying dance, the clot of horses and men turning slowly around and around, the flashing swords keeping time. At last Jill saw Cullyn, moving his horse around the edge of the melee.

Cullyn was silent, his face perfectly calm, as if he found battle tedious. Then he began to strike, and he wasn't dodging like the others. He cut hard, shoved his way into the mob, slashed around, and struck over and over as he made a set course for Lord Ynydd. Ahead of him Ynydd's warband fell back. One man reeled in the saddle with blood running down his face; Cullyn went on swinging with a bloodied blade and led Braedd's men behind him like a wedge. He was almost to Ynydd's side when one rider shoved his horse in between them. For a moment swords flashed and swung; then the rider screamed and fell over his horse's neck into the mob. Cullyn tossed his head, but his face showed nothing at all.

Lord Ynydd's line broke. With a shout of surrender, Ynydd turned his horse and fled, his warband close behind him. One riderless horse went along with them. Braedd and his men chased them, but slowly, down to the edge of the meadow. Cullyn stayed behind, dismounted, then knelt down by the body of the rider. Without thinking, Jill dismounted and raced over to him.

"Da, are you all right?"

"Get away." Cullyn rose and slapped her across the face. "Get back, Jill."

Although Jill ran back, it was already too late. She'd seen what Cullyn didn't want her to see—the rider lying face down in the grass with a pool of blood spreading from his throat and soaking into his soft blond hair. Blood smelled warm, sticky, and unexpectedly sweet. Abryn ran to meet her.

"Did you see?" His face was dead white.

Jill fell to her knees and began to vomit, kept it up until her stomach was sore. Abryn grabbed her shoulder when she was done and helped her stand up. She felt as cold as if it were snowing. They walked back to the two ponies and sat down to watch the warband come back, laughing and crowing at the victory. Jill was so tired that she closed her eyes, but she could see the dead man like a picture, the blood spreading around him. Hastily she opened her eyes again. Eventually Cullyn left the warband and walked over to her.

"I told you to stay away," he said.

"I just forgot. I couldn't think."

"I suppose not. What's that on your mouth? Did you throw up?"

Jill wiped her face on her sleeve. He was still her da, her handsome wonderful da, but she had just seen him kill a man. When he laid his hand on her shoulder, she flinched.

"I'm not going to slap you," Cullyn said, misunderstanding. "I threw up myself the first time I saw a man killed. Ah by the hells, another man dead over pig food! I hope that fool ends this here."

"Ynydd, you mean?" Abryn said.

"Him, too," Cullyn said.

The warband took the dead man's body back to the dun for the tieryn to send to Ynydd in honorable return. Since the dead man's horse had fled in the rout, Abryn had to give up his pony and ride behind Cullyn. When the riders tied the corpse over the saddle, Jill made herself look at it, flopping like her rag doll, not a man anymore at all. She felt sicker than before. When they reached the dun, Glyn and the servants ran out to meet them. In the confusion, Jill slipped away, going around behind the broch and finding a quiet spot to sit in the shade of the ruined wall. She knew that Abryn would run to his mother, and she envied him bitterly.

She'd been there for some time before Cullyn found her. He sat down next to her on the ground. She could hardly look at him.

"The herald's riding out now to take that poor lad home," Cullyn said. "This corpse should end the thing. The honor of

Braedd's piss-poor warband has been avenged, and Ynydd's had all the gas scared out of both ends of him."

Jill looked at Cullyn's hands, resting on his thighs. Without his heavy gauntlets, they looked like his hands again, the ones that gave her food and combed her hair and patted her on the shoulder. She wondered why she'd thought that they would have changed. He's killed lots of men, she thought, that's why he has all that glory.

"Still feel sick?" Cullyn said.

"I don't. I didn't think blood would smell like that."

"Well, it does, and it runs like that, too. Why do you think I didn't want you riding with us?"

"Did you know someone would get killed?"

"I was hoping I could stop it, but I was ready for it. I always am, because I have to be. I truly did think those lads would break sooner than they did, you see, but there was one young wolf in the pack of rabbits. Poor bastard. That's what he gets for his honor."

"Da? Are you sorry for him?"

"I am. I'll tell you something, my sweet, that no other man in Deverry would admit: I'm sorry for every man I ever killed, somewhere deep in my heart. But it was his Wyrd, and there's nothing a man can do about his own Wyrd, much less someone else's. Someday my own Wyrd will take me, and I've no doubt it'll be the same one I've brought to many a man. It's like a bargain with the gods. Every warrior makes it. Do you understand?"

"Sort of. Your life for theirs, you mean?"

"Just that. There's nothing else a man can do."

Jill began to feel better. Thinking of it as Wyrd made it seem clean again.

"It's the only honor left to me, my bargain with my Wyrd," Cullyn went on. "I told you once, and no doubt I'll tell you a thousand times over, never dishonor yourself. If ever you're tempted to do the slightest bit of a dishonorable thing, you remember your father, and what one dishonor brought him—the long road and shame in the eyes of every honest man."

"But wasn't it your Wyrd to have the dagger?"

"It wasn't." Cullyn allowed himself a brief smile. "A man can't make his Wyrd better, but it's in his hands to make it worse."

"Da?" Jill said. "Do the gods make a man's Wyrd?"

"They don't. Wyrd rules the gods, too. They can't turn aside a man's Wyrd no matter how much he prays and carries on. Do you remember the story of Gwindyc, back in the Dawntime? The Goddess Epona tried to save his life, but his Wyrd was upon him. She sent a spear at the Rhwmanes, but Gwindyc turned and took the spear in his own side."

"So he did, and he didn't even complain. But that lad you killed screamed."

"I heard him." Cullyn's face went dead calm, just as it had in the battle. "But don't hold it against him. I don't."

Jill thought for a moment, then leaned against his shoulder. Cullyn put his arm around her and pulled her close. He was still her father—and all she had in the world.

Close to nightfall, the herald returned. After conferring with the tieryn and the herald, Councillor Glyn sought Cullyn out.

"Lord Ynydd will sue for peace in the morning," Glyn said. "And Tieryn Braedd will grant it."

"Thanks be to all the gods," Cullyn said. "Here, Jill and I will be riding on in the morning."

That night Cullyn let Jill sleep in the same bunk with him. She cuddled up to his broad back and tried to think of things other than the battle, but she dreamt about it. All over again she ran up to Cullyn and saw the dead rider, but when she looked up, Cullyn was gone, and Aiva stood there, just as Jill had always imagined her—tall and strong, with golden braids coiled about her head and a long spear in her hand. She was carrying a shield with the device of the moon in its dark phase. Jill knew she couldn't see the moon if it was dark, but in the dream she could. Since she refused to disgrace herself in front of Aiva, Jill made herself look at the rider. As she watched, his whole body turned to blood and soaked into the earth until there was nothing but grass, growing thick and green. When she looked up, Aiva was smiling at her, and the moon on her shield was full.

Jill woke up and listened to the comfortable sound of Cullyn snoring beside her. She thought over the dream to make sure that she remembered all of it. Although she wasn't sure why, she knew it was very important.

I

For seven long years, ever since the lark omen down on the Eldidd coast, Nevyn had been wandering the kingdom and searching for the child who held his Wyrd in her soul. For all the power of his dweomer, it had its limits. He could never scry out a person whom he hadn't seen at least once in the flesh. Trusting the luck that's more than luck, he'd taken his riding horse and his pack mule, laden with herbs and medicines, and lived by tending the ills of the poor folk as he traveled endlessly from place to place. Now, with another summer coming to an end, he was on the road to Cantrae, a city in the northeast corner of the kingdom. He had a good friend there, Lidyn the apothecary, with whom he could spend the winter in comfort.

The Cantrae road ran through endless grassy hills stippled with white birches in the little valleys. Nevyn traveled past roaming herds of horses, tended by mounted men, which were Cantrae province's true wealth. That particular day, he was traveling slowly, letting his horse pick its own pace while the mule plodded behind. He was lost in thought that was close to being a trance, musing over the woman he would always think of as Brangwen, even though she was now a child with another name. All at once he was startled out of his reverie by the clatter and pounding of a mounted warband trotting straight downhill toward him. There were about twenty men with the silver dragon of Aberwyn blazon on the shields slung beside each saddle, and at their head was a young lad. One of the men screamed at Nevyn to get off the road and out of the way. Nevyn hurriedly swung his horse's head to the right, but the lad rose up in his stirrups and yelled at the warband to halt.

Sulkily, with a clatter of hooves and the jingle of tack, the men did as they were told. As Nevyn rode toward them, he realized with a sense of absolute amazement that the young lord at their head was ordering them to get off the road and let the aged herbman pass by. The lad was only about ten, dressed in the blue, silver, and green plaid of Aberwyn, and easily one of the most beautiful children Nevyn had ever seen. He had raven-dark wavy hair, large cornflower blue eyes, and perfect features, his mouth so soft and well formed that it was almost girlish. Nevyn stopped his horse beside him and made him a bow from the saddle.

"My humble thanks, my lord," Nevyn said. "You honor me too highly."

"Any man with hair as white as yours, good sir, deserves some courtesy." The young lord shot his men a haughty glance. "It's easier for us to handle our horses than it must be for you."

"Well, true spoken. Would his lordship honor me by telling me his name?"

"Lord Rhodry Maelwaedd of Aberwyn." The lad gave him a charming smile. "And I'll wager you wonder what Eldidd men are doing all the way up here."

"Well, truly, I did have a thought that way."

"Well, I was a page at my uncle's, Yvmur of Cantrae, but my father sent part of his warband to fetch me home. My brother Aedry just got killed."

"That saddens my heart, my lord."

"It saddens mine, too." Lord Rhodry looked at the reins in his hand and blinked back tears. "I loved Aedry. He wasn't like Rhys—he's my eldest brother, I mean. Rhys can be a true hound." He looked back up with a sheepish smile. "I shouldn't be saying that to a stranger."

"Well, truly, you shouldn't, my lord."

When Nevyn looked into the boy's dark blue eyes, he nearly swore aloud. For a moment he looked into another pair of eyes, looked through them into the soul of a man whose Wyrd was inextricably bound with his and Brangwen's. Then the vision left him.

"And will his lordship be staying at the Aberwyn court?" Nevyn said.

"Probably." Rhodry shrugged uneasily. "I guess my father wants me home because I'm the second heir now."

"It would doubtless be wise of him, my lord. I may see his lordship in Aberwyn. I often travel to Eldidd to gather herbs."

Nevyn bowed again, a gesture that Rhodry acknowledged with a lordly wave of his hand, then clucked to his horse and rode on by. At the top of the hill he turned in his saddle to watch the warband trotting off in a cloud of dust. Luck and twice luck, Nevyn told himself, thanks be to the Lords of Wyrd!

That night, Nevyn found shelter in a shabby little inn beside the road. He got himself a stool by the hearth—an old tired man from the look of him, nodding over a tankard of ale and staring into the flames. None of the other patrons said a word to him, not even the rowdy riders of the local lord. He shut the noise out of his mind and concentrated on his scrying. In the hearth, the flames played over the glowing logs. When Nevyn thought of young Lord Rhodry, he saw an image of the lad clearly, wrapped in his plaid cloak by a campfire and eating a chunk of bread while his men sat nearby. Nevyn smiled at the lad, then banished the vision.

At least he had one good clue now. Always before, in all those other lives they'd shared, he'd found Brangwen linked to this man's soul. Sooner or later, if Nevyn didn't find her first, she and Rhodry would be drawn together, and now Nevyn knew where to find Rhodry. And what was his name then? Nevyn asked himself. Blaen, truly, that was it.

In the tavern men were laughing, jesting over ale, wagering on the dice. Nevyn felt utterly cut off from them and the normal life they represented. He was also very tired that night, and the memories came to him unbidden, as bitter as always. All he truly wanted to do was die and forget, but death was forbidden to him. A long time ago now, he thought, but it was the beginning of it all.

Deverry, 643

If you write in the sand with a stick, soon the waves and wind will wash away the words. So are the mistakes of ordinary men. If you cut words into stone, they remain forever. A man who claims the dweomer becomes a chisel. All his misdeeds are graved into the very flank of Time itself. . . .

The Secret Book of Cadwallon the Druid

The storm came at sunset, a steady rain with a south wind that set the forest sighing with a tremble of spring leaves. By dawn, the roof of the hut was leaking, one thin steady trickle in the corner. The water dug a little trench in the dirt floor before it escaped through a crack under the wall. Rhegor stood with his hands on his hips and watched it run.

"The way out won't be so easy for you," Rhegor said.

"I know," the prince said. "But I'll be back here before the Beltane feast. I swear it."

Rhegor smiled as if he doubted it. He picked a couple of big logs off the woodpile in the corner and laid them on the small stone hearth. When he waved his hand over the logs, flames sprang up and flared along the bark. The prince let out his breath with a little hiss.

"You'll have to get over your infatuation with these tricks," Rhegor said. "The true dweomer lies deeper than that."

"So you've said, but I can't lie and say I've already gotten over it."

"True enough. You're a good lad in your way, Galrion."

As supple as a cat, Rhegor stretched his back, regarding the prince with shrewd eyes. Rhegor looked like an old peasant, short, barrel-chested, dressed in a dirty pair of brown brigga and a patched plain shirt with a bit of rope around his waist for want of a proper belt. His gray hair was cropped and untidy; his gray mustaches always needed a trim. At times, when he wasn't watching his thoughts, Prince Galrion wondered why he was so impressed with this man that he'd follow his orders blindly. It's the dweomer, he told himself. Who needs wealth when you've got the dweomer?

"Have you been thinking about this betrothed of yours?" Rhegor said.

"I have," Galrion said. "I'll do what you told me."

"You should be doing it because you understand the reasons, not just following my commands like a hunting dog."

"Of course. But you're sure? I can bring her with me?"

"If she'll come. Marry her first, then bring her along." Rhegor glanced around the skew-walled hut. "It's not a palace, but we'll build her a better home by winter."

"But what if she doesn't want to come?"

"If she chooses freely, then release her." Rhegor paused for effect. "Freely, mind you."

"But if she—if we—have a child?"

"What of it?" Rhegor caught his sulky glance and stared him down. "A vow is a vow, lad, and you swore one to her. If this were the usual arranged marriage, it would be different, but you sought her and won her. A man who can't keep his word is of no use to the dweomer, none."

"Very well then. I'll ride to Brangwen before I go and lay the matter before my father."

"Good. She deserves the news first."

Wrapped in his fine wool cloak of scarlet and white plaid, Galrion mounted his blooded black horse and rode off through the unbroken forest of ancient oaks. In a little while, he would return as a poverty-stricken exile to study the dweomer—if he could fight himself free of his old life. Galrion was the third of the four sons of Adoryc, High King of all Deverry. With two healthy heirs ahead of him, and one behind in reserve, he was a disposable young man, encouraged all his life to spoil himself with his beloved horses and hunting, so that he'd present no coveting threat to his eldest brother's claim to the throne. He saw no reason why he shouldn't ride away from court, out of the way for good and no longer a drain on the royal treasury. Yet he doubted if his father would see things so simply. Adoryc the Second, the ruler of a recent and unstable dynasty, seldom saw anything simply.

And there was the matter of Brangwen, the lord's daughter whom Galrion had won over many another suitor. Only a few months ago, he'd loved her so much that the wait of their betrothal time seemed like an unjust torment. Now he saw her as a potential nuisance. Rhegor admitted that Galrion would make slower progress with his studies if he had a wife and children than if he were alone. There were duties a man had to fulfill if he were married, Rhegor always said, but after twenty-two years of having every one of his royal whims satisfied, Galrion was in no mood to hear talk of duty. He was used to having exactly what he wanted, and he had never wanted anything as much as he wanted dweomer power. He hungered after it and thirsted for it.

Or, as he thought about it during his damp ride through the forest, wanting the dweomer was a lust, a burning inside him. Once he'd thought he lusted for Brangwen, but now a new lust had driven that passion out. To delve into secret lore, to learn and master the secret ways of the universe, to stand in control of forces and powers that few people even knew existed—against rewards such as those, mere love looked as valuable as a pebble lying in the dirt.

The prince's ride was a short one. One of the many things bemusing Galrion these days was the way that Rhegor had chosen to settle so close to the Falcon clan and Brangwen, where Galrion could stumble across him and the dweomer both. If he'd been but ten miles farther south, I'd never have found him, Galrion thought. Truly, dweomer must be my Wyrd. It occurred to him that his love for Brangwen was probably just a tool in the hands of his Wyrd, drawing him to Rhegor. Rhegor himself, of course, had already hinted that there were other, important reasons that Galrion had fallen in love with her; Galrion's heart sank as he remembered those hints.

Just as the drizzle was dying into a cloudy gray noon, he rode out of the woods into cleared fields and saw the Falcon dun, rising at the crest of an artificial hill, built for defense in this flat country. Around the base of the hill ran a pair of earthworks and ditches; at the top stood a wooden palisade with iron-bound gates. Inside stood the squat stone broch and a clutter of round wooden sheds and huts for the servants. As Galrion led his horse in, the muddy ward came alive with servants—a groom running to take his horse, a page to take his saddlebags, the chamberlain to greet him and escort him ceremoniously inside. As the aged chamberlain struggled with the heavy door, the prince glanced up. Over the lintel was a severed head, blackened, weather-shrunken, with rain dripping from the remains of a blond beard. Brangwen's father, Dwen, was one of the last of the old-style warriors. No matter how much the priests reproached him, no matter how often his daughter begged him to have it taken down, Dwen stubbornly kept his trophy up, the head of his worst enemy from a long blood feud.

The great hall was warm, smokey, and light-shot from the fires burning at either side. Up by the bigger hearth, Dwen and Gerraent were drinking in their carved chairs with a pack of staghounds sleeping in the dirty straw by their feet. Gerraent rose to greet Galrion, but Dwen stayed seated. He was sodden in his chair, a florid-faced man whose rheumy eyes glanced up through folds of skin. It was hard to believe that in his youth he must have looked much like his son, this tall blond warrior, square-shouldered, with an arrogant toss to his head.

"Good morrow, my liege," Gerraent said. "My sister's in her chamber. I'll send a page for her."

"My thanks." Galrion bowed to Dwen. "My lord."

"Sit down, lad, and have some ale." Dwen wheezed as he spoke, then coughed and nearly choked.

Galrion felt a cold shudder, a bristling of hairs along the back of his neck as if a draft had touched him. Although Dwen had been ill for years and never seemed to sicken further, Galrion knew with a sharp stab of dweomer that soon he would die. A page brought Galrion ale, a welcome distraction from Dwen's illness. When Galrion raised the tankard to Gerraent in friendly salute, Gerraent forced out a smile that was the barest twitch of his mouth. It didn't take dweomer to know that Gerraent hated him. Galrion merely wondered why.

The door across the great hall opened, and Brangwen came in with her maidservant in attendance. A tall lass, willow-slender in a dark green dress, she wore her long blond hair caught back in a simple clasp, as befitted an unmarried woman. Her eyes were as deep and blue as a winter river—the most beautiful lass in all Deverry, men called her, with a face that was dowry enough for any man in his right mind. Drawn by the love he'd thought he'd cast out of his mind, Galrion rose to greet her and take both her hands in his.

"I didn't think to see you soon, my prince," Brangwen said. "This gladdens my heart."

"And it gladdens mine, my lady."

Galrion seated her in his chair, then took a footstool from the maidservant and put it down to keep Brangwen's feet off the damp, straw-strewn floor. He perched on the edge of the stool and smiled up at her while she laughed, as merry as sunlight in the dark room.

"Will his highness honor me by riding with me to the hunt tomorrow?" Gerraent said.

"I won't, by your leave," Galrion said. "I have things to discuss with my lady."

"She's not your lady yet." Gerraent turned on his heel and stalked out of the hall.

When he slammed the door shut behind him, Dwen roused from his doze, glanced around, then fell back asleep.

"Oh here, Gwennie," Galrion whispered. "I hope I haven't offended your brother by not riding with him on the morrow."

"Oh, Gerro's in such a mood these days." Brangwen shrugged delicately. "I can't talk a word of sense into him about anything. Here, my love, don't you think it's time he married? He's put it off awfully late. He'll be twenty at the turning of the summer."

"True enough." Galrion was remembering his dweomer-warning of Dwen's coming death. "He'll be the Falcon someday, after all. Is there any woman he favors?"

"Not truly. You men can be such beasts." Brangwen giggled, hiding her mouth behind her hand. "But well, Gerro rides to hunt with Lord Blaen of the Boar, and his sister's just absolutely mad for Gerro. I've been trying to speak well of her to him, but he doesn't much listen."

"I've seen the Lady Ysolla at court. She's a lovely lass, but nothing compared to you, of course."

The compliment brought another giggle and a blush. At times Brangwen was a helpless little thing, unlike the women at the court, who were trained as partners in rulership. Once Galrion had looked forward to the chance to prune and form his wife's character; now, he found himself thinking that she was going to take an awful lot of his time.

"Do you know what Ysolla told me?" Brangwen said. "She said that Blaen's jealous of you."

"Indeed? That could be a serious matter if it's true."

"Why?"

"Ye gods, think! The Boar Rampant was involved in many a plot against the last dynasty. A little lover's rivalry is a political matter when one of the rivals is a prince."

"Truly. My apologies."

She was so woebegone about being snapped at that Galrion patted her hand. She bloomed instantly and bent down to allow him to kiss her cheek.

Circumstances conspired to keep the prince from having his necessary talk with his betrothed. All evening, Gerraent kept them sullen company. On the bright and sunny morrow, Brangwen settled her father outside in the ward, then sat down beside him with her needlework. Much to Galrion's annoyance, the old man stayed wide awake. Finally, when Gerraent stopped by on his way to hunt, Galrion decided that since he might soon be Gerraent's elder brother, he might as well put that authority to good use.

"Here, Gerro," Galrion said. "I'll ride a little way with you after all."

"Well and good." Gerraent shot him a glance that said the exact opposite. "Page, run and saddle the prince's horse."

Preceded by a pack of hounds and followed by a pair of servants, Galrion and Gerraent rode to the forest. The Falcon clan lay lonely on the edge of the kingdom. To the north, the clan's farmlands stretched out until they met those of the Boar, their only near neighbor. To the east and south was nothing but unclaimed land, meadow and primeval forest. It occurred to Galrion that Brangwen was doubtless looking forward to the splendid life at court that he could no longer give her.

"Well, young brother," Galrion said at last. "There's something I wanted to talk with you about. My lady Brangwen tells me that you've won the favor of Ysolla of the Boar. She'd make any man a fine wife."

Gerraent stared straight ahead at the road.

"You're nineteen," Galrion said. "It's time you married for your clan's sake. The head of a clan needs heirs."

"True spoken. I know my duty to my clan."

"Well then? Blaen's your sworn friend. It would be a fine match."

"Did Gwennie put you up to this talk?"

"She did."

Gerraent glanced his way with bitter eyes.

"My sister knows her duty to the clan, too," Gerraent said.

As they rode on, Gerraent was lost in thought, his hand on his sword hilt. Galrion wondered how this brooding proud man was going to take it when Galrion swept his sister off to a hut in the forest instead of the palace. The prince was vexed all over again at his stupidity in getting himself betrothed just as he had found the dweomer.

"Does Gwennie think Ysolla would have me?" Gerraent said.

"She does. She'd bring a fine dowry, too."

They rode in silence for some minutes while Gerraent considered, his mouth working this way and that as if the thought of marrying a rich, pretty wife pained him. Finally he shrugged as if throwing off a weight from his shoulders.

"Grant me a boon, elder brother," Gerraent said. "Will you ride to Blaen with me as my second in the betrothal?"

"Gladly. Shall we ride soon?"

"Why not? The soonest done, the best."

That evening the dinner was a celebration. While the Falcon's demesne stretched broad and prosperous, there had been few sons born to the clan over the past generations. If Gerraent should die without an heir, the clan would die with him, its lands reverting back to the High King for reassignment. Every now and then, Galrion noticed Gerraent looking at the blade of his table dagger, where a falcon mark was graved, the clan's symbol, and his whole life, his duty and power. Galrion knew that Gerraent must be thinking of his duty to preserve the clan every time he turned his brooding eyes to the dagger.

After Brangwen escorted her father from the table, Galrion had a chance at a private word with Gerraent.

"My lady Brangwen was teasing me the other night,"

Galrion said. "Saying Blaen's jealous of me. Is that just a maid's chatter?"

"It's true enough." Gerraent made the admission unwillingly. "But she's dwelling on the thing to please her vanity. Blaen will forget her soon enough. Men in our position marry where we have to, not to please ourselves."

At the bitterness in his voice, Galrion felt a cold touch like a hand down his back, the dweomer-warning of danger. Never had that warning failed to be true, not since he'd felt it first as a little lad, climbing a tree and knowing without knowing how he knew that the branch was about to break under him.

The dun of the Boar clan lay a full day's ride to the north. A stone broch rose three floors above a cobbled ward and proper wooden round houses for the important servants. Off to one side were the stables that also doubled as a barracks for the warband of twelve men. Lord Blaen's great hall was fully forty feet across with a dressed stone floor. Two tapestries hung on either side of the honor hearth, and fine furniture stood around in profusion. As he walked in, Galrion had the thought that Brangwen would be far happier in that dun than she would be in a wilderness.

Blaen himself greeted them and took them to the table of honor. He was a slender man, sandy-haired and with pleasant blue eyes that always seemed to be smiling at a jest, and good-looking in a rather bland way.

"Good morrow, my prince," Blaen said. "What brings me the honor of having you in my hall?"

"My brother and I have come to beg an enormous favor," Galrion said. "My brother has decided that it's time for him to marry."

"Oh, have you now?" Blaen shot Gerraent a smile. "A wise decision, with no heirs for your clan."

"If it's so wise," Gerraent snapped. "Why haven't you made one like it?"

Blaen went as stiff as a stag who sees the hunting pack.

"I have two brothers," Blaen said levelly.

The moment hung there. Gerraent stared into the hearth; Blaen stared at the prince; Galrion hardly knew where to look.

"Ah by the hells," Blaen said. "Can't we dispense with all this mincing around? Gerro, do you want my sister or not?"

"I do." Gerraent forced out a smile. "And my apologies."

When Galrion let his eyes meet Blaen's, he saw only a man who wanted to be his friend—against great odds, perhaps, but he did. Yet the dweomer-warning slid down his back like snow.

In his role as a courting man's second, Galrion went to the woman's hall, a pleasant half-round of a room on the second floor of the broch. On the floor were Bardek carpets in the clan colors of blue, green, and gold; silver candlesticks stood on an elaborately carved table. In a cushioned chair, Rodda, dowager of the clan, sat by the windows while Ysolla perched on a footstool at her mother's side. All around them were wisps of wool from the spinning that had been hastily tidied away at the prince's approach. Rodda was a stout woman with deep-set gray eyes and a firm but pleasant little smile; Galrion had always liked her when they'd met at court. Ysolla was a pretty lass of sixteen, all slender and golden with large eager eyes.

"I come as a supplicant, my lady," Galrion said, kneeling before the two women. "Lord Gerraent of the Falcon would have the Lady Ysolla marry him."

When Ysolla caught her breath with a gasp, Rodda shot her a sharp look.

"This is a grave matter," Rodda pronounced. "My daughter and I must consider this carefully."

"But Mother!" Ysolla wailed.

"My lady?" Galrion said to Rodda. "Do you have any objections to Lord Gerraent?"

"None," Rodda said. "But I have my objections to my lass acting like a starving puppy grabbing a bone. You may tell Gerraent that we are considering the matter, but my son may start discussing the dowry if he wants—just in case Ysolla agrees."

Blaen was expansive about the dowry. Ysolla, of course, had been filling her dower chest for years with embroidered coverlets, sets of dresses, and the embroidered shirt her husband would wear at his wedding. To go with it, Blaen offered ten geldings, five white cows, and a palfrey for Ysolla.

"Gerro?" Galrion said. "That's splendidly generous."

"What?" Gerraent looked up with a start. "Oh, whatever you think best."

Yet that evening Gerraent acted the perfect suitor, happy to have his lady within his reach at last. At table, he and Ysolla

shared a trencher, and Gerraent cut her tidbits of meat and fed
her with his fingers as if they were already married, a gesture that
made Ysolla beam with happiness. Galrion and Rodda, who were
seated next to each other, found themselves watching the couple
and occasionally turning to each other to share a thoughtful
glance. Since the bard was singing, and Blaen laughing with his
brother, Camlann, Galrion and Rodda could whisper in private.

"Tell me," Rodda said. "Do you think Gerraent will come to
love my daughter someday?"

"He'd be a fool not to."

"Who knows what you men will do?"

Galrion broke a slice of bread in half and offered her one
portion.

"Is this better than no bread at all?"

"You're a wise one for someone so young, my prince," Rodda
said, accepting the bread. "Does that come from living at court?"

"It does, because if you want to live to be an old prince, not a
poisoned one, you'd best keep your eyes on every little wave of
everyone's hand and your ears on every word they speak."

"So I've been telling your little Gwennie. Life at court is
going to be difficult for her at first. She's lucky to have a man like
you to watch over her interests."

Galrion felt a stab of guilt. I'm as bad as Gerro, he thought.
I'll have to offer Gwennie at least the half-a-piece of bread—
unless I find her a man who'd give her the whole loaf.

Courtesy demanded that Galrion and Gerraent take the
Boar's hospitality for several days. The more Galrion saw of
Blaen, the more he liked him, a cultured man as well as a generous one, with a fine ear for the songs of his bard and a proper
knowledge of the traditional tales and lore. Even more, Galrion
came to admire Rodda, who carried out her dowager role with
perfect tact. She would make Brangwen a splendid mother-in-
law. At times, Galrion remembered Rhegor's insistence that she
choose freely, but he doubted if Gwennie, poor little innocent
Gwennie, was capable of making such an important decision on
her own.

Late on the second day, the prince escorted the dowager to
the garden for a stroll. The spring sun lay warm on the glossy
leaves and the first shy buds of the roses.

"I'm much impressed with your son," Galrion said. "He should feel more at home at my court."

"My thanks, my prince." Rodda hesitated, wondering, no doubt, how to turn this unexpected honor to her son's advantage. "I'm most grateful that you favor him."

"There's only one slight thing. You'll forgive my bluntness, and I'll swear an honest answer will do Blaen no harm. Just how much does he hold Gwennie against me?"

"My son knows his duty to the throne, no matter where his heart lies."

"Never did I think otherwise. I was merely wondering how fine his honor might be in matters of the heart. Let me be blunt again. Suppose Brangwen was no longer betrothed to me. Would he spurn her as a cast-off woman?"

Briefly Rodda stared, as open-mouthed as a farm lass, before she recovered her polished reserve.

"I think my prince is troubled at heart to speak this way."

"He is, but he'll beg you never to ask him why. He'll tell you this much: he's troubled by the life ahead of Brangwen. Flatterers at court will come around her like flies to spilled mead."

"Not just flies, my prince. Wasps come to spilled mead, and Gwennie is very beautiful."

"She is." Suddenly torn, Galrion wondered if he could truly let her go. "And I loved her once."

"Once and not now?" Rodda raised a doubting eyebrow.

Galrion walked a little ways ahead, letting her catch up with him in the shade of a linden tree. He caught a low branch and stripped the leaves off a twig, to rub them between his fingers before he let them fall.

"My prince is deeply troubled," Rodda said.

"The prince's troubles are his own, my lady. But you never answered me. Would Blaen marry Gwennie if he could?"

"Oh, he would in a moment! My poor lad, I swear he's been ensorceled by Gwennie's blue eyes. He put off marrying until she came of age, and then, well—"

"The prince stepped in, giving the Boar another reason to chafe under the High King's rule. How would the Boar take it if his mother hinted that the prince was yielding to a prior claim?"

"I've no doubt he'd honor the prince always."

Smiling, Galrion made her a deep bow. It could work out

well, he told himself. Yet at the thought of Brangwen lying in another man's arms, his heart gave a flash of rage.

When the day came for Prince Galrion to ride back to court, Gerraent rode a few miles with him simply because he was expected to. The prince smiled and chattered until Gerraent wanted to murder him and leave his body in a ditch by the road. At last they reached the turning, and Gerraent sat on his horse and watched the prince's scarlet and white plaid cloak disappear into the distance. Three more weeks, only three more weeks, and the prince would return from Dun Deverry to take Brangwen away. With her, Gerraent's heart would go breaking.

When he rode back to the dun, Gerraent found Brangwen sitting outside in the sun and sewing. He gave his horse to Brythu, his page, and sat down at her feet like a dog. Her golden hair shone in the sun like fine-spun thread, wisping around the soft skin of her cheeks. When she smiled at him, Gerraent felt stabbed to the heart.

"What are you sewing?" Gerraent said. "Something for your dower chest?"

"It's not, but a shirt for you. The last one I'll ever make, but don't worry, Ysolla does splendid needlework. I'll wager that your wedding shirt is ever so much nicer than my poor Galrion's."

Gerraent merely watched her as she sewed. He wanted to get up and leave her alone, but he stayed trapped in his old torment, that his beautiful sister, the one beautiful thing in his world, would turn him into something ugly and unclean, despised by the gods and men alike, if ever they knew of his secret fault. All at once she cried out. He jumped to his feet before he knew what he was doing.

"I just pricked my finger on the cursed needle," Brangwen said, grinning at him. "Don't look so alarmed, Gerro. But, oh, here, I've gotten a drop of blood on your shirt. Curse it!"

The little red smear lay in the midst of red interlaced bands of spirals.

"No one's ever going to notice it," Gerraent said.

"As long as it's not a bad omen, you're right enough. Doubtless you'll get more gore on it than this. You do get so filthy when you hunt, Gerro."

"I won't wear it hunting until it starts to wear out. It'll be my best shirt, the last one you ever sewed for me." Gerraent caught her hand and kissed the drop of blood away.

Late that night, Gerraent went out to the dark, silent ward and paced restlessly back and forth. In the moonlight, he could see the severed head of old Samoryc glaring down at him with empty eye sockets. Once every dun and warrior's home would have been graced with such trophies, but some years past, the priests had had visions stating that taking heads had come to displease great Bel. Dwen was one of the last of the old-style warriors. Gerraent remembered the day when the priests came to implore him to take the trophy down. A tiny lad, then, Gerraent hid behind his mother's skirts as Dwen refused, roaring with laughter, saying that if the gods truly wanted it down, they'd make it rot soon enough. Chanting a ritual curse, the priests left defeated.

"I'm the curse," Gerraent said to Samoryc. "I'm the curse the gods sent to our clan."

Gerraent sat down on the ground and wept.

The days passed slowly, long days of torment, until Gerraent fled his sister's presence and rode to Blaen on the pretense of seeing his new betrothed, but it was really Blaen's soothing company that he wanted. They were more than friends; the year before, when they had ridden to war together, they had sworn an oath together that they would fight at each other's side until both were dead or both victorious, and they had sealed that oath with drops of their own blood. They spent a pleasant pair of days, drinking at Blaen's hearth, hunting out in his forest preserve, or riding aimlessly across his lands with the warband behind them. Gerraent envied Blaen for having a warband. He was determined to get one of his own; the ten horses that he'd receive in Ysolla's dowry would be a splendid start, and soon Brangwen's royal marriage would bring wealth to the Falcon. Yet, having the coin to support a warband seemed too small a compensation for losing her.

On the third day, late in the afternoon, Gerraent and Blaen rode out alone. Enjoying each other's silent company, they ambled through the fields until they reached a low rise that overlooked meadowlands. Tended by a pair of herders and a dog,

Blaen's herd of white cattle with rusty-red ears grazed peacefully below.

"Let's hope there's no war this summer," Blaen said.

"What?" Gerraent said, grinning. "What are you doing, turning into an old woman?"

"I'm not ready to start sucking eggs yet, but I'll tell you somewhat I'd never tell any other man. There are times when I wish I'd been born a bard, singing about wars instead of fighting them."

Thinking it a jest, Gerraent started to laugh, then stopped at the quiet seriousness in Blaen's eyes. All the way home, he puzzled over it, remembering Blaen's calm courage in battle and wondering how any man could want to be a bard rather than a warrior. They returned to the dun at sunset. As he dismounted, Gerraent saw Brythu running out of the broch.

"My lord!" the boy panted out. "I just got here. Your father's dying."

Gerraent clutched the reins so hard that the leather marked his palm.

"Take the best horse in my stable," Blaen said. "Break him if you have to."

When he rode out, Gerraent left the page behind so that he could make good speed. He galloped through the twilight, alternately trotted and galloped even when dark fell, although the road was treacherous in the pale moonlight. Not for one moment did it occur to him that he might be thrown. All he could think of was his father, dying without a last sight of his son, and of Brangwen, tending the dying alone. Whenever the horse stumbled, he would let it walk to rest, then spur it on again. At last he reached the small village on the edge of his lands. He banged on the tavern door until the tavernman came hurrying down in his nightshirt with a candle lantern in his hand.

"Can you change my horse?" Gerraent said.

"Lady Brangwen had the gray brought here to wait for you."

The gray was the fastest horse in the Falcon's stable. Gerraent switched saddle and bridle, flung the tavernman a coin, then kicked the gray to a gallop, plunging out of the candlelight and into the night-shrouded road. At last he saw the dun rising, the palisade dark against the starry sky. He spurred one last burst

of speed out of the gray and galloped through the open gates. As
he dismounted, the chamberlain ran out of the broch.

"He still lives," Draudd called out. "I'll tend the horse."

Gerraent ran up the spiral staircase and down the hall to his
father's chamber. Propped up on pillows, Dwen was lying in bed,
his face gray, his mouth slack as he fought for every breath.
Brangwen sat beside him and clutched his hand in both of hers.

"He's home, Da," she said. "Gerro's here."

As Gerraent walked over, Dwen raised his head and
searched for him with rheumy eyes. Dwen tried to speak, then
coughed, spitting up a slime of blood-tinged phlegm, slipping
and glistening as his head fell back. He was dead. Gerraent wiped
the spittle off his father's mouth with the edge of the blanket,
then closed his eyes and folded his arms across his chest. The
chamberlain came in, glanced at the bed, then flung himself
down to kneel at Gerraent's feet—at the feet of the new Falcon,
head of the clan and its only hope.

"My lord," Draudd said. "I'd best send a page to the king
straightaway. We've got to catch the wedding party before it
leaves."

"So we do. Get him on the way at dawn."

It would take three days to get the message to Dun Deverry
that Brangwen's wedding would have to wait for a time of
mourning. All at once, as he looked at his father's face, Gerraent
turned sick with self-loathing. He would have given anything to
stop that marriage, anything but this. He threw his head back
and keened, cry after wordless cry, as if he could drive his
thoughts away with the sound.

In the morning, the priests of Bel came from the temple to
preside over the burial. Under their direction, Brangwen and her
serving maid washed the body, dressed it in Dwen's best court
clothes, and laid it on a litter. While the servants dug the grave,
Gerraent groomed and saddled his father's best horse. The procession assembled out in the ward, servants carrying the litter,
the priests just behind, then Gerraent, leading the horse. Sup-
ported by her maid and the chamberlain, Brangwen brought up
the rear. The head priest gave Gerraent a cold smile, then
pointed to the lintel of the door.

"That head comes down today," he said. "Or I won't bury
your father."

"Done," Gerraent said.

Since he refused to order a servant to do such a hideous task, Gerraent climbed up the side of the broch, working his way up the rough stone while the priest waited below with a basket. When Gerraent reached the door, he clung to the lintel and examined the head. There was little left, a stretch of blackening skin over a skull, shreds of hair, a few cracked teeth.

"Well and good, Samoryc," Gerraent said. "Both you and your old enemy are going to be buried today."

Gerraent pulled his dagger and pried out the rusty crumbling nails until the head dropped down into the priest's basket with a sickening little thud. The maidservant screamed; then the ward was silent except for the stamp and snort of the restless horse.

The priests led the procession out and down around the hill to the small grove, the burial ground of the Falcon clan. At the sight of their mother's grave, Brangwen began to weep. The fresh grave lay beside it, a deep trench, some eight feet wide and ten long. As Gerraent led the horse up to it, the horse pulled at the reins and danced in fear, as if he knew the Wyrd in store for him. Gerraent threw the reins to a waiting servant. As the horse tossed up its head, Gerraent drew his sword and struck, killing it cleanly with one blow to the throat. With a gush of blood, the horse staggered forward, its legs buckling, and fell headlong into the grave. Gerraent stepped back and unthinkingly wiped the sword blade clean on his brigga. For the rest of the ceremony, he stood there with the sword in his hand, because he never thought to sheathe it.

At first Gerraent managed to cling to his warrior's calm, even when a sobbing Brangwen poured milk and honey over their father's body. But the first spadeful of earth, the dark mud settling over his father's face, broke him. Keening, he fell to his knees, tossed his head back and sobbed that high strange note over and over. Dimly he felt Brangwen's hands on his shoulders.

"Gerro," she said. "Gerro, Gerro, please stop."

Gerraent let her lead him away, leaning on her as if she were the warrior and he the lass. She took him back to the hall and shoved him into a chair by the hearth. He saw the priests come back, saw them fussing around Brangwen and talking in low voices. She came over to him with a tankard of ale in her hand.

Automatically Gerraent took it, sipped from it, then nearly threw it in her face. It tasted of bitter herbs.

"Drink it," Brangwen said. "Drink it down, Gerro. You've got to sleep."

For her sake Gerraent choked the bitter stuff down. She took the empty tankard from his hands just as he fell asleep in his chair, drowning, or so he felt, in the warm sunlight. When he woke, he was lying on his bed with a torch burning in an iron sconce on the wall. Blaen was sitting on the floor and watching him.

"Ah ye gods," Gerraent said. "How long did I sleep?"

"It's just past sunset. We all rode in an hour or so ago. My mother and your betrothed wanted to be with Gwennie."

Blaen got up and poured water from the clay pitcher on the windowsill. Gerraent drank greedily to wash the bitter aftertaste of the drug out of his mouth.

"How long will you set the period of mourning?" Blaen said.

"For my sake I'd say a year, but that would be cruel to our sisters, wouldn't it? I can go on mourning after they're both married."

"Say to the turning of the fall, then?"

Gerraent nodded in agreement, thinking that Gwennie would be his for one more summer. Then he remembered why he would have the summer. Keening he threw the clay cup against the wall so hard that it shattered. Blaen sat down beside him and grabbed him by the shoulders.

"Here, here, he's gone," Blaen said. "There's nothing more to do or say."

Gerraent rested his head against Blaen's chest and wept. I love him like a brother, he thought. I'll thank all the gods that Gwennie's not marrying him.

Prince Galrion's first week back at court was one long frustration, with never a chance to speak to his father except in full, formal court. He knew that he was holding back, too, letting slip a chance here and there, because his heart was still torn over the question of marrying Brangwen or letting Blaen have her. Finally, he decided to enlist the aid of the one ally he could always trust: his mother. On an afternoon so warm and balmy that it reminded him Beltane was close at hand, Galrion left the city and rode out to find the Queen's hawking party down by Loc Gwer-conydd, the vast lake where three rivers came together west of Dun Deverry.

The Queen and her attendants were having their noon meal at the southern shore. In their bright dresses, the serving women and maidservants looked like flowers scattered through the grass. Queen Ylaena sat in their midst, and a young page, dressed in white, stood behind her with the Queen's favorite little merlin on his wrist. Off to one side menservants tended the horses and other hawks. When Galrion dismounted, the Queen waved him over with an impatient flick of her hand.

"I've hardly seen you since you rode home," Ylaena said. "Are you well?"

"By all means. What makes you think I'm not?"

"You've been brooding somewhat. I can always tell." The Queen turned to her women. "Go down to the lakeshore or suchlike, all of you. Leave us."

The women sprang up like birds taking flight and ran off, laughing and calling to one another. The page followed more slowly, chirruping to the hawk to keep it calm. Ylaena watched them go with a small satisfied nod. For all that she had four grown sons, she was a beautiful woman still, with large dark eyes, a slender face, and only a few streaks of gray in her chestnut hair. She reached into the basket beside her, brought out a piece of sweetbread, and handed it to Galrion.

"My thanks," Galrion said. "Tell me somewhat, Mother. When you first came to court, did the other women envy your beauty?"

"Of course. Are you thinking about your betrothed?"

"Just that. I'm beginning to think you were right to doubt my choice."

"Now's a fine time for that, when you've already pledged your vow to the poor child."

"What son ever listens to his mother until it's too late?"

Ylaena gave him an indulgent smile. Galrion nibbled on the sweetbread and considered strategies.

"You know," Ylaena said. "There's not a lass alive who wouldn't want to be known as the most beautiful woman in all Deverry, but it's a harsh Wyrd in its own way. Your little Gwennie never had the education I had, either. She's such a trusting little soul."

"Just that. I spoke with Lady Rodda of the Boar about the matter, too, when I went with Gerraent for his betrothal. Lord Blaen of the Boar is much enamoured of the lass."

"Indeed? And does that mean trouble coming?"

"It doesn't, but only because Blaen is an honorable man. It's odd, truly. Most lords care naught about their wives one way or another, just so long as she has sons."

"Great beauty can act on the roughest lord like dweomer." Ylaena smiled briefly. "Or on a prince."

Galrion winced at her unfortunate choice of imagery.

"What are you scheming?" Ylaena went on. "Leaving Gwennie to Blaen and finding another wife?"

"Well, somewhat like that. There's one small difficulty to that plan. I still love her, in my way."

"Love may be a luxury that a prince can't afford. I don't remember Blaen well from his few visits to court. Is he like his father?"

"As different as mead from mud."

"Then that's one blessing. I'm sure that if his father hadn't been killed in that hunting accident, he'd be plotting against the king right now."

Ylaena glanced away, sincerely troubled. The Deverry kingship was a risky thing. The lords knew well that in the old days of the Dawntime, kings were elected from among their fellow nobles, and families held the throne only as long as their heirs held the respect of the lords. Under the pressures of colonizing the new kingdom, that custom had died away hundreds of years before, but it was far from unknown for the nobility to organize a rebellion against an unpopular king in order to replace him with a better one.

"Lady Rodda assures me that Blaen will hold loyal," Galrion said.

"Indeed? Well, I respect her opinion. You truly don't want to give Brangwen up, do you?"

"I don't know." Galrion tossed the remains of the bread into the grass. "I truly don't know."

"Here's somewhat else you might think about. Your eldest brother has always been far too fond of the lasses as it is."

All at once Galrion found himself standing, his hand on his sword hilt.

"I'd kill him if he laid one hand on my Gwennie," Galrion growled. "My apologies, Mother, but I'd kill him."

Her face pale, Ylaena rose and caught his arm. Galrion let go of the hilt and calmed himself down.

"Think about this marriage carefully," Ylaena said, her voice shaking. "I beg you—think carefully."

"I will. And my apologies."

Her talk with the prince seemed to have spoiled the Queen's pleasure in her hawking, because she called her servants to her and announced that they were returning to the city.

At that time, Dun Deverry was confined to a low rise about a mile from the marshy shores of Loc Gwerconydd. Ringed with stone walls, it lay on both sides of a rushing river, which was spanned by two stone bridges as well as two defensible arches in the city walls. Clustered inside were round stone houses, scattered along randomly curving streets, that sheltered about twenty thousand people. At either end of the city were two small hills. The southern one bore the great temple of Bel, the palace of the high priest of the kingdom, and an oak grove. The northern hill held the royal compound, which had stood there in one form or another for six hundred years.

Galrion's clan, the Wyvern, had been living on the royal hill for only forty-eight years. Galrion's grandfather, Adoryc the First, had ended a long period of anarchy by finally winning a war among the great clans over the kingship. Although the Wyvern was descended from a member of King Bran's original warband and thus was entitled to be called a great clan, Adoryc the First had forged an alliance among the lesser clans, the merchants, and anyone else who'd support his claim to the throne. Although he'd been scorned for stooping so low, he'd also taken the victory.

As the Queen's party rode through the streets, the townsfolk bowed and cheered her. No matter what they might have thought of her husband in private, they honestly loved Ylaena, who'd endowed many a temple to give aid to the poor and who spoke up often for a poor man to make the king show him mercy. For all his thickheadedness, the king knew what a treasure he had in his wife, too. She was the only person whose advice he would take and trust—at least, when it suited him to do so. Galrion's main hope lay in getting her to advise the king to let his third son leave court for the dweomer. Soon, he knew, he would have to tell his mother the truth.

A stone wall with iron-bound gates ringed the bottom of the royal hill. Beyond was a grassy parkland, where white, red-eared cattle grazed along with the royal horses. Near the crest was a second ring of walls, sheltering a village within the city—the royal compound of huts for servants, sheds, stables, barracks, and the like. In the middle of this clutter and bustle rose the great broch of the Wyvern clan.

The main building was a six-story tower; around it clustered three two-story half-towers like chicks nestling around a hen. In case of fighting, the broch would become a slaughterhouse for the baffled enemy, because the only way into the half-towers lay through the main one. Besides the king and his family, the broch complex housed all the noble-born retainers of the court. It was a virtual rabbit warren of corridors and small wedge-shaped chambers, where constant intrigues and scheming over power and the king's favor were a way of life not only for the retainers, but for the various princes and their wives. Getting out of that broch had always been the consummate goal of Galrion's life.

As befitted a prince, Galrion had a suite of rooms on the second floor of the main tower. His reception chamber was a generous wedge of the round floor plan, with a high, beamed ceiling, a stone hearth, and a polished wooden floor. On the wood-paneled walls hung fine tapestries from the far-off land of Bardek, gifts from various traders who hoped that the prince would speak of them to the king. Since he was honorable in his bribe taking, Galrion always dutifully spoke. The chamber was richly furnished with carved chests, a cushioned chair, and a table, where stood, between bronze wyverns, his greatest treasure: seven books. When Galrion first learned to read, the king was furious, raging that letters were no fit thing for a man, but in his usual stubborn way, Galrion had persevered until now, after some four years of study, he could read almost as well as a scribe.

To avoid the bustle and clamor of the formal dinner in the great hall, Galrion dined privately in his chamber that night. He did, however, receive a guest after the meal to share a silver goblet of mead: Gwerbret Madoc of Glasloc, in whose jurisdiction lay the lands of the Falcon and the Boar. Although below members of the royal family, of course, the rank of gwerbret was the highest in the kingdom, and the title went back to ancient times. The Dawntime tribes elected magistrates called Vergobreti to administer their laws and to speak for the wartime assemblies. Generally the vergobreti were chosen from the noble-born, and at about the time that word became gwerbret in Deverry, the position began to pass from father to son. Since a man who made judgments and distributed booty was in a good position to build up his power, in time the gwerbrets became great, wealthy, and in possession of small armies to enforce their legal rulings on the tieryns and lords beneath them. One last remnant of the Dawntime survived, however, in the council of electors who, if a gwerbret's line died out, would choose the noble clan to succeed it.

Thus, every gwerbret in the kingdom was a force to be reckoned with, and Galrion fussed over Madoc as if he were a prince himself, offering him the cushioned chair, pouring him mead with his own hands, and sending the page away so that they could speak privately. The object of these attentions merely smiled benignly. A solid man with a thick streak of gray in his raven-dark hair, Madoc cared more for fine horses than honors and for a good battle more than rank. That night he was in a jesting mood, pledging the prince with his goblet of mead in mock solemnity.

"To your wedding, my prince!" Madoc said. "For a man who doesn't say much, you're a sly one. Fancy you nipping in and getting the most beautiful lass in the kingdom."

"I was rather surprised she accepted me. No one could ever call me the most beautiful lad."

"Oh, don't give yourself short value. Brangwen sees beyond a lad's face, which is more than many a lass does." Madoc had a swallow of mead, long enough to burn an ordinary drinker's throat. "I don't mind saying that every man in the kingdom is going to envy you your wedding night. Or have you already claimed your rights as her betrothed?"

"I haven't. I had no desire to set her brother against me just for one night in her bed."

Although Galrion was merely speaking casually, Madoc turned troubled, watching him shrewdly over the rim of his goblet.

"Well?" Galrion went on. "How do you think Gerraent would have taken it, if I'd bedded his sister under his roof?"

"He's a strange lad." Madoc looked idly away. "He's been out there alone on the edge of that cursed forest too much, but he's a good lad withal. I rode with him in that last rebellion against your father. By the hells, our Gerro can fight. I've never seen a man swing a sword as well as he does, and that's not idle praise, my prince, but my considered judgment."

"Then coming from you, that's high praise indeed."

Madoc nodded absently and had another sip of mead. When he spoke again, it was to change the subject to the legal doings of his gwerbretrhyn—and he kept it there.

It was late, and Madoc long gone, when a page came with a summons from the King. Galrion assumed that Ylaena had mentioned something to him about his wavering betrothal.

Since the King scorned luxury as unfit for a fighting man, even a regal one, his large chamber was perfectly plain, with the torches in their iron sconces the only decoration on the stone walls. Near the hearth, where a small fire burned to ward off the spring chill, King Adoryc was sitting on a plain wooden chair, with Ylaena beside him on a footstool. When Galrion came in, the King stood up, setting his hands on his hips. Adoryc the Second was a massive man, broad-shouldered, tall, with a thick neck and a square face, perpetually ruddy. His gray hair and thick mustaches were still touched with blond here and there.

"So, you young cub," Adoryc said. "I've got somewhat to say to you."

"Indeed, my liege?"

"Indeed. What by all the hells have you been doing out in the forest with that daft old man?"

Caught off guard, Galrion could only stare at him.

"Don't you think I have you followed?" Adoryc went on with a grim smile. "You may be fool enough to ride alone, but I'm not fool enough to let you."

"Curse your very soul!" Galrion snapped. "Spying on me."

"Listen to your insolent little hound." Adoryc glanced at Ylaena. "Cursing his own father. But answer me, lad. What have you been doing? The village folk tell my men that this Rhegor's a daft old herbman. I can get you an apothecary if the prince has royal boils or suchlike."

Galrion knew that the moment had come for truth, even though he had never been less willing to tell it in his life.

"He earns his living with his herbs, sure enough," Galrion said. "But he's a dweomer-master."

Ylaena caught her breath in an audible gasp.

"Horsedung!" Adoryc said. "Do you truly think I'll believe such babble? I want to know what you're doing, spending so much time with him when you tell me you're at the Falcon dun."

"Studying with him," Galrion said. "Why shouldn't a prince study the dweomer?"

"Ah ye gods!" Ylaena burst out. "I've always known you'd leave me for that!"

Adoryc rose, turning to stare his wife into silence. Hastily Galrion scrambled up to face him.

"Why not?" the King said. "Why not? Because I forbid it."

"Oh here, you just called it horsedung," Galrion said. "Why are you raging now?"

Swinging too fast to be dodged, Adoryc slapped him hard across the face. When Ylaena cried out, Adoryc turned on her.

"Get out of here, woman," Adoryc said. "Now."

Ylaena fled through the curtained archway that led to the women's hall. Adoryc drew his dagger, then stabbed it into the back of the chair so hard that when he took his hand away, the dagger quivered for a moment. Galrion held his ground and stared steadily at him.

"I want a vow out of you," Adoryc said. "A solemn vow that you'll never touch this nonsense again."

"Never could I lie to my own father. So I can't swear it."

Adoryc slapped him backhanded.

"By the hells, Father! What do you hold so much against it?"

"What any man would hold. Whose stomach wouldn't turn at somewhat unclean?"

"It's not unclean. That's a tale the priests make up to frighten women away from witchcraft."

The barb hit its mark. Adoryc made a visible effort to be calm.

"I can't give it up," Galrion went on. "It's too late. I know too much already for it to let me rest."

When Adoryc took a sharp step back, Galrion finally realized that his father was afraid, and him a man who would ride straight into a hopeless battle and take no quarter from man or god.

"Just what do you know?" the King whispered.

Galrion had Rhegor's permission to display one small trick to persuade his father. He raised his hand and imagined that it was glowing with blue fire. Only when the image lived no matter where he turned his mind did he call upon the Wildfolk of Aethyr, who rushed to do his bidding and bring the blue light through to the physical plane, where Adoryc could see it too. It flared up like a torch, raging from his fingers. Adoryc flung himself back, his arm over his face as if to ward a blow.

"Stop it!" Adoryc bellowed out. "I say stop it!"

Galrion forced the fire away just as the King's guard flung open the door and rushed into the chamber with drawn swords. Adoryc pulled himself together with a will almost as strong as his son's.

"You can all go," Adoryc said, grinning. "My thanks, but I'm only arguing with the stubbornest whelp in the litter."

The captain of the guard bowed, glancing Galrion's way with a smile of honest admiration. As soon as the men were gone and the door shut, Adoryc pulled the dagger free of the chair back.

"I'm half minded to slit your throat and put a clean end to this," Adoryc remarked, in a casual tone of voice. "Don't you ever do that again around me."

"I won't, then," Galrion said, smiling. "But it makes a handy thing on a dark night when you've dropped your torch."

"Hold your tongue!" Adoryc clutched the dagger tight. "To think a son of mine—and as cold as ice about it!"

"But ye gods, Father, can't you see? It's too late to go back. I want to leave the court and study. There's no other road open to me."

Adoryc held the dagger up so that the blade caught the torchlight.

"Get out," Adoryc whispered. "Get out of my presence before I do a dishonorable thing."

Galrion turned and walked slowly toward the door. The flesh on his back prickled. Once he was safely out, Galrion allowed himself one long sigh of relief that the dagger was still in his father's hand, not in his back.

On the morrow, Galrion went early in search of his mother,

but he found her talking urgently with her serving women. To pass the time until he could speak with her, he decided to go for a walk through the parkland. As he walked down the hill to the first gate, he was thinking that it should have come as no surprise that the King would fear a prince with dweomer-power—Adoryc feared every possible rival to his throne. At the gate, two guards stepped forward and blocked his path.

"My humble apologies, my prince," one said. "The King's given orders that you not be allowed to pass by."

"Oh, has he now?" Galrion's voice snapped in fury. "And would you raise your hand to stop me?"

"My apologies, my prince." The guard licked nervous lips. "But at the King's orders, I would."

As Galrion stalked back to the broch, he was determined to have it out with his father over this insult no matter what it cost him. As he strode down the corridors, servants scattered in front of him like frightened birds. Galrion slammed into the council chamber, knocked aside a page who tried to stop him, and found the King standing by the window and talking with a dusty, travel-stained lad who knelt at the King's feet.

"Well and good," Adoryc was saying. "Tomorrow you can take back the message of our condolences to Lord Gerraent. Our heart sorrows for the Falcon."

Only then did Galrion recognize one of the pages from the Falcon dun. Ah ye gods, he thought, Dwen is dead! All at once, he felt his subtle plans slipping away from him, as when a child builds a tower out of bits of wood only to see it tumble down at the first breath of wind.

"And here is the prince," Adoryc said. "Does your lord have any message of import for him?"

"He does, Your Highness," the page said. "My prince, Lord Gerraent has set the period of mourning until the turning of the fall. He humbly begs your understanding on this matter."

"He has it, truly," Galrion said. "Come to me before you return to the Falcon. I'll give you a message for my lady."

Adoryc dismissed the page in the care of another, who would feed and shelter him for the night. Once they were alone, the King dropped his false civility.

"So," Adoryc said. "You seem to know what's going on well enough. Did your cursed dweomer show you Dwen's death?"

"It did," Galrion said. "But I never thought it would come so soon."

The King's face first paled, then went scarlet, but Galrion got his thrust in first.

"Here, Father," Galrion said. "Why have you told the guards to keep me in?"

"Why do you think?" Adoryc snapped. "I'm not having you ride out of here on the sly to your cursed old hermit. Here, this evil news of Lord Dwen made me remember your betrothed. What were you planning on doing? Marrying her and taking her to a hut in the forest while you dabble about with spells?"

"Just that, if she'll go."

"You little dog!" Adoryc's mouth moved, seeking insults. "You arrogant little—"

"Oh here, where do I get my arrogance but from you? Why shouldn't a woman follow where her man wills to go?"

"No reason in the world—unless she's the noble-born daughter of a great clan." Adoryc stepped closer. "You ugly little dolt, haven't you thought of the insult to the Falcon? Gerraent's uncle died for the sake of our throne, and now you dare to treat their kin this way! Do you want to drive them to rebellion?" He gave Galrion a backhanded slap. "Get out of my sight. I don't want to see you until you've gotten sense into your head."

Galrion stalked back to his chamber, slammed the door behind him, and flung himself down into his chair to think. There was nothing for it now but to break his betrothal—but the King would never allow that insult to the Falcon, either. I could slip away somehow, Galrion thought, climb the walls at night and be in the forest before they catch me—and break Gwennie's heart by deserting her without even a message to explain. He had the horrible feeling that Rhegor was going to be displeased by the way he was handling things. With the period of mourning, you've got time, he told himself. At the thought, the dweomer-warning flared up so strongly that he shivered. For some reason that the dweomer couldn't tell him, there was no time at all.

Galrion got up and paced over to the window. When he looked down, he saw two armed guards standing at the foot of the broch directly below his window. Galrion rushed to his door and flung it open to find four more guards in the corridor. The captain managed to give him a sickly smile.

"My apologies, my prince," the captain said. "The King orders that you remain in your chamber. We're only allowed to let your page through."

Galrion slammed the door and returned to his chair. He wondered how long the King would make him wait before summoning him.

Four days, it turned out, four tedious days with no company but his books and his page, who brought him food and took away the leavings silently, furtively because servants of an out-of-favor master often met ill ends at court. Every now and then, Galrion would open the door and chat with the guards, who were friendly enough, because their place was secure no matter what happened to the prince. Once Galrion sent a message to the Queen and begged her to come see him. The answer came back that she didn't dare.

Finally, on the fourth night, the guards opened the door and announced that they were taking him to the King. When they marched Galrion into the royal chamber, Adoryc dismissed them. There was no sign of Ylaena.

"Very well," Adoryc said. "Have you had enough time to think about swearing me that vow? Leave this dweomer nonsense behind, and everything will be as it was before."

"Father, believe me—I have no choice but to say you nay," Galrion said. "I can't leave the dweomer because it won't leave me. It's not like breaking your sword and retiring to a temple."

"So—you've got plenty of fancy words to justify disobeying the King, do you? For your mother's sake, I'll give you one last chance. We'll see what Brangwen can do to talk you round."

"Are you going to pen me like a hog until fall?"

"I'm sending for her to come to court. Curse the mourning. I'm sending a speeded courier to Lord Gerraent tomorrow. My apologies will go with him, but I want them both here as fast as they can ride. I'm going to tell Lady Brangwen what her dolt of a betrothed is planning on doing, and I'll order her to talk you round."

"And if she can't?"

"Then neither of you will ever leave the palace. Ever."

Galrion felt so heartsick that he nearly wept. Never leave—never ride through his beloved forest again—never see the snow hanging thick on leafless branch nor a river in spate—never? And

Brangwen, too, would be shut up as a prisoner for years all for her
husband's fault. Then, only then, when it seemed too late for
them both, did he realize that he truly loved her, not just her
god-cursed beauty, but her.

That night Galrion had no hope of sleep. He paced back and
forth in his chambers, his mind a confused babble of dread, remorse, and futile schemes of escape. It would take a hard-riding
courier three days to reach the Falcon, then another five for
Brangwen and Gerraent to reach Dun Deverry. I'd have to meet
them on the road, he thought, if I can get out—out of the best-
guarded fort in the kingdom. His dweomer could never help
him. He was the merest apprentice, with only an apprentice's
feeble tricks at his disposal. A little knowledge, a few wretched
herbs, Galrion reproached himself. You're no better than a
woman dabbling in witchcraft! All at once, his plan came to him,
and he laughed aloud. But he would need help. As much as he
hated to put her at risk, he had no one to turn to but the Queen.

In the morning, Galrion sent his page to Ylaena with the
urgent message that she come see him. She sent back the answer
that she would try, but it depended on the King's whim. For
three days Galrion waited, counting in his mind every mile that
the King's courier was riding, closer and closer to the Falcon
keep. Finally, he sent the page with a pair of torn brigga and the
request that his mother's servants mend them. Such an errand
would allay the King's suspicions, if indeed he ever heard of
anything so trivial. The ruse worked. On the next morning, the
Queen herself brought the mended brigga back, slipping into his
room like a servant lass.

"Mother," Galrion said. "Do you know the King's plan?"

"I do, and I weep for little Brangwen as much as you."

"Weep for her more, because I'm unworthy of her. Here, will
you help me for her sake? All I ask is this. If I give you some more
clothes to mend, will you take them and have your maids leave
them out in the women's hall tonight? Tell them to put them on
the table by the door."

"I will." Ylaena shuddered lightly. "I don't dare know
more."

After the noon meal, when the guards were bound to be
bored with their light duty, Galrion opened his door for a chat.

His luck was with him—they were sitting on the floor and playing dice for coppers.

"Can I join you?" Galrion said. "If I sit on this side of the doorway, we won't be breaking the King's orders."

Obligingly the guards moved their game over closer. Normally Galrion never wagered on the dice, simply because he could always tell which way they would fall with his Sight. Now, to get sympathy from his guards, he used the Sight to place his bets so that he lost steadily.

"By every god and his wife," the captain said. "Your luck is bad today, my prince."

"How could it be otherwise? It's been against me for weeks now. If you've ever envied the prince, let this be a lesson for you. It's a hard thing to fall from your own father's favor."

The captain nodded in melancholy agreement.

"I don't mind telling you, my prince," he said. "That I think I'd go daft, shut up like you are."

"I'm close to it," Galrion said with a sigh. "And the nights are more wearisome than the days, because I can't sleep well. Oh here, I know the King's orders allow you to bring me things. Would that hold true of a woman?"

"I don't see why not." The captain shared a grin with his men. "Is there one of your mother's maids you fancy?"

"Do you know Mae, the golden-haired lass? She's taken a tumble with me before this."

"Well and good, then. We'll do our best to smuggle her in tonight, when things are all quiet-like."

At the dinner hour, Galrion had his page bring him a flagon of mead and two goblets. He dug down into a chest and found his packets of dried herbs. Rhegor was teaching him simple herbcraft, and he'd brought his student work home mostly as a pleasant reminder of his days in the forest. Now, he had a real need for that packet of valerian, the most potent soporific in an herbman's stock. He ground up only a spare dose. He had no desire to make Mae ill with too big a dose, and besides, the musty, thick taste of valerian might give his whole game away.

Toward midnight, Galrion heard Mae giggling in the corridor and the captain telling her to hush. He opened the door and saw that she was wearing a cloak with the hood up to hide her face, exactly as he'd hoped.

"Greetings, my sweet," Galrion said. "How kind you are to a dishonored man."

When Mae giggled, Galrion clapped his hand over her mouth in pretend alarm.

"Keep her quiet when you take her back, will you?" Galrion said to the captain.

"Hear that, lass?" the captain said. "Not one word out of you on the way back."

Mae nodded, her big blue eyes as solemn as a child's, when it's been let into a secret. Galrion ushered her inside and barred the door behind them. Mae took off her cloak, revealing a loose flowing dress—loose enough, Galrion thought, to fit his shoulders nicely. He'd chosen her deliberately because she was tall for a lass, with squarish shoulders and a long graceful neck.

"I've had the page bring us mead," Galrion said. "Sit and drink with me awhile."

"You're always so gallant," Mae said. "It aches my heart to see you out of favor."

"My thanks. And what about my marriage? Does that ache your heart too?"

Mae merely shrugged and went into his bedchamber. Galrion handed her the drugged goblet, then took a sip from his own, a gesture that automatically made her drink some of hers. They sat down together on the edge of the bed.

"Ah well," Mae said at last. "We've had our good times, and a prince marries where the kingdom needs him to." She grinned, winking at him. "I only hope your new wife never hears of me."

"Oh here—you must have a new man to be so agreeable."

Mae had another long swallow of the mead and winked again.

"Maybe I do, maybe I don't," she said with a dramatic sigh. "But no one will know where I've been tonight, and so what if he does? He won't be arguing with the prince, I'll wager, even if you are out of favor for now." She had still another sip. "These bad times will pass, my prince. Your mother's ever so upset, but she'll talk the King round."

"So I hope," Galrion said piously.

Mae yawned, shaking her head, then had a sip of mead.

"This mead tastes so sweet," she said. "It's awfully good."

"Only the best for you," Galrion said. "Drink that up, and we'll have a bit more."

A bit more was unnecessary—by the time she had finished that first goblet, Mae was yawning, shutting her eyes, then forcing them open. When she leaned over to set the goblet on the table beside the bed, she dropped it. Galrion grabbed her just as she fell forward into his arms.

Galrion undressed her, tucked her up comfortably into his bed, then got out the packet of herbs and left it by her goblet to make it clear that she was a drugged, unwilling accomplice. He paced restlessly around, letting enough time lapse to satisfy the guards. When he could bear to wait no longer, he changed into her clothes, drew the hood of the cloak around his face, and slipped out into the hall. Suspecting nothing, the guards gave him a leer and a wink, then escorted him along the dark corridors. At the door of the women's hall, the captain gave him a friendly pat on the behind, told him that he was a good lass, and gallantly opened the door for him.

Dim moonlight filtered through the windows of the silent room. Galrion found the table, his clothes, and a dagger in a sheath, left under his brigga. Thanking his mother in his heart, he changed into his clothes and settled the dagger inside his shirt. When he looked out, the ward below was empty. Carefully he edged out onto the window ledge, turned precariously, and started down the rough stonework. Praying that no one would walk by, he clambered down, his hands aching and bleeding on the stone, until at last he reached the ward.

Galrion ran from hut to hut and shed to shed until he reached the stables. Abutting directly on the wall was a storage shed that he could climb easily. He swung from the roof to the wall, then crawled on his stomach until he reached a place where an oak grew on the far side. He swung into the branches, climbed down, then lingered in the safe shadows. He could see down the long slope of parkland to the outer ring, where, against the starry sky moved the dark shapes of the night guards, patrolling the ramparts. The most dangerous part of the escape lay ahead.

Galrion circled the inner ring until he could see the road leading down to the outer gates. He crawled downhill in the long grass until he was out of sight of the guard at the inner gates, then stood up and boldly walked down the road. When he came close to the guard station, he broke into a run.

"Here!" Galrion made his voice as high and unsteady as a lad's. "Open up! An errand for the cook."

"Hold, lad." A guard stepped forward to peer at him in the darkness. "That's a likely tale."

"Nerdda's having her child," Galrion said. "And it's bad. The midwife needs the apothecary. Please hurry."

"That's the kitchen wench," another guard called out. "She's been heavy for weeks now."

Hardly daring to believe in his success, Galrion raced through the postern gate and kept running until he was well into the silent city. He crouched among some empty ale barrels behind a tavern and caught his breath while he considered his next move. Not the best trick in the world would get him past the guards at the city gates, but the river flowed through the arches in the walls without asking anyone's permission. Cautiously he stood up and began slipping through the alleys behind the buildings. He was halfway to the river when he heard footsteps behind him. He flung himself into a doorway and crouched in the shadows as a pair of drunken riders from the King's warband staggered past. They weren't more than two yards beyond him when one of them burst out singing at the top of his lungs. Galrion cursed him and prayed that the city guards wouldn't come running to deal with the nuisance.

At last the riders were gone, and the street silent again. With a constant eye out for trouble, Galrion made his way down to the riverbank and waded out to the deep part of the channel. As he let the current take him, he saw far above guards pacing back and forth on the city wall. Closer, closer—the river was sweeping him along fast to the point where they might look down and see him. He held his breath and plunged down deep. In the murky water it was hard to see, but he thought he saw the darker stone of the arches sweep by him. His lungs ached, began to burn like fire, but he forced himself to stay down until the desperate pain drove him, panting and gasping, to the surface. He swung himself over on his back like a seal and barely swam while he breathed in the blessed air. Nervously he looked around, but the guards were far behind him, and no one else was out on the riverbank.

Galrion made his way to the bank and crawled out under a copse of willow trees. Free, he thought. Now all I've got to do is get to Brangwen. Galrion wrung the worst of the water out of his clothes and put them back on damp. The sky told him that he had about five hours till dawn. His page wouldn't find Mae for about another hour after that, and there was bound to be another hour's confusion before the King's warband rode out to hunt him down. It wasn't much of a lead, but if he could only reach the wild forest, they would never find him. He knew the tracks through it, while the riders would be blundering around, making too much noise to surprise any kind of game.

Galrion set off across the meadows to the neighboring farms and the horse he had in mind to steal. It was an easy theft; he'd often ridden this way and stopped to admire the sleek bay gelding, who remembered his kind words and pats. When Galrion approached, the bay came right up and let him take its halter. Since there was no lead rein and no time to steal one, Galrion tore a strip of cloth off the bottom of his shirt and prayed that it would hold. The bay was well trained, responding to the touch of this improvised rein along its neck. Galrion set off at a gallop down the east-running road. If the King's messenger wasn't already with Gerraent, he would reach the Falcon on the morrow.

After a few minutes he slowed the bay to a walk to save its strength. Alternately walking and trotting in short bursts, they traveled all night and reached, just at dawn, the border of the King's personal demesne. Galrion turned south, heading for the wild heath to avoid the well-traveled road. On this roundabout route, it would take longer to reach the forest, but he had no choice. By noon, the horse was weary and stumbling under him. Galrion dismounted and led it along until they came to an unkempt woodland on the edge of pasture land. He found a stream and let the bay drink. It was when the bay began grazing on the grassy bank that Galrion realized he was starving. In his hurry, he'd forgotten to bring any coin, not so much as a copper. He could no longer ride up to a noble lord's door and expect to be fed simply because he was a prince.

"I'm not quite as clever as I need to be," he said to the horse. "Well, I wonder how you go about stealing food from farmers?"

The horse needed to rest, and Galrion was weaving with exhaustion. Letting the improvised halter rope trail for want of a proper tether, he left the horse to its grass, then sat down with his back to a tree. Although he told himself that he would rest only for an hour, when he woke, it was late in the afternoon, and he heard voices nearby. He jumped to his feet and pulled the dagger out of his shirt.

"I don't know whose it is," a man was saying. "A stolen horse, from the look of this bit of cloth."

Galrion crept through the trees and came upon a farmer and a young lad, who was holding the bay by the halter. When the horse saw Galrion, it nickered out a greeting. The farmer spun around, and he raised his heavy staff to the ready.

"You!" he called out. "Do you claim this horse?"

"I do." Galrion stepped out of cover.

The lad started urging the horse out of the way, but he kept frightened eyes on his father and this dirty, dangerous stranger. When Galrion took a step forward, the farmer dropped to a fighting crouch. Galrion took another step, then another—all at once, the farmer laughed, dropped the staff, and made a kneel at the prince's feet.

"By the sun and his rays, my liege," the farmer said. "So you're out of the palace. I didn't recognize you at first."

"I'm out indeed. How do you know so much?"

"What's better gossip than the doings of the King? Truly, my prince, the news of your disgrace is all over the marketplace. Everyone's as sad as sad for your mother's sake, her such a good woman and all."

"She is at that. Will you help me for her sake? All I ask is a bit of rope for this halter and a meal."

"Done, but I've got a bridle to spare." The farmer rose, dusting dead leaves off his knees. "The King's warband rode by on the east road today. The tailor's daughter saw them when she went out to pick violets."

The farmer was even better than his word. Not only did he give the prince the bridle and a hot dinner, but he insisted on packing a sack of loaves of bread, dried apples, and oats for the gelding—more food, no doubt, than he could truly spare. When Galrion left at nightfall, he was sure that the King's men would hear nothing but lies from this loyal man.

It hardly mattered what the farmer would have told them, if indeed they did ride his way, because by midmorning of the next

day, Galrion led his weary horse into the tangled virgin forest. He
found water, gave the horse a meager ration of oats, then sat
down to think. He was tempted simply to go to Rhegor and let
Brangwen think what she liked about him, but he had the distinct feeling that Rhegor would be furious. For the first time in
his pampered life, Galrion knew what it was to fail. He'd been a
fool, dishonorable, plain and simply stupid—he cursed himself
with every insult he could think of. Around him the forest
stretched silent, dappled with sunlight, indifferent to him and his
short-lived human worries.

Husbanding every scrap of food, scrounging what fodder he
could for his horse, Galrion made his way east through the forest
for two days. He stayed close to the road and tried to calculate
where the Falcon's party might be, because he had made up his
mind to intercept it. Late one afternoon, he risked coming out
onto the road and riding up to the crest of a low hill. Far away,
hanging over the road, was a faint pall of dust—horses coming.
Hurriedly he pulled back into the forest and waited, but the
Falcon's party never rode past. With Brangwen and her maidservants along, they would be making early camps to spare the
women's strength. As it grew dark, Galrion led the bay through
the forest and worked his way toward the camp. From the top of
the next hill he saw it: not just Lord Gerraent and his retainers,
but the King's entire warband.

"May every god curse them," Galrion whispered. "They
knew she'd be the best bait to draw me."

Galrion tied his horse securely in the woods, then ran across
the road and began making his cautious way to the camp. Every
snap of a twig under his foot made him freeze and wait. Halfway
downhill, the trees thinned somewhat, giving him a good look at
the sprawling, disorganized camp. In the clearing along the
stream, horses were tethered; nearby, the warband was gathered
around two fires. Off to one side among the trees was a high-
peaked canvas tent, doubtless for Brangwen's privacy. She had to
be in there, away from the ill-mannered riders.

The true and dangerous question, of course, was where Gerraent might be. The firelight below was too dim for Galrion to
make out anyone's face. He lay flat in the underbrush and
watched until after about an hour, a blond man came out of the
tent and strolled over to one of the fires. No man but Gerraent

would have been allowed in that tent in the first place. As soon as Gerraent was safely occupied with his dinner, Galrion got up, drawing his dagger, then circled through the underbrush, moving downhill and heading for the tent. The warband was laughing and talking, making a lot of blessed noise to cover his approach.

Galrion slit the tent down the back with his dagger, a rip of taut cloth. He heard someone moving inside.

"Galrion?" Brangwen whispered.

"It is."

Galrion slipped back into cover. Wearing only her long nightdress, her golden hair loose over her shoulders, Brangwen crawled out the rip and crept to join him.

"I knew you'd come for me," she whispered. "We've got to go right now."

"Ah ye gods! Will you come with me?"

"Did you ever doubt it? I'd follow you anywhere. I don't care what you've done."

"But you don't even have a scrap of extra clothing."

"Do you think that matters to me?"

Galrion felt as if he'd never truly looked at her before: his poor weak child, grinning like a berserker at the thought of riding away with an exile.

"Forgive me," Galrion said. "Come along—I've got a horse."

Then Galrion heard the sound, the softest crack of a branch.

"Run!" Brangwen screamed.

Galrion swirled around—too late. The guards sprang out of the trees and circled him like a cornered stag. Galrion dropped to a fighting crouch, raised the dagger, and promised himself he'd get one of them before he died. A man shoved his way through the pack of guards.

"That'll do you no good, lad," Adoryc said.

Galrion straightened up—he could never kill his own father. When he threw the dagger onto the ground at Adoryc's feet, the King stooped and retrieved it, his smile as cold as the winter wind. Galrion heard Brangwen behind him, weeping in long sobs, and Gerraent's voice murmuring as he tried to comfort her.

"Nothing like a bitch to bring a dog to heel," Adoryc remarked. "Bring him round to the fire. I want a look at this cub of mine."

The guards marched Galrion around the tent and over to the bigger campfire, where the King took up his stance, feet spread apart, hands on hips. When someone brought Brangwen a cloak, she wrapped it around her and stared hopelessly at Galrion. Gerraent laid a heavy hand on her shoulder and drew her close.

"So, you little whelp," Adoryc said. "What do you have to say for yourself?"

"Nothing, Father," Galrion said. "I'll only ask you for a single boon."

"What makes you think you have the right to ask for any?" Adoryc drew his own dagger and began to fiddle with it as he talked.

"No right at all, but I'm asking for my lady's sake," Galrion said. "Send her away out of sight before you kill me."

"Granted," Adoryc said. "Fair enough."

Brangwen screamed, shoved Gerraent so hard that he stumbled, and ran forward to throw herself at the King's feet.

"Please, my liege, spare his life," Brangwen sobbed. "I beg you, I'll do anything you say, but don't kill him."

When Garraent started forward, the King waved him back.

"Please, please," Brangwen went on. "For the sake of his mother, if not for mine. I beg you. If you must have blood, take mine."

Brangwen clutched the hem of the King's shirt and turned her throat up to him. She was so beautiful, with her hair streaming down her shoulders, with tears running down her perfect face, that even the King's riders sighed aloud in pity for her.

"Ah ye gods," Adoryc said. "Do you love this lout as much as that?"

"I do," Brangwen said. "I'd go with him anywhere, even to the Otherlands."

Adoryc glanced at the dagger, then sheathed it with a sigh.

"Gerraent!" Adoryc said.

Gerraent came forward, took Brangwen by the shoulders, and led her away, but she refused to leave the circle. Galrion was so sick he could barely stand—he was unworthy of her, or so he saw it, and this second failure seemed to shatter him, as if he'd been broken into pieces and could never put those pieces back together in the same way.

"Well, by the hells," Adoryc said mildly. "If I can't slit your throat, Galrion, how am I going to solve this little matter?"

"You could let me and my lady go into exile," Galrion said calmly. "It would spare us all much trouble."

"You little bastard!" Adoryc stepped forward and slapped him across the face. "How dare you?"

Galrion staggered from the force of the blow, but he held his ground.

"Do you want me to tell everyone else what this quarrel between us is all about?" Galrion said. "Do you, Father? I will."

Adoryc went as still as a hunted animal.

"Or shall I just accept exile?" Galrion went on. "And no man need know the cause of it."

"You bastard." Adoryc whispered so low that Galrion could barely hear him. "Or truly, not a bastard, because of all my sons, you're the one most like me." Then he raised his voice. "The cause need not be known, but we hereby do pronounce our son, Galrion, as stripped of all his rank and honor, as turned out of our presence and our demesne, forever and beyond forever. We forbid him our lands, we forbid him the shelter of those sworn to us as loyal vassals, all on pain of death." He paused to laugh under his breath. "And we hereby strip him of the name we gave him at his miserable birth. We proclaim his new name as Nevyn. Do you hear me, lad? Nevyn—no one—nobody at all—that's your new name."

"Done," Galrion said. "I'll bear it proudly."

Brangwen shook herself free of Gerraent's arm. She smiled as proudly as the princess she might have been as she started over to her banished man. With a smile to match, Galrion held out his hand to her.

"Hold!" Gerraent forced himself between them. "My liege, my King, what is this? Am I to marry my only sister to an exile?"

"She's my betrothed already," Galrion snapped. "Your father pledged her, not you."

"Hold your tongue, Nevyn!" Adoryc slapped him across the face. "My lord Gerraent, you have our leave to speak."

"My liege." As he knelt before the King, Gerraent was shaking. "Truly, my father pledged her, and as his son, all I can do is honor the pledge. But my father betrothed her to a good life, one of comfort and honor. He loved his daughter. What will she have now?"

As Adoryc considered, Galrion felt the dweomer-warning like ice, shuddering down his back. He stepped forward.

"Father," Galrion said.

"Never call me that again." Adoryc motioned to the guards. "Keep our no one here quiet."

Before Galrion could dodge, two men grabbed him from behind and twisted his arms behind him. One of them clapped a firm hand over his mouth. Brangwen stood frozen, her face so pale that Galrion was afraid she would faint.

"I beg you, my liege," Gerraent went on. "If I allow this marriage, what kind of a brother am I? How can I claim to be head of my clan if I have this little honor? My liege, if ever the Falcon has paid you any service, I beg you—don't let this happen."

"Done, then," Adoryc said. "We hereby release you from your father's pledge."

"Gerro!" Brangwen sobbed out. "You can't! I want to go. Gerro, let me go."

"Hush." Gerraent rose, turning and sweeping her into his arms. "You don't understand. You don't know what kind of life you'll have, wandering the roads like beggars."

"I don't care." Brangwen tried to struggle free. "Gerro, Gerro, how can you do this to me? Let me go."

Gerraent weakened; then he tossed his head.

"I won't," he said. "I won't have you die in childbirth someday, just because your man doesn't have the price of a midwife, or starve some winter on the road. I'd die myself first."

It was touching, perfectly said, but Galrion knew that Gerraent was lying, that all those fine words were cruel deadly poisoned lies. The dweomer was making him tremble and choke. He struggled in his guard's arms, and bit the man hard in the hand, but all he got for his struggle was a blow on the head that made the world dance before him.

"You're wrong, Gerro," Brangwen said, shoving against his arms. "I know you're wrong. I want to go with him."

"Right or wrong, I'm the Falcon now," Gerraent snapped. "And you're not disobeying me."

Brangwen made one last wrench, but he was too strong for

her. As he dragged her away bodily, she wept, sobbing hysteri-
cally and helplessly as Gerraent shoved her into their tent.
Adoryc motioned to the guards to let Galrion go.

"Now," Adoryc said. "Get this Nevyn out of my sight forever." He handed Galrion his dagger. "Here's the one weapon
allowed to a banished man. You must have a horse, or you
wouldn't be here." He took the pouch at his side and drew out a
coin. "And here's the silver of a banished man." He pressed the
coin into Galrion's hand.

Galrion glanced at it, then flung it into his father's face.

"I'd rather starve," he said.

As the guards fell back in front of him, Galrion strode out of
the camp. At the top of the rise he turned for a last look at
Brangwen's tent. Then he broke into a run, crashing through the
underbrush, running across the road, and tripping at last to fall
on his knees near the bay gelding. He wept, but for Brangwen's
sake, not his own.

II

The women's hall was sunny, and through the windows,
Brangwen could see apple trees, so white with perfumed blos-
soms that it seemed clouds were caught in the branches. Nearby,
Rodda and Ysolla were talking as they worked at their sewing,
but Brangwen let her work lie in her lap. She wanted to weep,
but it was so tedious to weep all the time. She prayed that Prince
Galrion might be well and wondered where he was riding on his
lonely road of exile.

"Gwennie?" Lady Rodda said. "Shall we walk in the meadows this afternoon?"

"If you wish, my lady."

"Well, if you'd rather, Gwennie," Ysolla said. "We could go
riding."

"Whatever you want," Brangwen said.

"Here, child," Rodda said. "Truly, it's time you got over this
brooding. Your brother did what was best for you."

"If my lady says so."

"It would have been ghastly," Ysolla broke in. "Riding behind a banished man? How can you even think of it! It's the
shame. No one would even take you in."

"It would have been their loss, not ours."

Rodda sighed and ran her needle into her embroidery.

"And what about when you had a babe?"

"Galrion never would have let our child starve," Brangwen said with a little toss of her head. "You don't understand. I should have gone with him. It would have been all right. I just know it would have been."

"Now, Gwennie, lamb, you're just not thinking clearly," Rodda said.

"As clearly as I need to," Brangwen snapped. "Oh—my pardons, my lady. But you don't understand. I know I should have gone."

Both her friends stared, eyes narrow in honest concern. They think I'm daft, Brangwen thought, and maybe I am, but I know it!

"Well, there are a lot of men in the kingdom," Ysolla said, in an obvious attempt to be helpful. "I'll wager you won't have any trouble getting another one. I'll wager he's better than Galrion, too. He must have done something awful to get himself exiled."

"At court a man has to do very little to get himself out of favor," Rodda said. "There are plenty of others to do it for him. Now here, lamb, I won't have Galrion spoken ill of in my hall. He may have failed, but truly, Gwennie, he tried to spare you this. He let me know that he saw trouble coming, and he was hoping he'd have time to release you from the betrothal before the blow fell." She shook her head sadly. "But the King is a very stubborn man."

"I can't believe that," Brangwen snapped. "He never would have cast me off to my shame. I know he loves me. I don't care what you say."

"Of course he loved you, child," Rodda said patiently. "That's what I've just been saying. He wanted to release you in such a way as to spare you the slightest hint of shame. When he failed, he planned to take you with him."

"If it weren't for Gerro," Brangwen said.

Rodda and Ysolla glanced at each other, their eyes meeting in silent conference. This argument had come full circle again, in its tediously predictable way. Brangwen looked out the window at the apple trees and wondered why everything in life seemed tedious now.

Brangwen and Gerraent were visiting at the Boar's dun for a few days, and Brangwen knew that Gerraent had arranged the visit for her sake. That night at dinner, she watched her brother as he sat across the table and shared a trencher with Ysolla. He still has his betrothed, Brangwen thought bitterly. It would have been a wonderful release to hate him, but she knew that he had done only what he thought best for her, whether it truly was best or not. Her beloved brother. While their parents and uncles always doted on Gerraent, the precious son and heir, they had mostly ignored Brangwen, the unnecessary daughter. Gerraent himself, however, had loved her, played with her, helped care for her, and led her around with him in a way that was surprising for so young a lad. She remembered him explaining how to straighten an arrow or build a toy dun with stones, and he was always dragging her out of danger—away from a fierce dog, away from the river's edge, and now, away from a man he considered unworthy of her.

All through the meal, Gerraent would sometimes look up, catch her looking at him, and give her a timid smile. She knew that he was afraid she hated him. Eventually Brangwen could no longer bear the crowded hall and made her escape into the cool twilight of Rodda's garden. Red as drops of blood, the roses bloomed thickly. She picked one, cradled it in her hand, and remembered Galrion telling her that she was his one true rose.

"My lady? Are you distressed about somewhat?"

It was Blaen, hurrying across the garden. Brangwen knew perfectly well that he was in love with her. Every soft look, every longing smile that he gave her stabbed her like a knife.

"How can I not be distressed, my lord?"

"Well, true spoken. But every dark time comes to an end."

"My lord, I doubt if the dark will ever end for me."

"Oh here, things are never as bad as all that."

As shy as a young lad, Blaen smiled at her. Brangwen wondered why she was even bothering to fight. Sooner or later, Gerraent would hand her over to his blood-sworn friend whether she wanted to marry him or not.

"My lord is very kind," Brangwen said. "I hardly know what I say these days."

Blaen picked another rose and held it out. Rather than be rude, Brangwen took it.

"Let me be blunt, my lady," Blaen said. "You must know that my heart aches to marry you, but I understand what you say about your dark time. Will you think of me this time next year, when these roses are blooming again? That's all I ask of you."

"I will, then, if we both live."

Blaen looked up sharply, caught by her words, even though it was only an empty phrase, a pious acknowledgment that the gods are stronger than men. As Brangwen groped for something to say to dispel the chill around them, Gerraent came out into the garden.

"Making sure that I'm treating your sister honorably?" Blaen said with a grin.

"Oh, I've no doubt you'd always be honorable," Gerraent said. "I was just wondering what happened to Gwennie."

Gerraent escorted her back to the women's hall. Since Rodda and Ysolla were still at table, Brangwen allowed him to come in with her. He perched uneasily on the edge of the open window while a servant lit the candles in the sconces with a taper. After the servant left, they were alone, face to face with each other in the silent room. Restlessly Brangwen turned away and saw a moth fluttering dangerously close to a candle flame. She caught it softly in cupped hands and set it free at the window.

"You've got the softest heart in the world," Gerraent said.

"Well, the poor things are too stupid to know better."

Gerraent caught both her hands in his.

"Gwennie, do you hate me?"

"I could never hate you. Never."

For a moment Brangwen thought that he would weep.

"I know that marriage means everything to a lass," Gerraent went on. "But we'll find you a better man than an exile. Has Blaen declared himself to you?"

"He has, but please, I can't bear thinking of marrying anyone right now."

"Gwennie, I'll make you a solemn promise. Head of our clan or not, I'll never make you marry until you truly want to."

Brangwen threw her arms around his neck and wept against his shoulder. As he stroked her hair, she felt him trembling against her.

"Take me home, Gerro. Please, I want to go home."

"Well, then, that's what we'll do."

Yet once they were back in the Falcon dun, Brangwen bitterly regretted leaving Rodda and Ysolla's company. Everything she saw at home reminded her either of her father or her prince, both irrevocably gone. Up in her bedchamber, she had a wooden box filled with courting gifts from Galrion—brooches, rings, and a silver goblet with her name inscribed on it. He would have had his name put next to hers once they were married. Although she couldn't read, Brangwen would at times take out the goblet and weep as she traced the writing with her fingertip.

The dailiness of her life eventually drew her back from her despair. Brangwen had the servants to supervise, the chamberlain to consult, the household spinning and sewing to oversee and to do herself. She and her serving woman, Ludda, spent long afternoons working on the household clothes and taking turns singing old songs and ballads to each other. Soon, though, she had a new worry in Gerraent. Often she caught him weeping on their father's grave, and in the evenings, he turned oddly silent. As he sat in his father's chair—his chair, now—he drank steadily and watched the flames playing in the fireplace. Although Brangwen sat beside him out of sisterly duty, he rarely spoke more than two words at a time.

On a day when Gerraent was hunting, Gwerbret Madoc came for a visit with six men of his warband for an escort. As she curtsied to the gwerbret, Brangwen noticed the men staring at her—sly eyes, little half-smiles, an undisguised lust that she had seen a thousand times on the faces of men. She hated them for it.

"Greetings, my lady," Madoc said. "I've come to pay my respects to your father's grave."

After sending the servants to care for his men, Brangwen took Madoc into the hall and poured him ale with her own hands, then sat across from him at the honor table. Madoc pledged her with the tankard.

"My thanks, Brangwen," he said. "Truly, I wanted to see how you fared."

"As well as I can, your grace."

"And your brother?"

"He's still mourning our father. I can only hope he'll put his grief away soon." Brangwen saw that he was truly worried, not merely being courteous, and his worry made her own flare. "Gerro hasn't been himself of late. I don't know what's wrong."

"Ah, I wondered. Well, here, you know that your brother and yourself are under my protection. If ever you need my aid, you send a page to me straightaway. That's no idle courtesy, either. Sometimes when a man gets to brooding, he's a bit much for his sister to handle, so send me a message, and I'll ride by to cheer Gerro up a bit."

"Oh, my thanks, truly, my thanks! That gladdens my heart, Your Grace."

Soon Gerraent rode in from hunting, bringing a doe for the cook to clean and hang. Since the two men had important matters to discuss, Brangwen withdrew and went outside to look for Ludda. Out by the wall, Brythu was helping the cook dress the deer. They'd cut off the head and thrown it to the pack of dogs, who were growling and worrying it. Although she'd grown up seeing game cleaned regularly, Brangwen felt sick. The velvet eyes looked up at her; then a dog dragged it away. Brangwen turned and ran back to the broch. The whole world seemed to have turned strange and full of omens.

On the morrow, Madoc took leave of them early. As Brangwen and Gerraent were eating their noon meal, Gerraent told her a bit about his grace's talk. It looked as if there might be trouble out on the western border where a few clans still grumbled at the King's rule.

"I'd hate to see you ride to another war so soon," Brangwen said.

"Why?"

"You're all I have in the world."

Suddenly thoughtful, Gerraent nodded, then cut up a bit of the roast fowl on their trencher with his dagger. He picked up a tidbit and fed it to her with his fingers.

"Well, little sister," he said. "I try to be mindful of my duty to you."

Although it was pleasantly said, Brangwen suddenly felt a cold chill down her back, as if something were trying to warn her of danger.

Yet when the danger finally came, she had no warning at all. On a sunny afternoon they rode out together into the wild meadowlands to the east, a vast stretch of rolling hills that neither the Falcon nor the Boar had men enough to till or defend. At a little stream they stopped to water their horses. When they were children, this stream had marked the limit they were allowed to ride without an adult along. It was odd to think that now, when she could have ridden as far as she wanted, she had no desire to wander away from home. While Gerraent tended the horses, Brangwen sat down in the grass and looked for daisies, but she couldn't bear to pluck those innocent symbols of a lass's first love. She'd had her love and lost him, and she doubted if she'd ever find another—not merely a husband, but a love. Eventually Gerraent sat down beside her.

"Going to make a daisy chain?" he remarked.

"I'm not. It's too late for things like that."

Gerraent looked sharply away.

"Gwennie?" he said. "There's something I'd best ask you. It aches my heart to pry, but it's going to matter someday if I have to bargain out your betrothal."

Brangwen knew perfectly well what was on his mind.

"I didn't bed him," she said. "Don't trouble your heart over it for a minute."

Gerraent smiled in such a fierce, gloating relief that all at once she saw him as the falcon, poised hovering on the wind, seemingly motionless although it fights to keep its place. Then he struck, catching her by the shoulders and kissing her before she could shove him away.

"Gerro!"

Although Brangwen tried to twist free, he was far too strong for her. He held her tight, kissed her, then pinned her down in the grass to give her a long greedy kiss that set her heart pounding only partly in fear. All at once, as silently as he'd caught her, he let her go and sat back on the grass with tears running down his face. Her shoulders ached from those greedy hands, her brother's hands, as she sat up, watching him warily. Gerraent pulled his dagger and handed it to her hilt-first.

"Take it and slit my throat," he said. "I'll kneel here and let you do it."

"Never."

"Then I'll do it myself. Go home. Get Ludda and ride to Madoc. By the time he rides back, I'll be dead."

Brangwen felt as if she were a bit of wire, being pulled between a jeweler's tools until it's as fine as a single hair. This last loss was too much to bear, her brother, her beloved brother, kneeling before her as a supplicant. If he did kill himself, no one would know the truth of it, thinking him mad over his mourning, not an unclean man who'd broken the laws of the gods. But she would know. And she would never see him again. The wire was being pulled tighter and tighter.

"Will you forgive me before I die?" Gerraent said.

She wanted to speak, but no words came. When he misread her silence, his eyes filled with tears.

"Done, then," he said. "It was too much to hope for."

The wire broke. In a rush of tears, Brangwen flung herself against him.

"Gerro, Gerro, Gerro, you can't die."

Gerraent dropped the dagger and slowly, hesitantly, put his hands on her waist, as if to shove her away, then clasped her tight in his arms.

"Gerro, please, live for my sake."

"How can I? What shall I do, live hating my blood-sworn friend if you marry Blaen? Every time you looked at me, I'd know you were remembering my fault."

"But the clan! If you die, the clan dies with you. Ah by the Goddess of the Moon, if you kill yourself, I might as well do the same. What else would be left for me?"

He held her a little ways away from him, and as they looked into each other's eyes, she felt death standing beside her, a palpable presence.

"Does my maidenhead mean so much to you?" she said.

Gerraent shrugged, refusing to answer.

"Then you might as well take it. You wouldn't force me for it, so I'll give it to you."

He stared at her like a drunken man. Brangwen wondered why he couldn't see what was so clear to her: if they were doomed, they might as well live an hour longer in each other's arms. She put her hands alongside his face and pulled him down to kiss her. His hands dug into her shoulders so tightly that it hurt, but she let him kiss her again. As his passion for her flared, it was frightening, wrapping her round, catching her up like a branch in a fire. When she let herself go limp in his arms, Brangwen felt more like a priestess in a rite than a lover. She felt nothing but the force of him, the solid weight of him, her mind so far away that she felt she was watching their lovemaking in a dream.

When they finished, he lay next to her and pillowed his head on her naked breasts, his mouth moving on her skin, a gentle nuzzling kiss of gratitude. She ran her fingers through his hair and thought of the dagger lying ready for them. I never wanted to die a maid, she thought, and who better than Gerro? He raised his head and smiled at her, a soft drunken smile of pleasure and love.

"Are you going to kill me now?" Brangwen said.

"Why?" Gerraent said. "Not yet, my love, not after this. There'll be time enough later for the pair of us to die. I know we will, and the gods know it, too, and that's enough for them. We'll have our summer first."

Brangwen looked up at the sky, a pure blue, glittering like a fiery reproach from the gods. Her hand groped for the dagger.

"Not yet," Gerraent said.

He caught her wrist, those heavy calloused hands circling it, mastering her, taking the dagger away. He sat up and threw it. It glittered through the air and plunged into the stream. Brangwen thought of protesting, but his beauty caught her, a cruel flaming beauty like the angry sun. He ran his hands down her body, then lay down beside her and kissed her. This time she felt her desire rise to match his, a bittersweet lust, born of despair.

When they rode home that evening, Brangwen was surprised that everyone treated them so normally and easily. She was expecting that everyone would see if not their dishonor then at least their coming death, as if death should cast a glow around them that could be seen for miles. But Brythu merely took their horses and bowed; the chamberlain came hurrying over to Gerraent with some tedious news from the village; Ludda met Brangwen and asked if she should set the kitchen maid to laying the table. The evening turned so normal that Brangwen wanted to scream.

After the meal, the servants settled in at their hearth and Gerraent, with a tankard in his hand, at his. The great hall was dark except for the crossed and battling glows from the two small fires. Brangwen watched her brother's shadowed face and wondered if he was happy. She hardly knew what she felt. For the past year, she'd been readying herself for marriage, when she would swear an oath to her husband and bind herself under his will. Instead, she'd sworn a blood oath, giving up her will to a pledge of death. There was nothing left but to center herself on Gerraent, her first man, her brother, just as she'd planned to do with her prince. Until she let Gerraent slit her throat, she would serve him as her lord. The decision gave her a precarious peace, as if she had closed a door in her mind on the tragedy of the past. Galrion was gone, and all the promise he'd held out of a different kind of life.

"Gerro?" Brangwen said. "What are you thinking about?"

"That rebellion," Gerraent said. "If there's a war this summer, I won't go. I promise you that—I'll find a way out."

Brangwen smiled, her heart bursting with love for him. He was making the biggest sacrifice a man like him could, giving up his glory to live with her in the summer and die with her in the fall.

Brangwen would have liked to have slept in his bed, as was her place, but it was of course far too risky with so many servants in the house. If the priests in the village ever learned of their sin, they would come tear them apart. Often, over the next few weeks, they rode out together to lie down in the soft grass. Wrapped in his arms, Brangwen could think of Gerraent as her husband. Her calm continued, as fair as the weather, summer day after summer day slipping by, like water in a full stream, silent, smooth as glass, glistening. Nothing could disturb her calm, not even her occasional thought of Ysolla, whose betrothed she had taken away. At first, it seemed that Gerraent too was happy, but slowly his brooding and his rages returned.

Gerraent was growing more and more like their father, dark as a storm when he was idle, glowering into the fire and pacing restlessly around the ward. One evening, when Brythu brought him ale, the lad slipped and spilled it. Gerraent swung and slapped him so hard that the lad fell to his knees.

"You clumsy little bastard," Gerraent said, rising from his chair.

As the lad cowered back, Gerraent's hand went to his dagger almost of its own will. Brangwen threw herself in between them.

"Hold your hand, Gerro," she snapped. "You'll be weeping with remorse not five minutes later if you hurt the lad."

Sobbing, Brythu fled the hall. Brangwen saw the rest of the servants watching with pale faces and terrified eyes. She grabbed Gerraent by the shoulders and shook him hard.

"Oh by the hells," Gerraent said. "My thanks."

Brangwen fetched him more ale herself, then went out to the stable, where, as she expected, she found Brythu weeping in the hay loft. She hung her candle lantern on a nail in the wall, then sat down and laid a gentle hand on his shoulder. He was only twelve, a skinny little thing for his age.

"Here, here," Brangwen said. "Let me have a look."

Brythu wiped the tears away on his sleeve and turned his face up to her. An ugly red puff was swelling on his cheek, but his eye was unharmed.

"Lord Gerraent's sorry already," Brangwen said. "He won't do this again."

"My thanks, my lady," Brythu stammered. "What's so wrong with Lord Gerraent these days?"

"He's half mad from mourning his father, that's all."

Brythu considered, touching the swelling on his cheek.

"He would have killed me if it wasn't for you," he said. "If ever you want me to do anything for you, I swear I will."

Late that night, when everyone was asleep, Brangwen crept out of her chamber and went to Gerraent, who was sleeping in their father's room and in their father's bed—the great carved bedstead with embroidered hangings, marked with falcons and the privilege of the head of the clan. She slipped in beside him, kissed him awake, and let him take her for the sake of peace in the house. Afterward, he lay drowsy in her arms, every muscle at ease like a satisfied child. She felt for the first time the one power allowed to her as a woman, to use her beauty and her body to bring her man to the place where he would listen to her instead of only to his whims. It would have been different with my prince, she thought. Tears ran down her cheeks, mercifully hidden from her brother by the darkness.

Though Brangwen was careful to leave his bed and return to her own, that next morning she had her first intimation that the rest of the household was beginning to suspect something. The men seemed utterly unaware, but at times Brangwen caught Ludda watching her with a frightened wondering in her eyes. Brangwen took Gerraent aside and told him to go hunting and leave her alone.

Over the next few days, he ignored her for long hours at a time, going hunting or riding round the demesne; he even began talking of visiting Madoc or Blaen. But always she felt him watching her whenever they were in the same room, as if he were guarding her like a treasure. Although she tried to put him off, finally he insisted that she ride with him into the hills.

That afternoon they found a copse of willows for their lovemaking. She had never seen him so passionate, making love to her as if every time he had her made him want her more rather than satisfying him. Afterward, he fell asleep in her arms. She stroked his hair and held him, but she felt weary, so tired that she wanted to sink into the earth and never see the sky again. When Gerraent woke, he sat up, stretching, smiling at her. Beside him, tangled in his clothes, lay his dagger.

"Gerro, kill me now."

"I won't. Not yet."

All at once, Brangwen knew it was time to die, that they had to die now, this very afternoon. She sat up and grabbed his arm.

"Kill me now. I beg you."

Gerraent slapped her across the face, the first blow he'd ever given her. When she began to cry, he flung his arms around her, kissed her, and begged her to forgive him. She did forgive him, simply because she had no choice—he was more than her whole life; he was her death as well. All during the ride home, she felt her urgency ache her: they should be dead. When they rode into the ward, she saw horses tied up outside. Lord Blaen had come to visit.

Blaen stayed for three days, hunting with Gerraent, while Brangwen crept around and tried to avoid them both. Only once did she have to talk with Blaen alone, and then he held to his pledge and said not one word about marriage. On his last night there, however, he begged her to stay at the table after dinner. Gerraent brooded, staring into the fire and drinking as steadily as if he'd forgotten they had a guest. When Blaen started talking to Brangwen about his mother, she could only listen miserably, hardly able to answer, because she was wondering what Rodda would say when she learned the truth. Apparently Blaen misread her silence.

"Now here, my lady," Blaen said. "I promised you that I'd never even speak of marriage till the spring, and I keep my word."

"What's this?" Gerraent said.

"Well," Blaen said. "I've spoken to you before about paying court to your sister."

"So you have," Gerraent said, smiling. "I've made her a promise, you see. I told her that I'd never make her marry unless she chooses to."

"Indeed?" Blaen said. "Even if she stays under your roof all her life?"

"Just that."

Blaen hesitated, his eyes darkening.

"Well, my lady," he said to Brangwen. "You're lucky in your brother, aren't you?"

"I think so," Brangwen said. "I honor him."

Blaen smiled easily, but all at once, Brangwen was frightened. The glow from the smokey fire danced, but it seemed to her that the fire came from Gerraent, as if long tendrils of flame were reaching out for Blaen against all their wills.

With summer at its height, the sun lay hot along the dusty road, light as golden as the grain ripening in the fields. Nevyn, who had once been Prince Galrion, led a pack mule laden with baled herbs across the border of the Falcon lands. As he walked, he kept a constant lookout for Gerraent, who might well be out riding his roads. Nevyn doubted if anyone else would recognize the prince in this dusty peddlar with his shabby clothes, shaggy hair, and old mule. He was learning that a man could be invisible without mighty dweomer-workings but merely by acting in unexpected ways in unexpected places. No one would expect the prince to dare come near the Falcon again.

When he came to the village, Nevyn even risked buying a tankard of ale from the tavernman, who barely glanced his way after he'd taken his copper. Nevyn sat in the corner near an old woman and asked her foolish questions about the countryside, as if he'd come from a long way away. When he left, no one even noticed him go.

It was toward evening when he reached his destination, a shabby wooden hut on the edge of the wild forest. Out in front, two goats were grazing on the stubby grass, while old Ynna sat on her stoop and watched them. Ynna was thin as a stick, with long twiglike fingers, gnarled from her long years of hard work. Her white hair was carelessly caught up in a dirty scarf. An herbwoman and midwife, she was thought by some folk to be a witch, but in truth, she merely loved her solitude.

"Good morrow, lad," Ynna said. "Looks like old Rhegor's sent me a pretty thing or two."

"He has," Nevyn said. "This supply should last you through the winter."

Nevyn unloaded the mule and carried the herbs inside, then watered it and sent it out to graze with the goats. When he came back to the hut, Ynna was laying out bread and cheese on her small unsteady table. When she handed him a wooden cup of water and told him to set to, Nevyn gratefully pitched in, spreading the soft pungent goat's cheese on the dark bread. Ynna nibbled a bit of bread and studied him so curiously that Nevyn wondered if she knew he'd once been the prince.

"It's wearisome, having old Rhegor gone from this part of the forest," Ynna said. "And so sudden it was, him coming by one day to tell me he was going. Has he ever told you why?"

"Well, good dame," Nevyn said. "I do what my master says and hold my tongue."

"Always best with a strange one like our Rhegor. Well, if he sends you to me with herbs every now and then, I'll manage."

Ynna cut a few more slices from the loaf and laid them on Nevyn's plate.

"I miss Rhegor, though," Ynna said abruptly. "I could always count on his counsel, like, when there was some troubling thing."

Nevyn felt the dweomer-warning down his back.

"And how fares Lord Gerraent these days?" Nevyn said.

"You're almost as sharp as your master, aren't you, lad? Well, here, tell Rhegor this tale for me. He always kept an eye, like, on poor little Brangwen."

"Did he now? I never knew that."

"Oh, truly, he did, just from a fatherly distance, like. So tell him about this. About a month ago, it was, the page up at the dun got a bit of fever, and a stubborn thing it was. I must have been back there five times before the lad was right again. And Lord Gerraent gives me a silver coin for it. He says, do you have an herb to take madness away, Ynna? He was jesting, I suppose, but he smiled so cold-like it troubled my heart. And then the last time I went up the hill, I see Gerraent sobbing on his father's grave."

"You can rest assured I'll tell Rhegor about it. How does Brangwen fare, shut up with a man like that?"

"Now there's the strangest thing of all. You think she'd be heartsick, but she goes around like a woman in a dream. I've never seen the lass look so broody-like. I'd say she was with child, but who's would it be? She's just as broody as if her belly was swelling, but that betrothed of hers has been gone too long now. Well, tell Rhegor for me."

On the ride home, Nevyn pushed the balky mule as fast as it would go, but it still took him over two days to reach his new home, up in the wild forest north of the Boar's demesne. Nevyn and Rhegor had cleared a good space of land near a stream. They'd used the logs to build a rough house and the land to plant beans, turnips, and suchlike. Since Rhegor's reputation as a healer moved north with him, they had plenty of food and even a few coins, since farmers and bondsmen alike were willing to pay with chickens and suchlike for Rhegor's herbs. Nevyn saw clearly that he and Brangwen would have had a comfortable if spare life in the forest. If only you hadn't been such a dolt, Nevyn cursed himself, such a stupid fool! Hardly a day went by without him reproaching himself for losing her.

Rhegor was out in front of the house, treating the running eye of a little boy while the mother squatted nearby. From her ragged brown tunic, Nevyn saw that she was a bondswoman, her thin face utterly blank, as if she hardly cared whether the lad was cured or not even though she'd brought him all this way. On her face was her brand, the old scar pale on dirty skin. Though he was barely three, the lad was already branded, too, marked out as Lord Blaen's property for the rest of his life. Rhegor stood the lad on a tree stump and wiped the infected eye with a bit of rag dipped in herbal salve.

Nevyn went to stable the mule alongside the bay gelding. When he came back, the bondswoman looked at him with feigned disinterest. Even from ten feet away he could smell her unwashed flesh and rags. Rhegor called her over, gave her a pot of salve, and told her how to apply it. She listened, her face showing a brief flicker of hope.

"I can't pay you much, my lord," she said. "I brought some of the first apples."

"You and the lad eat those on your way home," Rhegor said.

"My thanks." She stared at the ground. "I heard you tended poor folk, but I didn't believe it at first."

"It's true," Rhegor said. "Spread the tale around."

"I was so frightened." She went on staring at the ground. "If the lad went blind, they'd kill him because he couldn't work."

"What?" Nevyn broke in. "Lord Blaen would never do such a thing."

"Lord Blaen?" She looked up with a faint smile. "Well, so he wouldn't. How would he even know we're alive to be killed? His overseer, my lord, that's who'd do it."

Nevyn supposed that she spoke the cold truth. As the prince, he'd given less thought to bondsmen than to horses. Rhegor was making him see a different world.

Once the woman went on her way, Rhegor and Nevyn went inside their cabin, a single light airy room, scented with new-cut pine. They had a scattering of cast-off furniture from grateful farmers: a table, a bench, a free-standing cabinet to hold cookware. On one wall was the half-finished hearth Nevyn was building as his share of the summer's work. Nevyn dipped them ale from a barrel, then brought the dented tankards over to join Rhegor at the table.

"And how was the journey?" Rhegor said. "How fares old Ynna?"

"Well enough, my lord," Nevyn said. "But she told me a cursed strange tale about the Falcon. Ah ye gods, my poor Brangwen! I truly wish you'd done what my father would have—beaten me half to death for my fault!"

"That would have solved nothing, and made you feel like you'd made amends when you hadn't." Rhegor hesitated on the edge of anger. "Ah well, what's past is past. Tell me the tale."

While Nevyn told him, Rhegor listened quietly, but his hands clasped his tankard tighter and tighter. At the end, Rhegor swore under his breath.

"Truly," Rhegor said. "Well, we'd best look into this. Here, old Ynna can practically smell when a lass is with child. There's no chance the babe's yours, is it?"

"Not unless longing for a woman can get her with child."

His eyes dark, Rhegor smiled briefly.

"And what will you think of your Gwennie," Rhegor said. "If she's big with another man's child?"

"If he's a good man, let her go with him," Nevyn said. "And if he's not, then I'll take her child and all."

"Well and good. First we'll have to see if that child's Blaen's. If it is, there'll be a wedding, and that'll be the end to it. If not, I still have hope we can get her away."

"Here, my lord, why are you so concerned with Brangwen? Is it just the honor of the thing?"

"Now, that I can't tell you just yet."

Nevyn waited, hoping for at least a word more, but Rhegor merely looked away, thinking.

"I'll ride down to the Boar early tomorrow," Rhegor said. "Out of courtesy, I should let Lady Rodda know there's an herbman nearby. You stay here. Blaen would hate to kill you if he saw you, but his honor would make him do what the King ordered. I should reach the dun by noon, so you might make yourself a fire and see if you can follow me that way."

On the morrow, Nevyn spent an impatient morning digging stones out of their little field for the hearth. So far, most of his training was just this sort of menial labor in the summer heat. Often it galled him: what was a prince doing, sweating like a flea-bitten bondsman? Yet in his heart, he knew that humbling the prince's pride was the real work. There is only one key to unlock the secrets of the dweomer: I want to know in order to help the world. Anyone wanting power for its own sake gets only dribs and drabs, hard-won, harder to keep, and not worth having. Yet here and there, Rhegor had given Nevyn work bearing more directly on dweomer-lore. Although Nevyn had always had the Sight, it came and went of its own will, showing him what it chose to show and not a jot more. Now he was learning to bring the Sight under his will.

Nevyn made a circle of stones outside on the ground and built a small fire, which he lit like any other man with a tinder box and flint. He let the fire burn down until the logs were glowing caves of coals. Then he stretched out on the ground, pillowed his chin on his hands, and stared directly into the fire caves. He slowed his breathing to the right rhythm and thought of Rhegor. At last the fire cave stretched, widened, and turned into the sheen of sunlight glowing on a polished wood chamber. In the flames, Nevyn made out Rhegor, a tiny image. Nevyn summoned his will and thought of Rhegor, imaged him clearly, and forced his mind to him. The vision swelled, turned solid, swelled again, and became as clear as though Nevyn were looking into the women's hall from an outside window. With one last effort of will, Nevyn went in, hearing a little rushy hiss, a dropping sensation in his stomach, and at last he was standing beside Rhegor on the floor.

Lady Rodda was sitting on her chair, with Ysolla perching on a footstool nearby. With his shirt off to reveal a bad case of boils, a young miserable page was kneeling in front of Rhegor on the floor.

"These will have to be lanced," Rhegor said. "Since I don't have my tools with me, I'll have to ride back tomorrow with your lady's leave."

The boy gave a miserable squeak in anticipation.

"Now don't be a silly lad," Rodda said. "They've been hurting you for weeks, and if the herbman lances them, they'll be over and done with. Don't you go hiding in the forest all day tomorrow."

The lad grabbed his shirt from the floor, made Rodda a bow, then fled unceremoniously. Smiling, Rodda shook her head at him, then motioned Rhegor to a chair next to hers.

"Sit down and rest, good sir," Rodda said. "So, you say you're from the south. Have you any interesting news?"

"My thanks." Rhegor bowed and took the chair. "Well, no true news, but a lot of evil rumor."

"Indeed?" Rodda said unsteadily. "How fares Lord Gerraent of the Falcon?"

"I see the rumors have reached my lady's ears," Rhegor said. "Badly alas, and of course the locals insist on talking of witch-craft."

Ysolla leaned forward, clasping her arms around her knees, her eyes half-filled with tears. When he remembered the happy night of her betrothal, Nevyn felt such a stab of pity for her that the Vision broke. It took him a long time to retrieve it.

"Mourning is understandable," Rhegor was saying. "But after all, the natural order of things is for the son to lose his father sooner or later." He glanced at Ysolla. "Once he has you at his side, no doubt the black mood will lift."

"If he ever marries me," Ysolla burst out.

"Hold your tongue, lamb," Rodda said.

"How can I?" Ysolla snapped. "After what Blaen said—"

Rodda raised her hand as if to slap her. Ysolla fell silent.

"Kindly forgive my daughter, good sir," Rodda said. "She's worrying her heart, thinking that what happened to poor Brangwen might happen to her."

"A sad sad thing that was," Rhegor said, sighing. "Let's hope she finds a better man soon. The villagers told me that your son hopes to announce his betrothal to the lady."

"Well." Rodda's voice went flat. "I'll pray that such happens."

So, Nevyn thought, that babe's not Blaen's. True enough, Rhegor answered, ah by the hells, I'd hoped so much it was! Nevyn was so shocked at the answer that he lost the Vision again, and for good, this time.

Rhegor returned at sunset. He tended the mule, then came into the hut where Nevyn, steaming with curiosity, was laying out their evening meal. Rhegor took a gold coin out of his brigga pocket and tossed it onto the table.

"Our Lady Rodda is generous," Rhegor remarked. "Little does she know whom this will feed, but she'd be glad. We talked a bit more after you left us, and she still honors you, Prince Galrion."

"The prince is dead," Nevyn said.

Rhegor smiled and sat down, picking up a slice of bread and butter.

"I think I'll risk getting Nevyn's throat cut tomorrow," Rhegor said. "Lord Blaen will be at the hunt when I ride back to tend that lad's boils, so you can come with me."

"Well and good, my lord," Nevyn said. "Here, why did you wish that child was Blaen's?"

"Think, lad. If Blaen's not to blame, well, then, who is? What men are at the Falcon's dun—a couple of twelve-year-old lads, a grubby stableman, and the old chamberlain, so aged that he can barely lift his hand to a maid, much less anything else. So who does that leave?"

"Well, nobody."

"Nobody?"

"Oh by the hells." Nevyn could barely say it. "Gerraent."

"By the hells indeed. This is a terrible dark thing to accuse any man of doing, and I won't make a move until I'm sure."

Nevyn picked up the table dagger, twisting it in his fingers for the solid comfort of the metal.

"If it's true," Nevyn said. "I'll kill him."

"Look at you," Rhegor said. "Your father's son indeed."

Nevyn stabbed the dagger hard into the table top and let it quiver.

"And would killing him be such a wrong thing?" Nevyn said.

"It would—for you." Rhegor took a calm bite of bread and butter. "I forbid you to even think about it."

"Done, then. His blood is safe from me."

Rhegor considered him carefully. Nevyn picked up a slice of bread, then flung it back onto the plate.

"You said you'd take her, child and all," Rhegor said. "Is that still true if she's carrying her own brother's bastard?"

"I'm not a prince anymore," Nevyn said. "And I'm the man who left her there."

"You're a decent enough lad at heart. Truly, you might redeem yourself yet."

By keeping his hood muffled around his face, Nevyn managed to avoid being recognized by any of the servants in the Boar's dun. When he and Rhegor went up to the women's hall, Nevyn kept the cloak on and busied himself with unpacking Rhegor's herbs and implements. Ysolla was mercifully gone, and Rodda was occupied with Rhegor and one of the pages.

"What do you mean, you don't know where Maryc is?" Rodda said to the page. "I told him to be here when the herbman came."

"He's scared, my lady," the page said. "But I can look for him. It's going to take a long time."

"Then run and start right now," Rodda said. "Ye gods!"

As soon as the page was gone, Nevyn took off his cloak and tossed it onto the floor. Rodda stared, her eyes filling with tears.

"Galrion!" she whispered. "Oh, thank the holy gods. It gladdens my heart to see you well."

"My humble thanks, my lady," Nevyn said. "But my name is no one."

"I heard about your father's spite," Rodda said. "You've got to be gone when my son rides home."

"I know," Nevyn said. "But I had to come. I'll beg you for news of my Brangwen."

Rodda's face went slack as she looked away.

"Our poor little Gwennie," she said. "I wish the gods had allowed her to marry you. I swear, maybe she should have ridden into exile with you." She glanced Rhegor's way. "Here, good sir, I can trust you, for bringing my prince if nothing else, so I'll speak freely. Blaen rode down to the Falcon not long ago, and he came home in a rage. He's sure Gwennie will never have him, he said. She walks around like she's half-dead and barely speaks. I tried to get her to come here, but she refused. She's still mourning you in her heart, my prince, or so I hope."

"So we all may hope," Rhegor said drily. "How often has Gerraent ridden here to see his betrothed?"

As startled as a cornered deer, Rodda glanced this way and that.

"It's all nonsense," she burst out. "I won't believe that they'd do such a thing, not Gwennie, not Gerro! Blaen and Ysolla are just working themselves up with silly suspicions, because they're so disappointed and eager. I won't believe it!"

"What?" Rhegor said. "Tell me, my lady. Get these dark fears out of your heart."

Rodda hesitated, fighting with herself, then gave in.

"All the servants at the Falcon say that only Brangwen stands between them and Lord Gerraent's rage—just like she was his wife," Rodda said. "And Ysolla, my own child, has been working her brother up like a little scorpion. Gerro was always so fond of Gwennie, she says, it's not fair—Gwennie even has the man I want. It's Gwennie this and Gwennie that, and all because poor Ysolla's always envied little Brangwen's wretched beauty."

"Wretched indeed," Nevyn said. "You say you can't believe it—is that true? Or do you only want to turn away from an unclean thing? Ye gods, I couldn't blame you."

Rodda broke and wept, covering her face with her hands.

"He's always loved her too much," Rodda sobbed. "Why do you think I worked so hard on Lord Dwen to let Gwennie marry so young? She had to get out of that cursed household."

"Cursed indeed," Rhegor said, sighing. "Twice cursed."

Nevyn paced restlessly back and forth while Rhegor helped the lady into her chair.

"Tell me something, my lady," Nevyn said. "If I steal her away from her brother, will you blame me?"

"Never," Rodda said. "But if you do, Gerraent will call on his friends, and they'll hunt you down like the gray deer."

"I'd die for her," Nevyn said. "And I'm more clever than the gray deer."

That very evening, Nevyn took his bay gelding and headed south for the Falcon's dun. He was going to have to be clever. He could never risk riding straight into the fort, even if Gerraent were gone. He would be of no use to Brangwen if Gerraent returned and killed him at her feet. Though Galrion had never been particularly good with a sword, Nevyn had a few tricks of dweomer at his disposal. He was sure that if he could only get a few minutes alone with Brangwen, he could easily convince her to steal out of the dun and escape with him. Once they were on the road, Gerraent would never find them.

When Nevyn reached Ynna's hut, he told her that Rhegor had sent him to keep an eye on things. As he'd hoped, Ynna was so glad of it that she offered him shelter with her.

"Here, the women down in the village are starting to whisper that Brangwen's carrying a bastard," Ynna said.

"Are they?" Nevyn said. "Well, that betrothed of hers swore he'd come back for her, you see. Rhegor says to tell you that he's been seen sneaking around this part of the country."

When Ynna raised her eyebrows and smiled, Nevyn was sure that this delicious gossip would soon be all over the village, thus salvaging at least one part of Brangwen's reputation. He could only hope it would give the truth no room to spread.

For three days, Nevyn kept a close watch on the Falcon dun. Down at the edge of the forest, close to the road, he found a large spreading oak. By climbing up into the crown, he could lie hidden and see the fort, just a mile away across the meadowland. Drawing on all his will, he sent his thoughts across and tried to reach Brangwen's mind, calling her, planting the thought that she should come out to the forest. Once, he felt that he reached her; he also felt her brush the irrational thought aside. He kept trying, begging her, but failing, until he was desperate enough to consider sneaking into the fort the next time Gerraent rode out to hunt.

On the fourth afternoon, as he was lying on his perch, Nevyn saw a man and a page riding slowly up the hill to the dun. He recognized the horse and the set of the rider's shoulders—Blaen. He climbed down and ran for the hut.

"Ynna, for the love of every god, I need your aid," Nevyn said. "Can you give me an excuse to get into the Falcon dun? A message I can deliver, anything to tell the servants."

"Well." Ynna thought for a maddeningly long time. "Here, I made a love philter up for Ludda, Brangwen's serving lass. She's got her eyes set on a lad in the village. You can fetch it to her."

While Ynna got the packet of herbs, Nevyn rubbed dirt into his hair and face—a poor disguise, but then, no one had ever seen the prince the least bit dirty. He muffled himself up in his cloak, then galloped up to the fort. As he led his horse into the ward, he saw Blaen's page leading the lord's horses to the stables. Brythu came running and looked Nevyn over coldly.

"And just what do you want?" Brythu said.

"A word with Ludda, if you please. Ynna gave me somewhat to fetch to her."

"I'll go ask her. You wait here and don't try to come in."

When Ludda appeared, she looked the unkempt stranger over nervously.

"I brought you some herbs from Ynna," Nevyn said. "She said you might give a poor man a drop of ale, too."

At the sound of his voice, Ludda started, laying her hand at her throat.

"My prince!" she whispered. "Thanks be to the Goddess herself!" Then she raised her voice. "Well, I will, because you've spared me a long hot walk to her hut."

Nevyn tied his horse up by the door, then followed Ludda inside to the servants' hearth in the great hall. He sat down in the straw in the curve of the wall, out of the way of the other servants, who were busy preparing dinner. They gave him hardly a look—Ludda had the privilege of being generous to a stranger if she chose. Down at the far side of the hall, Gerraent and Blaen were drinking at the honor table. From his distance, and because they talked in low voices, Nevyn couldn't hear their words, but it was plain enough that Blaen was furious from the way he leaned forward in his chair and clutched his tankard like a weapon. When Blaen's page returned, he gave his master an anxious glance and sat down by his feet in the straw. Ludda brought

Nevyn his ale and knelt down beside him with a nervous look at the lords.

"Where's your lady?" Nevyn whispered.

"Hiding from Lord Blaen," Ludda said. "But she'll have to come out sooner or later, or Lord Gerraent will take it amiss."

"No doubt. Oh, no doubt."

Ludda winced and began to tremble.

"I know the truth," Nevyn said. "I don't care. I've come to take her away."

Ludda wept in two thin silent trails of tears.

"I'll help if I can," she whispered. "But I don't know what good can ever happen now."

On the pretense of keeping out of the cook's way, Nevyn moved from the hearth to a spot nearer the two lords. At last Brangwen slipped into the hall, pressing against the wall and watching her brother. Nevyn was shocked at the change in her. Her cheeks were hollow and pale, her eyes deep-shadowed, and her stance that of a doe poised for flight. She glanced his way and allowed herself a tremulous smile. Nevyn rose slowly, fighting with himself to keep from rushing to her side. Then Brangwen shrank back against the wall.

Nevyn had forgotten Blaen and Gerraent, who were leaning forward in their chairs and staring each other down. Slowly and deliberately Blaen rose, his hand on his sword hilt.

"May the gods curse you," Blaen said. "It's true, isn't it?"

Gerraent rose to face him, his hands on his hips, and he smiled in a calm that made Nevyn's blood run cold.

"Answer me," Blaen said, his voice ringing in the hall. "You've taken your sister to your bed, haven't you?"

Gerraent drew, the sword flashing, swung and struck before Blaen could get his blade half out of the scabbard. Brangwen screamed, one high note, as Blaen took one step and staggered, the bright blood pouring down his chest. He looked at Gerraent as if he were bewildered, then crumpled at Gerraent's feet. His page began inching for the door. Gerraent turned and went for him.

"Gerro!" Brangwen rushed in between. "Not the lad!"

Gerraent hesitated, and that minute gave the page his life. He grabbed the bay gelding and swung himself into the saddle as Nevyn ran forward. Screaming and weeping, the servants rushed for the door. The bloody sword still in his hand, Gerraent began to laugh, then saw Blaen's body on the floor and came to himself. Nevyn could see the reason return to his eyes as he fell to his knees and started keening. Nevyn grabbed Brangwen by the arm.

"We've got to get out now," he said.

"I can't." Brangwen gave him a smile as mad as her brother's. "I swore I'd die with him."

"No god or man would hold you to such an unclean oath."

"I hold myself to it, my prince."

Nevyn grabbed her and started pulling her toward the door, but Gerraent leapt up and ran to block it, his sword at the ready. Here's where I die, Nevyn thought.

"Prince Galrion, by the gods," Gerraent hissed.

"I am. Go on—add my blood to your sworn friend's."

"Not him, Gerro!" Brangwen burst out. "Just kill me and be done with it."

"I won't raise my sword against either of you," Gerraent said. "My prince? Will you take her away?"

"Gerro!" Brangwen stared at him in disbelief. "You promised me. You swore you'd kill us both."

Gerraent's eyes snapped in fury. He grabbed her by the shoulder and shoved her into Nevyn's arms.

"You little bitch, get out of here!" Gerraent snarled. "I've slain the only man in the world I loved, and all over you." He slapped her across the face. "The sight of you sickens me. This means the death of the Falcon—because of you!"

The lie was so perfect that Nevyn believed him, but when Brangwen fell weeping against him, he saw the truth in Gerraent's eyes: a real love, not mere lust, the hopeless ache of a man sending away the only thing he ever loved.

"Take the gray from the stable," Gerraent said. "It would have been yours in the dowry."

Gerraent turned and threw his sword across the great hall, then flung himself down by Blaen's body. Slowly, one step at a time, Nevyn half carried, half dragged Brangwen out of the hall. He looked back once to see Gerraent cuddled against Blaen's back, just as when a warrior lies beside his slain friend on the battlefield and refuses to believe him dead, no matter how many men try to get him to come away.

Out in the ward, the last of the sunset flared through shadows. Torch in hand, Brythu led the gray out of the stables. Ludda rushed from the broch with a pair of saddlebags and some rolled up blankets. An eerie silence hung over the deserted ward.

"My prince, forgive me," Brythu said. "I didn't recognize you."

"I'm cursed glad you didn't," Nevyn said. "Ludda, is there anyone else left in the dun? You'd all better flee to your families. The Boar will ride back as soon as ever it can, and they'll fire the place for Blaen's sake."

"Then we will, my prince," Ludda said. "Here, I've brought food and suchlike for my lady."

Nevyn lifted Brangwen into the saddle like a child, then mounted behind her. He rode out slowly, letting the burdened horse pick its own pace. At the bottom of the hill, Nevyn glanced back for a last look at the dun, rising dark against the sunset sky. With the Sight, it seemed to him that he saw flames already dancing around it.

That night they rode only for a few hours until they were well away from the dun and into the safe hills. Nevyn found a copse of trees beside a stream for their camp. After he tended the horse, he built a little fire out of twigs and scraps of dead wood. Brangwen stared at the fire and never spoke until he was done.

"You must know," she said.

"I do," Nevyn said. "I want you, child and all."

"Let me spare you that. I want to die. You can't still love me. I'm carrying my own brother's bastard."

"That's my shame as much as yours. I left you there alone with him."

"You didn't push me into his bed." Brangwen gave him an uncertain smile, a pathetic attempt to be cold. "I don't love you anymore anyway."

"You don't lie as well as your brother."

Brangwen sighed and looked at the fire.

"There'll be a curse on the child, I just know it," she said. "Why won't you just kill me? Gerro promised me he'd kill us both, and here he was lying to me the whole time. He promised me." She began to weep. "Ah ye gods, he promised me!"

Nevyn caught her in his arms and let her weep. Finally, she fell silent, so silent that he was frightened, but she'd merely fallen

asleep in a merciful exhaustion. He woke her just enough to get
her to lie down on the blankets and sleep again.

In the morning, Brangwen fell into a dream state. She never
spoke, refused to eat by turning her head away like a stubborn
child, and had to be lifted onto the horse. All morning they rode
slowly, avoiding the roads and sparing the burdened horse as
much as possible. If they hadn't have been riding to Rhegor,
Nevyn would have been overwhelmed by despair. She was broken, crushed like a silver cup that falls beneath a warrior's boot
when his troop is looting a hall. Rhegor could help her—Nevyn
clung to that hope—but Rhegor was over a day's ride away.
Occasionally Nevyn thought of the Boar's warband, riding for
revenge. The page had doubtless reached them before dawn;
they were doubtless already on their way to the Falcon, with
Blaen's young brother Camlann—Lord Camlann now—at their
head. Nevyn supposed that Gerraent would flee ahead of them
into a miserable exile's life.

Close to sunset, Nevyn and Brangwen came to the river that
would, on the morrow, lead them to Rhegor. After he made their
camp, Nevyn tried to get Brangwen to eat or speak. She would do
neither. All at once he realized that she was planning on starving
herself to death to keep her vow to the gods. Though it ached his
heart, he used the only weapon he had.

"And what are you doing?" Nevyn said. "Starving the babe
in your body? The poor little thing is cursed indeed if its own
mother won't feed it."

Her eyes brimming tears, Brangwen raised her head. She
looked at him, then took a piece of bread and began to nibble on
it. When Nevyn gave her cheese and an apple, she ate it all, but
she never spoke a word. He gathered more wood for the fire,
then made her lie down near it where she could be warm. When
he went through their meager provisions to see what was left, he
found, wrapped in a piece of cloth, every courting present he'd
ever given her. Ludda had sent them all along with their unfortunate owner. Nevyn looked for a long while at the jeweled brooch
in the shape of a falcon and thought of Gerraent.

When the night turned dark, Nevyn finally gave in to his
wondering and built up the fire to scry. With so much terror and
pain behind it, the Vision built up slowly, but at last he saw the
great hall of the Falcon. Blaen's body was laid out by the hearth,

with a pillow under his head and his sword on his chest. As Nevyn thought about Gerraent, the Vision changed. Out in the ward, Gerraent was pacing back and forth with his sword in his hand: so he had refused to flee his Wyrd.

Nevyn never truly knew how long he kept that last watch with Gerraent. Once, the fire burned so low that he lost the Vision, but when he laid more wood in, he scried Gerraent out immediately, pacing, pacing, pacing, his sword swinging back and forth, the blade glittering in the torchlight. At last, Nevyn heard the sound, just as Gerraent did, tossing up his head like a stag. Horses, a lot of them, clattering up the hill—calmly Gerraent strolled to the gates and positioned himself between them with his sword raised at the battle-ready. With his warband behind him, Lord Camlann rode into the pool of torchlight while Gerraent smiled at him. When Camlann drew his sword, the warband did the same.

"Where's my brother's body?" Camlann said.

"By my hearth," Gerraent said. "Bury one of my horses with him, will you?"

His young face troubled, Camlann leaned forward in the saddle to stare at the friend who had become his enemy. Then the troubled look disappeared, swept away by the cold honorable rage of the avenger. He flung up his sword, keened once, and spurred his horse forward. The men charged and ringed Gerraent round. In the mob, Nevyn saw Gerraent's sword flash up, bright with blood in the torchlight. A horse reared; men shouted; then the mob pulled back. Gerraent was lying dead on the ground. His cheek bleeding from a sword cut, Camlann dismounted and walked over to kneel beside him. He raised his sword two-handed and cut Gerraent's head off. Then he rose, swinging the head by the hair, and with a howl of rage, he flung it hard against the wall.

The scream broke the Vision—Brangwen's scream. Nevyn scrambled up and ran to her just as she rose, sobbing.

"Gerro," Brangwen said. "He's dead. Gerro, Gerro, Gerro!" Her voice rose to a shriek. "Camlann—ah ye gods—he cut—he ah ye gods! Gerro!"

Nevyn flung his arms around her and pulled her tight. Brangwen struggled, throwing herself back and forth in his arms while she keened for her brother and the father of her child. Nevyn held on tightly and grimly until at last she fell silent.

"How did you know?" Nevyn said.

Brangwen only wept silently, an exhausted tremble of her body. Nevyn stroked her hair and held her tight until at last she seemed calm. When he let her go, she threw her head back and keened again.

And so it went for hours. He would just soothe her when something would make her remember and she would keen, struggling with him. Slowly her struggles grew weaker. He got her to lie down on the cloaks, then lay down next to her and let her weep in his arms. When she at last fell asleep, he watched the fire burning itself out until he, too, drifted off, as exhausted as she. But he woke not an hour later and found her gone.

Nevyn jumped to his feet and ran for the river. He could just see her there, poised on the bank, a dark shape against the sky.

"Gwennie!" he called out.

She neither turned nor hesitated, but flung herself into the river before he could reach her. Weighted by her long dresses, she went down, swirling away into the darkness. Nevyn dove in after her. Black—the cold shock of the water—he could barely breathe or see. The current swept him along, but as he broke the surface and came up, he saw nothing but black water, scouring ahead of him. If she'd sunk already, he could easily be swimming over her. Yet though he knew it was hopeless, he kept diving, kept swimming back and forth across the river like a dog seeking a water bird. Then the current swirled him and rammed him hard against a sharp something in the dark. A rock. With his shoulder aching like fire, Nevyn managed to pull himself to the riverbank and out, but only barely. He lay gasping and weeping on the bank for a long time.

Just as the first gray of dawn lightened the sky, Nevyn got up and walked downstream. He was too mad with grief to know what he was doing; he merely walked, looking for her. As the sun came up, he found her. The current had washed her into a sandy shallows. She lay on her back, her golden hair sodden and tangled, her beautiful eyes wide open, staring sightlessly at the brightening sky. She had fulfilled her vow to the gods. Nevyn picked her up, slung her weight over his uninjured shoulder, and carried her back to camp. All he could think was that he had to get Gwennie home. He wrapped her in both cloaks and tied her over the gray's saddle.

It was close to nightfall when Nevyn at last reached the hut in the forest. Rhegor came running out and stopped, looking at the burden in the saddle.

"You were too late," Rhegor said.

"It was too late from the first day he bedded her."

Nevyn brought her down and carried her inside, laid her down by the hearth, then sat down beside her. While the light faded in the hut, he looked at her, simply looked as if he were expecting her to wake and smile at him. Rhegor came inside, carrying a lantern.

"I've tended the horse," Rhegor said.

"My thanks."

Slowly, a broken phrase at a time, Nevyn told him the tale, while Rhegor listened with an occasional nod.

"The poor lass," Rhegor said at last. "She had more honor than either you or her brother."

"She did. Would it be a wrong thing for me to kill myself on her grave?"

"It would. I forbid it."

Nevyn nodded vaguely and wondered why he felt so calm. He was dimly aware of his master leaning over him.

"Lad, she's dead," Rhegor said. "You've got to go on from here. All we can do for Gwennie now is pray that she has better afterwards."

"Where?" Nevyn bitterly spat out the words. "In the shadowy Otherlands? How can there even be gods, if they'd let her die and not kill a wretch like me?"

"Here, lad, you're mad from your grief, and truly, I'm afraid you might stay that way if you keep brooding. The gods have nothing to do with this, either way—that's true enough." Rhegor put a gentle hand on Nevyn's arm. "Come now, let's sit at the table. Let poor little Gwennie lie there."

Nevyn's habit of obedience saved him. He let Rhegor haul him up and lead him to a table, sat down when the master told him to, and took a tankard of ale just because the master had handed him one.

"That's better," Rhegor said. "You think she's gone forever, don't you? Cut off from life, forever and ever, and her a lass who loved life so much."

"And what else would I think?"

"I'll tell you the truth to think instead. There's a great secret to the dweomer. One that you can never tell any man unless he asks you point-blank. They never ask, truly, unless they're marked for the dweomer themselves. And the secret is this, that everyone, man and woman both, lives not once, but many times, over and over, back and forth between this world and the other. What looks like a death here, lad, is but birth to another world. She's gone, truly, but she's gone to that other world, and I swear to you, someone will come to meet her."

"I never thought you'd lie to me! What do you think I am? A babe that can't bear grief without some pretty tale to sweeten it?"

"It's not a lie. And soon, when you're training allows, you'll do and see things that will prove the truth of it. Until then, believe me."

Nevyn hesitated, but he knew that Rhegor would never lie about the dweomer.

"And in a while," the master went on. "She'll die to that other world and be born again to this one. I can't know if ever your paths will cross again. That's for the Great Ones, the Lords of Wyrd, to decide, not you and me. Do you still doubt my sworn word?"

"Never could I doubt that."

"Then that's what you have." Rhegor gave a long weary sigh. "And since men believe the bitter easier than the sweet, I'll tell you somewhat else. If you do meet again, whether in this life or the next, then you have a great debt to make up to her. You failed her, lad. I'm half minded to turn you out, but that would only mean I'm failing you. You're going to make this up to her, and the burden won't be an easy one. Maybe it sounds pleasant, saying you'll meet again, but think about what you owe her. You little fool, you should have recognized her. You thought of her like a jewel or a fine horse, the best woman to come your way like a prize. Ye gods, under that face, under that god-cursed beauty, lay a woman to match you in the dweomer. Why do you think I hung around the falcon keep? How could she ever leave to study the dweomer except through the right man? Would her father have

ever so nicely let her go off on her own to study her birthright?
Why do you think you fell in love with her the moment you saw
her? You knew, you little dolt, or you should have known—you
were a pair, calling to one another!" Rhegor slammed his hand
down on the table. "But now she's gone."

Nevyn turned cold, a sick ripple of shame.

"And someday soon she'll have to start all over again,"
Rhegor went on remorselessly. "A little babe, blind, unknowing,
years before she can even speak and hold a cursed spoon to feed
herself. She'll have to grow up all over again, while the kingdom
needs every dweomer-master it can get! You dolt! By then, who
knows where you'll be? You fool!"

Nevyn broke, falling onto the table to weep on his folded
arms. Hastily Rhegor got up, laying a gentle hand on his shoulder.

"Oh here, I'm sorry, lad," Rhegor said. "There'll be time to
talk when you're done mourning. You don't need vinegar poured
on your wounds. Here, here, I'm sorry."

Yet it was a long hour before Nevyn could stop weeping.

In the morning, Nevyn and Rhegor took Brangwen into the
woods to bury her. As he helped dig her grave, Nevyn felt a
deathly calm. He lifted her up for the last time and laid her in,
then put all the courting presents in with her. Other lives or no,
he wanted her to have grave goods, like the princess she should
have been. Working together, they filled in the grave and built a
cairn over it to keep the wild animals from digging her up.
Around them the forest stretched silent and lonely, far from her
ancestors. When the last stone lay on the cairn, Rhegor lifted his
arms to the sun.

"It is over," Rhegor called out. "Let her rest."

Nevyn fell on his knees at the foot of the cairn.

"Brangwen, my love, forgive me," Nevyn said. "If we ever
meet again, I swear I'll put this right. I swear to you—I'll never
rest until I set this right."

"Hold your tongue!" Rhegor snapped. "You don't know what
you're offering."

"Curse it—I'll swear it anyway. I'll never rest until I put this
right!"

From the clear sky came a clap of thunder, then another,
then another—three mighty hollow knocks, rolling and booming
over the forest. His face white, Rhegor stepped back.

"Well and good," Rhegor said. "The Great Ones have accepted your sacrifice."

After the thunder, the silence was unbearably loud. Nevyn rose, shaking like a man with a fever. Rhegor shrugged and picked up his shovel.

"There you are, lad," Rhegor said. "A vow's a vow."

When the forest was turning gold and scarlet, and the winds whipped down from the north, Gwerbret Madoc rode their way. Nevyn came back from gathering firewood to find his splendid black horse, shield hanging at the saddle bow, standing in front of the hut. He dumped his armload of wood into the bin and ran inside to find Madoc drinking ale with Rhegor at the table.

"Here's my apprentice, Your Grace," Rhegor said. "Since you're so interested in meeting him."

"Have you come to kill me?" Nevyn said.

"Don't be a dolt, lad," Madoc said. "I came to offer my aid to Brangwen, but now I hear I'm far too late."

Nevyn sat down and felt his grief welling up heavy in his heart.

"How did you find me?" Nevyn said.

"By asking here and there. When you were banished, I stayed at court and tried to convince His Highness to recall you. I might as well have tried to squeeze mead out of turnips. So your most noble mother let it slip to me that you'd gone for the dweomer, and that there was no hope at all. Then when I rode to Lady Rodda after Blaen's murder, I heard a tale or two from the servants about this strange herbman and his apprentice. Worth a look, think I, but I haven't had the time till now."

"Nicely done," Rhegor said. "The gwerbret keeps his eyes open wider than most men."

Madoc winced as if he'd been slapped.

"Here, Your Grace," Rhegor said. "Just a way of speaking."

"You can't know how deep that cuts," Madoc said. "About Gerraent and his god-cursed passion? I saw it, and here like a fool I held my tongue, hoping I was wrong."

"If it's any comfort," Rhegor said. "No one would blame you."

"No comfort at all when a man blames himself. But then I heard that our prince had gotten her away in the end. Well, think

I, the least I can do is find the lass before winter and make sure she and the child will be warm." His voice broke. "Too late now. I'll never make it up to her."

A cold silence hung in the room.

"How fares Lady Rodda?" Rhegor said at last. "I grieve for her, but I haven't dared to ride her way."

"Well, she's a warrior's wife and the mother of warriors," Madoc said. "Her heart will heal in time. Ah curse it, I failed Blaen, too! A piss-poor excuse for a man I am, taking a man's fealty and then letting things sweep him to his death."

"And the Falcon no longer flies," Rhegor said. "It's a hard thing to see the death of a clan."

"And a death it is, truly," Madoc said. "The King has given the Falcon's lands to the Boar as a blood price for Blaen's murder. What lord will ever take that device again, cursed as it is?"

"True enough," Nevyn joined in. "And in a while, the bards will sing the ballad of Brangwen and Gerraent. I wonder what they'll make of it."

Rhegor snorted profoundly.

"Somewhat better than it deserves," he said. "Oh, no doubt."

Deverry, 1058

If a man would claim the dweomer, he must learn patience above all else. No fruit falls from a tree before it is ripe.

The Secret Book of Cadwallon the Druid

This early in the spring, the river water was still cold. Giggling and splashing at the chilly shock, Jill jumped up and down in the shallows until she could bear to kneel down on the sandy bottom. Curious Wildfolk clustered around, faces that appeared in the ripples, sleek silver forms that darted like fish, while she washed her hair as well as she could without soap. She'd never worried before about being clean, but it had come to seem important. Once she was done, she rolled on the grassy bank like a horse to get dry, then hurried back to the camp among the hazel trees. Out in the meadow beyond, her gray pony and Da's warhorse were grazing quietly. Cullyn himself was still over at a nearby farmhouse buying food. Jill rushed to get dressed before he returned. Just lately, it was troubling to think of Da seeing her without any clothes.

Before she put on her shirt, she looked at her chest and the two definite swellings of little breasts. At times, she wished that they would just go away. She was thirteen, an ominous age since many girls married at fourteen. Hurriedly she pulled on the shirt and belted it in, then rummaged in the saddlebags and found a comb and a fragment of cracked mirror. The gray gnome, all long nose and warts, materialized next to her. When Jill held up the mirror to him, he looked behind it as if searching for the rest of the gnome he saw there.

"That's you," Jill said. "See, there's your nose."

The bewildered creature merely sighed and hunkered down on the grass next to her.

"If it was bigger maybe you'd understand. Da said he'd buy me a proper mirror for my birthday, but I don't want one. Stupid town lasses primp all the time, but I'm a silver dagger's daughter."

The gnome nodded agreement and scratched his armpit.

When Cullyn returned, they set out riding for Dun Mannanan, a coastal town on the eastern border of Deverry province. It turned out to be a collection of shabby wooden houses that straggled along a river, where decrepit, aging fishing boats were docked. Rather than having town walls, it merely faded into the surrounding farmlands, and the smell of drying fish was everywhere. On a muddy street that curved up to the river's edge, they found a shabby wooden inn, where the innkeep took Cullyn's coin without even a glance at his silver dagger. Since it was market day, the tavern room was crowded with men, a sullen lot, by and large, and Jill noticed that a remarkably large number of them wore swords. As soon as they were alone, she asked Cullyn if Dun Mannanan were a pirate haven.

"It's not," he said with a grin. "They're all smugglers. Those stinking boats out in the river are faster than they look. They carry in many a pretty thing under the mackerel."

"Doesn't the local lord stop it?"

"The local lord's in it up to his neck. Now don't you say one word about this out in public, mind."

Once the horses were tended, they went down to the market fair. Down by the river, people had set up wooden booths, but many simply displayed their goods on rough cloths thrown onto the ground. There was food of all sorts—cabbages and greens, cheeses and eggs, live chickens tied upside down onto poles, suckling pigs, and rabbits. Cullyn bought them each a chunk of roast pork on a stick to eat as they looked at the booths with cloth, pottery, and rough metal work.

"I don't see any fancy lace," Cullyn said. "Pity. I wanted to buy you some for your birthday."

"Oh Da, I don't want that sort of thing."

"Indeed? Then what about a pretty dress?"

"Da!"

"A new doll? Jewelry?"

"Da, you'd best be jesting."

"Nothing of the sort. Here, I know a jeweler in this town, and I'll wager he's not even at the fair. Come along."

Down near the edge of town, where the green commons met the last houses, they came to a little shop with a wooden sign painted with a silver brooch. When Cullyn pushed open the door, silver bells jingled melodiously above. The chamber was just a thin slice of the round house cut off by an intricate wickerwork partition. The doorway in the wickerwork was covered by an old green blanket.

"Otho?" Cullyn called. "Are you here?"

"I am," a deep voice said from within. "Would I be leaving the door unlocked if I weren't?"

The owner of the voice shoved aside the blanket and came out. He was the shortest man Jill had ever seen, just about four and a half feet tall, but broad-shouldered and heavily muscled, like a miniature blacksmith. He had a thick shock of gray hair, a tidy gray beard, and piercing black eyes.

"Cullyn of Cerrmor, by the gods," Otho said. "Who's this with you? Your son, from the look of him."

"My daughter, in truth," Cullyn said. "And I want to buy her a trinket for her birthday."

"A lass, are you?" Otho looked Jill over carefully. "Well, so you are, and one old enough to be thinking about her dowry at that. We'd best turn some of your Da's coin into jewels, then, before he drinks the lot away."

Otho led them into the workshop, a thick slice of the house. In the center, just under the smokehole in the roof, were a hearth and a small forge. Off to one side stood a long low workbench, scattered with tools, small wooden boxes, and a half-eaten meal of bread and smoked meat. Lying in the clutter were a handful of small rubies. Cullyn picked one up and held it so that it caught the light.

"Nice stones," he remarked.

"They are," Otho said. "But I'll trouble you to not ask where I got them."

With a grin Cullyn rolled the ruby back onto the bench. Otho perched on the stool and had a thoughtful bite of bread.

"Brooches, rings, bracelets?" he said with his mouth full. "Or does she want a jeweled coffer? Earrings, maybe?"

"None of those, truly," Cullyn said. "But a silver dagger."

Jill laughed, a crow of victory, and threw her arms around him. With a sly smile Cullyn untangled himself and gave her a kiss on the cheek.

"Now that's a strange gift for a lass," Otho said.

"Not for this little hellcat here. She's even badgered her old father here into teaching her swordcraft."

Otho turned to Jill in surprise. The gray gnome popped into existence, squatting on the workbench, and laid one long warty finger on a ruby. Jill reached out and swatted it away, then realized from the way that Otho's eyes were moving that he, too, could see it. With an injured look, the gnome vanished. Otho gave Jill a bland conspiritorial smile.

"Well, lass," he said. "No doubt you'll want the same falcon device as your Da."

"By the asses of the gods, Otho," Cullyn broke in. "It was fourteen years ago when you made me my dagger. You've got a cursed long memory."

"I do. Memory serves a man well if he'll only use it. Now, you're in a bit of luck. I've got a dagger all made up, so all I have to do is grave the device on. A year or so ago, Yraen the silver dagger brought me a lad to pledge to your band. I got the dagger finished, but cursed if the lad didn't go and ask questions about the fishing boats, and so he never lived to pay me for it. Luckily I'd never put on the device, or I'd have been out a good bit of coin."

Late in the afternoon, Jill went back to the smith's to get the finished dagger. She ran greedy hands over the hilt and a cautious finger down the blade. While an ordinary Deverry craftsman would have drawn a falcon as a circle for a head on top of a pair of triangles for wings, Otho's work was a lifelike side view, detailed to give the illusion of feathers, and yet it was only an inch tall.

"This is truly beautiful," Jill said with a grin.

The gnome materialized for a look. When Jill obligingly held the dagger up, Otho laughed under his breath.

"You're a strange one, young Jill," Otho said. "Seeing the Wildfolk as clear as day."

"Oh, I'm strange, am I now? Good smith, you see them, too."

"So I do, so I do, but why I do is my secret, and not for the telling. As for you, lass, is there elven blood in your mother's clan? You can tell by looking at him that there's no such thing in Cullyn's."

"What? How could there be? Elves are only a children's tale."

"Oh, are they now? Well, the elves you hear about are a tale and no more, perhaps, but that's because no one knows the true elves. They're called the Elcyion Lacar, they are, and if you ever meet one, don't trust him a jot. Flighty, they are, all of that lot."

Jill smiled politely, but she was sure that Otho must be daft. He put his chin on his hand and considered her.

"Tell me somewhat," he said at last. "Does it suit you, riding with your father? Cullyn's a cursed harsh man."

"Not to me. Well, most of the time, not to me. But it's splendid, getting to go everywhere and see everything."

"And what's going to happen when it's time for you to marry?"

"I'll never marry."

Otho smiled in pronounced skepticism.

"Well, some women never marry," Jill said. "They get a craft, like spinning or suchlike, and they open a shop."

"True enough, and maybe you will find the right craft someday. Here, young Jill, I'll tell you a riddle. If ever you find no one, ask him what craft to take."

"Your pardons, but what—"

"Told you it was a riddle, didn't I? Remember, if ever you find nev yn, he'll tell you more. Now you'd best get back to your Da before he gives you a slap for dawdling."

All the way back to the inn, Jill puzzled over Otho and his riddle both. Finally she decided that the riddle meant that no one could ever tell her what to do, because she'd cursed well do exactly what she wanted. Otho himself, however, was not so easily solved.

"Da?" she asked. "What sort of a man is Otho?"

"What? What do you mean by that?"

"Well, he doesn't seem like an ordinary man."

Cullyn shrugged in vague irritation.

"Well, it must be hard on a man, being born that short," he said at last. "I suppose that's what makes him so gruff and grasping. Just to begin with, what lass would ever have him?"

Jill supposed that his answer made sense, but still, she was left with the feeling that there was something very odd about Otho the silversmith.

That evening, the tavern room filled up fast with merchants who'd been to the fair and farmers having a last tankard before they went home. Although the room was hot from the fire in the hearth, and clouds of midges swarmed around the candle lanterns, Cullyn showed no inclination to leave after dinner. With coin in his pocket, he would drink all night, Jill knew, and she got ready to argue with him later to keep him from spending the lot. Eventually four riders in the local lord's warband, wearing fox blazons on their shirts, came in to drink and chivy the serving lass. Jill kept a nervous eye on them. Three of them were laughing and talking, but the fourth stood on the edge of things. Since he looked no older than fifteen, doubtless he had yet to prove himself in battle or in a brawl. Jill hoped that he wouldn't be stupid enough to challenge Cullyn, because he was a handsome lad in his way. All at once, she realized that he was boldly looking back at her. She grabbed her tankard of ale and buried her nose in it.

"Not so fast," Cullyn snapped.

"My apologies, Da. Here, shall I fetch you another? The tavernman's so busy he never looks our way."

Jill got the ale from the tavernman and began making her way back, carefully keeping her eye on the foaming-full tankard. When she felt a touch on her shoulder, she looked up to find the young rider, grinning at her.

"Hold a minute," he said. "Can I ask you somewhat?"

"You can, but I might not answer."

The other Fox riders gathered round and snickered. The lad blushed and went on in wavering determination.

"Uh, no insult, mind, but are you a lad or a lass?"

"A lass, but it's nothing to you."

The riders laughed. One nudged the lad and whispered, "Oh go on."

"Uh well," the lad said. "I thought you were a lass, because you're so pretty."

Jill was caught speechless.

"Well, you are," the lad went on, a bit more boldly. "Can I stand you a tankard?"

"Now here." It was Cullyn, striding over. "What's this?"

"He was just talking to me, Da."

The lad stepped back sharply, stumbling into his friends.

"Listen, you young dolt," Cullyn said. "I happen to be Cullyn of Cerrmor. Ever hear that name?"

The lad's face went pale. The other Fox riders joustled each other in their hurry to fall back and leave the lad to face Cullyn alone.

"I see you have," Cullyn said. "Now, none of you are going to say one more word to my daughter."

"We won't," the lad stammered. "I swear it."

"Good." Cullyn turned on Jill. "And you're not saying one more word to them. Get back to the table."

Slopping the ale a bit, Jill hurried back to the table and sat down. Cullyn stood with his arms folded over his chest while the Fox riders unceremoniously ran out the door; then he came and sat beside her.

"You listen to me, Gilyan. The next time any young lout says a wrong word to you, you walk on by and find me. By the hells, you're getting older, aren't you? I never truly noticed how much older before."

When their eyes met, Jill felt that she'd somehow become shameful and failed him. She disliked the way her father was looking at her, too, a cold appraisal that made her feel unclean. Abruptly he looked away, and she knew that he was as troubled as she was. She sat there miserably and wished that she could talk to her mother. It was only later that she remembered the young rider telling her she was pretty. In spite of herself, she was pleased.

II

On a day when the trees stood scarlet, and a cold drizzle turned the streets to muck, Nevyn rode into Dun Mannanan. He rented a chamber in the inn, stabled his horse and packmule, then wrapped himself in his patched cloak and hurried to the shop of Otho the silversmith. For reasons of its own, the dweomer watched over the band of silver daggers; since most of them were decent enough lads who had only committed one grave fault, they came in handy on those rare times when the dweomer needed some help from the sword. Nevyn knew every smith in the kingdom who served them, though few were as strange as Otho, a dwarf in long exile from the kingdoms of his race far to the north. When Nevyn appeared at his door, the silversmith greeted him heartily and took him into the workshop, where a cheerful fire burned on the hearth.

"Would you care for a bit of mulled ale, my lord?" Otho said.

"I would. These old bones are feeling the damp."

Otho allowed himself a smile at the jest. They had, after all, known each other for some two hundred years. Nevyn pulled the only chair in the room up to the fire and held out his hands to the heat while Otho bustled around, filling a metal flagon with ale from the barrel by the wall, adding a stick of Bardek cinnamon, then popping on a lid to keep the ashes out when he stood the flagon in the coals.

"I was hoping you'd ride my way," Otho said. "I might have a bit of news for you. That lass of yours, the one you've been vexing yourself over for so long, is it time for her to be reborn again?"

"It is. Here, have you seen her?"

"I may have, I may not. I don't have the second sight, my lord, or the dweomer neither, as well you know. But she was a cursed strange little lass of about thirteen who rode my way this summer. Her name was Gilyan. Her father's a silver dagger, you see, and he has his daughter riding with him. Cursed strange to see a human being treat his child so well, but that's neither here nor there. His name's Cullyn of Cerrmor. Ever heard of him?"

"The man they say is the best swordsman in Deverry?"

"The very one, and he is, too. His mark is the striking falcon."

"Oh by the gods! It could be. It just could be."

Otho got a clot of rags and gingerly took the flagon from the fire, then poured the steaming ale into a pair of tankards. Thirteen would be the right age, Nevyn thought, and it would be like Gerraent to end up with that dagger in his belt. If she were wandering with a silver dagger, it was no wonder he'd never found her in all his long years of trying. Suddenly he felt weary. For all that Cullyn of Cerrmor had great glory, it would be a hard job to track him down. Otho handed him a tankard.

"When they left here," Otho said. "They rode north. Cullyn

took a hire with a merchant who was taking a caravan of our . . . ah well, special imports up to Cerrgonney."

"Special imports indeed. Here, Otho, when are you going to mend your ways?"

"It's your people, not mine, who make such a cursed fuss over excises and the King's tax."

"Ye gods, trying to talk with you about such things is like trying to talk sense into a stone."

Although Nevyn was tempted to ride north straightaway, by that time of year it would already be snowing in Cerrgonney, and for all he knew, Cullyn had left the province long before. Nevyn decided to carry out his original plan of returning to his home in western Eldidd for the winter. After all, he reminded himself, this Gilyan might not even be his Brangwen reborn. She wasn't the only soul in the kingdom marked for the dweomer, and the falcon mark might well be a simple coincidence. Besides, he also had Lord Rhodry Maelwaedd of Aberwyn to consider. He was as much a part of Nevyn's Wyrd as Brangwen was.

Although Nevyn had been planning on riding straight to Aberwyn, he took the precaution of scrying Rhodry out first and so saved himself a wasted trip. When he called up Rhodry's image in the burning coals of a fire, he saw the lad out riding in the forest preserve of the gwerbrets of Aberwyn—a stretch of virgin forest near the little town of Belglaedd. Nevyn assumed that he would have no chance to meet Rhodry, simply because the preserve was closed land to all but gwerbretal guests, but even so, he went to Belglaedd on the off chance that the young lord might ride into town for some reason. There, as he later came to realize, the Lords of Wyrd took a hand in the matter.

The people of Belglaedd and the outlying farmers both knew and honored Nevyn, because he was the only source of medical care that most of them had. The tavernman insisted on putting him up for free and then rattled off a list of symptoms about the pains in his joints. For the next week Nevyn had little time to think about Rhodry as family after family came to buy his herbs and ask his advice. On the eighth morning, Nevyn had just gone out to the muddy tavern yard for a bit of sun when a rider trotted up in a splash of muck. He wore a blue cloak blazoned with the dragon device of Aberwyn.

" 'Morrow, aged sir," the rider said. "I hear there's a good herbman in town. Do you know him?"

"I am him, lad. What's the trouble?"

"I've just come from the lodge. Lord Rhodry's cursed ill."

Talking all the while, the rider helped Nevyn load his supplies onto his mule. Lord Rhodry had been caught out in the rain and stubbornly gone on hunting even though he was soaking wet. The only people at the lodge with him were a pair of servants and five of his father's men, none of whom knew the first thing about physick.

"And what's his lordship doing out here this time of year anyway?" Nevyn said.

"Ah well, sir, I'm not free to say, but he got into a bit of trouble with his older brother. Naught that was serious."

Although the gwerbret probably considered his hunting lodge to be charmingly rustic, it was as imposing as many a dun of a lesser lord. In the middle of a cobbled and well-drained ward rose a three-story broch, surrounded by enough outbuildings and stables to house a party of a hundred guests. An aged manservant led Nevyn up to the second floor and Rhodry's chamber, sparsely furnished with one carved chest, a bed with faded hangings, and his lordship's shield hanging on the wall. Although there was a brazier heaped with coals glowing in the middle of the room, the damp seeped out of the very walls.

"By the hells," Nevyn snapped. "Isn't there a chamber with a proper hearth?"

"There is, but his lordship won't let us move him."

"Indeed? Then I'll deal with his lordship."

When Nevyn pulled back the bed curtains, Rhodry looked up at him with gummy eyes. At sixteen, he'd grown into a lanky lad, getting close to six feet tall, and still as handsome as ever—or he would have been handsome if his hair weren't plastered to his forehead with sweat, his lips not so badly cracked that they were bleeding, and his cheeks not flushed with a hectic glow.

"Who are you?" Rhodry mumbled.

"An herbman. Your men fetched me."

"Ah curse them! I don't need—" And then he began to cough so violently that his body went rigid. He propped himself up on one elbow and spasmed, choking until Nevyn grabbed him and hauled him upright. Finally he spat out green rheum.

"You don't need me?" Nevyn said drily. "I may only be a commoner, your lordship, but you're following my orders."

Rhodry's lips twitched in a faint smile as he trembled with fever. Nevyn laid him down again and turned to the frightened manservant.

"Get that chamber with the hearth warm," Nevyn said. "Then pile extra pillows on the bed, and start heating me a big kettle of water. When you've done all that, send one of the men back to Aberwyn. Gwerbret Tingyr needs to know that one of his heirs is cursed ill."

All that afternoon, Nevyn worked over his patient. He fed Rhodry infusions of coltsfoot and elecampe to bring up the phlegm, hyssop and pennyroyal to make him sweat, and quaking aspen as a general febrifuge. Nevyn rubbed the lad's lips repeatedly with flaxseed meal in lard to soothe them. As the medicines cleansed his humors, Rhodry coughed until it made Nevyn's own sides ache to hear him, but at last he began to breathe freely instead of gasping for every breath. Nevyn let him lie down then, propped up on the mound of pillows. The fever still played on his face like firelight.

"My thanks," Rhodry whispered. "Owaen? Does he still live?"

For a moment Nevyn was too puzzled to answer him; then the memory came back, of another life when he'd tended battle wounds on the body this soul wore then, and his best friend lay dying nearby.

"He does, lad," Nevyn said gently. "Just rest."

Rhodry smiled and fell straight asleep. So, Nevyn thought, he's reacting to my presence, is he? In his feverish state, Rhodry had somehow come across that long-buried memory.

All the next day, Nevyn brooded over his patient, forcing him to drink the bitter infusions of herbs even though Rhodry swore at him and complained that he couldn't get another loathsome mouthful down. Finally, that evening, the fever broke. Rhodry was well enough to eat a little thin soup, which Nevyn fed to him a mouthful at a time.

"My thanks," Rhodry said when he was finished. "It's a marvel, you turning up like this. Do you remember meeting me on the Cantrae road all those years ago?"

"I do, truly."

"Cursed strange. I was just trying to be courteous. I never dreamt you'd save my life someday. I must have cursed good luck."

"So you must," Nevyn said, suppressing a smile. "So you must."

When Rhodry fell asleep, Nevyn went down to the great hall for his dinner. The men in the young lord's warband insisted on treating Nevyn like a hero. They brought him his food like pages and crowded round to thank him while he ate. One of them, a beefy lad named Praedd, even insisted on bringing Nevyn a goblet of mead.

"Here, good sir," Praedd said. "If you ever need our aid for anything, me and the lads will ride out of our way to give it."

"My thanks. I take it you men honor Lord Rhodry highly."

"We do. He's young yet, but he's got more honor than any lord in Eldidd."

"Well and good, then. And what of Lord Rhys, the heir?"

Praedd hesitated, glancing this way and that, and he dropped his voice when he answered.

"Don't spread this around, like, but there's plenty of men in Aberwyn who wish Lord Rhodry had been born first, not second."

Praedd bowed and hurried away before he could say anything else indiscreet. As Nevyn thought over what he'd said, he felt a cold dweomer-warning ripple down his back. There was trouble coming in Aberwyn. Suddenly he had a brief flash of Vision, saw swords flashing in the summer sun as Rhodry led a wedge of men into a hard-fought battle. When the Vision faded, Nevyn felt sick at heart. Was there going to be a rebellion to put Rhodry in the gwerbretal chair when Tingyr died? Perhaps— dweomer-warnings were always vague, leaving the recipient to puzzle out their meaning. Yet he could guess that once again, he would have important work to do in Aberwyn when the time came.

The guess turned to a certainty late on the next afternoon. Nevyn was up in Rhodry's chamber when a manservant rushed in with the news that Rhodry's mother, Lady Lovyan of Aberwyn, had arrived with a small retinue. In a few minutes, the wife of the most powerful man in Eldidd swept into the room. She threw her travel-stained plaid cloak to the waiting servant and ran to Rhodry's bedside. A solid woman in her early forties, Lovyan had an imposing beauty, her raven-dark hair just streaked with gray, her cornflower blue eyes as large and perfect as her son's.

"My poor little lad," she said, laying a hand on his forehead. "Thanks be the Goddess, you're not fevered anymore."

"The Goddess sent a cursed good herbman," Rhodry said. "Mother, you didn't need to ride all this way just for me."

"Don't babble nonsense." Lovyan turned to Nevyn. "My thanks, good sir. I'll see you're well paid for all of this."

"It was my honor, my lady," Nevyn said, bowing. "I'm just thankful that I was close at hand."

Nevyn left them alone, but later he returned to find Rhodry asleep and Lovyan sitting by his bedside. When Nevyn bowed to her, she came over to talk where they wouldn't waken him.

"I've spoken to the servants, good Nevyn," Lovyan said. "They told me that they feared for his life until you came."

"I won't lie to you, my lady. He was very ill indeed. That's why I thought you should be notified."

Lovyan nodded, her mouth slack with worry. In the fading light, she looked intensely familiar. Nevyn allowed himself to slip into the second sight and saw her clearly—Rodda, bound to Blaen again as mother to son. At that moment, she recognized him as well, and her eyes grew puzzled even as she smiled.

"Now here, do you ever ride to Aberwyn?" Lovyan said. "I must have seen you before, but surely I'd remember a man with such an unusual name."

"Oh, my lady, you may have seen me when you rode by in the street or suchlike. I'd never be presented to a woman of your rank."

Nevyn felt like laughing in triumph. Here they were, three of them come together at the same time as he'd had news of the lass who might be Brangwen. Surely the time was ripening, surely his Wyrd was leading him to one of those crisis points when he would have the chance to untangle it. In his excitement, he forgot himself badly. The fire was growing low; he tossed on a couple of big logs, then waved his hand over them. When the flames leapt up, he heard Lovyan gasp. Hastily he turned to face her.

"My apologies, my lady, for startling you," Nevyn said.

"No apology needed, my lord." Lovyan pronounced the honorific slowly and deliberately. "I'm most honored that a man like you would stoop to treating my son for a fever."

"I see that my lady doesn't dismiss tales of dweomer as nonsense fit only to amuse children."

"Her ladyship has seen too many odd things in her life to do anything of the sort."

For a moment they studied each other like a pair of fencers. Then Nevyn felt the dweomer prod him, force him to speak, as if his mouth would burn if he didn't speak out the truth.

"It is véry important for Rhodry to live to his manhood," Nevyn said. "I cannot tell you why, but his Wyrd is Eldidd's Wyrd. I would like to be able to keep an eye on the lad from now on."

Lovyan went tense, her face pale in the leaping firelight. Finally she nodded her agreement.

"His lordship is always welcome at the court of Aberwyn," Lovyan said. "And if he prefers, I shall keep up the fiction that this shabby old herbman amuses me."

"I do prefer, and my thanks."

That night, Nevyn stayed up late, leaning on the windowsill of his guest chamber and watching the moon sail through wind-torn and scudding clouds. He had been sent to his post like a soldier, and he would do nothing but obey. From now on, he would stay in Eldidd and trust that the Lords of Wyrd would send Brangwen to him when the time was ripe. Deep in his heart he felt true hope for the first time in a hundred years. Great things were on the move. He could only wait and watch for their coming.

Deverry, 698

And the bard is picked out by his Agwen, not only to delight his lord, but to remember all the great deeds and great men in his clan, all in their proper order. For if men were without knowledge of anything but the name of each man's father, then the children of bondsmen would be as noble or as base as the children of a gwerbret. Therefore, let no man or woman either commit the impiety of raising his hand against a bard. . . .

The Edicts of King Bran

Low in its grassy banks, the river Nerr flowed slowly, a purl of brackish brown water under a hot sun, parching pale grass. Stripped to his wrinkled waist, an old herdsman led eager cows down to the water. Gweran stood on the bank and watched them sucking water that was mostly mud. Across the river stood a field of stunted grain. If the drought didn't break soon, the farmers would lose the crop. Hopelessly Gweran looked up at the sky, a crystal dome of pure blue, stubbornly clear. Although he'd come for a walk in the fields to work on a song he was composing, Gweran knew his heart was too troubled for bard work. If the weather stayed this way, a long cold winter of starvation faced him, his family, and everyone for miles around. With a shudder, he turned away from the river and walked back to the dun of the White Wolf clan.

Ringed with earthworks, the small fort lay on top of a low hill. Behind the inner log palisade rose a squat stone broch, its slits of windows brooding like eyes over the dusty ward. Except for a few drowsy flies, the ward was deserted in the hot sun. Gweran hurried into the great hall, which was blessedly cool in the circle of stone walls. Down by the empty hearth, Lord Maroic sat at the head of the honor table. With him were two priests of Bel, dressed in their long white tunics and gold torques, their freshly shaven heads shiny with sweat. When Gweran knelt at his lord's side, the head priest, Obyn, smiled faintly at him, his eyes narrowed shrewdly under pouched lids. Gweran felt uneasy.

There was something about priests that made a man feel better if they never looked his way. Lord Maroic, a florid-faced man in his thirties, with pale hair and pale mustaches, stopped in mid-sentence to turn Gweran's way. Gweran's unease deepened.

"I was hoping you'd return straightaway," Maroic said. "I don't suppose a bard can invoke the rain."

"I only wish I could," Gweran said. "I should think His Holiness here would be the one to do that for us."

"His lordship and I have been discussing just that," Obyn said. "We are considering a horse sacrifice to placate the gods."

"No doubt such an act of piety would be bound to please Great Bel."

Obyn considered him, while his young companion looked wistfully at the flagon of ale on the table.

"The question is why Bel is angry with us," Obyn said finally. "A sacrifice will fail if a curse hangs over the land."

"And does His Holiness think there is such a curse?" Gweran said.

"His Holiness doesn't know." Obyn allowed himself a thin-lipped smile. "A priest may read the omens of the future, but only a bard can read the past."

Gweran sighed sharply, realizing what Obyn was asking of him: that life-draining ritual of the Opening of the Well, where a bard may dream himself into the past and talk with the spirits of those long dead. He was tempted to refuse, but if there was no crop, the bard and his family would starve along with everyone else.

"A bard can try to read the past, Your Holiness," Gweran said. "I can only see what my Agwen shows me. By her grace, I'll try to help. Will you witness?"

"I will, and gladly. Tonight?"

"And why not?" Gweran shrugged idly. "When the moon is rising, I'll come to the temple."

To rest before his ordeal, Gweran went up to his chambers on the third floor of the broch, two rooms opening off the central landing by the spiral staircase, one for his children, one for himself and his wife. The main chamber showed many signs that Lord Maroic was properly generous to his bard: a heavy bed, hung with embroidered hangings, a carved chest, a table and two chairs, and a small Bardek carpet. On the table stood his two harps, the small plain lap harp, the tall heavily carved standing harp for formal presentations. Gweran idly plucked a few strings and smiled at the soft resonant echo.

As if the sound were a signal, his wife, Lyssa, came in through the door of the children's chamber. Although she was a pretty woman, with raven-dark hair and large blue eyes, her greatest beauty was her voice, soft, husky, with a musical lilt to it like wind in the trees. Her voice had snared Gweran's heart from the first time he'd heard it, those long ten years ago when she was a lass of fifteen and he at twenty-five could finally think of marrying after his long training.

"There you are, my love," Lyssa said. "Are the priests still down in the hall? I came up here to get away from them."

"Oh, they're gone, I'm going to the temple tonight to work with them."

Lyssa gasped, her soft lips parting. Laughing, Gweran took her hands in his.

"Oh now here," Gweran said. "They won't lay me on the altar like in the Dawntime."

"I know. There's just something about priests. Do you want to sleep? I'll keep the lads outside if you do."

"My thanks, because I'd better."

That night, Gweran fasted through the evening meal. Just at twilight, he fetched his gray gelding from the stables and rode out, taking his time on the gray twilit roads. Overhead in the opalescent sky, the full moon hung bloated on the horizon, shedding its silver light over farmland and forest. But it was hot, as hot as a normal summer day. The village of Blaeddbyr lay four miles to the north of the dun, a cluster of round houses around a well, with a fenced common pasture off to one side. On the far edge of the pasture stood the temple, built of wood and roofed with thatch, set among a small stand of oaks. When Gweran led his horse into the trees, a young priest was there to meet him, moving surefooted in the darkness. He took the reins of Gweran's horse.

"I'll take it round to the stable," the priest said. "His Holiness is waiting for you in the temple."

Inside the small round shrine, candle lanterns cast a pool of golden light before the stone altar. Draped in the long white cloak of ritual working, Obyn stood off to one side, his hands raised to the statue of the god. A rough man-shape, the statue was carved of a single oak trunk whose bark still clung for clothes on the abstract body. The head was beautifully modeled, with great staring eyes and a mobile mouth; two wooden heads hung by their wooden hair from its delicate hands. Lying in front of the altar was a thick pile of tanned white sheepskins.

"Is the temple suitable for the working?" Obyn said.

"It is," Gweran said. "If the god will allow my goddess to share his abode."

"I have no doubt that Great Bel will allow everything that will aid his people." Obyn's eyes blinked and fluttered. "Since he is, after all, the lord of all gods and goddesses."

Rather than engage in religious controversy at the wrong moment, Gweran smiled and knelt down by the pile of sheepskins. He spread them out to make a rough bed, then lay down on his back and crossed his arms over his chest. He let himself go limp until he felt like a corpse, laid out for burial. Obyn knelt down by his feet. The old man moved slowly and stiffly as he sat back on his heels.

"Can His Holiness kneel there all night?" Gweran said.

"His Holiness can do what needs to be done."

Gweran stared up at the ceiling and watched the candle-thrown shadows dancing. It had been a long time since he'd performed this ritual last, to talk to the spirit of an ancient bard of the Wolf clan to clarify a confusing point of Maroic's genealogy. Now a great deal more than a lord's vanity depended on the working. He let his breathing slow until he seemed to float, not rest, on the soft fleece. The candle-thrown shadows danced in silence, broken only by the soft rhythmic breathing of the old priest.

When he was on the drift point of sleep, Gweran began to recite in a dark murmur under his breath. He spoke slowly, feeling each word of his Song of the Past, a gift from his Agwen, the gate to the rite.

> *I was a flame, flaring in the fire,*
> *I was a hare, hiding in the briar,*
> *I was a drop, running with the rain,*
> *I was a scythe, slicing the grain.*

Axe and tree
Ship and sea
Naught that lives
Is strange to me.
I was a beggar, pleading a meal,
I was a dweomer-sword of steel . . .

At those words he saw her, the Agwen, the White Lady, with her pale face, lips red as rowan berries, and raven-dark hair. He was never sure where he saw her, whether it was in his mind or out in a dark place of the world, but he saw her as clearly as the temple ceiling. Then more vividly than the ceiling—she was smiling as she ran her fingers through her hair and beckoned to him. The candle-thrown shadows turned to moonlight and fell, wispy white, to envelop him. He heard his own voice chanting, but the words were meaningless. The last thing he saw was the priest, leaning close to catch every whisper.

Then Gweran was walking to the well head by the white birches. A little patch of grassy ground, three slender trees, the gray stone wall of the well—all were as clear and solid to him as the temple, but on every side stretched an opalescent white void, torn by strange mists. The Agwen perched on the edge of the well and considered him with a small cruel smile.

"Are you still my faithful servant?" she said.

"I'm your slave, my lady," Gweran said. "I live and die by your whim."

She seemed pleased, but it was always hard to tell, because instead of eyes, she had two soft spheres of the opalescent mist.

"What do you want of me?" she said.

"The rain refuses to fall in our land," Gweran said. "Can you show me why?"

"And what would I have to do with rain?"

"You are the wise one, shining in the night, the heart of power, the golden light, my only love, my true delight."

She smiled, less cruel, and turned to stare down into the well. Gweran heard a soft lap and plash of water, as if the well opened into a vast dream river.

"There was a murder," she said. "But no curse. It was avenged properly. Ask him yourself."

She was gone, the birches rustling at her invisible passing.

Gweran waited, staring into the shifting white mist, tinged here and there with rainbow like mother-of-pearl. A man was walking out in the mist, wandering half seen like a ship off a foggy coast. When Gweran called to him, he came, a young warrior, sandy-haired with humorous blue eyes, and smiling just as if his chest weren't sliced open with a sword cut. Endlessly, blood welled and gouted down his chest to vanish before it dripped to his feet. The vision was so clear that Gweran cried out. The warrior looked at him with that terrifying smile.

"What land are you from, my friend?" Gweran said. "Are you at rest?"

"The land of the Boars bore me and buried me. I rest because my brother cut my killer's head from his shoulders."

"And was that vengeance enough?"

"Was it? Ask yourself—was it?" The specter began to laugh. "Was it?"

"It should have been, truly."

The specter howled with laughter. As if his sobbing chuckle brought the wind, the mist began to swirl and close in over the birch trees.

"Who are you?" Gweran said.

"Don't you remember? Don't you remember that name?"

The laughter went on and on, as, no longer solid, the specter whirled, a flickering shadow in the closing mists, a red stain dripping on white, then gone. There was only the mist and the soft rustle of wind. From out of the mist came the voice of his Agwen.

"He was avenged," she said. "Take warning."

As her voice faded, the mist turned thick, swirling, damp and cold, wrapping Gweran round, smothering him, pushing him this way and that like a windblown leaf. He felt himself running, then slipping, falling a long way down.

The candle-thrown shadows were dark on the ceiling of the temple. Obyn sighed, stretching his back, and leaned closer.

"Are you back?" he said. "It's two hours before dawn."

Shaking with cold, his stomach knotted with fear, Gweran sat up and tried to speak. The temple danced around him. Obyn caught his hands hard.

"For the love of Bel," Gweran whispered. "Get me some water."

Obyn clapped his hands together twice. Two young priests hurried in, carrying wooden bowls. Obyn draped his cloak around Gweran's shoulders, then helped him drink, first water, then milk sweetened with honey. The taste of food brought Gweran back to the world better than any act of will could have done.

"Get him some bread, too," Obyn barked.

Gweran wolfed down the bread, washing it down with long greedy swallows of milk, until he suddenly remembered he was gobbling this way in the middle of a temple.

"My apologies, but it takes me this way."

"No apology needed," Obyn said. "Do you remember the vision?"

The blood-gushing specter rose again in Gweran's mind.

"I do," Gweran said, shuddering. "How do you read it?"

"It was a true murder, sure enough, it happened when I was a tiny lad, so I remember somewhat of it. You saw Lord—oh, was it Caryl? I can't remember, but the head of the Boar clan he was, cruelly murdered by the Falcons. But truly, just as your White Lady said, it was avenged, twice over, some would say. The gods had justice, and I see no reason for Great Bel to be displeased."

"Well, then, there's no curse on the land, because that's all my lady could show me."

"Just so." Obyn nodded in perfect agreement. "We will perform the horse sacrifice at the waning of the moon."

Until the sun rose, Gweran rested at the temple. He was so tired he was yawning, but sleep refused to come to him. His mind raced, throwing up bits of the vision, seeing flecks of the white mist, then simply babbling to itself. The ritual always left him this way. Though some bards developed a lust for the strange white lands and the marvels therein, a madness that eventually took over their minds, Gweran felt mostly a disgust, based on a healthy fear of losing himself forever in the swirling mist. Yet as he thought it over, this particular vision seemed to have a message for him: he knew that murdered lord, knew him like a brother. Was it vengeance enough? he thought. Truly, it should have been. When the sun came in pale shafts through the temple windows, he shook off these incomprehensible thoughts and went to fetch his horse for the ride home.

Gweran slept all morning, or rather, he tried to sleep. It

seemed that someone was always coming in: one of the children, chased away by the maidservant; or Lyssa, fetching a bit of her sewing; a page, sent by the lord to make sure the bard was resting. Finally, the maidservant, Cadda, who seemed more than usually dim-witted that morning, crept in to find a clean pair of brigga for one of the lads. When Gweran sat up and swore at her, she cowered back, sniveling, her big blue eyes filling with tears. She was, after all, only fifteen.

"Ah by the gods, I'm sorry," Gweran said. "Here, Cadda, run and tell your mistress that her grouchy bear of a husband has given up trying to hibernate. Go fetch me bread and ale, will you?"

Cadda beat a hasty retreat with an awkward curtsey. She had no time to shut the door before the boys raced in, shouting Da Da Da and scrambling up on the bed to throw themselves at him. Gweran gave them each a hug and sat them down on the end of the bed. He was in no mood for a wrestling match. Aderyn, just seven, was a skinny little lad with huge dark eyes and pale hair. Acern, two and a six-month, was chubby, always laughing, and always, or so it seemed, running around half naked.

"Acern," Gweran said. "Where's your brigga?"

"Wet," Acern said.

"He did *that* again, Da," Aderyn announced.

"Ah ye gods," Gweran said. "Well, I hope your mother wiped you off before you got on the bed."

"Of course, dearest," Lyssa said, strolling in. "If you hadn't been so mean to Cadda, she would have had the lad dressed by now."

Gweran nodded in a meek admission of guilt. Pieces of his dreams and of his vision were floating in his mind. He wanted to compose a song about them; he could almost feel the words in his mouth. Lyssa sat down next to him—the whole family, settling in.

"What's wrong with Cadda, anyway?" Gweran said. "She's so cursed touchy these days."

"Oh, she's got a man on her mind," Lyssa said. "And not much of a man at that."

"Indeed?" Gweran said. "Who?"

Lyssa looked significantly at Aderyn, whose little ears grew bigger every day, and changed the subject.

As soon as he'd eaten, Gweran went out alone for a long walk through the fields. He wandered vaguely, hardly aware of where he was, stumbling occasionally in the long grass as he worked out his song. He would sing snatches of it aloud, changing the words around, working over every line until it was perfect. A stanza at a time, he memorized it, linking it together in his mind with chaining images and alliteration. He would never write it down. If a bard learned to read, learned so much as the names of the letters, his Agwen would desert him. Without her, he could never compose a song again.

His mind finally at rest, Gweran came back to the dun just at twilight. In the cooler gray air, the servants and riders were sitting around in the ward, talking softly together and resting after the long hot day. As he walked toward the broch, Gweran saw Cadda, perched on the edge of a horse trough and giggling up at one of the riders. Remembering Lyssa's snide comment about Cadda's man, Gweran paused to look the lad over: tall, blond, good-looking in a rough sort of way with the narrow blue eyes and high cheekbones of a southern man. Though Cadda seemed besotted with him, the rider listened numbly and half-heartedly to her chatter—surprising, because Cadda was a beautiful girl, all soft curves and thick blond hair.

Although Gweran would have preferred to ignore the matter, his wife was concerned, and for good reason: riders were prone to getting serving lasses pregnant and then doing their best to weasel out of marriage. Gweran walked around the ward until he found Doryn, captain of the troop, who was sitting idly on a little bench and watching the twilight fade. Gweran sat down beside him.

"Who's that new rider in the warband?" Gweran said. "A southern lad, and my wife's lass is making a fool of herself over him."

Doryn grinned in easy understanding.

"Name's Tanyc," he said. "He rode in here a while back, and our lordship took him on. He's a good man with his sword, and that's all that should count, truly."

"Should?" Gweran raised an eyebrow.

"Well, now, he's an odd lad." Doryn considered, struggling with this unfamiliar kind of thought. "Keeps to himself, and then he's dead quiet when he fights. When we rode that raid on Lord Cenydd's cattle, Tanno was as quiet as quiet in the scrap. Creeps a man's flesh to see someone make his kill without even a cursed warcry."

The mention of the cattle raid reminded Gweran that he had yet to sing about it. Although songs about raids were his least favorite, this one deserved the honor as part of the new feud between the Wolf clan and Lord Cenydd's Boars to the north.

"I don't suppose this Tanno's thinking of honorable marriages and suchlike," Gweran said.

"Ah by the hells, keep little Cadda away from him if you can," Doryn said, grinning. "He flies alone, Tanyc. One of the lads started calling him the Falcon, you see, just as a jest, but it's stuck. I was sure there'd be trouble over it, but Tanno just smiles and says it suits him well enough."

"Well, here, Cadda's mother is a good sort, and she trusted her daughter to my care. If you want to do a bard a favor, have a word with this falcon, will you? Tell him to course for another field mouse."

"What man wouldn't do a bard a favor? Done."

With this tedious matter disposed of, Gweran went back to the tower. His mind was running to thoughts of cattle raids. He could piece a song easily out of bits of standard praise lines and other songs. Just get in everyone's name, he reminded himself, none of these drunken louts know one song from another, anyway.

Early in the morning, while it was still halfway cool, Tanyc fetched his saddle, a rag, and a bit of saddle soap from the tack room and took them outside to a shady spot by the well. He drew himself a bucket of water, then sat down to clean his tack. Although some of the other riders were gathering in the tack room to do the same thing, he preferred to be alone, where it was quiet. He was always painfully aware that he was the new man in the warband, still on trial and working his way in. He was just working the soap up into a lather when Doryn came strolling over and hunkered down in front of him.

"Wanted a word with you, lad," Doryn said.

"Of course, captain, is there trouble?"

"Not yet, and there doesn't have to be. What do you think of the bard's little servant lass? Our Gweran doesn't like the way you've been hanging around her."

"She's hanging around me, captain. She's a stupid little bitch, as far as I'm concerned."

Doryn considered this in his slow way. Although he was telling the sincere truth, Tanyc expected to be disbelieved, simply because no one ever trusted him.

"Surprised to hear you say that," Doryn said. "I was afraid you'd lain her down in the straw already. She seems to want it bad enough."

"What honor she has is safe from me, she gets on my nerves. Babbles all the time."

"Well, a man could keep her too busy to talk."

"No doubt. You fuck her if you want her."

With a shrug, Doryn got up, setting his hands on his hips and looking over the saddle.

"Well and good," Doryn said at last. "Then you won't have any trouble doing what the bard wants and leaving her alone."

"None at all, I swear it."

Satisfied, Doryn walked off toward the barracks. Tanyc went back to soaping his saddle leather. Do what the bard wants, he thought, that stuffy little bastard of a nightingale, prattling all the time. He was tempted to meddle with Cadda just on the principle of the thing now, but he had already nocked his arrow for more dangerous game. He worked slowly, taking his time, and keeping a constant watch for the bard's woman. Usually she came down with her lads to let them see the horses.

Tanyc's patience was rewarded in a few minutes, when Lyssa came along with the boys. As they went into the stable, Tanyc sat back on his heels and watched her. There was just something about Lyssa, a soft sway of her hips when she walked, the way she had of smiling while she tossed her head, those eyes of hers that promised a very different kind of thing in bed than a scared young lass could offer. Watching her was as warm and pleasant as the sun on his back. He wondered if she were bored with her stuffy older man. What the bard wants, indeed, Tanyc thought, we'll just see about that.

At noon, Tanyc made a point of watching Lyssa as she ate with her husband. The bard and his family, the chamberlain and his, had a privileged table next to Lord Maroic's by the hearth of honor. Tanyc took a place at one of the rider's tables where he could see her easily. While she ate, Lyssa seemed far more con-

cerned with her children than her husband, who seemed lost in
one of his usual fogs somewhere, idly nibbling bread and looking
across the room. It was such a good sign that Tanyc began considering ways to get a word alone with Lyssa. One of the other riders
elbowed him in the ribs.

"What's all this?" Gennyn said. "Looks to me like you're
watching a doe in someone else's woods, my friend."

"What's the danger in hunting a doe when the stag doesn't
have horns?"

"The stag doesn't need horns when there's a keeper to watch
out for poachers. Lord Maroic would turn you out if you stuck
your thumb in the bard's ale."

"Indeed?" Tanyc turned to give him a slow stare. "Are you
going to run to the captain with the tale?"

Gennyn cringed in a satisfying way and shook his head no,
but Tanyc paid strict attention to his food. There was no use in
being so cursed obvious. If he wanted Lyssa, he was going to have
to fight to get her, but then, he was used to fighting for everything he wanted. Nothing in my whole cursed life ever came
easy, he thought, no reason for it to start now.

Late on a drowsy-hot day, Nevyn rode into Lord Maroic's
village of Blaeddbyr. It wasn't much of a place, a handful of
houses, a blacksmith's forge, not even a proper tavern—a problem, since he was going to have to find somewhere to stay. Nevyn
was there to banish the unnatural drought, but such major dweomer-workings took time. Camping out in the forest, though possible, was going to be wearisome. After fifty years on the road as a
traveling herbman, he was old, stiff, easily tired, and at heart, sick
of his constant solitude. Around the village well were three
women, gossiping and holding their water buckets for an excuse.
When Nevyn led his pack mule and horse over, they smiled and
greeted him with the aching curiosity of the perennially bored.
At the news that he was an herbman, the smiles grew even
broader.

"Now that's a welcome thing," one woman said. "Will you be
staying long, good sir?"

"I was thinking of it," Nevyn said. "I need to search the
woods and fields for more herbs, you see. Do you know of anyone
who'd take in a lodger? I can pay, of course."

The three women thought hard, running over their own domestic arrangements aloud and finally reaching the reluctant conclusion that they had no room.

"Now, there's Banna," one of them said. "She's got that little hut in back of her house."

"She'll talk the poor man's ear off," said another.

"But who else has a hut?" said the first.

When the conclusion was reached that no one else did, Nevyn got directions to the farm where Banna, a widow, lived with her only son. Nevyn rode out, heading in the direction of Lord Maroic's dun, and found the farmstead about a mile down the road, a big enclosure behind a low, packed-earth wall. Since the gate was open, he led his horse and mule inside and looked around. In the muddy yard stood a big stone round house, a cow barn, various sheds for chickens and suchlike, and off to one side, a shabby wooden hut in the shade of a poplar tree. When Nevyn called out a halloo, a young, sandy-haired man hurried out of the cow barn with a rake in his hands.

"Good morrow, are you Covyl?" Nevyn said. "The villagers told me you and your mother might take in a paying lodger. I'm a traveling herbman, you see."

"Ah," Covyl said. He leaned on the rake, looked Nevyn over, turned his attention to the horse and mule, considered Nevyn a bit more, then nodded. "Might. Depends on what Mam says."

"I see. Can I speak to your mother?"

Covyl considered for a long slow moment.

"In a bit," he said. "She's out picking berries."

Covyl turned and walked back to the barn. Nevyn sat down on the ground by the wall and waited, watching the flies drift lazily in air scented with cow. He was just making up his mind that he'd be better off in the forest when a stout woman, with wisps of gray hair peeking under her widow's black headscarf, came hurrying in. Behind her was a beautiful blond girl, too nicely dressed to be living on the farm, and a small skinny lad with the biggest eyes Nevyn had ever seen. All of them carried wooden buckets, and the lad's mouth was a predictable purple stain. Nevyn bowed to the widow and ran through his tale once again.

"An herbman, good sir?" Banna said. "Well, the gall of my

son for making you wait out here! He should have had the decency of offering you a bit of ale. Come in, come in."

Inside the house, it was cooler, but the flies still drifted and the scent was just as strong. The big half-round of the main room was scattered with straw, a few pieces of much-repaired furniture, sacks of oats and farm tools. The forest began to look better and better. Banna, the lass, and the child put their buckets onto a wobbly table. When the lad reached for more berries, the lass caught his hand.

"That's enough, Aderyn," she said. "You'll get a stomach-ache, and we've got to go back soon."

"I want to stay and talk to the herbman," Aderyn said.

"Maybe another day," the lass said firmly.

"But he'll be gone another day," Aderyn said.

Nevyn started to make some trivial remark, but the words froze in his mouth as he glanced at the lass. Those eyes were familiar—or rather, the soul that looked out from them was familiar—Ysolla, by the gods!

"Well, good sir," Aderyn said. "Won't you be gone?"

"Oh, I doubt it," Nevyn said, hastily collecting his wits. "I'm just here to ask good Banna if she'll let me stay in her hut."

"Oh, I'm sure we can work something out," Banna said. "A bit of coin will be welcome. So, here, Addo, the next time Cadda brings you to visit, you can talk to the herbman."

While Banna was showing him the hut, she was more than glad to tell Nevyn about Cadda, her youngest daughter, who had gotten herself a good place up in Lord Maroic's dun as the servant for the bard's woman. Banna also made it quite clear that Aderyn was the son of the bard and his wife—she repeated that several times in case Nevyn should think her daughter had a bastard.

The hut itself was small, with a packed-earth floor, a tiny hearth, and one narrow window, which had a cowhide to drape over it for want of proper shutters. Nevyn decided it would have to do. While he unpacked his horse and mule, Banna swept the dust out of the hut and covered the floor with fresh straw. After he gently shoo'ed Banna out, Nevyn spread his bedroll in the curve of the wall, arranged his canvas packs of herbs opposite, and dumped his saddlebags and cooking pots by the hearth. He sat down in the middle of the floor and looked over his new home, such as it was.

So, Ysolla's here, Nevyn thought, or rather, Cadda—I mustn't make that mistake! She was the first sign he'd had in fifty years that he might be drawing close to the soul who'd once been Brangwen of the Falcon. Since his youth, he'd looked constantly for her to be reborn as he wandered the kingdom, with only the chance that is more than chance to guide him. Although he'd been expecting her to come back immediately, so that when she, in her new body, was about fifteen, he'd be only thirty-six, young enough to marry her, the Lords of Wyrd had chosen otherwise with their usual contempt for a man's vanity. He had never found her. Though he was growing weary with age, he felt no signs of sickness, no omens of approaching death. At his level of the dweomer, he should have been able to see his death date by now, in order to make the proper plans for leaving life, but he saw nothing. The Lords of Wyrd had accepted his rash vow literally: he would never rest until he found her and set things right.

"Ysolla had a hand in the tragedy," Nevyn remarked to the fireplace. "It's just possible that the Lords of Wyrd would bring them together again."

The fireplace stared back in silence, which Nevyn took as doubt. It would still be worth taking a look around while he worked on banishing the drought. He could simply announce his presence as an herbman and get himself invited to visit Lord Maroic's dun.

Oddly enough, it was the bard's son, Aderyn, who provided Nevyn with an even easier entry to the dun. The very next day, Aderyn came down to see him. Nevyn was honestly surprised, because he'd assumed that the lad's interest was only a childish curiosity.

"Do you mind if I see the herbs and things?" Aderyn said. "Am I in the way? Da says I'm always in the way."

"Not in the way at all," Nevyn said. "Maybe you can help me, in fact. Are there any ruined or abandoned farms around here? Certain kinds of herbs grow in land that's been allowed to go fallow, you see, and those are the kind of herbs I need to pick."

"There's one, truly. There was this farm, and Lord Cenedd of the Boar said it was his, but our lord said it was his, and so they fought over it. So the farmer got scared and just left, and now there isn't anyone there to fight over."

"Oh ye gods! Well, that's a pack of noble-born warriors for you."

"Don't you like riders and battles and stuff?"

"Not truly, but I suppose you do. Lads usually do."

"I don't." Aderyn wrinkled up his nose. "I'll never be a rider when I grow up. It's just being cattle thieves. I don't care what anyone says."

In surprise, Nevyn considered the lad carefully. Aderyn twisted one foot behind the other, balanced precariously, and looked wide-eyed around the hut.

"Well, here," Nevyn said. "Would you like to show me where this farm is and help pick herbs? We'll have to go tell your mother where we're going first."

"Oh, I would. There's never anything to do up in the fort. Let's go ask Mam."

Nevyn got a cloth sack, some clean rags to wrap herbs in, and his small silver sickle. With Aderyn chattering all the way, they went up to the dun. As soon as they came through the gates, Cadda ran over and grabbed Aderyn's arm.

"Where have you been?" Cadda said. "I've been worried sick."

"I just went down to see the herbman," Aderyn said. "Where's Mam? I've got to ask her if I can go for a walk."

"She's waiting upon Lady Cabrylla, but your Da's in the great hall," Cadda said, glancing at Nevyn. "Shall I tell our lord's lady that you're in the village, sir? I'll wager she'd like a look at your herbs."

"I'd be most grateful if you would." Nevyn made her a bow. "Tell her I have perfumes and hair rinses and suchlike as well as medicine."

Although Cadda's eyes lit up at the thought, Aderyn grabbed Nevyn's shirt and dragged him firmly off to the great hall, where Gweran the bard was drinking at Lord Maroic's table. A solid-looking man in his thirties, with blond hair and a long blond mustache, Gweran rose to greet his son and this stranger. Nevyn got his second shock in as many days—Blaen! Nevyn then became deeply troubled about Aderyn's mother. Oh ye gods! he thought, Brangwen can't be married to another man! But even as he thought it, he had the uneasy feeling that the Lords of Wyrd were laughing at him.

While Aderyn chattered out his request, Gweran listened with a pleasant smile.

"Very well," he said. "If it's truly all right with you, good sir."

"It is. Your son's remarkably bright, good bard. I always enjoy teaching someone a bit about herbs."

After a pleasant afternoon gathering yellow dock, feverfew, and mallow in the abandoned fields, Nevyn took Aderyn back to the dun, then returned to his hut. He trimmed up the plants, cut off the useless parts, and laid the leaves and stalks out carefully on clean cloth to begin drying. As he worked, his mind ran restlessly of its own accord: Blaen and Ysolla here together. He had never expected to see the other actors in his and Brangwen's tragedy again. It was ominous, troubling, making him wonder if his burden of Wyrd was heavier than he'd ever dreamt. So many lives were ruined along with hers, he thought, and all because of me and Gerraent. He decided that tomorrow he'd take his wares up to the dun and get a look at this bard's woman. Until then, he put the matter firmly out of his mind. He had other work to do.

Just at sunset, Nevyn left the farm and went down to the riverbank, where he found an ash tree and sat down under its spreading branches to watch the river. A sluggish sullen flow, bloody-tinged in the last of the sunset, the river was weak even on the inner planes. Using the second sight, Nevyn could see how its raw elemental force ran tangled. Permeating, interpenetrating, and surrounding the world men call real are other worlds, or states of being, or even forces, if you would call them that. The dweomer calls them planes, knows their dwellers, studies their forces, and has the Sight to see them and know that they're as real as the only world most people can see. That the human mind is the gate between the planes is a safe secret to tell, because it takes years of study and work before the gate will open, years that impatient fools won't spend to learn secrets they shouldn't have.

One of these planes, the etheric, is the root of the elementals (what men call the Wildfolk), the source of natural forces and the web that holds every living creature's soul. Within or beyond that plane is a locus of force that the dweomer terms the Wildlands, and more of the human mind is rooted there than people

would like to admit. To see what was troubling the river, Nevyn
built himself a gate to the Wildlands. He let his breathing slow
until he felt rooted to the earth. The air flowed in and out of his
lungs; before him was the water, with the last fire of the sun
glinting upon it. His mind was the fifth element, reconciling the
four. Slowly, carefully, he built up in his mind an image, a pale
blue glowing five-pointed star, its single point upright as is holy.
After all his long years of work, it took little effort to make the star
flame and live apart from his will. He moved the image out of his
mind until it seemed to stand flaming on the riverbank.

Inside this traced sigil, he could see the Wildlands opening
out blue and misty under a cool sun. He was about to project
himself through when the Wildfolk came to him, rushing
through the gate in a swirl of half-seen forms. Nevyn felt the
rushy tingle of power down his spine as they swept around him
and projected raw emotions, trouble, hatred, and pleading to
help them. The Wildfolk of Air cursed those of Fire and Water
alike, while those of Earth were in despair.

"Here, here," Nevyn said. "I'll have to speak to your kings.
There's nothing I can do alone."

They were gone, racing back to their lands. Although Nevyn
considered following, he decided that it would be best to let
them bring the message to the Kings first. Slowly he erased the
pentacle, drawing the blue light back into himself, then slapped
his hand thrice on the earth to end the operation. In the cool
night air he felt strong and at peace.

I'll try again tomorrow night, Nevyn thought. If things are
this bad, sooner or later the Kings will accept my aid. Although
man is meant to rule the Wildfolk, not worship or placate them,
they deserve respect and due courtesy, which Nevyn could offer
them as one prince true-born to another. But it would have to be
soon if he was going to spare the people of Blaeddbyr a famine. If
this drought continued too long, it would be too late to save the
crops.

Early on the morrow, when the day was still cool, Nevyn
returned to the lord's dun to lay his wares before Lady Cabrylla.
She received him in the women's hall, where her serving women
and the maidservants were gathered to see what this traveling
peddler had to offer. As he laid out packets of herbs, pomanders,
and cosmetic preparations on a table, Nevyn surreptitiously stud-

ied each woman in turn. He was just giving up hope when a young matron, her raven-dark hair caught up in an embroidered headscarf, came slipping in a side door and stood on the edge of the crowd. For all her different coloring and face, Nevyn could think of her as no one but his Brangwen.

"There's our Lyssa," Lady Cabrylla said comfortably. "Nevyn, this is the bard's wife."

Nevyn wondered why he'd ever been so stupid as to think his Wyrd would work out cleanly. He bowed over Lyssa's hand and mumbled some pleasantry, which she returned. As their eyes met, she recognized him—he could see it—a sudden flash of joy in her dark blue eyes, then a bewilderment, as she doubtless wondered why she was so pleased to see this old man. That flash of joy was so much more than Nevyn had hoped for that for the joy of seeing her again, he was willing to endure the harshest of Wyrds.

The horse sacrifice took place out in the sacred oak grove at the edge of the village. On the appointed day, just before sunset, the villagers and the lord's household formed a ragged procession by the village well. Solemnly Lord Maroic knelt before Obyn the high priest and handed over the reins of a splendid white stallion. While Obyn held the horse, the young priests decorated the bridle with mistletoe. When they began to chant, the horse tossed its head and snorted, feeling its strange Wyrd like a rider on its back. To the slow pace of the chanting, Obyn led the horse away. Lord Maroic scrambled up and fell in behind, with the rest of the crowd following him. The procession wound through the grove, filled with long pillars of golden sunlight, and came to the altar in the middle. Unlike the one in the temple, this altar was a rough slab of barely worked stone. Wood for a large fire lay ready upon it.

While Obyn held the horse, the young priests came forward, struck flint on steel, and lit the kindling. Obyn watched narrow-eyed: if the fire caught poorly, the day was cursed, and the sacrifice would have to be postponed. As the flames danced up bright and strong, the crowd sank to its knees. Gweran moved well back to the edge. Since he had Aderyn with him, he wanted to be a good distance when the horse met its Wyrd. As the chanting droned on, Aderyn twisted around to look over the crowd. Men on one side, women and tiny children on the other, everyone who lived within twenty miles was here to beg the god to spare their crops. When Gweran looked over the women, he saw Lyssa and Cadda well to the back, Cadda with a scarf ready to hide her eyes. Acern was asleep in his mother's lap. The chanting grew faster and louder as the flames rose high.

"Da?" Aderyn whispered. "This is a waste of a good horse."

"Hush," Gweran whispered. "Don't talk at rituals."

"But nothing's going to happen till the full moon."

When Gweran threatened a slap, Aderyn fell silent. A young priest took the nervous horse's reins from Obyn, who stepped in front of the altar, raised his arms high into the air, and began to beg the god for mercy, his voice rising and quickening, faster and faster, until he cried out in a great sob of supplication. A young priest blew on a brass horn, a rasping ancient cry down from the Dawntime. Then silence. Obyn took a bronze sickle from his belt and approached the horse, who tossed up its head in terror. When the brass horn blared, the horse pulled back, but the bronze sickle swung bright in the firelight. The horse screamed, staggering, blood gushing, and sank dying to its knees.

Aderyn began to sob aloud. Gweran threw his arms around him, pulled him into his lap, and let the child bury his face against his father's shirt. He was wise to hide his eyes as the priests began dismembering the horse with long bronze knives. From his bard-lore, Gweran knew that in the Dawntime, the victim would have been a man, and that this horse represented the god's growing mercy to his people. The knowledge made it no easier to watch the priests work, their arms bloody to the elbows.

At last Obyn cut a strip of bleeding meat and wrapped it in thick fat from the horse's thigh. With a long wailing chant, he laid the sacrifice in the midst of the flames. The fat sputtered and caught, flaring up with a smokey halo.

"Great Bel," Obyn cried. "Have mercy."

"Have mercy," the crowd sighed.

The young priest blew a great blare on the horn. It was over, and Gweran could lead his sobbing child away. Since Aderyn was weeping as if his heart would break, Gweran picked him up and carried him as he looked desperately around for Lyssa in the scattering crowd. Instead he found Nevyn, who was leaning against a tree and watching the flame-lit altar with a sour smile.

"Oh here, here, Addo," Nevyn said, the smile disappearing. "It's all over now. It's a pity, sure enough, but the poor beast is dead and beyond suffering."

"They shouldn't have," Aderyn sobbed. "It won't even do any good."

"It won't," Nevyn said. "But what's done is done, and you'd best not talk of it right here, where the people can hear you. They need to think it will help."

Slowly, Aderyn sniffled himself to silence, wiping his face on his sleeve. Gweran kissed him and set him down, taking his hand and drawing him close.

"Well, bard?" Nevyn said. "Do you think this will bring rain?"

"Maybe it will, maybe it won't," Gweran said. "But either way, the god will be pleased."

"True spoken," Nevyn said with a laugh. "And pious of you, truly."

The old man walked off, leaving Gweran puzzled and more than a bit uneasy. As the crowd dispersed toward the village, Gweran finally saw Lyssa, hurrying to meet them. Just behind came Cadda, with one of the riders who was carrying the still-sleeping Acern. When Gweran recognized Tanyc, he was annoyed. Here he'd told Doryn to keep this young lout away from Cadda. As he thought about it, he realized he'd seen a lot of Tanyc lately, still hanging around the lass, sitting near her when she and Lyssa were in the ward, or walking conveniently to meet them when she and Lyssa were leaving the dun.

That very next morning, Gweran sought Doryn out when he came down into the great hall for breakfast. He waved the captain over to the side of the hall where they could be private and put his complaint to him. Doryn looked honestly surprised.

"Well, curse the little bastard," Doryn said. "I did talk to him, Gweran, and here he managed to convince me he didn't give a pig's fart for little Cadda."

"There's nothing like lust to make a man lie. Here, I'll have a word with the lad myself later."

It was afternoon before Gweran could get away from his lord's side long enough to go look for Tanyc, but when he found him, he found Cadda with him. Out in the ward, Tanyc was grooming his horse while Cadda stood beside him. She was tell-

ing him some long complex tale about her elder sister while
Tanyc listened with an occasional nod. As Gweran strode over,
Cadda made him a hurried curtsey.

"I'm sure your lady wants you," Gweran said.

With one last smile in Tanyc's direction, Cadda ran for the
tower. Tanyc looked up, the currycomb in his hand.

"My thanks," Tanyc said. "By the hells, doesn't that lass ever
hold her tongue?"

"Every now and then," Gweran said. "You can't find it as
displeasing as that. You seem to seek out her company whenever
you can."

Tanyc looked at him with a barely concealed contempt.

"Maybe I do, maybe I don't," Tanyc said. "What's it to you?"

"Maybe nothing at all—as long as you fancy yourself as a
married man someday. I warn you, if Cadda ends up with child,
I'm speaking to Lord Maroic about it. I don't care how many men
in the warband you get to lie and swear they've had her, too—
she'll be your wife."

Tanyc's hand tightened on the currycomb so hard that
Gweran was surprised the wood didn't crack. Rather than push
things to a formal exchange of insults, Gweran turned and
walked away. If things ever came to a fight, doubtless Tanyc
could cut him to pieces with a sword. Tanyc, of course, knew it,
too. Although Gweran should have been used to the contempt of
the riders, it always rankled his soul.

When he told Lyssa that he'd spoken to Tanyc, she seemed
pleased, remarking that since she didn't care for the man, she'd
be glad to have him stop turning up constantly at Cadda's side.

Over the next few days, Gweran made a point of keeping his
eye on Tanyc, mostly because of that warrior's contempt. At first
Tanyc seemed to have taken the warning to heart, but the morning came when Gweran saw Lyssa, Cadda, and the boys walking
across the ward and Tanyc hurrying over to walk with them.
Gweran hurried downstairs and ran to catch up with them. At
the first sight of him, Tanyc made the women a hasty bow and
went back to the barracks.

"Now, ye gods, Cadda," Gweran snapped. "Your mistress has
spoken to you, I've spoken to you—can't you get it through your
pretty head that he's the wrong sort of man for you?"

Cadda sniveled, grabbing her handkerchief from her kirtle and dabbing at her eyes. Lyssa patted her gently on the arm.

"Gweran's right," Lyssa said. "Here, let's go up to the chamber where it's cool and have a nice talk."

"I want to walk with Da," Aderyn said. "Can I, Da?"

"You may." Gweran held out his hand. "We'll have a nice stroll and let the women have their chat."

They walked down to the river, a trickle of water in mud, and sat down in the rustling dry grass. Without a breath of wind, the heat clung around them. Aderyn stretched out on his stomach in the grass and plucked a dead stalk to play with.

"Da?" he said. "You don't like Tanyc, do you?"

"I don't. Do you?"

"I don't. He scares me."

"Well, the captain tells me he's a hard man."

Aderyn nodded, twisting the grass stalk into a loop.

"You know what, Da? He doesn't bother us to see Cadda. When we walk, you know? He comes to see Mam."

Gweran felt as if he'd been punched in the stomach. Aderyn tried to tie a knot in the slippery stalk, then gave up and started chewing on it.

"Are you sure about that?" Gweran said.

"I am. You told me to watch what people do, remember? So I was watching Tanyc, because I don't like him, and I wondered why I don't like him. I don't like the way he looks at Mam. And he always bows to her so nice, and he talks to Cadda, but all the time, he's looking at Mam."

"Oh he is now?"

Aderyn started slitting the grass stalk with his fingernail and trying to braid the pieces. Gweran looked at the sluggish river and felt his rage flaring, just as when a spark gets into dry grass— it creeps along, smokes, then flares to a sheet of flame, racing along the meadowland. That bastard, Gweran thought, and does he think I'll back down without a fight over this?

"Da," Aderyn said suddenly. "What's wrong? Don't look like that."

"Oh, nothing, lad. Just worrying about the cursed drought."

"Don't. Nevyn's going to fix it."

Gweran forced out a smile and nodded vaguely. He had no time to worry about silly prattle about the herbman.

"Let's get back to the dun," Gweran said. "It's a bit hot out here, and there's a thing or two I want to keep my eye on."

"What I want to know is this," Aderyn said. "Why do herbs work on fevers and stuff?"

"Well, now," Nevyn said. "That's a very long question to answer. Do you want to listen to a talk?"

"I do. This is all splendid."

They were kneeling on the floor of Nevyn's hut and working with the herbs, turning them over to dry evenly. Almost every day, Aderyn came down to help and study herbcraft. After his long loneliness, Nevyn found the boy's chatter amusing.

"Very well," Nevyn said. "There are four humors, you see, in every human body. They match the four elements: fire, water, air, and earth. When all the humors are in perfect balance, then a person is healthy. Each herb has more or less of the various humors; they balance things out if someone is sick. If someone has a fever, then they have too much fiery humor. A febrifugal herb has lots of cool watery humor and helps balance the fiery out."

"Only four humors? I thought there should be five."

Nevyn sat back on his heels in sheer surprise.

"Well, so there are," Nevyn said. "But only four in the body. The fifth rules the others from the spirit."

Aderyn nodded, carefully memorizing the lore. More and more, Nevyn was wondering if the lad was meant to be his new apprentice. The wondering made him weary. Since a dweomerman could have only one apprentice at a time, he could never take Aderyn on while bringing Brangwen to the dweomer to fulfill his vow.

At times, in the hope of seeing Lyssa, Nevyn would take Aderyn back to the dun on horseback. Often in the hot afternoons, the various members of the household would be sitting on the grassy hill. Since Nevyn was now well known, one or the other of them would come over to ask him some medical question or to buy a few herbs or suchlike. It was there that he met Tanyc one afternoon and saw his Wyrd tangle around him like a fisherman's net around its prey.

Leading the horse, Nevyn and Aderyn were walking up the hill when Nevyn noticed Cadda sitting with one of the riders, a hard-eyed southern man. Aderyn noticed it, too, and went skipping over.

"Cadda," Aderyn said with a smirk. "I'm going to tell Mam on you. You shouldn't be here with Tanyc."

"Hold your tongue, you little beast!" Cadda snapped.

"Won't. Won't, won't, won't. I'm going to tell."

Tanyc got up, and something about the way he looked at Aderyn frightened Nevyn, who made a point of hurrying over.

"Slapping a bard's son is a good way for a man to get his name satirized," Nevyn remarked mildly.

"And what's it to you, old man?" Tanyc swung his head and looked at him.

As their eyes met, Nevyn recognized Gerraent's soul in the arrogance blazing out of his eyes.

"You better not insult Nevyn," Aderyn said. "He's dweomer."

"Hold your tongue," Tanyc said. "I'm in no mood to listen to nonsense from a flea-bitten cub."

Tanyc started to swing open-handed at the boy, but Nevyn caught him by the wrist. The Wildfolk flocked to him and lent him so much raw strength that no matter how Tanyc struggled, he couldn't break the herbman's grip. Nevyn pulled him close, caught his gaze, and stared deep into his eyes while he let his hatred burn—and dweomer was behind it. Tanyc went dead white and stopped struggling.

"I said leave the lad alone," Nevyn whispered.

Tanyc nodded in terrified agreement. When Nevyn released him, he turned and ran for the gates of the dun.

"Cadda, take Addo back to his mother," Nevyn said. "I'm going back to the farm."

For the next few days, Nevyn stayed away from the dun and his old enemy. All the actors in their grim little farce were there, even Gerraent, face to face again in a way that Nevyn had never foreseen. He realized that he'd fallen into a last vestige of royal pride, which values only the prince and princess and sees those around them only as supernumaries.

In the end, Lyssa came to him, turning up at the farm one day with the plausible excuse that she'd come to fetch Aderyn home. Nevyn sent the boy out on an errand and offered Lyssa the only chair he had, a wobbly three-legged stool. She perched on it and looked idly around at the hanging bunches of drying herbs.

"The smell in here is lovely," Lyssa pronounced. "It's kind of you, sir, to be so patient with my Addo. You should hear him chatter about it at dinner—today we learned about dog's tooth herb, today we dried the comfrey roots. His father hardly knows what to think."

"Does it vex Gweran?" Nevyn said. "Most men want their sons to show an interest in their own calling."

"Oh, it doesn't, because my man is the best-hearted man in the world. I think he's glad to see Aderyn taking such an interest in something. He's been a strange child from the moment he was born."

Nevyn smiled, quite sure of that.

"I'm surprised you don't have more children," Nevyn said. "You seem to love your lads so much."

"Well, I hope and pray to have more soon." Lyssa looked away, her eyes dark. "I had a daughter, you see, between the two lads, but we lost her to a fever."

"I'm truly sorry. That's a hard thing for a woman to bear."

"It was." Her voice went flat from remembered grief. "Well, doubtless it was my Wyrd, and my poor little Danigga's, too."

Nevyn felt a cold touch as he wondered if indeed it was her Wyrd: she'd drowned a child with her on that terrible night. So she had—the dweomer-cold ran down his back as he realized who that child might have been if it had lived to be raised with himself and Rhegor: a great master of dweomer indeed. Lyssa smiled, looking out the door.

"Here comes our Aderyn now," she said.

Though she was only speaking casually, "our" Aderyn meaning only the "Aderyn we both know, not some other Aderyn," her words turned Nevyn cold to the heart. I swore I'd raise the child as my own, he thought. A vow's a vow.

That night, Nevyn went down to the ash tree by the river bank and sat down to watch the slow water run. As it came clear, his Wyrd lay heavy on him. In this life, Brangwen was gone from him; she would have to repay Blaen for the hopeless love of her that had led him to his death, and repay Aderyn, too, for cutting short his previous chance at life. Nevyn owed Blaen and Aderyn a debt as well, since his scheming had left Brangwen there with her brother's lust. Only once those debts had been repaid could he take her away for the dweomer. Yet Aderyn would be under his care for the next twenty years, because the dweomer is a slow craft to learn. In twenty years, Nevyn was going to be over ninety. And what if he had to wait for her to be reborn again? He would be well over a hundred, an unthinkable age, so old and dry that he would be helpless in a chair, like a thin stick or drooling babe, his body too old for the soul it carried, his mind a prisoner in a decaying lump of flesh. At that moment Nevyn panicked, shaking cold and sick, no longer a master of the dweomer but an ordinary man, just as when a warrior vows to die in battle, but as the horns blow the charge, he sees Death riding for him and weeps, sick of his vow when retreat is impossible.

Around him a tremor of night wind picked up cool, rustling the canopy of branches above him. Nevyn rested his face in his hands and called on his trained will to stop himself from shaking. A vow's a vow, he told himself. If I wither, then let me wither, so long as I fulfill that vow. The wind stroked his hair like a friendly hand. He looked up, realizing that it was no natural wind, but the Wildfolk, sylph and sprite, half-seen forms and the flick of shining wings, a face showing here only to vanish there. They came to him as friends and felt his agony, clustering sympathetic lives forming from the raw surge of elemental life. Nevyn felt his weariness ebb away as they freely poured out some of their life to him, a gift between friends. He rose, walked forward, and stared up at the sky, where glittered a great white drift of stars, the Snowy Road, splendid, unreachable, but shining with promise. When he laughed aloud, his laugh was as full and clear as a lad's. He saw his Wyrd open in front of him, maintained by his work in the Wildlands. He would have life for the task, no matter how long it took as men measure time.

It was that night that he learned this lesson: no one is ever given a Wyrd too harsh to bear, as long as it is taken up willingly and fully, deep in the soul.

At times, Lyssa would leave Acern with Cadda and walk to the farm to fetch Aderyn back from the herbman. She liked these moments of solitude as she walked alone, away from the busy press and chatter of her life among the women of the household. She also found herself drawn to old Nevyn, for reasons she couldn't quite understand. Well, he's a wise kind man who's traveled much, she would tell herself, interesting to meet someone new. It was reason enough, of course, but at times she went to see him because she felt safe there, out of the fort and away from Tanyc. She knew perfectly well that young rider was pursuing her and lived in dread that her husband might notice. Lyssa simply had too much to lose to be interested in adultery—a high social position, a good husband, wealth, comfort, and above all, her children.

On an afternoon when the heat lay as palpable as a blanket over the land, Lyssa left the fort earlier than usual and dawdled her way down the dusty road to the farm. About halfway along stood a copse of aspen trees, where she decided to rest for a few minutes. She walked into the parched shade, glanced around for a place to sit, and saw Tanyc, waiting for her. He stood as still as one of the trees, his head a little to one side, and he was smiling, looking her over with the sort of admiration a man gives to a beautiful horse in a market.

"What are you doing here?" she snapped.

"What do you think? I wanted a word with you."

"I've nothing to say. You'd best get back before the captain finds you gone."

When he stepped toward her, she drew back, her hand at her throat, her heart pounding.

"I've got to be on my way," she said. "My lad will come along soon enough if I'm not there to meet him."

This likely witness gave Tanyc pause. Abruptly Lyssa realized that she was afraid he would rape her. For all his good looks, Tanyc repelled her in a way that she couldn't understand—like seeing a dead animal rotting in the road. She knew the repulsion was daft; rationally, she could admit that he was a decent enough man for a rider.

"May I walk with you aways, then?" Tanyc made her a courteous bow.

"You can't!" Lyssa heard her voice rise to a scream. "Leave me alone."

Then she found herself running, racing out of the copse like a startled deer and running running running down the road until she was sobbing for breath and drenched with sweat. Half in tears she spun around, but mercifully, he hadn't followed.

That night, it was so hot that it took a long time to get the children to sleep. The boys tossed and turned and whined on top of the blankets no matter how soothingly Lyssa talked to them. Finally Gweran came in and sang them to sleep. Lyssa went to their chamber, changed into a thin nightdress and lay down wearily. In a bit, Gweran joined her. He hung the candle lantern up on the wall and sat down on the edge of the bed.

"Don't you have to return to our lord?" Lyssa said.

"I begged his leave. I need to talk with you."

In the shadowed light his eyes were cold, questioning. She sat up, feeling her hands shaking, and twisted a bit of her dress between her fingers.

"Here, my sweet," he went on. "You've been keeping dangerous company these days."

"Oh, am I now? Who?"

"Tanyc. Who else would I mean?"

She clenched the cloth so hard that her fingers ached.

"My lord," she stammered out. "I swear to you that I want nothing to do with him. Do you doubt me?"

"Never. But I don't want my woman raped out in the stables."

When Lyssa started to cry, partly in relief, partly from seeing her worst fear shared, Gweran pulled her gently into his arms.

"My poor sweet little lass," he said. "Here, here, don't weep like that."

"How can I not weep? Ah ye gods, if you come to doubt me, what will you do? Cast me off? Cut my throat, and all for something I'd never do?"

"Hush, hush." Gweran stroked her hair. "I'd die myself before I'd do you the slightest harm."

As suddenly as they'd come, her tears vanished before a new fear. She looked up and found his face set and grim.

"If you challenge Tanyc, he'll win," Lyssa said. "Please, Gwerro, I beg you. Don't. Just don't. What good would it do me, if I had my honor and no husband?"

"I'm not going to do anything of the sort! Do you despise me, think me a coward, and all because I can't match him in a fight?"

"Don't be a dolt. I could have married lots of bloodthirsty men, but I never wanted anyone but you."

Gweran smiled as if he didn't quite believe her. They were

both trapped, she saw, caught by the customs that gave a man no recourse but to defend his wife with a sword. They would have to creep around the edge of Tanyc's arrogance, the pride of a true-born warrior, which thinks it can win a woman with a sword in a world where other men secretly agree. Lyssa hated Tanyc more than ever: no matter what the end of this, her marriage would never be the same. She could only pray that Gweran would never slip over the edge into hopeless violence.

The fear combined with the heat to give Lyssa a restless night of bad dreams. Finally she woke, deep into the night, and heard a strange sound outside the tower. As she lay awake, trying to place it, the two children came bursting into the chamber.

"Da, Mam, it's the wind!" Aderyn shrieked. "The wind's here! It's going to rain."

Just as Gweran woke with a muffled oath, Acern clambered onto the bed.

"Clouds, clouds, clouds, Da," Acern chanted.

Aderyn grabbed Lyssa's hand and dragged her to the window. She could see storm clouds, piling up in the sky, scudding in front of the moon, and smell the cool heady scent of the north wind. The ward was full of noise as the household ran outside to laugh and point and gloat in the feel of the wind. Since there was no hope of getting the children back to sleep, Lyssa got them dressed and took them down to the ward and the blessed coolness. Close to dawn, there was a clap of thunder, and it came, pouring down cold in great sheets of water. Grown men and women ran around and laughed like the children as it rained and rained and rained.

Laughing, his yellow hair dripping and plastered down, Gweran scooped Aderyn up in his arms and held him up to see the dawn breaking silver through the rain.

"There you go, Addo," Gweran said. "The horse wasn't wasted after all."

"It wasn't the priests who did it," Aderyn said. "It was Nevyn."

At first, Lyssa thought he meant "no one," but then she remembered the herbman.

"Now here," she said. "What could Nevyn have to do with it?"

"I saw him do it," Aderyn said. "I dreamt it."

"Dolt," Acern said, simpering. "Da, Addo's a dolt."

"Hush!" Gweran said. "It doesn't matter who started the rain. We've got it, and that's what matters."

Lyssa gave him a grin: Blaeddbyr wouldn't starve this winter. But as she turned to glance idly around the ward, she saw Tanyc, close at hand, watching her, while the water ran down his face and hair. All at once, she couldn't breathe—she felt herself choking in what she could describe only as terror. She grabbed Acern's hand tightly.

"Time to go in," Lyssa said. "Let's all get dry."

Too late—Gweran had seen Tanyc, too, and as he looked at his enemy, Lyssa knew that he was thinking of blood.

It rained steadily for three days. Life moved inside the tower and centered itself in the great hall, where Lord Maroic drank with his warband and the bard sang to keep them all amused. Much to Cadda's annoyance, Lyssa insisted on staying in her chambers, giving Cadda no choice but to stay with her. Finally, on the third day, Cadda's boredom got the better of her subservience.

"Oh please, my lady, can't we go down to the hall?" Cadda said. "We can listen to your lord sing."

"I'd rather not, but you can if you want."

"Oh, my thanks!" Gleefully, Cadda threw her sewing into the workbasket. "Are you sure you won't come?"

"I won't. All the riders will be there." Lyssa looked away. "It's so noisy, and I've got a headache."

Cadda hurried down to the great hall and took a place in the straw in front of the servant's hearth. One of her friends, Dwlla, was already there, listening while the bard sang sad tales of love —Cadda's favorite kind. From where she was sitting, Cadda could see the riders at their tables and Tanyc's broad back, only a few feet from her, but he might as well have been on the other side of the world. In her heart, Cadda cursed him and wondered how he could be so cold to her. Certainly plenty of other men told her she was beautiful. When Gweran paused to rest, Dwlla leaned over and whispered to Cadda.

"Tanno was asking me where you are," Dwlla said. "Or where your lady was, but it comes to the same thing."

All at once, Cadda wondered if it did indeed come to the

same thing. Whenever Tanyc came walking with them, he always spoke to the lady, not the maid. He wouldn't dare meddle with the bard's woman, she thought, and besides, I'm prettier than her. Yet as she gazed fondly at Tanyc's broad back, she wondered if any woman every really understood what men thought.

When the next day dawned clear, Lyssa gave Cadda permission to go down to the farm with Aderyn and visit her mother. While the lad worked with the herbman, Cadda spent a pleasant hour in her Mam's kitchen and gossiped about her sisters, who were already married, much to Cadda's great distress. It just wasn't fair—she was the prettiest and still unmarried, while they all had men of their own! Brooding on the injustice of it all gave her an idea. She left the house and went out to the herbman's hut, where she found Nevyn and Aderyn digging up a bit of ground by the wall for an herb garden.

"Good morrow," Nevyn said. "Is it time for Aderyn to go home?"

"Oh, not truly. I just wanted a word with you about buying some herbs."

Nevyn took Cadda inside his hut and gave her the stool to sit on while he leaned against the wall. Cadda decided that his manners were ever so much nicer than Tanyc's. She only wished she could tell Tanyc that and have him care.

"I was wondering if you made love philters," Cadda said. "I couldn't pay much, but my mistress gives me a coin every now and then."

"A maid with your beauty should have no need of such trash," Nevyn said sternly. "And trash they are. They're impious things, and besides, they never work right."

Cadda's heart sank. Though she didn't care about the impiety, she saw no need to waste her coin on something useless.

"Come now," Nevyn went on. "Is Tanyc as cold to you as all that?"

Cadda wondered if he were dweomer or if she'd simply been obvious. When she decided the latter, her cheeks burned with shame.

"Well, here," Cadda stammered. "It's a nasty thing to love a man who'll never love you."

"No doubt it is. But Tanno would only make a bad husband even if you got him. He's a hard man and a cold one."

"Oh huh! He's not as cold to some as he is to me."

"Oh indeed?" Nevyn smiled paternally at her. "I begin to understand—a bit of jealousy in this."

"Well, it's cursed unfair! There he is, hanging around a woman who's already got her own man, and besides, she doesn't even like him."

"Now listen, lass. If Tanyc's the sort of man who'd want a married woman, can't you see that you could do better for yourself than him? I—" All at once, the old man hesitated, turning to her with an ice-cold stare. "Just what married woman? Your lady?"

In panic, Cadda tried to think of a lie, but those cold eyes seemed to be boring into her very soul.

"Well, it is," Cadda stammered out. "But truly, sir, she hates him. She'd never betray her husband with him. Truly. Oh ye gods, don't tell Gweran, will you?"

"Rest assured—I'd never do anything of the sort. And listen, child, you hold your tongue, too. Hear me? For the life of you, not one word of tattling to Gweran."

Too frightened to speak, Cadda nodded her agreement. As soon as Nevyn turned away, she got up and ran out of the hut.

The High Lords of Water had promised Nevyn another storm, which broke on schedule the following day, a nice gentle rain that would properly soak the fields. In spite of the weather, Nevyn bundled himself up in his cloak and rode up to Maroic's fort. It was time for him to sound Gweran and Lyssa out about taking Aderyn in a formal apprenticeship. Besides, he wanted to take a look at the nasty situation Cadda had so inadvertently described. As he rode into the ward, where the cobbles were running with rain, Aderyn came dashing to meet him with a cloak pulled over his head.

"I've been watching for you," Aderyn announced. "I just knew you'd come today."

"And here I am. Going to help me stable my horse?"

Together they found an empty stall and tied Nevyn's horse up out of the weather. While Nevyn took off the damp saddle,

Aderyn leaned back against the wall and watched, his big eyes full of some question.

"What's on your mind, lad?" Nevyn said.

"I want to ask you something. How did you make the rain come?"

"Here! What makes you think I did?"

"I saw you in a dream. You were sitting on the riverbank, and there was this big star around you. It was like fire, but it was blue. Then these kings came to you, and you talked to them. There were four kings. I saw the one who was dripping wet. Then it rained."

Nevyn sighed. His last doubt that Aderyn was his apprentice was utterly gone.

"I was invoking the wind and asking it to blow, you see," Nevyn said. "The King of Air was quarreling with the King of Fire, and the King of Earth asked me to settle the quarrel. It's like the High King of Deverry giving a judgment to warring lords."

"And are you the High King, then?"

"I'm not. Just a way of speaking to make it clear."

"Were the Kings angry at us, too?"

"They weren't. Why did you think so?"

"Because we could have starved if there wasn't any rain. Da said so."

"Oh, Da was right, but the Kings of the Wildlands don't know that, you see. Truly, I doubt if they'd care. They have so little to do with us that we look to them like the field mice do to us, say. If you found a starving field mouse, you'd feed it, but do you course the fields to see if mice need your help?"

Aderyn laughed aloud.

"Now listen carefully," Nevyn went on. "I've come to speak to your father. You need to decide if you want to come with me in the spring and learn all the things I know. It's a big thing. Someday we'll leave Blaeddbyr, and you won't see your Mam and Da again for a long time."

"But will we come back someday?"

"We will, for visits."

Aderyn balanced on one foot and twisted the other around behind it. He chewed on his lower lip, a skinny little boy, suddenly frightened. But when he looked up, a man's soul—the man he would someday be—looked out of his eyes for the briefest of moments as the two levels of his mind merged to make the most important decision of his life.

"I don't want to go," Aderyn said. "But I know I will. I want to know things so much, Nevyn. It's like wanting water when it's all hot outside. You've just got to get some."

"So it is. Done, then."

The great hall was crowded and smokey with torchlight in the rain-dark day. At the front of the hall, Gweran sat cross-legged on a table, his harp in his lap, and sang with sweat running down his face. The men gazed up at him attentively while he recited a tale of a cattle raid and named member after member of the warband in decorated stanzas.

"We'd better just go see Mam," Aderyn said. "She's up-stairs."

As they went up the spiral staircase, Gweran's pure liquid tenor followed them, chanting of glory. In the bard's chamber, it was mercifully cool and quiet. One of the shutters was open to let in a streak of gray light. Lyssa sat near it with sewing in her lap. Although she smiled as she greeted them, Nevyn saw that she was troubled—about Tanyc, he assumed. For a few moments they chatted idly, while he studied her with a real greed—not for her pretty body, but for the soul looking out of her eyes, for the company she would have been, the end to his loneliness.

"Well, here," Lyssa said at last. "Surely you didn't come all this way to talk about the rain."

"I didn't, but about Aderyn," Nevyn said. "He shows a real talent for the herbman's trade, and I was wondering if you and your husband would consider apprenticing him to me."

"I want to go, Mam!" Aderyn broke in.

"Hush! We'll have to talk this over with your Da. Here, Nevyn, I know perfectly well this means he'd have to travel with you. I'm not sure I can let him go."

"Mam!" Aderyn wailed.

"Out with you, then, if you can't sit quiet," Lyssa said. "Go listen to your father for a while."

Whining, reluctant, Aderyn dragged himself out of the chamber and slammed the door behind him. Lyssa settled back in her chair and looked Nevyn over thoughtfully.

"I've already lost one child," she said. "Two seems a bit much to ask."

"I know, but he'll be leaving you anyway for some kind of training, sooner or later. I doubt me if he'll ever be a bard like his father. Here, do you doubt that I'll take good care of him?"

Lyssa considered, and as their eyes met, she remembered again, a little flicker of puzzled recognition.

"Well, I don't," she said slowly. "But will I ever see him again?"

"Of course. We'll ride back regularly for visits."

"That's some comfort, I suppose. Here, I'll tell you somewhat, because you're the only man I've ever met who might understand it. When Aderyn was born, I had the strangest feeling about him. I knew that someday he'd leave me for a cursed strange Wyrd indeed. It was my first time, of course, and truly, I was so tired and sick, just so glad it was over. So the midwife laid Addo to my breast, and he looked up at me with eyes that saw. Most babes are like puppies, nuzzling at your breast with cloudy little eyes, but Aderyn saw. I knew he knew just where he was, and he was glad of it. And I thought then that he was marked out for a strange Wyrd. Do you think I'm daft?"

"I don't. I've no doubt it's the plain truth."

Lyssa sighed and looked out the window, where the rain fell soft and steady.

"Herbs?" she said. "Is that all you'll teach him?"

"A bit more than that, truly. Tell me, what do you think of dweomer? A tale, fit for one of Gweran's songs and nothing more?"

"A bit more than that, truly." Lyssa smiled as she consciously echoed his words. "So I thought. If that's the truth of it, well, there's no way I can stand between him and his Wyrd."

"It would be a harsh thing if you tried—for all of us."

Nodding, Lyssa stared at the rain.

"Will you wait until spring?" she said, her voice catching. "He's such a little lad."

"I will. And we won't ride far the next summer. You'll see him in the fall."

The tears ran down her cheeks. Nevyn wanted to kneel at her feet, to call her Brangwen and beg her to forgive him. He decided that he could stay in Blaeddbyr, never take her son away, never leave her. The dweomer-warning hit him like a slap. Just as he did, she had a Wyrd to fulfill that he could no more soften than he could his own. *And what will happen if you stay?* he told himself. *You'll hate Gweran for having her.*

"Shall I leave you alone?" Nevyn said.

"Please. My thanks."

Nevyn went down the spiral staircase and lingered in its shadow to watch the great hall. Over by the servant's hearth, Aderyn was playing a game of Carnoic with one of the pages. Gweran was singing a ballad from the Dawntime, the sad tale of Lady Maeva and Lord Benoic and their adulterous love. Adultery. Nevyn felt the dweomer-warning and looked around for Tanyc, who was sitting with the riders and watching the bard with a tight insolent smile. Every now and then, Gweran would glance his way with a smile of his own. *Ah ye gods,* Nevyn thought, *I'm too late—Gweran knows.* Stanza after stanza reeled out until Gweran came to the climax: Benoic lying dead at the outraged husband's feet. Tanyc got up and strode out of the great hall.

With a sigh, Gweran set the harp down and wiped his sweaty face on his sleeve. He got off the table, took a tankard of ale from a waiting page, and wandered over to Nevyn.

"I need a bit of a rest," Gweran said. "Cursed smokey in here, and it affects your voice."

"So it must. You sing beautifully, bard, though I wonder about your choice of tales."

Gweran raised one eyebrow.

"Lord Benoic's sad end fell upon some ears that are doubtless raw from hearing it," Nevyn said.

"I only wish I could cut them from his head, if you mean the man I think you mean."

"It takes a great deal of skill with a sword to bring the falcon down as he flies, my friend."

"And that's what all men think, isn't it?" Gweran's voice turned cold and flat. "That I'm to grovel in fear before this lout of a rider, because he can swing a blade and I can't. I tell you, I'd rather die than be that kind of coward."

"I only pray your words never come to the test."

Gweran shrugged and had a long swallow of ale.

"Now here," Nevyn said. "If you mentioned to Lord Maroic

that Tanyc was sniffing around your woman, the lord would turn him out. Maroic honors a bard the way he should be honored."

"So he does, but that would only dirty Lyssa's name. I can hear the old gossips wagging their heads and saying where there's mud, there's water below, and the cursed warband looking at her and wondering. What kind of a man am I if I can't protect my own?"

"A dead man protects nobody."

"Oh, don't trouble your heart. I've no desire to die and leave my poor Lyssa a defenseless widow. This is all a warning, like, for our falcon. I truly think the lout didn't know I knew. Well, he does now. It'll put him in his place."

It was perfectly reasonable, but Nevyn knew, with an icy touch of dweomer, that somehow Gweran was lying.

As he went over his stock of story songs, laid up in his mind where no thief could steal them, Gweran was surprised at just how many tales had adultery for a theme. It seemed to be a common pastime among the noble-born, like hawking, though with an even bloodier result. Every night, Gweran would sing one song about adultery and watch Tanyc carefully when he came to the predictable doom at the end. From the tightness of his jaw and the cold flicker in his eyes, there was no doubt that Tanyc was listening. Tanyc wasn't the only man with sharp ears. After a week of this sport, Doryn came up to Gweran one night for a private talk.

"Here, bard, how about a pleasant tale or two?" Doryn said. "I'm as sick as I can be of all this lusting after other men's wives."

"Are you now, captain? So am I."

Doryn winced, tossing his head like a fly-stung horse.

"Do you think I'm blind?" Gweran said.

"My apologies. It's a shameful thing, truly, wanting another man's woman."

"Just that. I'm glad to see you share my opinion. Is there anything wrong with a shameful man feeling shame?"

"Nothing at all, and a bard's prerogative at that."

The next time Gweran sang one of the tales, he had the satisfaction of seeing the rest of the warband avoiding Tanyc's eye at the mention of adultery. For the next few nights, Tanyc glowered into his tankard and barely breathed during the crucial song. When he judged the time was right, Gweran sang a bawdy song about an adulterous miller, who thought he was close to seducing the tavernman's wife. All the time, the wife had been confiding in her husband, who was there with two strong friends to greet the would-be swain. They clapped the miller into an empty barrel, rolled him down the village street, and set him adrift in the river. When the other riders howled with laughter, Tanyc's face went dead white.

The very next morning, Tanyc met Gweran face to face out in the ward.

"You little bastard," Tanyc growled.

"Am I now?" Gweran said mildly. "And what injury have I ever done you?"

Trapped, Tanyc hesitated—he could hardly admit his own guilt by mentioning the choice of songs.

"If you have an injury," Gweran said. "By all means, lay it before Lord Maroic for judgment. I'll gladly accept his decree."

Tanyc turned scarlet, spun on his heel, and strode off. Gweran smiled after his retreating back. You fool, he thought, a bard has weapons stronger than steel. Although he knew that Maroic would settle this matter quietly if only he asked, Gweran wanted more. Getting rid of Tanyc wasn't enough vengeance.

That night, after still another tale of adultery-gone-wrong, Gweran humbly begged Maroic's leave to sing a new song of his own composing about hunting in the summer. Since he loved hunting, of course Maroic agreed. As Gweran tuned up the harp, he saw that Tanyc was relaxed over a tankard of ale and doubtless thinking his mockery was over for the night. Gweran began to sing about flying hawks out in the meadow, where the falcon flies the highest of all and swoops down on pretty birds for sport. The warband fell silent, watching Tanyc, whose hand gripped the tankard so hard his knuckles were white. Gweran went on sing- ing about the pretty white dove whom a little lad in the town loved for a pet, but the cruel hunter launched his falcon for her. Greedy to rend her in his claws, the falcon chased her all over the field, while her little heart was breaking in fear as she fluttered pathetically ahead. Just as the falcon was about to strike, up from the hedgerow sprang the lad who loved her and shot the falcon through the heart with an arrow.

"And the pretty white dove fluttered safe to her love,"
Gweran sang, then broke off in midline.

White as the dove, Tanyc sprang from his seat and strode
down the hall. Gweran set his harp aside and gave him a mild
smile.

"You bastard," Tanyc whispered. "That's enough!"

"Enough of what?" Gweran said. "There's a bit more song to
come, my friend."

Tanyc drew his sword and swung in one smooth motion, but
Gweran was ready. He threw himself backwards off the table as
the hall broke into shouting. Gweran tumbled inelegantly into
the straw and scrambled up in time to see the warband mobbing
Tanyc. They tackled him, threw him down, and disarmed him.
Lord Maroic was on his feet, yelling for order as the maidservants
screamed. At last the hall was quiet. The servants pressed back
against the wall; a few women were weeping. Twisting his arms
tight behind him, three men hauled Tanyc to his feet.

"What's all this?" Maroic snapped. "Have you gone daft?
Drawing your sword on a bard, and him unarmed at that!"

In his comrades' arms, Tanyc was shaking too hard to answer. Gweran stepped forward and did his best to look bewildered.

"If you disliked the song as much as all that," Gweran said.
"You might simply have told me."

"You bastard!" Tanyc shouted. "You little bastard! You
planned all this. You've been working on me for days!"

"Hold your tongue," Maroic snarled, stepping closer. "And
why would the bard do such a thing?"

The last piece of the trap sprung shut. Desperately Tanyc
looked this way and that, as if he were begging someone to help
him. Afraid to earn a bard's revenge, the white-faced riders
stayed silent.

"Ill temper is one thing, impiety another," Maroic said. "I
hate to do this, but the laws are the laws. Take him out and hang
him. Do it now. I want it over with."

Tanyc went as limp in his captor's arms as if he were going to
faint. By the hearth, Cadda screamed, burst out weeping, and
went running for the staircase.

"It's a hard thing, truly," Maroic remarked to all and sundry.

"But no man draws on my bard and lives to boast about it. Does anyone here dare quibble over my judgment?"

When everyone shook their heads in a terrified "no," Maroic nodded in satisfaction.

"Go on, hang him," he said. "Take the torches and shove him off the wall. No use in letting him brood about it all night long. I want it over and done with."

Shouting a warcry, Tanyc made a desperate struggle, breaking free and hitting out barehanded at his captors. Doubtless he was hoping that they'd cut him down with a sword, but the warband wrestled him to the floor and bound him hand and foot. As they dragged him away, Gweran had to exert all his will to keep from smiling.

By two hours after dawn, the news was all over Blaeddbyr that Lord Maroic had hanged one of his riders for threatening his bard. When Nevyn heard it, his first reaction was that he wasn't surprised Gerraent would be such a dolt. Then he remembered that Tanyc wasn't truly Gerraent, and that Gweran had more brains than ever Blaen did. Cursing under his breath, Nevyn ran to saddle his horse.

Mercifully, they'd taken Tanyc's body down from the wall by the time Nevyn arrived. The servant who took his horse told him that since the priests refused to say last rites over a hanged man, Tanyc was already buried in an unmarked grave behind the dun. Nevyn sought out Gweran, whom he found up in his chamber alone.

"The women are taking the lads for a long walk," Gweran said. "They're all upset over this trouble."

"No doubt. I take it Tanyc took your warning a bit much to heart."

Gweran merely smiled.

"Now here!" Nevyn snarled. "Why didn't you just have a word with Lord Maroic?"

"Because I wanted Tanyc dead. Ye gods, did you ever doubt otherwise?"

Nevyn let out his breath in an explosive little puff.

"You're a clever little murderer," Nevyn said. "Fit for one of your own ballads."

"My thanks. Are you going to tell Maroic?"

"And do you think he'd believe a word of what I said? But it's your Wyrd, my friend, and truly, you'll pay for this someday."

"Where? In the shadowy Otherlands?"

Gweran smiled so smugly that Nevyn felt like slapping him. Here Gweran had been given a chance to free himself from the tangled Wyrd that he shared with Gerraent—he could have let the past slip and honorably used the laws to send his enemy far away from his woman. Instead, he'd used the law like a sword to murder.

"Sooner or later," Nevyn said. "This murder will come round to you again."

"Will it now? I'll take that chance."

Nevyn's mouth ached from wanting to tell him the truth that he was forbidden to tell unasked: in this life, you may be safe enough, but in your next, or the next after that, this blood will fall on your head, you'll still be bound to Gerraent by a chain of blood. And suddenly Nevyn was afraid: would he still be bound to them, too, simply because he might have seen Gweran's mind and prevented the murder?

It was two days before Nevyn saw Lyssa. When he brought Aderyn back to the dun, she met them at the gates and sent Aderyn off with Cadda. Leading his horse, Nevyn strolled with her down the grassy hill. In the strong sunlight she was pale and haggard from sleepless nights.

"I want to tell you that Gweran's decided to apprentice Addo to you," Lyssa said. "You'll need to discuss details, but the matter's settled. Once Gwerro makes up his mind, it's done."

"He's a stubborn man, truly."

When Lyssa winced, he realized that she knew perfectly well what had happened.

"Forgive an old man's bluntness," he said.

"No need for apologies. Ah ye gods, it aches my heart, but what can I say? Gwerro only did it to protect me."

"Well, true spoken. No man in the warband will be stupid enough to trouble you after this."

Lyssa nodded, looking away to the distant view, where the Nerr sparkled in the afternoon haze.

"He's a good man, my husband," she said.

Nevyn sighed, thinking that she had to believe it.

"I know how lucky I am," she went on. "It aches my heart sometimes, thinking that I was lucky to pick him."

"What? It should gladden your heart."

"All men would think so, truly. But ye gods, it sickened me, this whole thing! There I was, hiding in my chamber like a scared babe, and all the while thinking I was lucky that my man believed the truth, lucky that I had a good man to protect me." Her eyes snapping, Lyssa turned to face him. "I'm sick to my heart of depending on luck. I wish I had a man's power, and then luck could go back to the Lord of Hell."

"Hold your tongue! That sort of wish has a way of turning dangerous."

With a little shrug, Lyssa went back to watching the view, as if she were seeing a distant future there.

Eldidd, 1062

The dweomer is a vast wilderness crossed by a few safe roads. To either side of the road lies uncharted country, filled with wild beasts, chasms, and swamps, danger that can slay the unwary soul as surely as a wild boar will slay the unwary hunter. Mock them not until you have faced them. . . .

The Secret Book of Cadwallon the Druid

Grunting, sweating in the hot sun, the mules nipped and kicked as the muleteers tried to beat them into some semblance of order. The caravan turned into an unruly mob, swirling at the city gates in a cloud of brown dust. Cullyn of Cerrmor pulled his horse out of line and trotted over to the side of the road. By rising in his stirrups he could see Dregydd the merchant arguing about taxes and dues with the city guards, but the mules were raising so much dust that it was impossible to make out who was where in the caravan itself.

"Jill!" Cullyn yelled at the top of his lungs. "Jill, get out of that mob."

After an anxious wait of a few minutes, Cullyn saw her guiding her chestnut gelding free and trotting over to join him. Sweat made streaks on her dusty face, and her blond hair looked the same color as her horse.

"I hope Dregydd just pays them," Jill said. "I want a bath."

"Me, too, and some ale as well."

They looked wistfully at the high city walls of Cermeton, one of the few real towns in northwest Eldidd. Despite the typical town reek, a drift of sewage on the hot summer air, it promised comforts after a long week on the road. Dregydd, a nervous sort, had hired Cullyn as an armed guard for this trip, even though bandits were a rarity in this part of the kingdom.

At last the caravan began to move, the men shouting, the mules braying, as they shoved their way into the close-packed warren of round houses, then wound along the curved streets until they reached a rambling stone inn. Cullyn dismounted and worked his way through the crowd of men and mules toward Dregydd. The grizzled merchant paid over a silver piece without haggling.

"I've never had an easier time with my men, silver dagger," Dregydd said.

As Cullyn turned away, the skinny innkeep, all greasy hair and narrow eyes, caught his arm.

"No silver daggers in my inn," he said.

"I've no desire to let your lice get a taste of me. Now get your hand off my arm."

A bit pale, the innkeep jumped back.

Over by the east gate was a shabby wooden inn in a muddy yard where Cullyn and Jill had stayed before. Although the stables were only a row of tumbledown sheds, and somewhat cleaner than the tavern room itself, there the innkeep greeted Cullyn like a long-lost brother and gave them his best room, a tiny chamber in the upper story, with one skewed window. Bradd himself was a stout fellow who had lost an ear in a fight, to judge from the bitten-off scarred remains.

"Well, little Jill," Bradd said. "You're not so little anymore, are you? Why aren't you married by now?"

"Do you want to hold your tongue?" Jill said. "Or do you want to lose that other ear?"

"By the hells, Cullyn! You've raised a hellcat, haven't you?"

"Not truly," Cullyn said with a grin. "She was born a hellcat, and she'd be worse if it weren't for me."

Jill threw a fake punch his way. At seventeen, she'd grown into a tall young woman, lean and muscled from their peculiar life, with a boyish stance and a boyish swagger to her walk that somehow did nothing to detract from her golden-haired beauty. She helped Bradd haul up the heavy buckets of hot water and the big wooden tub as easily as Cullyn did, then chased her father out of the chamber so she could lounge in her bath.

The big half-round tavernroom was mostly empty. A couple of hounds were asleep by the hearth, and a couple of colorless young men sat at a table conveniently near the door and talked in cant over their tankards. Both glanced at the gleaming hilt of the silver dagger in Cullyn's belt, then strictly ignored him. Cullyn settled in at a table with his back to the wall and gratefully accepted a tankard of dark ale from Bradd. He was working on his third one by the time that Jill came down, her wet hair clinging around her face. She gave him a narrow-eyed look.

"And how many have you had?" she snapped.

"None of your cursed business. Here, finish this while I haul up some clean water for that tub."

He got up and left before she could say anything more. He refused to admit the real reason that he was drinking so much: he could feel himself growing older, needing to ease the ache of every old wound after a long ride or after sleeping beside the road. At thirty-five, Cullyn was middle-aged by any man's standard in Deverry, and as a silver dagger, he was a marvel. He'd never known or even heard of a silver dagger who'd lasted as long as he had. And how much longer will it be before you face your Wyrd? he asked himself. You've got to find Jill a good man to take care of her. As usual, he shoved that thought away fast; he would deal with it later.

At dinner that night, Cullyn and Jill ate in silence, enjoying each other's company without a need for words. Every now and then, Jill would look into the fire at the hearth and smile, her eyes moving as if she saw things there. Over the years, Cullyn had grown used to this particular habit of hers, just as he was used to her seeing things in the clouds and the running streams. Although it griped his soul to admit it, he was sure that his daughter had what the country folk call the second sight. That evening, she gave him a further bit of evidence.

"You know, Da," Jill said. "We should ride with Dregydd when he leaves town."

"Indeed? Then what a pity that he never asked us to."

"Oh, he will."

Cullyn was about to make some exasperated remark when Dregydd came into the tavern. He paused at the door and looked around at the unaccustomed squalor. A man in his thirties with pepper-and-salt hair, Dregydd was as lean and taut as a warrior from his hard-riding life. When Cullyn hailed him, he smiled in relief and hurried over.

"Cursed glad I finally found you," Dregydd said. "I've been thinking, silver dagger. In about a week, I'll be riding west. If

you'll wait in town to guard the caravan, I'll pay for your lodg-
ings."

Jill smiled smugly out at nothing.

"Sounds like you're expecting trouble," Cullyn said to Dregydd.

"Well, not truly expecting it, like. It's just that you'd best be
ready for trouble when you trade with the Westfolk."

"The who?"

Dregydd gave him an odd smile, as if he were nursing an
important secret.

"There's a tribe who lives far to the west," Dregydd said.
"They're not ordinary Eldidd men, not by the hells they aren't,
but they raise the best horses in the kingdom, and they're always
willing to trade for iron goods. Now, I've never had any trouble
with the Westfolk themselves, mind, but sometimes the muleteers get a little, well, strange, way out there on the edge of
nowhere. I'd like to have you along."

"I'm on, then," Cullyn said. "A hire's a hire."

"Splendid! After we've done our trading, we'll be coming
back through Cannobaen—that's this little border town. You
might find better work for your sword there, too. I hear there's
some kind of trouble brewing around Cannobaen."

"Well and good, then. Send one of your lads over to tell me
the night before we leave."

After Dregydd left, Jill avoided looking her father in the eye.

"And just how did you know that he was coming?" Cullyn
snapped.

"I don't know. I just did."

Cullyn let the subject drop. My daughter, he thought, but by
the hells, sometimes I wonder if I know her at all.

As it often did, the summer fog lay thick and cold over Dun
Cannobaen. In the nearby lighthouse, the great bronze bell
tolled in booming slow notes. Inside the broch, servants scurried
around lighting peat fires in the hearths. Lady Lovyan, by now
dowager of Aberwyn and, by a twist of the laws, tieryn of the area
around Cannobaen in her own right, put on the gray, red, and
white plaid of her demesne when she went down to the great
hall. By the servants' hearth, her warband of fifty men lounged
close to the fire. At the hearth of honor knelt the suppliant come

for Lovyan's justice. The local soapmaker, Ysgerryn was a skinny fellow with gray hair who smelled faintly of tallow, for all that he'd put on his best embroidered shirt and striped brigga for this important visit.

"Speak up, good sir," Lovyan said. "I'm always willing to oversee any matter of justice, no matter how slight. For what do you seek redress?"

"Ah well, Your Grace, it's about my daughter." Ysgerryn blushed scarlet.

"She's with child, is she?"

"She is, and not married either, as I'm sure Your Grace can guess, or I'd hardly be troubling Your Grace about it."

Across the hall, the warband went stock still and listened in desperate suspense.

"Come along," Lovyan said gently. "Name the father out."

"Well, Your Grace." Ysgerryn paused for a deep breath. "The little minx swears it's your son."

The warband sighed in relief, and Lovyan in weariness.

"She really does swear it," Ysgerryn said miserably. "I doubt me if you believe—"

"Oh, I believe it well enough, my good man." Lovyan glanced around and saw the page snickering under the spiral staircase. "Caradoc, run find Lord Rhodry and bring him to me."

For a profoundly uncomfortable five minutes they waited while the warband whispered and snickered, Ysgerryn studied the pattern of braided rushes on the floor, and Lovyan did her best to look dignified instead of furious. A lord who treated his subjects' daughters as his private preserve was a lord who caused grumbling at the best of times. Now, when Lovyan's rule was being challenged by some of her noble vassals, the last thing she wanted was for her townsfolk to feel sympathy for the rebels. Finally Rhodry strode in, whistling cheerily. Just twenty that month, Rhodry was filling out at six feet tall, a man so handsome that Lovyan felt no scorn, only sympathy for the soapmaker's daughter. When Rhodry saw Ysgerryn, his good cheer disappeared so fast that Lovyan's last doubt vanished with it.

"Well and good, my lord," Lovyan said. "Our good Ysgerryn here claims you've gotten his daughter with child. Is it true?"

"And how would I know the true or false of it?" Rhodry said. "She could have had many another man as well as me."

"Indeed? Do you really expect me to believe that you'd stand by and do nothing if another man trifled with your lass?"

"Uh well." Rhodry started poking at the rushes with the toe of his riding boot. "Truly, I'd have slit his throat."

"So I thought."

"Your Grace?" Ysgerryn said. "Truly, she was always such a good lass until this. It's fair broken her mother's heart, it has, but who was I to say his lordship nay, even when I knew he was riding our way cursed often. I knew he wasn't there to collect Your Grace's share of our soap."

Pushed beyond human endurance, the warband laughed and elbowed each other. When Rhodry spun around and glared, they fell silent.

"My poor Ysgerryn," Lovyan said. "Well and good, then, I'll make provision for the lass. I'll settle a dowry on her, and with coin in her pocket doubtless she'll find a good husband even though the whole town knows the scandal. When the babe's born, bring it to me if it's healthy enough to live. We'll find a wet nurse and fosterage."

"Your Grace!" Ysgerryn's eyes filled with tears. "I never expected so much, Your Grace. Truly, I—"

Lovyan cut him short with a wave of her hand.

"The bastard of a noble lord can be very useful," Lovyan said. "Provided the child's been raised to be useful. Tell your daughter that her child will be well cared for."

Bowing repeatedly, stammering out thanks, Ysgerryn backed away from Lovyan's presence, then ran out of the hall. When Rhodry looked inclined to run himself, Lovyan grabbed his arm and hauled him toward the staircase.

"I wish to speak to your lordship," she snapped.

Like a whipped hound Rhodry followed her to her private chambers on the second floor of the broch. The reception chamber was a little room, crammed with memories of the long line of Maelwaedd lords—moth-eaten stag's heads, old swords, a dusty ceremonial mace, and a row of shields with devices no longer current. In one corner stood a lectern, carved with grappling badgers, which had been the Maelwaedd device before the clan came to the gwerbretrhyn of Aberwyn, and on the lectern was a copy of a book written by the first Maelwaedd, Prince Mael the

Seer himself. As soon as they were inside, Lovyan slapped Rhodry across the face.

"You little beast!"

Rhodry flung himself into a chair, stretched out his legs, and stared moodily at the cluttered wall.

"It aches my heart, knowing I've dishonored her," Rhodry said. "Truly, you have my heartfelt thanks for being so generous to my poor little lass."

Lovyan wondered if he were saying only what she wanted to hear. With a sigh, she sat down across from him and let him squirm for a while. All told, Lovyan had given birth to four sons. The eldest, Rhys, now ruled as gwerbret in Aberwyn; the second had died in infancy; the third had grown to manhood only to be killed in a war. Rhodry was her youngest. Some time before his birth, her husband had taken a young mistress and spent so little time in Lovyan's bed that Rhodry was her last.

The mistress had produced a pair of bastards, and it had fallen to Lovyan to make provision for the girls. Now Rhodry was grown into a man much like Gwerbret Tingyr.

"It's time you married," Lovyan said at last. "You can at least provide a few legitimate heirs for the tierynrhyn since you're so fond of this sport."

Rhodry winced.

"I wonder if the Goddess keeps cursing your betrothals because she knows what kind of man you are," Lovyan went on. "Three times now I've tried to marry you off, and three times she's taken a hand to spare the poor lass."

"Mother, by the hells! I'm sorry, truly I am! I know you need the coin I've just made you spend, and I know you need the town's goodwill, and truly, my heart aches for poor Olwen, too."

"You might have thought of all that before you lifted her dresses."

"Mother!"

"I don't want to hear of this happening again. Save that winning smile of yours for the lasses who stand to make silver out of it in more usual ways."

Rhodry flung himself out of his chair and ran, slamming the door so hard behind him that the swords on the wall rattled. Lovyan allowed herself a small smile of revenge.

For the rest of the day, Rhodry avoided her, which was easy

to do in a dun the size of Cannobaen. Out on what might as well have been the western border of Eldidd, since there was nothing much beyond it, the dun stood on the twisted headland of its name at the top of a sheer cliff overlooking the Southern Sea. Stone walls enclosed a crowded ward of about two acres. In the middle rose a four-story broch surrounded by storage sheds and a kitchen hut. Off to the seaward side stood the Cannobaen light, a hundred-foot tower, wound with a staircase, where on clear nights the lightkeeper and his sons kept an enormous fire burning under a stone canopy or rang the bronze bell when it was foggy.

Beyond the dun, the empty grasslands ran for miles in either direction along the cliff tops, while inland were the farms of Lovyan's personal demesne. It was a lonely place, suitable for retiring from worldly pursuits—if only Lovyan had been allowed to go into retirement. She'd been given Cannobaen as a dower gift from the Maelwaedds on her marriage, and when her husband died, she'd gone there to live far from the temptation to meddle in the new gwerbret's affairs. Just this last year, however, her only brother and his son had both been killed in an honor war. Since there was no other heir, their father's property had come to Lovyan under that twist in the laws designed to keep land holdings in a clan even if a woman had to inherit them. Lovyan may have married into the Maelwaedds, but by blood she was still one of the Clw Coc, the clan of the Red Lion, which had held a vast demesne in Western Eldidd for over a hundred years.

Blood and clan, children and their children—they ruled every aspect of a noblewoman's life, and it was about such things that Lovyan was musing for the rest of that dripping-cold summer's day at Cannobaen. She profoundly hoped that Rhodry's bastard would turn out to be a healthy lass, and as pretty as her father was handsome. If she were, then Lovyan could ultimately arrange a marriage between her and one of her many land-poor relations. The Red Lion had done Lovyan a great favor when she inherited the tierynrhyn by adopting Rhodry into the clan, thus making it possible for him to inherit upon her death, rather than having the land revert to the gwerbret for reassignment. In his vanity, Rhodry assumed that Lovyan made that move out of maternal love, but in truth, she had much sterner motives, and arranging the adoption was the lesser of two evils.

When she took over the demesne, some of her vassals grumbled about having a woman for overlord, even though it was right under the laws and, though rare, far from unknown. Once Rhodry was empowered to succeed, the grumblers could take comfort in knowing just which man would be ruling them in what was bound to be only a few years. After all, Lovyan was not immortal; at forty-eight, she was already old in a world where most women died in their thirties, worn out by childbearing. Soon enough, her vassals would have a man for tieryn if they'd only wait. Even so, however, some were refusing to wait.

Just at the time for the evening meal, a visitor came to the dun, Lord Sligyn, who held land in fealty to Lovyan about ten miles to the east. Possible rebellion, it seemed, was very much on his mind. During dinner Sligyn could say nothing with so many eavesdroppers around, but Lovyan knew he was troubled simply because he was the sort of man who showed his thoughts on his face. Lovyan sincerely liked him, a stout red-faced man in his early thirties, with a thick pair of blond mustaches and shrewd blue eyes. To honor him, she had taken his son Caradoc into her hall as a page. That night, Carro waited upon them at table, poured the mead perfectly, and carved the beef with skill. When the lad was out of earshot, Sligyn admitted that he was pleased with his son.

"And speaking of sons," Sligyn said with a nod at Rhodry's empty chair, "where's your lad?"

"Probably eating whatever he can beg from the cook out in the kitchen. He doesn't care to face me at the moment."

"What's he done now?"

"Sired a bastard on a common-born lass."

Sligyn sighed and drained his goblet.

"Bound to happen sooner or later," he said. "Given young Rhodry's ways with the lasses. My wife and I would count ourselves honored to foster the child for you."

"My sincere thanks. If the babe's born alive, I'll send it and the wet nurse to you straightaway. I'm most pleased to find I have such a loyal man."

"Unlike some, eh?" He paused significantly. "Well, if I can have a private word with Your Grace later?"

"You may, and as soon as we're finished here."

Just as Lovyan suspected, Rhodry never joined them for the

meal. As soon as they were done eating, she took Sligyn up to her reception chamber. She already knew that the chief grumbler against her rule was Lord Corbyn of Bruddlyn, and that he'd been putting out feelers to see how many lords would ally themselves with him in rebellion.

"They know better than to approach me," Sligyn said. "But I hear things in my own way. Now Nowec's gone over to them, and that truly aches my heart. I thought he was a better man than this."

"So did I."

"Huh, I wonder how these dolts think they can pull this chestnut out of the coals. What have they done, forgotten that the gwerbret with jurisdiction over the tierynrhyn also happens to be your own son?"

"They may have some reason for thinking that Rhys might not exercise his right of intervention. It's the coin, I suppose. Matters of loyalty so often come down to the dues and taxes."

"That's a cynical little remark, Your Grace."

"Well," Lovyan said with a toss of her head. "I knew that I was making a hard choice when I made Rhodry my heir. The lords of the rhan already pay one set of dues to the Maelwaedd clan because Rhys is gwerbret. Then they pay a second set to the Clw Coc through me. When I die, they feel that they'll be paying both to the Maelwaedds, because they'll always see Rhodry as a Maelwaedd, no matter how many of my cousins vouched for his adoption. I've no doubt that it rankles them."

Sligyn snorted like an angry mule.

"I see," he said. "And if they carry on this rebellion long enough to make Rhys rule in their favor, he'll add your lands to the gwerbretal demesne, and there'll only be one set of taxes to pay. By every god and his wife, would Rhys really dispossess his own mother just for the cursed coin?"

"I doubt that, but it would gladden his heart to dispossess me." It was Rhodry, striding in boldly. "Her Grace is doubtless right about the cursed coin. All that grumbling because you're a woman never rang true."

"Here!" Lovyan snapped. "How long have you been listening at the door?"

"Long enough." Rhodry flashed her a grin. "I wanted to hear what you said to his lordship about my dishonor."

"We discussed that at dinner."

"At dinner?" Rhodry flopped into a chair. "My lady has a strong stomach."

"Now listen, you young cub." Sligyn would be Rhodry's equal until Lovyan died, and he minced no words. "You treat your lady mother with some respect while I'm around."

"My apologies, I do but jest," Rhodry said. "But truly, Mother, I see what you mean. Rhys must be licking his chops, thinking he has a chance at what's rightfully mine."

"I cherish no illusions of brotherly love between the two of you, truly," Lovyan said. "But if it comes to open war, I trust Rhys will intervene."

"No doubt, if you ask him." Rhodry turned sullen. "But I want the chance to prove myself to these vassals of yours."

He said it so carelessly that Lovyan was sick at heart. If things came to war, Rhodry would be the cadvridoc, the war leader, delegated in her stead to lead the army. She knew him too well to hope that he would lead his men from the rear.

"I heard you tell Mother that Nowec's gone over to the rebels," Rhodry said to Sligyn. "I never would have thought it of him."

"No more would I," Sligyn said. "Cursed strange rumors going around."

"Dweomer again?" Rhodry said with a laugh.

"Just that." Sligyn paused, chewing on the edge of his mustache. "Cursed well makes a man wonder, seeing Nowec break his bond this way."

"Horseshit! Uh, my apologies, Mother. But I don't believe a word of it."

"Well, neither do I, of course. Eh!" Sligyn said. "But it has its effect on the men. Morale, that kind of thing. Once a rider starts thinking about dweomer, well, where's he going to stop?"

Lovyan nodded in agreement. Since no one knew the powers of that mysterious craft—since, in truth, so few people knew that it existed—once a man started brooding on what it might or might not be able to do, there was no limit to it.

"They say it's this councillor of Corbyn's," Sligyn said. "Loddlaen his name is. He's the one that everyone thinks has the dweomer."

"Indeed?" Rhodry sneered. "Well, I've met the man, and I

find it hard to believe that this mincing fop has any kind of power at all. Cursed if I know why Corbyn even listens to a man who stinks of perfume."

"It's strange, all right," Sligyn said. "But isn't that the point?"

Rhodry's sneer disappeared.

"You know," Lovyan broke in. "I think I should send for Nevyn."

"What?" Rhodry said. "How do you send for no one?"

"Nevyn the old herbman, you little dolt. Don't tease with things so serious."

"My apologies, Mother, and send for him if you like. I know the old man amuses you, and you'll need good company if we ride to war."

"I will, then, if I can get him a message. He's probably wandering the roads with his herbs, but he may be at his home."

"You know, Your Grace," Sligyn said. "I've never understood why you honor the old man so highly. He's well spoken and all, but he's practically one of your peasants."

"It's as Rhodry says. He amuses me."

Lovyan was in no mood to explain. If the stolid Sligyn and her rake of a son were too stupid to know a man with dweomer when they saw one, she wasn't going to waste her breath enlightening them.

Three days out of Cernmeton, the caravan of Dregydd the merchant reached an oddly named river, the Delonderiel, which flowed fast and deep between grassy banks. Near the village of Bruddlyn was a stone toll bridge, owned and maintained by the local lord. Since the caravan would have to stop soon anyway to ensure that there was enough daylight left for the horses and mules to graze, Dregydd decided to camp for the night near the village and trade for fresh food. He had a couple of packs of cheap goods for just this kind of barter, and as he told Jill, the villagers were more than willing to trade chickens and bread for colored ribands and copper brooches.

"Besides," Dregydd said. "It'll give Lord Corbyn a chance to come down and buy somewhat if he wants. Always be courteous when you're passing through someone's demesne."

Although the lord himself never appeared, one of his councillors did. Jill was hanging around, watching Dregydd haggle with a farm wife for a barrel of ale when the man rode up on a beautiful silver-gray horse. He was tall but slender, with dark violet eyes, and he had the palest hair that Jill had ever seen, practically the color of moonlight, and cut long to fall over his ears. He dismounted and strolled over to Dregydd, who was just handing over an iron skillet in return for the ale. At the sight of him, the farm wife turned pale and backed off. Jill noticed her making the sign of warding against witchcraft with her fingers as she hurried away.

"My name is Loddlaen," he said, in an oddly soft and musical voice. "Are you carrying any fine weapons?"

"Some swords of Caminwaen steel," Dregydd said.

While he looked over the swords, Loddlaen ignored Jill completely, and she was glad of it. Although he was courteous enough, there was something about him that creeped her flesh, and it wasn't only that he smelled of rose scent. At last he picked out the best sword in the lot.

"Well and good, councillor," Dregydd said. "And is it for you?"

"It's not, but for my lord, a token of my esteem."

"An honorable gift, indeed. Now, I usually get a decent horse for one of these blades."

"How about a gold piece instead?" Loddlaen flashed him a cold hard smile. "I have coin, unlike the rest of the stinking rabble in this part of the world."

"Splendid. A fair price, indeed."

"Far too high, actually, but there are some things that must never be haggled over."

Although Dregydd looked shocked at such an idea, he took Loddlaen's gold Deverry regal quickly enough. He even found a bit of cloth to wrap the sword in, escorted the councillor to his horse, and held the bridle while Loddlaen mounted. With a small contemptuous nod, he rode off, sitting with the ease of a man who's spent most of his life in the saddle. Dregydd scratched his beard in puzzlement.

"Now that was a strange one, lass," he announced. "I've seen many a man in my trading, but that was a strange one."

"He was. I half wondered if he wanted that sword to stab his lord or suchlike."

"Odd, I had the same thought, but listen to us, Jill, insulting a man we don't even know. Huh. Did you see his horse? It's a western hunter, one of the breed I'm after. His lord must honor him highly to give him an expensive animal like that."

That night, Jill had a dream, and grotesque though it was, it was so clear and coherent, so filled with small details, that she was forced to admit that it had to be a true dream. In it, she saw Loddlaen take off his clothes in the middle of a chamber, then go to a window. She saw him chanting aloud; then all at once, he was enveloped in a flash of blue light and turned into an enormous red hawk. When he leaped from the sill and soared above the countryside, she somehow was flying up above him. Suddenly he stooped and plunged, just like a real hawk, and came up with a rabbit in his beak. Only then did she realize just how unnaturally large this hawk was. She woke with a start and sat up, listening to the reassuring sound of Cullyn snoring nearby. The dream was so disgusting that she was cold all over.

To rid herself of the dream, she rose and went over to the riverbank. In the moonlit shallows the Wildfolk of Water disported themselves, an ebb and flow of faces in silver foam. When she put her hand in the water to call them, they clustered round and rubbed silvery backs against her fingers.

"Do you know Councillor Loddlaen?" Jill said.

She felt their terror break over her like a wave. Then they vanished utterly, leaving the river only ordinary water. Jill ran back to the camp. She didn't care to be out there alone.

Much to Jill's relief, on the morrow the caravan packed up early, clattered over the toll bridge, and headed west, far away from Loddlaen. All morning the men and mules wound their slow way through the prosperous farmlands of Eldidd, past stone-fenced fields and round farmhouses and through meadowland where white cattle with rusty-red ears grazed. At times Jill rode rear guard with Cullyn; at others, she rode beside Dregydd, who, true merchant that he was, loved to have an ear to talk into. He began telling her more about the horses he hoped to obtain.

"We call them western hunters," Dregydd said. "Even the mares stand sixteen hands high, and they've got the best wind you'd ever hope to find in a horse. But here's the big thing, lass. Some of them are golden, well, a yellowy brown, really, but in the sunlight, you'd swear they were made of gold."

"By the hells! I don't suppose a silver dagger would ever get the coin to buy one."

"Not likely by half. The Westfolk know their value, and they make you trade high. Worth it, though. If I can get a golden stud, the gwerbret of Caminwaen will give me two gold pieces for him."

Jill caught her breath. Two gold pieces would buy a decent farm. Suddenly she remembered Loddlaen again, handing over a Deverry regal for a sword worth a third of it, if that. Why had he insisted on cheating himself that way? Odd bits of bard lore drifted to mind, and at last she remembered the persistent tale that if a dweomerman wanted to enchant an item, he was forbidden to haggle for it.

"Tell me somewhat," Jill said to Dregydd. "Do you think there's such a thing as real dweomer?"

"Well now, most people dismiss those tales out of hand, lass, but I've seen an odd thing or two in my day." Dregydd gave her a sly smile. "I think me you're going to be cursed interested in the Westfolk when you meet them."

Although Jill questioned him further, he put her off with a simple "wait and see." Yet later that same day she had an inkling of his meaning. The farther west they rode, the bolder grew the gray gnome, popping into materialization to sit in front of her saddle even when she was riding beside another person. His long thin mouth open in a gaping smile, his green eyes gleaming with excitement, he would grab one of her reins in both skinny hands and shake it, as if trying to make the horse go faster. Finally she dropped far enough behind the caravan to speak to him.

"You know where we're going, don't you? Do you like the Westfolk?"

He nodded his head in a vigorous yes, then leaped up to throw his arms around her and kiss her on the cheek.

That night, the caravan camped in a pasture beside the last farm on the Eldidd border. Dregydd traded cheap goods for loads of hay and fodder, and Jill saw why on the morrow. Just an hour's ride brought them to primeval forest, a tangle of old oaks and bracken. All day they followed a narrow track through ancient trees, standing so thickly that it was impossible to see more than ten feet beyond the trail. They made their night's camp in a clearing that was just barely big enough to accommodate men and mules. Everyone huddled around a campfire to talk in strangely hushed voices. Every now and then, one of the men would turn sharply to peer into the forest as if he felt he was being watched. Jill knew they were being watched. Just beyond the circle of firelight she could see Wildfolk, clustering thick in the branches of the trees to stare down at these intruders in their land.

The next day brought more forest, but now the land was rising in a gentle slope that promised hills at some far distance. Men and mules alike sweated as the trail wound on and on through the dapple-dark forest. Finally, some four hours after noon, they came to a river, churning white in a deep gorge. Over it in a graceful arch was a stone bridge, as well made as any in Deverry. The side rails were carved in a looping pattern of leaves and vines, and here and there, in roundels, were chiseled marks that had to be letters in some utterly alien alphabet. As the caravan clattered over the bridge, Jill studied the carvings. Here and there, as a decoration, the face of one of the Wildfolk peered out through a cluster of stone leaves.

"Dregydd?" Jill said. "Did the Westfolk build this bridge?"

"They must've, lass. No one else out here to build it."

Then, Jill supposed, the Westfolk had to be able to see the little creatures she could see. It might explain why the Wildfolk here were so bold. That night, when they camped in another clearing, the Wildfolk wandered in for a close look at these interlopers. They strolled around, peering at the muleteers, touching anything shiny with long pointed fingers, occasionally pinching one of the horses just to make it stamp. Although only Jill could see them, most of the men could feel that something peculiar was going on. They turned sullen, sitting close together and concentrating on dice games, snapping at each other, too, over every roll. Eventually Cullyn would step in, speaking to every man personally and judging the games. Jill began to see why Dregydd wanted her father along.

Fortunately, at about noon on the morrow the caravan broke free of the forest. As the land rose, the trees began to thin, until finally they left the last of them behind and came to a wide, flat plateau. Ahead, wind-ruffled grasslands stretched like a green sea out to the horizon. Although Jill was glad to be out of the forest, the plain had its own eerieness, too, simply because she had never seen any view so empty.

"Are there any towns or suchlike out there?" Jill said.

"Naught that I know of," Dregydd said. "But then, I've never been much farther than this. Just a few miles along now, there's a place where I always camp and wait for the Westfolk to find me. They always know when I'm here. Cursed strange."

The Wildfolk told them, Jill assumed, but of course she wasn't going to tell Dregydd any such thing. When they came to the campsite beside a pleasant stream, hundreds of Wildfolk flocked around, considered the caravan for a few minutes, then abruptly disappeared. That night, Jill had trouble sleeping. She kept waking to lie on her back and look at the stars and the great drift of the Snowy Road, which seemed to hang closer to earth out there. For all her restlessness, she never heard anything moving near the camp, but when dawn broke, two men of the Westfolk were there.

Jill woke and saw them standing quietly a few yards away, waiting for the sleeping camp to wake. They were tall, but slender, with deep-set eyes and moonbeam pale hair like Loddlaen's. Their faces would have been handsome if it weren't for their ears, which rose to a delicate point like the curled tip of a seashell. Even though Dregydd had warned her that the Westfolk cropped their children's ears as babies, Jill still found the sight unnerving. They were dressed in leather boots and trousers, and cloth tunics, heavily embroidered in a free pattern of flowers and vines that splashed across one shoulder and trailed down the front.

Since she slept mostly dressed, Jill got up and walked over barefoot to greet them. When she was close enough to notice their eyes, she was in for another shock. Their irises were enormous, with barely any white showing around them, and their pupils were a vertical slit like a cat's. They don't do that when their children are babies, Jill thought, I wonder how Dregydd explains that away. Her feeling of being faced with something totally alien was so strong that she nearly yelped aloud when one spoke to her in perfect Deverrian.

"Good morrow, fair maid," he said. "Have you and your menfolk come to trade?"

"We have," Jill said. "Dregydd is the leader."

"I know him, truly." He cocked his head to one side and studied her with a faint smile. "I've never seen one of your womenfolk before. Are they all as lovely as you?"

When Jill stood there tongue-tied, he laughed and made her a bow.

"Tell Dregydd we'll bring the others," he said.

They walked away, glided away, really, without the slightest sound, as if the grass were parting to let them go through. At some distance they'd left their golden horses. Jill stared after them as they mounted and rode out of sight.

Just after noon, the Westfolk rode in from the grasslands in a long procession of mounted riders driving a herd of horses ahead of them. The group was a whole clan, men, women, and a few children, all dressed exactly alike, except that the women wore their long hair severely braided like Deverry women of the Dawntime. Instead of wagons, they dragged their possessions along behind them on wooden travois. A couple of hundred yards from Dregydd's camp, they pulled up and pitched their own. Fascinated, Jill watched the organized swarm of activity as everyone in the clan lent a hand to raise round leather tents, unpack their belongings, and tether out the horses. In less than an hour, the camp stood as if it had always been there, a gaudy, noisy affair of brightly painted tents, running children and dogs, and swarms of Wildfolk.

"Now we wait some more," Dregydd said. "They'll come when they're ready."

Sure enough, a few at a time the Westfolk strolled over to see what Dregydd had brought them. Singly or in pairs, they walked through the rows of cooking pots and knives, swords, woodsmen's axes, shovels, and arrow points. Occasionally they would squat down and pick something up to examine it, then lay it down again, and all without a word. As she grew used to them, Jill found herself thinking them beautiful. They were graceful and lithe, with a self-possessed dignity that reminded her of wild deer. She was surprised to find that the muleteers, and even Cullyn, looked on them with scorn. That entire afternoon, the men stayed down by the river and played dice with their backs to the proceeding. Only Jill sat with Dregydd in the grass and watched his customers.

When the sun was getting low in the sky, a young man came over with a leather meadskin.

"Good morrow," he said. "We're pleased with the trinkets you're offering us."

"That gladdens my heart, Jennantar," Dregydd said. "So we'll trade on the morrow?"

"We will." Jennantar handed him the skin. "For your men, to sweeten their hearts a bit."

Seeing that he knew the men despised his people embarrassed Jill profoundly, but he merely smiled in a wry sort of way as Dregydd hurried over to the muleteers. When Jennantar sat down beside her, the gray gnome appeared in her lap and leaned back with a contented smile.

"Here," Jennantar said sharply. "Do you see the Wildfolk?"

"By the hells, you mean you do?"

"All our people know them. We call them by a name that means the little brothers."

When she looked into his smokey-gray cat-slit eyes, Jill could feel the kinship there, for all that the Wildfolk were ugly and deformed, and these beings men called Westfolk were beautiful.

"You know," Jennantar said. "There's a man of your people who rides with us. I think he'd like to meet you."

Without another word Jennantar got up and walked away, leaving Jill wondering if she'd insulted him.

It was getting on toward sunset when an old man came from the Westfolk's camp. Since his eyes and ears were normal, even though he dressed like one of the Westfolk, Jill assumed that he must be the man whom Jennantar had mentioned. He was not very tall, with heavy shoulders and arms, though the rest of him was slender, and he had enormous brown eyes and white hair that swept up from his forehead in two peaks like an owl's horns. When he hunkered down next to Dregydd, his posture was somehow birdlike, too, especially the way his hands hung loosely between his thighs. It turned out that Dregydd knew him; he introduced him round as Aderyn, a name that made Jill giggle, because it meant "bird."

"I've come to ask a favor, Dregydd," Aderyn said. "I need to travel to Cannobaen, and I'd rather ride with a caravan than on my own."

"You're most welcome, but what is this?" Dregydd said. "Are you suddenly feeling longing for the folk you left behind?"

"Not truly." Aderyn smiled at the jest. "This is an unpleasant little matter of justice, I'm afraid. One of our people murdered a man, and now he's a fugitive. We've got to fetch him back."

"Unpleasant indeed. He should be easy enough to find, eh? He'll stand out among Eldidd folk."

"Not truly. He's a half-breed, you see."

"Councillor Loddlaen." The words burst out of Jill's mouth before she could stop them.

When Aderyn turned her way, Jill felt that he was looking through, not at her, as if his casual glance would nail her down like a farmer nails a shrike to a barn wall. Then he smiled pleasantly and released her.

"Well, his name is Loddlaen, sure enough," Aderyn said. "And you must be Gilyan."

"I am." Jill was certain that she'd never told any of the Westfolk her name. "Have we met, good sir?"

"We have, but not so you'd remember." For a moment, Aderyn looked melancholy, as if he wished that she would remember. "But why did you say *Councillor* Loddlaen?"

"Well, that's what he called himself. He seems to be part of Lord Corbyn of Bruddlyn's retinue now."

"Indeed? And isn't that cursed strange? Well, at least we know where to find him, then." Aderyn rose, glancing off into the night. "Most strange, it is—cursed strange."

Then he walked off without even a backward glance.

"Here," one of the muleteers said. "Is that old man daft or suchlike?"

"Oh, I wouldn't call him that," Dregydd said, thoughtfully scratching his beard. "He has his little ways, but his mind is as sound as an oak."

The muleteers exchanged doubting glances.

"Must be daft," Cullyn muttered. "Running off with the Westfolk like he did."

Although Jill knew better than to say so aloud, she was thinking that running off with these people didn't seem like a daft idea to her.

Later that night the music started. Across the moonlit meadow a woman's voice started a melancholy melody. Three other voices picked up a harmony that sounded out of key until Jill realized that they were singing in quarter tones, just like the Bardek minstrels one heard every now and then down in port towns. Suddenly instruments joined in, a cool, clear sound like a harp, then something that made a constant drone, and finally a small drum. The music came faster, faster, flowed from one song to the next with barely a pause. Cullyn and the men crowded close together and concentrated on dice. Jill slipped away and went to stand on the edge of the camp. Across the meadow torches flared among the jewel-bright tents. Drawn as if by dweomer, Jill took a few steps forward, but suddenly Cullyn grabbed her by the shoulder.

"And just what are you doing?" Cullyn snapped.

"Listening and nothing more."

"Oh, horseturds! Listen, don't you dare sneak off. Those people are more wild animals than they are men, but I wouldn't be surprised if you pleased their men well enough anyway."

"Oh ye gods, Da! You think every man I meet is lusting after me."

"Most of them are, and don't you forget it. Now come along. You can hear this cursed squawling well enough by the fire."

Even for a tieryn with a vast demesne, coin was hard to come by in western Eldidd. Since Dun Cannobaen was only Lovyan's summer retreat, she had to send back to her main residence, Dun Gwerbyn, for silver for the soapmaker's daughter. When it finally arrived, Rhodry was incensed to find that his mother expected him to deliver it personally.

"Why can't the chamberlain go?" Rhodry snapped. "Or the cursed equerry? Let them earn their meat and mead."

Lovyan merely crossed her arms over her chest and glared at him. With a sigh, Rhodry picked up the pair of saddlebags from the table and went to the stable to get a horse.

The morning lay clear and sunny over the wild green meadow, and far below at the base of the cliffs the ocean sparkled like a casket of blue and green jewels, but Rhodry rode out with a heavy heart. Olwen's going to weep, he told himself, and it's going to be horrible. What Rhodry could never admit to another living soul was that he was honestly fond of Olwen. It was one thing to tumble a common-born lass around in bed; quite another to admit that you liked her and felt more at ease with her than with a woman of your own class.

The town of Cannobaen lay nestled around a small harbor in a break in the cliffs, where the Brog, a stream that only qualified as a river in the winter, came to the sea. There were three wooden piers for fishing boats and a larger pier for the ferry that went out to the holy islands of Wmmglaedd about ten miles out to sea. From the piers about four hundred buildings spread out in ragged semicircles. Although Ysgerryn's soapworks lay about a mile from town to spare the residents the stink of tallow, his family lived in a round house down near the harbor. Rhodry's courtship had been so successful because Ysgerryn and his wife were up to their arms in grease and potash all day a good long ways away from Olwen, who tended the younger children at home.

As soon as Rhodry dismounted to lead his horse through the narrow curving streets, he realized that he was in for the worst morning of his life. The townsfolk all bowed or curtsied as usual, but he was aware of hastily repressed smirks and snickers everywhere he went. Although he was the lord and they the commoners, satire was an injured man's right, and apparently Ysgerryn had been exercising it to the hilt. Rhodry tied his horse up behind the house and slipped in like a thief.

Olwen was chopping turnips at the battered table in the kitchen. She was fifteen, a slender little thing with a heart-shaped face, big blue eyes, and a charming triangular smile. This morning, however, she looked up without the usual smile when Rhodry came in.

"Uh, I've brought you somewhat." Rhodry laid the saddlebags on the table.

Olwen nodded and wiped her hands on her apron.

"Do the terms of the settlement please you?" Rhodry said.

She nodded again and began unlacing the bags.

"My mother sent along some honey and things like that." Rhodry began to feel desperate. "Things that are strengthening, she said."

She nodded a third time and began taking various pots and sacks out of the saddlebags.

"Olwen, please, won't you talk to me?"

"And what do you want me to say?"

"Ah by the hells, I don't know!"

Olwen took out the small wooden box of coins, opened it, and stared at the heap of silver for a long time, her chance at a decent life. Rhodry paced around the kitchen while she counted out every coin.

"By the goddess herself," Olwen said at last. "Your mother's a generous woman."

"It's not just her. *I* wanted you well provided for."

"Truly?"

"Truly. Ye gods, what kind of a man do you think I am?"

Olwen considered the question with a weary sort of look in her eyes.

"A better one than most," she said at last. "Are you waiting for me to weep? I've done all of that that I'm going to do."

"Well and good. Will you give me one last kiss?"

"I won't. Just go, will you?"

Rhodry took the saddlebags and headed out, pausing to glance back and see her calmly putting the coins back in the box. She looked more relieved than sad to have him gone. He mounted his horse and trotted out fast, letting the townsfolk get out of his way as best they could. His heart wasn't lightened any when he returned to the dun and found the page waiting for him with the news that his mother wanted to speak with him straightaway. Although he wanted to make an excuse and duck out, he could never avoid the fact that Lovyan was no longer merely his mother, but his overlord, to whom he owed fealty as well as filial respect.

"I'll wait upon her directly," Rhodry said with a groan.

Lovyan was standing by the window in the reception chamber. The harsh morning sun brought out the wrinkles slashed across her cheeks and the gray in her once-dark hair, but she was still an imposing woman, if a bit stout from bearing four sons. She was wearing a white linen dress, kirtled with the green, silver, and blue plaid of the Maelwaedds, but thrown over the chair behind her was the red, brown, and white plaid of the Clw Coc, the symbol of the tierynrhyn. It struck Rhodry as odd that after all these years of thinking himself a Maelwaedd, one day he too would wear that foreign plaid.

"Well?" Lovyan said.

"I handed it all over."

"Did the poor lass weep?"

"Frankly, I think the poor lass was cursed glad to get rid of me."

"She might be, indeed. You're very handsome, Rhoddo, but I've no doubt that you're a very wearing sort of man to be in love with."

Rhodry had the horrible feeling that he was blushing.

"The midwife tells me that your Olwen is about three months along," Lovyan continued. "She'll be having the babe around the Festival of the Sun. Since it's her first, it'll doubtless be a bit late."

"I wouldn't know, I'm sure."

"About such women's matters?" Lovyan raised one eyebrow. "It's time you realized that upon these 'women's matters' rests the strength of every clan in the kingdom. If your uncle had had a bastard son, I wouldn't be tieryn. You might think about that."

Rhodry flung himself into a chair and refused to look at her. With a sigh, Lovyan sat down nearby.

"The real trouble is you were never raised to rule," Lovyan said. "No one ever thought you had the remotest chance of inheriting anything, so your father got you the best warrior's training he could and left it at that. You simply have to marry soon, and she's going to have to be exactly the right sort of woman, too." She hesitated, looking at him shrewdly. "I suppose it would ache your heart to marry a plain lass, or one older than you."

"It would!"

"Now, do try to be sensible. I—here, what's all that clatter outside?"

Rhodry realized that for some minutes he'd been hearing noise out in the ward. Giving thanks to the gods for the interruption, he went to look out the window. Servants scuttled around, greeting a troop of men on horseback. Rhodry could see the dragon device on their shields, and the blue, silver, and green plaid of the rider at their head.

"Ah by a pig's cock!" Rhodry said. "It's Rhys."

"If you could please watch your tongue around your brother, I'd be most grateful."

When they came down to the great hall, they found Rhys standing by the honor hearth. At the head of the table, the plaid of Aberwyn lay over the chair to announce that the gwerbret's presence superceded that of the tieryn. Rhys was just Rhodry's height, but stocky where Rhodry was slender. He had the raven-dark hair and cornflower blue eyes of the Maelwaedds, but his face was coarse rather than fine—the jaw a little too square, the lips a little too full, the eyes a little too small for the breadth of cheek. When Lovyan curtsied to him, Rhys bowed with an affectionate smile. Rhodry's bow he ignored.

"Good morrow, Your Grace," Lovyan said. "What brings you to me?"

"Naught that I care to discuss in your open hall."

"I see. Then let us retire upstairs."

When Rhodry started to follow, Rhys turned to him.

"See that my men are well taken care of," he said.

Since it was a direct order from the gwerbret himself, Rhodry gritted his teeth and followed it. You bastard, he thought, I have to ride this war you're discussing ever so privately with Mother.

The cluttered reception chamber looked even smaller with Rhys in it. Refusing a chair, he paced back and forth, stopping occasionally to glance out the window. Lovyan took the opportunity to collect her thoughts. This was bound to be a touchy interview, straining the delicate balance of power they'd worked out between them. Since as gwerbret Rhys was her overlord, she was bound by law to follow his orders, but since she was his mother, he was bound by custom to follow her advice and pay her every possible respect. For the past year, they'd done an uneasy dance to this difficult bit of counterpoint.

"Why do I hear rumors of rebellion out here?" Rhys said finally.

"So they've reached Aberwyn?"

"Of course." He trotted out the old proverb with a certain point. "Everything comes under the nose of the gwerbret of Aberwyn sooner or later."

"And have you heard that Sligyn believes the rumors?"

"Sligyn isn't given to fancies. Does he have proof? Letters, things he's personally overheard?"

"Naught—yet. I can send for him if his grace would like to speak with him."

"Do you want to make a formal deposition to my court? I doubt if the case would stand if all you have is Sligyn's gossip."

"Doubtless not, especially if his grace has already decided that the information is gossip."

"Oh here, Mother! Corbyn was one of your brother's most loyal men. He pledged to you willingly when you inherited the rhan, didn't he? Why should he throw all that over and declare himself in rebellion?"

Talking of dweomer would draw Rhys's scorn and nothing more. Rhys misinterpreted her hesitation.

"Unless, of course," Rhys said, "the trouble's Rhodry."

"And what makes you think the trouble would be Rhodry?"

"He's an untried man, and I didn't hear any rumors until you made him your heir. I don't think he's fit to rule, myself." Rhys held up his hand flat for silence. "Now, I know Rhodry's a good man with a sword. But leading men to battle is a cursed sight easier than giving judgments on your vassals. If you disinherited him, I'm sure all this cursed grumbling about rebellion would stop."

"I have no intention of doing anything of the sort."

"Indeed? Well, if Sligyn gets real proof, of course I'll rule that you have every right to your rank and lands."

"My humble thanks, Your Grace."

Rhys winced at the sarcasm.

"But if the lords throw Rhodry in my face," Rhys went on, "that may have to be a point of negotiation."

Lovyan rose to face him. Although he towered over her, he ducked back out of reach.

"There is no law in the land," Lovyan said steadily, "that will allow you to force me to disinherit Rhodry."

"Of course there's not. I was merely thinking that Her Grace might have to see reason and do it of her own free will."

"Her Grace also has the right of appeal to the High King."

Rhys flushed scarlet with rage. It was his sorest point, knowing that although he ruled like a king in Western Eldidd, there was a true king in Deverry with jurisdiction over him.

"Very well, Mother," he said. "Then if Rhodry's to have your lands, let him fight to keep them."

"Oho! So you do believe the rumors!"

Rhys spun around and stared out the window. Lovyan laid a maternal hand on his arm.

"Rhys, my sweet, why do you hate Rhodry so much?"

"I don't hate Rhodry," he snarled, his face redder than before.

"Indeed?"

"I just happen to think he's unfit to rule."

"I happen to disagree."

Rhys merely shrugged.

"Very well, then, Your Grace," Lovyan said with a sigh. "There's no use in discussing the matter further until it comes to a formal case of either law or sword."

"Apparently so." Back under control, he looked at her. "At the first overt act of rebellion, you may send for my aid, and my warband will be at your disposal to enforce the laws."

And yet he'd made it impossible to ask his aid, unless she wanted to let him disinherit his brother in open court.

That afternoon, while Rhys and his men drank in her great hall, Lovyan wrote a private message to Sligyn to come to her on the morrow. She needed his advice. When she returned to the hall, Rhodry was sitting at his brother's left and discussing hunting dogs, a fairly safe subject. Lovyan sat down at the gwerbret's right and stayed on guard for the trouble that soon, predictably, surfaced.

"Well, brother," Rhys said. "I hear from your men that you've been hunting a different kind of game than the gray deer. The soapmaker's daughter, was she? Well, at least she'd be clean."

When Rhys laughed at his own jest, Rhodry's eyes went dangerously blank.

"I can't lie and say that I didn't dishonor her," Rhodry said. "Tell me, brother, has your wife conceived yet?"

Rhys's hand tightened on his tankard so hard that his knuckles went white.

"Rhodry!" Lovyan snapped.

"Well, Mother, it seemed a reasonable question." Rhodry shot his brother a sideways smile. "Since we're talking about siring sons and all."

With a flick of his wrist, Rhys threw the ale in his tankard full into Rhodry's face. Shouting insults and the worst oaths they knew, they were on their feet and shoving at each other before Lovyan could intervene. She jumped up and ran round the table to push herself between them, and for all that Rhys had the higher rank, she slapped him across the face, too.

"Stop it!" Lovyan yelled. "What a splendid example you are for your men, brawling like a pair of servants! My lords, kindly remember who you are."

They both had the decency to blush. Rhodry wiped his face off on his sleeve and stared down at the floor. Rhys collected himself with a sigh and held out his hand.

"My apologies," Rhys said.

"And you have mine from the bottom of my heart." Rhodry took the offered hand.

But the handshake was as brief as they could make it, and Rhodry stomped out of the hall. Rhys and Lovyan sat down and waited while a servant refilled the gwerbret's tankard and scuttled away again.

"My apologies to you, Mother," Rhys said. "That was an ill way for me to treat your hospitality, but ye gods, the cursed young cub made me furious."

"What he said was uncalled for and cruel."

Rhys studied the tabletop and rubbed at a bit of rough wood with his thumb. Finally he looked up with a brittle smile.

"Well?" Rhys said. "Aren't you going to tell me that it's time I put my wife aside?"

"I know you love her, and never would I wish that bitter Wyrd on any woman. I take it your councillors have been pressing the issue again."

"They have. That's another reason I rode to Cannobaen, to ask your advice. I know Aberwyn needs heirs, but it aches my heart to think of Donilla living shamed on her brother's charity."

With a sigh, Lovyan considered. Rhys had been married for ten years; he was now twenty-eight and his wife twenty-six; if Donilla was going to conceive, surely she would have done so by now.

"If you do put her aside," Lovyan said at last, "I'll make provision for her. At the very least, she can come to me as part of my retinue, but I might be able to do better than that."

"My thanks. Truly, Mother, my thanks." He rose abruptly. "If you'll excuse me? I need a bit of air."

Yet Lovyan knew that he was close to tears. For a long while she sat at the table alone and brooded on those women's matters that lay at the heart of the kingdom.

On the morrow, Rhys and his men rode out early, much to Lovyan's relief. His stubbornness over the rebellion puzzled her; it was, after all, to the gwerbret's advantage to intervene before things came to open war, both to assert his authority and to issue a warning that rebellions would not be tolerated in his rhan. Later, while speaking with Rhodry and Sligyn in her reception chamber, she found an answer to the puzzle that nearly broke her heart.

"Cursed high-handed of him, eh?" Sligyn said. "Never known his grace to be so unreasonable."

"Indeed?" Rhodry said with a cold tight smile. "All my life, Rhys could always hold one thing over my head, and that was that he'd get the gwerbretrhyn and I'd have naught but his charity. And then Uncle Gwaryc has to go and get himself killed, and lo and behold, I've got a rhan after all. Of course it aches the bastard's heart."

"Here!" Sligyn snapped. "Don't call your brother that. Your lady mother had more honor than to put horns on your father's head."

"My apologies to you, Mother. Let me refer to the esteemed gwerbret as a piss-poor drunken excuse for a noble lord then."

"Rhodry!" Lovyan and Sligyn said together.

"Well, by the gods!" Rhodry got to his feet. "How do you expect me to be courteous to a man who wants me dead?"

Suddenly Lovyan turned cold.

"Can't you see it?" Rhodry was shaking with rage. "He's letting the war go on in the hopes of seeing me killed. I'll wager Corbyn and Nowec see it, too. They kill me off, then sue for peace, and Rhys ever so honorably makes them give restitution to his poor mother. Then when you die, the rebels have what they want, direct fealty to Rhys, and he has what he wants, my lands." Rhodry leaned over her chair. "Well, Mother? Aren't I right?"

"Hold your tongue!" Sligyn rose and hauled him back. "You're right enough, but don't go throwing it into your lady mother's face!"

Rhodry strode to the window and looked out, gripping the sill with both hands. Lovyan felt as if Rhys and Rhodry physically had her by the arms and were ripping her apart. Sligyn watched her with concern.

"Now here, Your Grace," Sligyn said. "We'll keep your young cub alive. He knows how to swing that sword he wears, and he'll have plenty of loyal men around him."

Lovyan nodded mutely.

"My lady?" Sligyn said. "We'd best leave you."

It seemed to take them forever to get out of the chamber and close the door.

"Ah ye gods," Lovyan whispered aloud. "I never thought he hated Rhodry as much as all this."

She dropped her face into her hands and let the blessed tears come.

Much to Jill's delight, it took Dregydd some days to finish trading with the Westfolk, who did things at a slow pace. One at a time, either a man or a woman would lead a horse over and sit down in the grass to haggle leisurely with the merchant. When that deal was done, an hour or two would pass before the next horse made its appearance. Since most of the Westfolk knew no Deverrian, the man named Jennantar stayed with Dregydd to translate. In her self-appointed role as Dregydd's assistant, Jill came to know him fairly well, which—predictably—infuriated her father. The second afternoon, during a break in the trading Cullyn came over and insisted that Jill take a walk with him down by the river.

"I wish to every god and his wife that you wouldn't spend so much time hanging around old Dregydd," he said. "I know cursed well it's the wretched Westfolk you want to talk with."

"Da, I just don't see what you have against them. They're not animals. Look at their clothes and their jewelry, and then they built that bridge over the river. Somewhere they must have farms and cities and suchlike."

"Indeed? And I suppose you'd like to ride off with that Jennantar and take a look at them."

"What? Da, you're daft! He's got a wife and a babe, and he's never said one wrong word to me."

"Oh horseturds! There's more than one man in the world who's had a wife and didn't mind having a pretty lass, too."

"Da, I don't even know what to say to you when your temper takes you this way."

Cullyn stopped walking, turning a little to look out over the endless green of the grasslands, and his mouth went slack and weary. Jill laid a hand on his arm.

"Da, please, what's so wrong?"

"Oh, cursed if I even know, my sweet. It aches my heart, being out here. For years I thought it was the edge of nowhere, and now I find out there's this cursed strange folk riding around out here, and they've been here all along, and"—he shrugged in inarticulate frustration—"and, well, you're going to think me daft, curse it, but they stink of dweomer and witchcraft. So does that Aderyn fellow."

Jill couldn't have been more shocked if a performing bear in the marketplace had suddenly started declaiming a bard song. Her stolid warrior of a father—talking of dweomer?

"Well," Cullyn snapped. "I said it sounds daft!"

"It doesn't, truly. I think you're right."

He looked at her for a moment, then slowly nodded, as if he'd been waiting for her judgment upon the matter. Jill felt a cold shudder run down her back, because he was seeing something in her that she was desperately trying to deny. As if to mock her, the gray gnome popped into manifestation nearby, grinned at her, then vanished again.

"Da? I'd never leave you. If you thought I would, then truly, you were daft."

Cullyn relaxed, smiling at her softly.

"Well and good, then, my sweet," he said. "My apologies. You can watch our merchant haggle if you want to. We'll be getting out of here soon enough."

Jill took him up on his offer and went back to the trading. When she sat down beside Jennantar, he raised a quizzical eyebrow.

"Doesn't your father think I'm fit company for you?" he said.

Jill merely shrugged. He started to say more, then suddenly jumped to his feet with an oath. There was trouble brewing. Two of the Westfolk were arguing with a frightened Dregydd, who held the last remaining sword of Caminwaen steel. As Jill followed Jennantar over, she heard them arguing about who was going to buy it.

"Now here!" Dregydd snapped. "I never promised it to either of you."

The two men looked only at each other in an anger the more frightening because it played over such beautiful faces.

"Jill!" Jennantar hissed. "Go fetch Aderyn. Quick!"

Without thinking, Jill ran to the Westfolk's camp. At the edge, she stopped, suddenly bewildered by the profusion of bright colors, the gaggle of children and dogs, the unfamiliar language that swirled around her. A few at a time, Westfolk strolled over and surrounded her. When a dog growled, she stepped back sharply.

"Aderyn," Jill said. "Jennantar told me to get Aderyn."

The people merely looked at her.

"Please?" Jill tried again. "Where's Aderyn?"

They glanced at each other, their cat-slit eyes totally expressionless. Jill felt a little flutter of panic around her heart. All of them, even the women, were wearing long knives at their belts.

"Please, Jennantar told me to come here."

One man glanced her way, but he said nothing. Jill wanted to turn and run, but they were standing close behind her, too. Then she heard Aderyn's voice, calling out in their language, and the crowd parted to let him through.

"Jennantar said to fetch you," Jill said. "A couple of your lads are fighting over somewhat."

Aderyn swore under his breath. The people, who only a moment before had seemed to understand not one word she said, all muttered at the news. Aderyn grabbed Jill's arm and hurried her across the meadow, surprisingly fast for such an old man. When she glanced back, she saw the crowd trailing after them.

Back by the trade goods, Jennantar stood in between the two who wanted the sword, while Dregydd hovered nearby, clutching the sheathed blade in nervous fingers. As soon as they saw Aderyn, all three men of the Westfolk began to yell at the top of their lungs. Jill hurried over to Dregydd.

"They're like this at times," he said in a resigned tone of voice. "I'm glad the old man's here to settle things."

Yet it seemed that Aderyn's efforts to do just that were proving futile. All the time that he talked in a soothing, patient voice, the two went on staring at each other, arms crossed tight over their chests, cat-slit eyes unblinking. With a shake of his head, Jennantar left the bad job to the old man and joined Jill. Around them the crowd grew, Westfolk and muleteers alike, and Wildfolk popped into manifestation in droves, grinning so hard that they bared pointed teeth.

"They've hated each other for years," Jennantar remarked. "They're not going to listen now."

Eventually he proved right. Aderyn threw his hands in the air and returned to the crowd of Westfolk, who stamped their feet on the ground in a sharp rhythm. The two men slowly and methodically stripped off their tunics, tossed them on the ground, then drew their knives, which were about a foot long and slightly curved on one side of the blade. The blades winked in the sun as the pair dropped to a fighting crouch. Jill felt sick, wondering if she was going to see a man killed right in front of her.

In dead silence the pair circled around one another, their strange eyes narrow, their jaws set. There was none of the ritual boasting and yelling that would have accompanied a fight between two Deverry men, just the quiet animal circling, a few quick feints, a few quick withdrawals, while the sweat sprang up on their bare backs and made their pale skin glisten. Around and around they went, until one made a charge, and the other held his ground. A quick scuffle, too quick to see—then one fell back with his arm gashed open from elbow to shoulder. Dregydd cursed, but the watching crowd of Westfolk merely stamped on the ground again, and briefly. Aderyn ran to separate the combatants, who fell back willingly.

"It's just to the first blood?" Jill said, with profound relief.

"It is," Jennantar said. "My apologies. I forgot you didn't know."

The bloody knife still in his hand, the victor strolled over to Dregydd, who handed him the sword without a word. His head bowed, the loser stood alone, slumped in defeat, and let the blood run down his arm until Aderyn grabbed him and forcibly hauled him away.

"So much for that," Jennantar remarked. "Until the next time they find somewhat that annoys them. One of these days, the first blood is going to be someone's throat."

When Jill looked at the man she'd been thinking of as a friend, she was caught all over again by his alienness as his smokey, slit eyes stared back unblinkingly. They truly are kin to the Wildfolk, she thought, and for the first time, she wondered if her father were right to think them dangerous. That night, as she listened to the music wailing from the Westfolk's camp, she was glad to be sitting by the fire with her own kind.

By sunset of the third day, Dregydd had twelve Western hunters in his herd, including the golden stud that he particularly wanted, and it was a good thing, too, because Jennantar abruptly announced that no one else wanted to trade with him. Dregydd made no attempt to argue with the news, merely walked away to tell the men that they would be riding out on the morrow.

"I'll be going with you," Jennantar remarked to Jill. "Aderyn's taking three of us along for guards."

"I don't blame him. I met this Loddlaen, and I wouldn't trust him with a copper, much less my life. Well, if you lay your complaint with the tieryn, she'll haul him into her malover for you."

"Her what? I've never heard that word."

"Malover. It's when someone feels wronged and asks a tieryn or a gwerbret to judge the matter. The priests of Bel come, too, because they know all the laws."

"Oh. Well and good, then. No doubt Aderyn knows all the right things to say."

At dawn of the next day, the caravan prepared for the long march back to Eldidd. In the cool gray morning, the mules brayed in protest as the yawning men loaded up the last of the trade goods and the provisions Dregydd had obtained from the Westfolk. Jill was helping rope the riderless horses together when Aderyn rode up with his guards, Jennantar and then two men he introduced as Calonderiel and Albaral. Jennantar led a horse that was dragging a loaded travois.

"Come ride at the head of the line with me and Jill," Dregydd said to the old man. "I'll put your men in the rear with Cullyn, on guard, like, if you don't mind."

"You're the caravan master," Aderyn said, smiling. "We ride at your orders."

Since they were heading for Cannobaen, the caravan took a different route back. For the first day, Dregydd led them straight south through the long grasslands. Once, they saw at a great distance the tiny figures of mounted riders and riderless horses heading west, like a ship seen across a green ocean, but if that clan of Westfolk saw the caravan, they gave no sign. Jill found herself wondering what it would be like to ride endlessly from nowhere to nowhere, always free like the falcon in the skies. She had such a life herself, but she knew with a bitter certainty that someday her wandering would end. At times she dropped back to ride beside Cullyn, and she would notice the gray sprinkling his hair and the web of fine lines around his eyes. The day was coming when some younger man would bring his Wyrd to him in battle. The thought brought such panic that at times it was hard to breathe.

On the second day, the caravan turned east. Here and there they came to magnificent stands of forest, but Dregydd knew his route well and led them from wild meadow to wild meadow. Once the track passed through straggly young beeches and alders that had to be a second-growth forest, and on the other side was land that had once been plowed. Packed flint walls still stood, marking out long-gone fields. In pastures Jill saw tumbledown stone sheds and white cattle, gone wild and as suspicious as deer. Since she was riding next to Aderyn, she asked him if the Westfolk had once farmed there.

"Not the Westfolk, but Eldidd men," Aderyn said. "A long long time ago it was, but some of the younger sons of Eldidd lords tried to colonize out here. It was too far west, and they couldn't keep their holdings."

"And was there trouble with the Westfolk over it?"

"Trouble and twice trouble. The Westfolk used to roam much farther east than they do now, and they felt they'd given up enough land."

"Here, I never heard any tales about that."

"It was a very long time ago, and Eldidd men have forgotten. They've worked at forgetting, truly. But haven't you ever wondered about the names of the rivers—the El, the Delonderiel? Those aren't Deverry words, child."

"Of course! Delonderiel's like Calonderiel."

"Just so, and Eldidd was called Eltidiña, a long time ago when Deverry men first sailed here." Aderyn thought for a moment. "That was eight hundred or so years ago, if I remember rightly. It's been a long time since I studied such things."

Soon Dregydd called for the halt for the night's camp. Where a stone wall marked out what had once been a field, and scrubby hazels grew along a stream, they tethered out the horses and mules and made their camp. Over dinner, Dregydd discussed the route ahead.

"This stream turns into a river farther south," he said. "We'll follow it down to the coast, then turn east and march along the sea cliffs to Cannobaen. There's plenty of fodder along there for the stock. I'd say we're a good two days out, so let's hope this dry weather holds."

Jill felt a sudden coldness along her back, as if someone had stroked her spine with a clammy hand. She was sure that worse trouble than a possible rainstorm lay ahead. Although she tried to talk herself out of the feeling, late that night when she was trying to get to sleep, the gray gnome appeared. He was troubled, too, pulling at her shirt, pointing off to the east, and opening his mouth in little soundless whimpers. Finally Jill got up and followed him to the edge of the sleeping camp. He jumped up and down, pointing, always pointing to the east.

"I don't see anything," Jill said.

He clutched at his head in agony and promptly disappeared. Jill went back to her bedroll. Except for the occasional drowsy stamp of a horse or a mule, the night was utterly quiet. Once she heard the cry of an owl and looked up to see the tiny dark shape of the bird flying against the stars. She dozed off to have troubled dreams, that an enormous owl flew overhead, calling out warnings of danger. Just at dawn she woke with a start. The gnome was pulling her hair.

"Oh all right," Jill said. "Let me get my boots on, and then you try to show me again."

The gnome led her down to the stream, where, a giant among the tangled hazels, stood one old oak. He danced around and pointed to the tree. When Jill looked up, she saw Aderyn in the branches. He gave her a sheepish smile, then climbed down, as nimble as a lad.

"I've been keeping a watch," Aderyn said, and Jill could see that he was deeply troubled. "We're in grave danger, child. Hurry! Go wake your father!"

Together they ran back to the waking camp. The men were

getting up and stretching, the horses and mules starting to graze. Jill found Cullyn just pulling on his boots.

"Da, come with me," Jill said. "Aderyn says there's trouble ahead."

Cullyn got up and grabbed his sword belt from the ground. He buckled it on as they ran back across the camp to find Aderyn arguing with Dregydd, who looked utterly baffled.

"You've known me for years now," Aderyn was saying. "Please, my friend, you've got to trust me now."

"I do," Dregydd said. "But how the hells can you know? I've never had any trouble with bandits out here, and now you say that there's a whole pack of them waiting in ambush. Doesn't make any cursed sense."

"I can know and I do know. We've got to do something, or we'll all be slaughtered on the road."

From the look on Dregydd's face it was obvious that he thought the old man had gone completely and suddenly mad. Aderyn leaned forward and stared into his eyes. The look of disbelief vanished.

"Of course," Dregydd said. "I'll do whatever you say."

For a moment Jill's hands shook. Against all reason she knew that she'd just seen a man ensorceled. When Aderyn glanced her way, she ducked her head and refused to look at him. He laughed softly, acknowledging the gesture.

"Cullyn," he said. "Do you believe me?"

"I do, and I don't care how you scried them out, either."

It was Aderyn's turn to be startled. Cullyn gave him a weary sort of smile.

"How many of them are there?" Cullyn said.

"At least thirty, and they seemed to be as well armed as a lord's warband."

Dregydd turned dead white. Frightened muleteers clustered around to whisper the news among themselves.

"We've got to have shelter." Cullyn looked as bored and lazy as if he were asking for ale in a tavern. "The muleteers have quarterstaves, but they can't use them if they're being ridden down by men on horseback. A patch of forest, rocks—anything to make them attack on foot."

Aderyn hesitated, thinking hard.

"Here," Jill broke in. "If there were lords out here once, they must have had duns. Are any still standing?"

"Of course," Aderyn said. "Forgive me. I know nothing of matters of war. There's one about five miles or so to the south and west. The walls were still there the last time I passed that way."

"Splendid," Cullyn said. "We might be able to hold them off long enough for Jill to get back from Cannobaen with some of the tieryn's men."

"What?" Jill snapped. "You can't send me away!"

Cullyn slapped her across the face so hard she staggered.

"You follow orders," Cullyn said. "What's two days' ride for a lot of stinking mules should be one for a rider with a spare horse to share her weight. You're riding to the tieryn and begging for aid. Do you hear me?"

"I do." Jill rubbed her aching cheek. "But you'd best be alive when I ride back."

The way Cullyn smiled, a cold twitch of his mouth, told Jill that he doubted he would be. For a moment she thought that her body had turned to water, that she was going to flow away and dissolve like one of the Wildfolk. Cullyn grabbed her by the shoulders and shook her.

"You're riding for the life of every man in this caravan," he said. "Do you understand me?"

"I do. I'll take two of the hunters. They're the best horses we've got."

Jennantar saddled one horse and put the other on a lead rope, then held the bridle as Jill swung herself up. As she bent over to take the lead rope, their eyes met.

"I'll see you on the morrow," Jennantar said.

"I'll pray that's true."

"Oh, we've got a trick or two to play on these piss-pot bandits. We'll hold them off."

All at once Jennantar flung his hands over his head and danced, just a few quick steps to some unsung music, and he was grinning like a fiend. Seeing him so battle eager was one of the strangest things on this cursed strange day.

Getting the caravan on the road seemed to take an eternity. Cullyn kept on the move, yelling orders, as the men got the mules loaded and themselves mounted on the spare horses. During the march, he rode up and down the line, yelling and bullying everyone to ride as fast as they could, occasionally slapping the rump of a balky mule with the flat of his sword to keep it trotting. At last they came to the ruined dun, rising from the wild grass with all the loneliness of a cairn marking a warrior's grave. Although the stone walls and the broch itself looked sound, the wooden gates and outbuildings had long since rotted away. Weeds and ivy ran riot in the ward. Cullyn herded the caravan inside.

"Get the mules and horses inside the broch," he yelled. "Feed them to keep them calm."

When he saw his orders being followed, he ran round to the back of the ward and found the well. As he'd expected, it had fallen in and was choked with rubble as well as ivy. He ran back into the broch and detailed three muleteers to rush to the nearby stream and fill every pot and waterskin they had. Off to one side he saw Aderyn testing the rusty spiral staircase that led up to the second floor.

"It should hold my weight," Aderyn announced. "I wouldn't let a man of your size try it."

"I doubt me if the floor above will hold anyone." Cullyn glanced up at the rotten timbers.

"I have to try. I need a high place that's also private. I can't be scaring the men out of their wits with dweomer."

Cullyn felt a bit queasy himself.

"Jill said Loddlaen is a lord's councillor," Aderyn went on. "Could he persuade his lord to send men to murder us?"

"It depends on how much this Corbyn honors him, I suppose, but it's hard to believe. Do you think Loddlaen's trying to stop you from hauling him in for that murder?"

"That was my first thought, but it doesn't make sense. Yet I've never seen bandits out here, and I tell you, the men I saw were cursed well armed. Well, I'll have another look."

As nimbly as a squirrel, Aderyn scrambled up the creaking stairs. Cullyn hurried outside and saw the Westfolk down by the gate. They were unpacking gear from the travois—a pair of longbows, beautifully polished staves of some dark wood he'd never seen before, and as tall as they were.

"Archers, are you?" Cullyn said.

"We are," Jennantar said. "I think me our bandits are in for a little surprise." He gestured at Albaral, who was unpacking a sword belt. "He's not Cullyn of Cerrmor, but we fight with long knives in our land, too."

"Well and good then. Maybe we'll take some of these bandits to the Otherlands with us. Albaral, do you have any armor?"

"Eldidd mail. Thought it might come in handy, so I packed it."

"And here I thought you were a fool," Calonderiel said. "For dragging all that weight along."

Albaral smiled with a tight twist to his mouth. Cullyn noticed that Albaral had a scar down his cheek much like the one he himself carried.

"So," Cullyn said. "Your people fight among themselves, do they?"

"Every now and then," Albaral said. "But an Eldidd lord marked me like this. I killed the bastard for it. Long time ago now."

The four of them peered up at the rotted splinters along the top of the wall that were all that was left of the catwalks under the ramparts. Never would they hold an archer again.

"Well, the top of that wall's about five feet thick," Jennantar said at last. "We can stand there and shoot if we're careful. Those projection things will provide some cover for our legs, anyway."

"Merlons." With a real surprise Cullyn realized that they knew nothing about duns. "They're called merlons. But we still have to get you up there."

Albaral took a rope off the travois, turned it into a lasso, then stepped back and cast. The loop sailed up and encircled a merlon as easily as if he'd been aiming at a horse in a herd. Cullyn whistled in admiration.

"Now we can weave ourselves a ladder," Calonderiel said. "I wonder if those bandits are still lying in their cursed ambush. May the flies cluster thick around them if they are."

"Aderyn will know," Jennantar said. "Or look—he's just going to find out."

Just then Cullyn heard a strange sound above him, a rushy flap like the wings of an enormous bird. When he glanced up, an enormous bird was exactly what he saw—a great silver owl, a good five feet long, flapping up from the broch, circling once, then heading off to the east with a long mournful cry. Albaral waved farewell to it as casually as if he were waving to some friend who was riding off to a tavern. For a moment Cullyn came close to vomiting.

"By the black ass of the Lord of Hell," Cullyn said. "Can Aderyn turn himself into an owl?"

"Of course," Jennantar said. "You just saw him, didn't you?"

Cullyn's mind refused to acknowledge the fact. He had, of course, seen the owl; he believed that Jennantar was telling the truth; he even remembered seeing Aderyn go upstairs for some purpose of his own—but his mind stubbornly refused to draw the proper conclusion. He stared at the sky for a long time before he could speak.

"Well and good, then," Cullyn said. "Albaral, we'd best get our cursed mail on our backs."

Every morning, unless it was pouring rain, Rhodry led his warband out to exercise the horses. Lately, thanks to the threat of rebellion, he'd been making the rides good long ones to ensure that men and mounts both would be fit to ride to war. It seemed perfectly logical, then, when the idea occurred to him of taking the men out for a day-long jaunt. He was talking with Caenrydd, his captain, as he usually did after breakfast when suddenly—out of nowhere, as he would later think of it—it occurred to him that none of them had spent a full day in mail in months.

"Have the men pack provisions for the noon meal," Rhodry said. "We'll ride till then fully armed, rest a bit, and then return."

"Well and good, my lord. Which way shall we ride?"

"Oh, doesn't much matter." Rhodry named the first direction that came to mind. "West."

Although a dark line of fog crouched ominously on the ocean horizon, it was a fine sunny morning when they set out. Every now and then Rhodry would turn in the saddle just to look at his men, riding two abreast, with the red lion shield of his adopted clan at every saddle peak. Soon he would be leading a full army. Cadvridoc, he thought to himself, it has a fine ring to it, truly. Eventually he called Caenrydd up to ride beside him. The captain was a solid man in his late twenties, with blond hair and drooping mustaches almost as thick as Sligyn's. Since he'd served the Clw Coc all his life, Rhodry could speak freely with him.

"Are the men talking of dweomer among themselves?" Rhodry said.

"They are, my lord. I do my best to stop it."

"I knew I could count on you for that. How do you feel about these rumors yourself?"

"Pack of horseshit, my lord."

"Good. I couldn't agree more."

At noon they stopped to rest in a meadow about half a mile inland, where a river wound down from the north. Just like one of his men, Rhodry unsaddled his own horse and let it roll, then tethered it out. He sat on the grass with his men, too. He knew that they saw him as an interloper, and he was determined to show them that the sudden elevation of his prospects in life hadn't swelled his head.

They were all trading friendly jests over their bread and smoked meat when Rhodry felt as much as heard hoofbeats coming their way. He scrambled up and looked off to the north. Trotting fast beside the river came a rider leading a spare horse.

"Who by all the hells is out here?" Rhodry said.

Caenrydd joined him and shaded his eyes to stare at the tiny figures.

"Old Nevyn the herbman, maybe?" Caenrydd said.

"It's not, because those are two western hunters, not a palfrey and a mule."

"By the hells! His lordship has cursed good eyes."

"So I do." Rhodry saw a wink of silver at the rider's belt. "A silver dagger with two western hunters. What do we have here, a horsethief?"

No horsethief, however, would have broken into a gallop and ridden straight for them as the silver dagger did. He was a young lad, blond and road filthy, and riding without a shield though he had a sword at his side. He swung himself down from his horse and ran to kneel at Rhodry's feet. Down one side of his face was a livid purple bruise.

"My lord," he said, and his soft, unchanged voice made it likely he was about fourteen. "Do you serve the tieryn in Cannobaen?"

"I do, and I'm her son to boot, Lord Rhodry Maelwaedd."

"A Maelwaedd? Thanks be to every god! Then I know I can trust your honor, my lord. I've just come from a merchant caravan to beg for help. It's bandits, my lord, at least thirty of them, and they've got us penned up in a ruined dun to the north."

"Bandits? In my demesne? I'll have their heads on pikes." Rhodry spun around to yell orders. "Saddle up and get ready to ride! Amyr, ride back to the dun and give Her Grace the news. Tell her to send a cart with supplies and the chirurgeon after us."

Everyone ran to do his bidding.

"Get up, silver dagger," Rhodry said. "What were you, a hired guard?"

"Well, my father is, to tell you the truth. I just travel with him."

"Well, mount up and get ready to lead us back. What a cursed bit of luck this is, me having the warband out here. You'd think it was dweomer or suchlike."

The lad giggled in an outburst of hysteria, then ran back to his horses.

As the hot afternoon dragged on, there was no sign of Aderyn. While the others rested inside the broch, Cullyn and Jennantar kept an uneasy watch, Cullyn at the gates, Jennantar pacing back and forth along the top of the wall. Cullyn began to wonder if they'd ever see the old man again, or if he'd been captured by the enemy. Finally, when the sun lay low in the sky, Jennantar called out in triumph.

"Here he comes!"

Although Cullyn strained his eyes, it was several minutes more before he saw the flapping speck in the sky that meant the owl. All over again, Cullyn felt sick at the unnatural size of the thing as the bird swooped down and disappeared into an upper window of the broch. It was some minutes before Aderyn ran out, pulling his tunic over his head.

"They're on their way," Aderyn called out. "But so is help. Lord Rhodry and his warband are heading up from the south."

"What did Jill do?" Cullyn said. "Founder both those horses?"

"She didn't. She met Rhodry on the road." Aderyn looked briefly troubled. "Something cursed strange is afoot here. Jennantar! Did you see any hawks fly overhead?"

"One or two," Jennantar called down. "Oh ye gods! You don't think—"

"I do. Loddlaen has to be behind this." Aderyn turned to Cullyn. "The men I saw were well armed, well provisioned, and they carried shields with a number of different blazons."

"Then they're not bandits, sure enough," Cullyn said. "What's Loddlaen trying to do, kill the witnesses to his murder before they reach court?"

"So I thought at first. But here, I'm the chief witness against him, and it's hard to trap a man who can fly away." The old man allowed himself a ghost of a smile. "There's something strange and twice strange afoot here."

The rest of the men were already running out of the broch. Hurriedly Cullyn disposed the pitiful force he had on hand—two decent swordsmen, counting himself, three men skilled with a quarterstaff, and five who knew the right way to hold the staff and little more. Because of the rubble, the gate was only big enough for two men to fight side by side. He and Albaral would have to hold it as long as they could, with Dregydd and the other skilled stavemen right behind to step in when they fell. Up on the wall, the archers stood ready with full quivers at their hips. Aderyn climbed up to join them.

"Now listen, lads," Cullyn said. "No heroics like in the bard songs. Just fight to hold your place."

It was some time before Cullyn saw the pack of thirty-four men in mail ride out of the east at a steady trot. About three hundred yards away, they drew up and clustered around a leader for a hasty conference, then came on again at a walk. Cullyn could see men loosening shields and getting ready to dismount for the final charge on the gates, but like most Eldidd men, they were going to stay in the saddle for as long as possible—a habit that was to prove fatal. At a hundred yards they pulled up, well out of javelin range.

Arrows sang out from the wall, then again, and again. The lead horses reared, screaming in agony, and went down hard, rolling on their riders, as the arrows came again, and again, and again. Horses behind them bucked and kicked in panic; men yelled and cursed. The arrows flew again, a noiseless rain of death. The warband broke into a riot of men on foot and pan-icked horses, and still the arrows flew down. Shouting, scream-ing, the warband turned tail and fled, leaving behind twelve dead men and more horses. Far down the meadow they regrouped. When the muleteers broke into howls of laughter, Cullyn turned and yelled them into silence.

"It isn't over yet," Cullyn said. "We don't have all the arrows in the world with us, and if even ten of those bastards reach the gate, you'll need your wits about you—if you dogs even have any."

Then came more waiting, while the sun inched itself another notch lower in the sky, their enemies argued, and somewhere— or so Cullyn devoutly hoped—Rhodry and his men rode closer to them. Finally Cullyn saw the enemy dismounting. They spread out into two squads, each circling out of bowshot range around a different side of the dun, then splitting up again. Jennantar muttered something in his own tongue that had to be a vile oath from its tone.

"They've learned somewhat," Albaral remarked.

"So they have," Cullyn said. "The only thing they can do. Rush us from all sides and circle under the shelter of the walls."

"We can't stop them with only two archers."

They exchanged a grim smile. At that moment, Cullyn wondered how he could have hated the Westfolk—he and Albaral understood each other perfectly well. Most of the enemy were moving round to the back of the dun. Jennantar began sidling along the wall to meet them, but Calonderiel held his post over the gates until the other squad began moving to the side. Cursing under his breath, Calonderiel moved to face them. For a moment, everything was preternaturally quiet; then a silver horn rang out.

Distantly from the far side of the broch, warcries exploded as the charge began. Closer and closer—a few screams as arrows hit their mark—then the jingle and clink of men in mail running— the first enemies rounded the wall and raced for the gates. Three, four, too many to count, they mobbed in, but the gate was too narrow for mobs. The fight was a shoving match as much as it was swordwork. Cullyn parried more than he swung, using his shield like a bludgeon to shove back the blades that hit it. Screaming warcries, the men at the rear pressed forward and forced their own men at the front off balance. Cullyn and Albaral swung and parried and swayed back and forth in a perfect rhythm with each other.

Arrows flew down into the rear of the mob, and Cullyn saw

one shaft split a lad's mail and skewer him like a chicken on a spit. Cursing and yelling, part of the mob tried to peel off and run back around the walls. The rest surged forward. Cullyn got a kill at last, keeping his arm close to his side and stabbing rather than slashing. As the corpse fell, it knocked another man off his feet, and the mob swirled in confusion. Over the screaming, Cullyn heard a silver horn ring out.

"Red lions!" Calonderiel yelled.

"Cannobaen!" Dregydd howled out.

Trapped between Lord Rhodry's charge and the dun, the enemy broke in screaming panic. One clot of men surged blindly forward. Cullyn saw Albaral knocked off balance and swung round toward him. With a shout Dregydd leaped into line. Out of the corner of his eye, Cullyn saw the blur of a staff swinging down and the snap of a head as an enemy fell. An enemy slashed at Albaral, but an arrow caught him in the back. With a quick stab and slash, Cullyn killed the last of them. He threw his shield and grabbed Albaral's arm as he tried to stagger to his feet. Albaral flopped like a rag doll onto Cullyn's shoulder, and his mouth and nose were running blood. The cat-slit eyes, no longer alien somehow, sought his.

"I always knew this dun would see my death," Albaral said. "Never thought I'd be defending it."

When he coughed, blood bubbled and gouted on his lips. Staggering under his weight, Cullyn knelt to lay him back down, but Albaral was dead before they reached the ground, his mouth frozen in a blood-stained smile at his own jest.

"Ah shit!" Cullyn said.

Around him eddied the cheers of the muleteers. Cullyn closed Albaral's eyes, crossed his arms over his chest, then rose to find himself face to face with Rhodry. For a moment, they merely looked at each other. Cullyn was sure that he knew him; irrational though it was, he'd never been so sure of anything in his life, that he knew this young lord like a brother. Then the feeling vanished like dweomer. Rhodry laid a sympathetic hand on his shoulder.

"Lose a friend?" Rhodry said.

"I did. Well, it happens."

"So it does, silver dagger."

Cullyn nodded and let out his breath in a long sigh, surprised at the truth of it: Albaral had become a friend, there in the breach. The other two Westfolk came running. At the sight of Albaral, Jennantar burst out keening and flung himself down by the body, but Calonderiel merely set his hands on his hips, his whole body as tense as a strung bow.

"There's another one," he whispered. "Slain by the cursed round-ears."

Then he looked up and howled out a single word in his own tongue, the meaning plain for any man to hear: vengeance. Cullyn and Rhodry glanced at each other, then walked away to leave the Westfolk to their mourning. Once they were out of earshot, the puzzled lord turned to Cullyn.

"Westfolk?" he said. "What are Westfolk doing mixed up in this?"

"It's a cursed strange tale all round, my lord. These men weren't bandits, either. What would you say if I told you Councillor Loddlaen of Dun Bruddlyn's behind this?"

Rhodry seemed about to argue; then he glanced down to see the shattered shield of one of the enemy—a green shield with a tan chevron.

"By the Lord of Hell's balls," Rhodry said. "That's Corbyn's blazon, sure enough. Looking for a hire, silver dagger? I think me you've already captained the first battle of an open war."

Lovyan was wondering irritably when Rhodry and the warband would return when Amyr rode in to deliver Rhodry's message. Although she said nothing to Amyr, the news troubled her badly. She knew that there weren't any bandits in western Eldidd for the simple reason that there wasn't enough caravan trade to support them. At dinner, she and her two serving women, Dannyan and Medylla, sat at table in a great hall eerily silent with the warband gone. Lovyan picked at her food, then decided that she wasn't in the least hungry.

"My lady's sorely troubled," Medylla said.

"I am," Lovyan said. "It was stupid of Rhodry to ride off into nowhere like that."

They nodded their agreement. Dark-haired and delicate Dannyan, blond and homely Medylla were both in their late thirties, noble-born friends rather than servants, who twenty years ago had chosen to take Lovyan's service rather than marry

the unsuitable men their fathers had picked out for them.
Shrewd women both, they were her councillors, and Lovyan
knew that no matter how much intrigue might rage around a
powerful court, she could count on both for absolute honesty.

"I rather find myself missing Tingyr tonight," Lovyan said.
"It's so rare that I do, but as a husband, he had his good points."

"He understood matters of war, truly," Dannyan said.

"So, Dann, you don't think that these so-called bandits are
real bandits?"

"I don't. I was wondering if we should send a message to
Sligyn."

"That's a very good idea. We can send one of the stable lads.
The young rider who just came back must be dead tired."

Lovyan was about to call over Caradoc when she heard a
clatter in the ward—men and horses riding in, and servants
shouting as they ran to meet them. Half thinking it might be
Rhodry, Lovyan rose from her chair, but it was Sligyn who strode
into the great hall, and right behind him was Nevyn.

"By the gods, my lord," Lovyan said. "I was just going to
send you a message."

"No doubt, Your Grace." Sligyn bent his knee in a bob that
passed for a kneel. "Our good herbman here's been telling me
that Rhodry went off like a madman to chase bandits. Bandits?
Hah!"

"I just happened to see them on the road, Your Grace,"
Nevyn said. He gave her a wink to ask her to share the ruse. "I
was gathering valerian root out in the wilderness."

"Could have been cow dung for all I care," Sligyn said. "I'm
cursed glad you had the wit to ride straight to me. Your Grace,
I've had troubling news beyond what our Nevyn tells me."

Lovyan realized that armed men were filling the hall—
twenty, thirty, close to forty, most of Sligyn's warband.

"Dannyan, send a servant to fetch those men ale," Lovyan
said. "Nevyn, come have a bit of mead with us. I think me you've
earned it."

Once they were settled, Sligyn told his tale. Not twenty
minutes after Nevyn came in with his news, a messenger arrived
from Lord Edar, whose demesne was in the north close to
Corbyn's. Corbyn and his allies had mustered their army. Edar
himself was sending his wife and children to shelter with her

brother in the east, and he and his warband were coming to Cannobaen.

"He'll arrive in two days," Sligyn said. "The messenger was going to ride on to you, but I decided to take the news on myself. I took the liberty of sending it along to the rest of your loyal men. Thought we didn't have any time to waste."

"My thanks," Lovyan said. "I'm afraid I don't have the men to ride messages, anyway."

"So Nevyn told me, and a grim thing that is. Here, Your Grace, if an army had turned up at your gates, how long could you and the servants have held Dun Cannobaen?"

"Long enough for you to relieve us, my lord, but I'm glad I don't have to put that boast to the test."

"Just so." Sligyn had a thoughtful sip of mead. "Well, the rest of your allies should ride in on the morrow. I told them to ride at night if they had to. We'll leave you a good fort guard before we go."

"Will you ride north after Corbyn?"

"West, my lady. Rhodry's out in the wilderness with what? fifty men and whatever excuses for guards that merchant had. Corbyn's mustered at least two hundred men, and I'll wager he's on his way west right now."

Lovyan bit her lip hard to keep from crying out.

"Don't distress yourself unduly, Your Grace," Nevyn broke in. "Later, I'll have a few interesting things to tell you."

"My lord," Aderyn said. "I know you have no reason to believe me, but I swear I'm telling the truth."

Rhodry felt like grabbing the man by the shoulders and shaking him. For an hour now he'd listened to so much talk of dweomer that he felt as if the strange words and stranger tales were water that would physically drown him. He turned to Cullyn, sitting beside him at the campfire out in the ward. In the dancing firelight, the silver dagger's impassive face was unreadable.

"I'd believe him, my lord," Cullyn said. "Didn't he tell us about the ambush? For that matter, didn't he tell us that you were on the way?"

"True enough," Rhodry said with a groan. "Well and good

then, Aderyn, if you say that Sligyn's coming with an army, then we'll stay here and wait for him."

"My thanks, my lord," Aderyn said. "If I might make a suggestion, on the morrow you might want to have some of your men cut down trees to barricade that gap in the walls. Dregydd has some axes left from his trading."

"Good idea," Rhodry said. "By the black hairy ass of the Lord of Hell, I feel like such a dolt!"

"His lordship is nothing of the sort," Aderyn said. "The trap was very well laid, and you had no way of knowing that Loddlaen was using dweomer to put thoughts into your mind. It's just a cursed good thing that Loddlaen had no way of knowing about Nevyn."

Rhodry shuddered profoundly.

"But there's one small thing I don't understand," Aderyn went on. "Why didn't Corbyn have his whole army out here to wait for you?"

"Simple," Cullyn broke in. "If he'd marched west with his full force, every lord in the north would have seen him, and they would have mustered and followed him straightaway. But he and his allies could slip a few men out, a couple at a time, no doubt, and then follow with the rest. If his cursed plan had worked, he would have been a full day's march ahead of Rhodry's allies. Oh, they'd have caught us on the road, sure enough."

"They might catch us here instead," Rhodry said. "Aderyn, do you know how close Corbyn is?"

"I don't, but if his lordship will excuse me, I intend to find out."

For a while Rhodry and Cullyn sat together in a companionable silence and watched the leaping fire. All around them, the men slept, rolled up in their blankets. For all that Cullyn was a dishonored silver dagger, Rhodry found his presence comforting. Here, at least, was a man he could understand.

"It's cursed strange," Rhodry said. "Here I've heard of your glory, of course, and I've always wanted to meet you, but I was thinking it might be under better circumstances than this."

"Oh, I don't know, my lord. I couldn't think of a better time for you to ride my way."

Rhodry laughed.

"True enough," Rhodry said. "Huh, if the caravan hadn't

sent a messenger to me, I suppose Loddlaen would have sent one
of his men, claiming to be a guard or suchlike. You just spared him
the trouble by sending your lad."

"My lad?" Cullyn gave him a grin. "Here, my lord, Jill's my
daughter."

"Oh by the hells! Here I rode with her all day, and I never
once thought she was a lass."

Sometime later Jill came to sit with her father. She'd apparently washed her face and hair in the stream, because the dirt
was gone, revealing a face that was obviously not only female, but
beautiful. Or, at least, it would have been beautiful if it weren't
for the black-and-blue bruise on her face.

"Where did you get that bruise?" Cullyn said to her.

"You gave it to me this morning," Jill said.

"Oh by the hells, so I did. Forgive me, my sweet. I was half to
pieces, thinking you'd be slain."

Jill turned to Cullyn and gave him a smile that made her
beauty as delicate and glowing as that of any court lady. Rhodry's
heart sank. It was cursed unfair of the gods to give a lass like this a
father who happened to be the best swordsman in the whole
wide kingdom of Deverry.

All morning the tieryn's loyal men rode to the muster at Dun
Cannobaen. Following Sligyn's orders, they'd ridden fast, leaving
their provision carts to follow the army at their own slow pace,
under the guard of the common-born spearmen that their various towns owed them in time of war. Nevyn sat off to one side of
the great hall and kept an eye on Lovyan as she greeted first Lord
Oledd, then Peredyr, then Daumyr, and finally Manydd, who
was the captain of the warband stationed at Dun Gwerbyn. At
last over two hundred men were crowded into the great hall.
Lovyan was taking the strain well, greeting each leader calmly.
The only emotion she allowed herself was the occasional outburst
of wrath at the rebel Corbyn, a wrath that was fitting for a tieryn.
About an hour before noon, Sligyn rose to his feet and announced
that they had enough men to set out.

"The lads from farther away will ride in tomorrow," Sligyn
announced to all and sundry. "But we can't wait, eh?"

When the lords nodded their agreement, Nevyn could see
tension on their faces. Just how many of those vassals would

indeed arrive, and how many go over to the rebels? Only the final count of the muster would answer that question. Lovyan named Sligyn cadvridoc until the army should meet up with Rhodry, and in a bustle of talk and the jingle of mail, lords and warbands alike got up and began filing out of the hall. In the confusion Nevyn hurried to Lovyan's side. She led him back to the hearth for a few private words.

"Does Rhodry still live?" Lovyan said.

"He does. Aderyn contacted me naught but an hour ago. There's no sign of trouble so far today. With this army coming, it would behoove Corbyn to withdraw to safer territory. No doubt Loddlaen will advise his lord to do so."

After so many years of hearing him talk of dweomer, Lovyan took this news of dweomer turned to evil ends calmly. Nevyn himself, however, was seriously concerned about the depths of the evil into which Loddlaen had fallen.

"Which would you rather have me do?" Nevyn said. "Stay with you, or ride with the army?"

"Ride, of course, and not just for the sake of my feelings. I keep remembering what you said to me the first time we met, when Rhodry had the terrible congestion of the lungs. Rhodry's Wyrd is Eldidd's Wyrd, you told me." Lovyan paused, watching armed men swagger out the door. "I love Eldidd more than my son. Keep him safe for her."

Although the army was traveling light, there were packhorses in the rear carrying a few days' provisions to tide it over until the carts caught up. Since as far as anyone knew, Nevyn was an herbman and nothing more, he rode in the rear as well, with his pack mule behind him. Up at the head of the line, Sligyn set a fast pace, alternately walking and trotting. Although with their late start they would never reach Rhodry by nightfall, Sligyn intended to get to him as early as possible on the morrow. Nevyn was glad of the speed for his own private reasons. Aderyn, of course, had told him who was waiting at the ruined dun. Soon, if all went well, just on the morrow, he would at last see his Brangwen again.

"I wish we could cremate him," Jennantar said in a thin flat voice. "But there's no wood and no sacred oil."

"A grave will do," Calonderiel said. "He's dead, my friend. It won't matter one cursed jot to him what we do with his flesh."

Jennantar nodded in a miserable agreement and went on digging Albaral's grave. Jill kept an eye on him as the two men of the Westfolk worked, sweating in the hot sun as the narrow trench grew deeper and deeper. The night before, Jennantar had been so hysterical with grief that Aderyn had given him a strong draught of sleeping potion. Now he seemed merely light-headed and a little sick, like a man who had drunk too much mead the night before. At last they were done; they threw the shovels to one side, then picked up Albaral's body, wrapped in a blanket, and laid him in. For a moment all three of them stood in respectful silence for the dead. All at once, Jennantar tossed back his head and howled with rage. Before either Jill or Calonderiel could stop him, he drew his knife and made a shallow gash on his forearm.

"Vengeance!" he screamed. "I'll have blood to match mine for this!"

Jennantar held his arm over the grave and let the blood drip, spattering the blanket.

"I witness your vow," Calonderiel said softly.

Jennantar nodded and let the blood run. Suddenly Jill saw or thought she saw Albaral's shade, a pale blue flickering form, something just barely visible in the sunlight. She was afraid she would choke, afraid that she was going daft. Jennantar howled out a wordless cry, then ran blindly away, crashing into a thicket of trees far downstream. The shade, if indeed it had ever been there, was gone.

"We'd best leave him alone with his grief," Calonderiel said. "I'll fill this in."

"I'll help." Jill took a shovel gladly; she wanted to forget what she might have just seen.

When they were finished, they went back to the dun and found an open spot by the back wall where Calonderiel could work at straightening the arrows he'd salvaged from the battle-field. The Westfolk had a special tool for that, the shoulder blade of a deer pierced with a hole just the diameter of a shaft.

"We didn't bring a cursed lot of arrows with us," he remarked. "I never dreamt we'd be riding into the middle of a war. Are there good fletchers in this part of the world?"

"I wouldn't know. I've never shot a bow myself."

Calonderiel frowned down at the mangled fletching on the arrow in his hands. His eyes were a deep purple, as rich and dark as Bardek velvet.

"I might as well cut these off," he said. "Curse it—I've left the proper knife in my gear."

"Borrow this." Jill drew her silver dagger. "It's cursed sharp."

He whistled under his breath and took the dagger from her. When he ran one finger down the flat of the blade, the weapon glowed with a light strong enough to be visible even in the daylight.

"Dwarven silver!" he said. "You don't see a lot of this around, do you?"

"What did you call it?"

"Dwarven silver. Isn't that what it is? Where did you get this, anyway?"

"From a smith named Otho on the Deverry border."

"And this Otho was a short man." He gave her a sly grin. "But stocky for all his lack of height."

"He was. Don't tell me you know him!"

"Not him, truly, but his people."

Jill was too puzzled by the way her dagger was behaving to wonder about Otho's clan. She took it back and turned it this way and that to watch the soft sheen of light playing on the surface. In her hands, it was much dimmer.

"I've never seen it glow like this," she said.

"It's because of me. Otho's folk don't care for the likes of me. They like to know when one of us is around, because they think we're a pack of thieves."

Jill looked up sharply.

"Elcyion Lacar," she whispered. "Elves."

"Call us what you like," he said with a laugh. "But we've been given those names before, true enough."

One at a time, like slow raindrops falling into a still pond, Wildfolk manifested around him, a blue sprite, two warty gnomes, the thick shimmer of air that meant a sylph, as if they were hounds, come to lie at their master's feet.

"And what's the true name of your people, then?" Jill said.

"Oh, now, that's somewhat I'll never tell you. You have to

earn the right to hear that name, and of all your folk, Aderyn's the only one who has." Calonderiel smiled, taking any insult from his words. "Now, I've heard some of the tales you folk tell about us. We're not thieves, and we're not demons from hell or closer to the gods than you are, either, but simple flesh and blood like you. Old Aderyn tells me that our gods fashioned us from the Wildfolk, just like your gods fashioned you from animals, and so here we are, together on the earth for good or ill."

"Here, our priests say the gods made us from earth and water."

"The dweomer knows a cursed lot more than priests; remember that well. May I have the borrowing of that dagger again? I've got a cursed lot of work to do."

Jill handed it back. For a long time she sat and watched it glow like fire in his hands, while she wondered over the strange things he'd told her.

Toward noon, Jill saw the great silver owl circle the broch and disappear inside, a sight that made her shudder. She ran after it and found Cullyn and Rhodry talking together at the foot of the stairs. In a few minutes Aderyn came down, swinging his arms and flexing his shoulders like a man who's just swum a very long way in a strong sea.

"I found them, my lord," Aderyn said. "They're staying in camp about fifteen miles to the northeast."

"Well and good, then," Rhodry said. "We might as well ride out and meet Sligyn."

"That might be unwise, my lord," Cullyn broke in. "They won't risk besieging the dun with an army coming at their back, but they might make a desperate ride to catch you if you were out in the open."

"And how will they know if we—oh by every god and his wife, what a dolt I am! Of course they'll know."

"You know, silver dagger," Aderyn went on. "I'd take it most kindly if you stuck close to Lord Rhodry when things come to battle. If the rebels are going to succeed, they have to kill him before they've caused so much damage that Gwerbret Rhys is forced to intervene. No doubt that's why they're not attacking Sligyn's army. They can't risk killing the noble-born unless Rhodry's there as a possible prize."

"Just that," Cullyn said. "Here, I thought you said you didn't understand matters of war. Sounds to me like you were being cursed modest."

"Oh, I'm just repeating what Nevyn told me."

Rhodry and Cullyn nodded thoughtfully at this meaningless remark.

"Aderyn, I don't understand," Jill broke in. "You say that no one told you?"

"Oh!" The old man chuckled under his breath. "My apologies, child. I have a friend named Nevyn. His father gave him the name as some kind of bitter jest, if I remember rightly."

Since Otho the smith was very much on her mind, Jill suddenly remembered his riddle, that someday no one would tell her what craft to follow. If he were a friend of Aderyn's, this "no one" had to be a dweomerman, too. While the men went on talking of the coming war, Jill slipped away and ran out of the dun. By the stream that ran behind it she sat down and watched the water sparkling with Wildfolk, who raised themselves up like waves to greet her. For a moment, she couldn't breathe. The dweomer seemed to have swooped out of the sky like a falcon, and it had her in its claws.

The waiting got on everyone's nerves as the hot summer day dragged on. With nothing but stream water to drink and meager, stale provisions from Dregydd's stores to eat, the warband was in a sullen mood, while the merchant and his muleteers crept around in numb panic. Everywhere Rhodry walked, he heard the men talking of dweomer, and he could no longer cheerily dismiss their fears. Finally he went down to the gates, newly barricaded with big logs, and found Cullyn there, leaning meditatively against the barricade on folded arms and watching the ravens wheel over the dead horses out in the meadow.

"At least old Dregydd had shovels with him," Rhodry said. "Enemies or not, it would have ached my heart to leave those men unburied."

"That's cursed honorable of you, my lord."

"Well." Rhodry shrugged the compliment off. "I've been thinking about what old Aderyn asked you, about sticking close to me in the scraps, I mean. They're going to be riding to mob me, sure enough, and I'd never ask a man to put himself in that kind of danger. Ride where you will on the field."

"Then I'll ride next to you."

When Rhodry swung around to look at him, Cullyn gave him an easy smile.

"My Wyrd will come when it comes," Cullyn said. "It gripes my heart to think of a decent man like you being killed for a handful of coin. What are these lords, silver daggers?"

"Well, my thanks. Truly, my thanks. I'm honored that a man like you would think so highly of me."

"A man like me, my lord?" Cullyn touched the hilt of his silver dagger, as if to remind Rhodry of his shame.

"Ah by the hells, what do I care what you did twenty years ago or whenever it was? You've ridden through more rough scraps than a lord like me ever even hears about."

"Well, maybe, my lord, but I—"

In the ward behind them, yells exploded, jeers and curses and ill-natured taunts from the warband. Over it all, like the shriek of a raven, floated Jill's voice, shrill with rage.

"Oh by the hells!" Cullyn turned on his heel and ran.

Rhodry was right behind him. As they came round the side of the broch, they saw half the warband gathered round Jill, who yelled foul insults back as fast as they yelled them at her. Caenrydd came running from the other direction and elbowed himself into the mob, pulling or slapping his men away impartially, like a hunter slapping the dogs off the kill.

"Now what's all this, you young swine?" Caenrydd said. "I'll put stripes on your backs if you've been doing the wrong things to this lass."

"It isn't that at all," Jill said, shaking in fury. "They've been saying I don't have the right to carry this sword. Just let one of the little bastards try to take it away from me."

When the warband surged forward, Rhodry shoved his way through the pack, which fell back at the sight of him.

"My apologies, fair maid." Rhodry made her a bow.

"I don't want any cursed apology!" Jill snarled, adding a "my lord" as an afterthought. "I meant what I said. Just let one of them try to take it away. A challenge, I mean. Come on, you bastards, I'll take any one of you on with my bare hands—if you have the balls to face me."

Rhodry was struck speechless. Cullyn reached his side, and he was smiling wryly.

"My lord?" he said. "I've learned it's best to let Jill settle these things her own way."

"What?" Rhodry and Caenrydd spoke together. "She'll get hurt."

"If I thought that," Cullyn said levelly, "I'd have my sword out and swinging right now. I've seen this kind of scrap a hundred times, my lord, and I'll wager Jill wins handily."

"Done, then," Rhodry said. "One silver piece gets you two if your lass wins."

Shaking his head in bewilderment, Caenrydd set up a fair fight between Jill and Praedd, a beefy man who was the best brawler in the warband. Praedd was grinning at the easy fight ahead as he handed his sword belt over to Caenrydd. By then, every man in the dun was crowded round the contest ground. Rhodry noticed Aderyn, watching in horrified alarm, and the two men of the Westfolk, who were making wagers on Jill against any man who'd take them on.

"Well and good, then," Caenrydd said, stepping clear. "It's on."

Jill and Praedd began to circle around each other, hands raised and ready. Praedd charged, swinging confidently, only to find Jill dodging in from the side. She grabbed his wrist as he punched, dropped to one knee, and somehow, just like dweomer, two-hundred-pound Praedd flew through the air and landed with a grunt amid the weeds. Still game, he scrambled back up, but this time he moved in cautiously. They feinted, dodged; Praedd swung in low from the side. Jill leapt straight up, kicked him in the stomach, and twisted down like a dancing girl. Gasping, Praedd doubled over, then forced himself upright. Jill danced in and clipped him neatly and precisely on the chin. With a sigh, Praedd closed his eyes and fell forward on the ground.

The Westfolk yelled in triumph, and Cullyn laughed softly under his breath, but the warband was utterly silent, staring at Jill in disbelief and sideways at Rhodry in shame. Jill set her hands on her hips and glared at them.

"Anyone else?" she said.

"Jill, enough!" Cullyn called out. "You've made your cursed point, and I have to ride with them."

"True spoken," Rhodry said, stepping forward. "All right, men, go pour water over your sleeping comrade there. And don't feel shamed on my account—I've just lost a good bit of silver myself."

Still, they must have felt the dishonor at.the hands of a lass, because they frankly fled, stopping only long enough to scoop up Praedd and carry him away, with the Westfolk trailing after to make sure they collected their coppers. Rhodry made Jill a deep bow.

"And where by the hells did you learn to fight like that?" Rhodry said.

"Da taught me somewhat, my lord, and I figured the rest out for myself."

Jill wiped the sweat off her face onto her shirt sleeve like a man, but still Rhodry's heart skipped a beat. He'd never seen a lass like her, and she was lovely, oh so lovely. Then he realized that Cullyn was watching him with a certain paternal suspicion.

"I'll get those coins out of my saddlebags for you," Rhodry said. "And you'd best keep your hellcat here away from the warband for a while."

"I will, my lord. Have no fear of that."

As Rhodry hurried away, he was cursing himself for an utter fool. He knew that he should put this common-born lass with the dangerous father out of his mind for good, but he also knew that for some bizarre reason, he was falling in love again.

That night, Lord Sligyn's army camped on the banks of the stream that would eventually lead them to Rhodry. The men gathered in little groups, their campfires like flowers of light out in the dark wild meadow. As Nevyn wandered through the camp, he came across a man he knew, Sandyr, who rode for Lord Sligyn. A year ago, Nevyn had pulled a bad tooth for him and cured the infection, and apparently Sandyr remembered it kindly.

"It's Nevyn," Sandyr said. "Here, sit down at our fire, good sir. This is Arcadd and Yvyr. Lads, this is the best herbman that ever rode the kingdom."

Sandyr's two comrades greeted Nevyn with small smiles and nods of their heads. Like Sandyr, they were no more than twenty, but they had the hard-eyed dignity of men tried by war.

"I was cursed glad when I saw you in the train," Sandyr said. "I'd rather have you along than our lord's chirurgeon any day."

"Oh, he's a good man," Nevyn said. "He just doesn't know teeth the way I do."

"Maybe so." Sandyr rubbed his jaw at the memory of that long-gone abscess. "But let's hope that none of us need your cures after a scrap."

"Or here," Arcadd said with a twisted grin. "I don't suppose you have any herbs to protect a man against dweomer."

All three laughed uneasily.

"Well, now, there aren't any herbs like that," Nevyn said. "I take it you all believe the rumors going around."

"Doesn't every man in the army?" Sandyr said. "But it's not just wild talk. A couple of us have ridden to Corbyn's dun with messages and suchlike. I've talked to men who saw this Loddlaen do things."

"Do things?"

"I saw this myself," Yvyr broke in, and his broad face was pale. "Back in the spring, it was, when our lord was trying to talk Corbyn out of rebelling. Lord Sligyn sends me to Bruddlyn with messages. And Corbyn treated me well enough, giving me dinner with his men. So there were these big logs laid in fresh on the honor hearth, and Loddlaen comes down with Corbyn. I swear it, good sir, I saw Loddlaen snap his fingers, like, and flames sprang up all over the logs, and they were big logs, no kindling or suchlike."

"And then one of Lord Oledd's men went to Bruddlyn, too," Sandyr said. "He walks in and Corbyn says, well, Loddlaen told me you were coming. The men in his warband swear he knows everything that goes on for miles and miles."

"It makes you wonder what else he can do," Arcadd said. "Here, Nevyn, if you know herbcraft, you must know bones and muscles and suchlike. Do you think a dweomerman could turn someone into a frog?"

"I don't," Nevyn said firmly. "That's nothing but a silly bard's fancy. Now here, think. All those tales say that the frogs are just ordinary frogs, right? Well, if someone did get turned into a frog, it would have to be a cursed big one. You can't just go shrinking a man's flesh down to nothing, but the tales never say a thing about frogs big enough to ride."

All three laughed and relaxed at the jest.

"Well and good, then," Sandyr said. "I pledged I'd die for my lord, and I don't give the fart of a two-copper pig if it's dweomer or a sword that kills me, but cursed if I liked the idea of hopping around in a marsh the rest of my days."

"The lasses you'd have," Arcadd said mournfully. "All green and warty."

Nevyn joined in the general laughter. Jests were the best weapon these men had against the fear preying upon them.

Toward midnight, when the camp was asleep except for the night watch, Nevyn sat over the dying coals of his fire to contact Aderyn. After their long years of friendship, all he had to do was think of Aderyn briefly before he saw the image of Aderyn's face building up and floating just above the red glow.

"There you are," Nevyn thought to him. "Are you in a position to talk?"

"I am," Aderyn thought in return. "The camp's asleep. I was just going to contact you, truly. Corbyn's army is still camped where I saw it last."

"No doubt they're going to wait till we're out of the dun, and then make a try at killing Rhodry. Is Loddlaen still with them?"

"He is. Ah ye gods, my heart's half torn apart. What a dolt I was to train the lad!"

Nevyn bit back the all-too-human temptation to say, "I told you so." Aderyn's image smiled sourly, as if he knew cursed well that Nevyn was thinking it.

"But I did," Aderyn went on. "And now his misdoings are my responsibility—you don't have to tell me that twice. What counts now is ending the matter."

"Just so. Do you still think he's merely insane?"

"I do. If he'd truly gone over to the Dark Path and its foul ways, he'd be hiding himself, not flaunting his gifts and meddling with petty lords."

"Now that's true spoken. Here, you know Loddlaen better than I ever will. It seems clear that he's stirred up this cursed rebellion. Why? Is he trying to escape being brought to justice for that murder he did? If so, his scheme won't work. It doesn't matter who Corbyn's overlord is—Gwerbret Rhys would haul him into the malover as readily as Lovyan would."

"True spoken, and I've been puzzling myself over this very question. At first I thought he had some scheme of killing me or at least the other two witnesses I'm bringing, but if that were

true, why involve Rhodry and half the tierynrhyn? It doesn't
make sense."

"It doesn't, and I think me we'd best find out just what he
thinks he's up to."

Aderyn laughed, a harsh mutter.

"If we can," he said. "That's the crux, my friend. If we can."

After he finished talking with Aderyn, Nevyn sat up brooding for a long time, hoping that Aderyn was right about Loddlaen
only being mad. Truly, the lad had been unstable from the beginning. Studying dweomer demands a perfect stability of mind, a
core of simple common sense, in fact, because the forces that
dweomer invokes can tear an unstable mind to pieces, leaving it
prey to delusions and fantasies. Loddlaen had never had iron in
his soul, only the malleable silver of a raw psychic talent that
should have been suppressed, not encouraged. At least, if Aderyn
was right, Loddlaen was only misusing his dweomer, not immers-
ing himself in strange and unclean things. Just as every light casts
a shadow, so does a dark dweomer exist. The men who study it
(and they never open their foul ranks to women) lust after power
above all else and hoard it like misers, never helping but only
harming other souls. They grub around the dark places of the
Innerlands for peculiar magicks and keep themselves alive unnaturally by feeding on the vitality of spirits and living people
alike. Nevyn was sworn to destroy such as them wherever he
found them, and they knew it, and hid from him.

Scattered over a wild meadow, the army of Lord Corbyn and
his allies lay asleep under the starry sky. Surefooted in the dark,
Loddlaen picked his way through the camp and out with a muttered word to one of the guards. The stink of so many unwashed
humans was making him feel ill, and he walked a good long ways
away from camp before he flung himself down in the grass to
rest. He was tired—he was always tired these days—yet when
night came, he could not sleep. He pressed both hands against his
forehead and tried to steady himself. The despised smell that
he'd left behind him seemed to cling to his clothes. Suddenly he
saw the smell, a thick gray cloud of smoke, swirling around him in
some unfelt wind. It was only a vision, an illusion, but he had to
fight to banish it. Many visions came to him unbidden these days,
just odd little things, voices half heard, things half seen, and

always he could understand the cause, but still they were terrifying, because he knew that they should never have come at all. A dweomerman works long years to open his mind to the Innerlands, but at the same time he has to close his mind at will, to draw a veil between himself and unseen things. No matter how hard Loddlaen tried to close that veil, things slipped through.

When he looked up at the stars, they were dancing and leaping, sending long points of light like reflections off a polished blade. Hastily he looked away, but things seemed to be crawling through the grass, like little weasels, sniffing him out. He flung up one hand and made the banishing sigils in the air. When he looked, the weasel things were gone, and the stars steady. With a sigh that was half a groan, he flung himself facedown to lie full length in the grass. The broken light from the stars seemed to dance in his mind, dazzling him. He summoned up an image of darkness, a soft warm darkness like sleep, and let the image suffuse his mind until at last it seemed to him that he stood inside that warm, comforting dark, safe at last. He'd stumbled upon this trick of summoning a dark some months before; it was the only way he could get any rest. Now, it came to him easily, swiftly, every time he called, as if it came of its own will.

Yet even wrapped in dark, he could not sleep. His hatred was there in the blackness with him, the hatred he bore toward the stinking human beings he was forced to use as allies, and even more, the hatred he bore toward the Elcyion Lacar. It seemed he heard his hatred talking to him in a child's voice, until that voice became his own. There he'd been, practically an outcast in the elven camps, and all because his father was a wretched human being. Oh, everyone had been kind to him; that was the worst wound of all, the galling way that everyone had been ever so kind, as if he were a half-wit who needed tender care. They were smug, the Elcyion Lacar, so smug, secure in knowing that they'd live to six, maybe even seven hundred years, while as for him, well, how long did a half-breed live, anyway? No one truly knew; at any moment, he might look in the mirror and see the beginnings of that inevitable human corruption into death that men called old age. He hated them all, men and elves alike.

The hatred burned so bright that it threatened to wipe the darkness away. Loddlaen steadied himself and thought only of the dark, let it soothe and blanket him. Voices came out of the darkness, as they usually did, comforting him, agreeing with him that he'd been ill used, promising him that he would get his revenge on the Elcyion Lacar and Eldidd men both.

"Loddlaen the Mighty," the voices said. "Master of the Powers of Air, no man can touch you, no man can best you, not you, Loddlaen the Mighty."

"It's true," he answered them in his mind. "I shall have vengeance."

"Splendid vengeance for all that these dogs made you suffer." This voice was as soft and smooth as perfumed oil. "Remember, slay Rhodry Maelwaedd, and all the vengeance you have ever sought will be yours. Rhodry must die—remember, remember."

"I remember, and I swear to you I will."

He heard a ripple of satisfied laughter, and then the darkness turned thick and warm. At last, he could sleep.

At dawn on the morrow, the camp came awake fast. Lord Sligyn walked through, yelling orders and keeping the men busy until the horses had grazed their fill and everyone was ready to march. All morning they pushed on fast upriver. Nevyn felt his excitement at seeing Brangwen turn to a curious sort of dread. What was her personality in this life like? What would she think of him? For all his vast age and true dweomer, Nevyn was man enough to want her to like him. Finally, about an hour before noon, they came to the ruined dun.

Rhodry and his men were at the gates to greet them with cheers. Since there wasn't enough room in the ward for the army to ride in, the men dismounted outside and sat with their horses while the noble-born went in. Looking for Aderyn, Nevyn slipped in, too, and found him and the two elves waiting for him by the dun wall. Jennantar and Calonderiel bowed low.

"Hail, Wise One of the East," Jennantar said. "I'd hoped to meet you again in better circumstances than these."

"I'd been hoping the same thing, truly. It aches my heart that your friend died for the sake of an Eldidd feud."

"We'll have vengeance for him," Calonderiel broke in. "Just like we will for all the others."

In his cat-slit eyes burned a wild rage. Even though the war to which he referred had been over for three hundred and fifty years, doubtless he still remembered the name of every elf slain in it. Foe or insult, the Elcyion Lacar never forgot and only rarely forgave. Although Aderyn liked to talk of what he called the essential goodness of the folk, they made Nevyn profoundly nervous.

"I know you must be eager to meet Jill," Aderyn said. "I saw her not a moment ago, but now she's off somewhere. Shall we go look for her?"

Yet Nevyn had to postpone the meeting for a little while, because Sligyn came striding up to them. He looked like a baffled bear when the hunting dogs first surround it.

"Now here, Nevyn," Sligyn bellowed. "I'm gravely worried. Young Rhodry's gone daft. Stark out of his mind."

"Indeed, my lord?" Nevyn said. "Let me guess the kind of delusions the lad's suffering from. He swears that Aderyn and I are both dweomer, and that Aderyn can turn himself into an owl."

"Just that. I—" Sligyn's mouth slackened as he finally realized that Nevyn was being sarcastic. "Oh now here! You're not telling me it's the truth, are you?"

"I am."

Sligyn swung his head back and forth, looking at both of them in turn, just as the bear swings his when the dogs close in.

"By the black hairy ass of the Lord of Hell, what have I done?" Sligyn said. "Ridden all this cursed way to rescue a pack of madmen? Even that silver dagger swears it's true."

"That's because it is true," Nevyn said. "I suppose I have to do some stupid trick to convince you." He glanced around and saw a stick of firewood in the grass. "Here, watch."

When Nevyn invoked the Wildfolk of Fire, they rushed to do his bidding and set the stick on fire. Sligyn swore, and he swore again when Nevyn had them douse it.

"You can touch it," Nevyn said. "It's hot."

Sligyn turned and ran back to the broch without so much as a backward glance. When the two elves burst out laughing, Aderyn snapped at them in their own language. Reluctantly they held their tongues.

"Go get ready to ride," Aderyn said. "Get my horse for me too, will you?"

Still grinning, Calonderiel and Jennantar hurried off. It was then that Nevyn saw Jill, standing at a little distance and watching him as warily as a stag in a forest. Without waiting for Aderyn to call to her, she walked over, studying him all the while. In spite of her dirty men's clothing, in spite of her face that was different than Brangwen's for all its beauty, Nevyn recognized her immediately. His first muddled thought was a surprise that she would be so tall.

"Good morrow, Jill," Nevyn said. "Our Aderyn's told me somewhat about you."

"Has he now? Good things, I hope."

"They were."

Nevyn wished that he could simply tell her the truth, use his dweomer to make her remember and pour out his heart to say how glad he was he'd found her again—all forbidden by his dweomer-vows. Jill was studying him coolly and curiously.

"But here," she said. "Haven't we met before? On the road or suchlike when I was a child?"

"We haven't."

"Then I must be thinking of someone else. Cursed strange— I could have sworn I'd met you."

For a moment Nevyn nearly wept. Even after all these years, she still remembered him.

After a good bit of argument, the noble lords worked out their next moves in the war. Since they had dweomermen on their side to keep track of Corbyn's movements, they could safely fall back to pick up their supply train, then head east, circling round in a feint designed to make Corbyn think that they were trying to bypass him in order to take his dun. Corbyn would be forced to follow, allowing them to pick the position for the inevitable battle. In the meantime, they could send messengers to any reinforcements coming from Dun Cannobaen. Cullyn idly wondered how many reinforcements they would get; the number depended on how many of Lovyan's vassals held steady for her.

After the council of war broke up, Cullyn found Jill by the gates of the dun. She had gotten both their horses saddled and ready and was holding their reins while she waited for him.

"I asked Lord Rhodry for a boon, and he granted it," Cullyn said. "You're going to be taking messages to Dun Cannobaen as soon as we join up with the supply train."

"Da! By the hells, I wanted to—"

"Do what? Ride to war with us? Sometimes, I swear that you've got nothing between your two ears!"

"I'll wager I could hold my own."

"Oh don't dribble on like a spewing drunkard! So what if you could? I'm not going to let you risk your life in battle when you're the only thing I've got in the world. You know what's wrong with you, my sweet? You're like all young riders—you think that death's only for other men, not for you. Well, I've given more than a few of those cocksure young lads their last drink of water and sat with them while they died. Cursed if I'll risk having to do the same for you."

His bluntness hit home. Jill looked down and began fiddling with the reins in her hand.

"I know what's aching your heart," he went on. "You think that I don't value your swordcraft. That's not true. You're good enough with the blade, but riding into a battle's a cursed different thing than playing out a mock combat to amuse a lord in his hall."

"Well, true enough." Jill looked up with a faint smile. "Da, do you truly think I'm good with a blade?"

"I do."

The way she smiled in childlike delight wrung his heart. It was at moments like these that Cullyn felt an ugly knowledge pressing at the edge of his mind, that maybe he loved his daughter far too well. He grabbed his horse's reins from her.

"Don't go getting all puffed up because I said that," he snapped. "You've got a cursed lot more to learn."

Leading the horse, he strode away to join Rhodry's warband. Although he knew how badly he'd hurt her, he refused to look back.

When the army headed south to meet the baggage train, Dregydd the merchant left them. Jill went over to say farewell to him, and he shook her hand vigorously for quite a long time.

"My thanks to you, lass," he said. "And to your Da, too. And here's a bit more than thanks. I know cursed well you both saved my life."

Dregydd slipped her a small pouch, heavy with coin, then trotted off to get his caravan in order. Rather than turning it over to her father, Jill kept the pouch. When this hire was over, they'd need the coin, and Da would only drink half of it away if she let him know that she had it.

When Jill fell back into line at the rear of the army, she found herself next to Nevyn, who greeted her too courteously for her to be able to just move away from him, as she rather wanted to do at first. All the dweomer around her was frightening in itself; that she seemed to understand some of it instinctively was terrifying. Yet much to her surprise, she found Nevyn pleasant company. In the bard songs, dweomermen were supposed to be grim and silent, with dark, haunted eyes marked by strange lore and stranger workings. But here was Nevyn with his candid blue eyes and ready smile, dressed like a farmer in a plain shirt and brown brigga instead of the long robes embroidered with peculiar signs and sigils of her fancies.

Since he'd seen even more of the kingdom than she had, they talked of their various travels. As the afternoon wore on, she found herself thinking of him as a long-lost grandfather whom sheer bad luck had kept her from meeting before.

"Tell me somewhat, child," Nevyn said at one point. "Your father seems an unusually decent man—the way he cared for you and all. Do you know what drove him to take the silver dagger?"

"I don't, and if I were you, I'd never ask him. But he took me with him because he loved my Mam so much. She died when I was just a little lass, you see, and at the time, I didn't understand at all. Da just rode in one day and off we went. But I've been thinking about it. Da had a cursed lot of coin from a noble lord's ransom, and I realized when I grew up that he was planning on settling down with us—getting a farm, maybe, somewhat like that. And there he rides in to find her dead. He was more than half mad that day."

"So he must have been, the poor lad. Ye gods, that was a cruel jest his Wyrd had on him, and on you and your Mam, too."

He spoke with a warm, sincere sympathy that took Jill by surprise. Somehow she'd always thought that people like a silver dagger and his bastard would be beneath the notice of a man who'd studied strange magicks. And yet Nevyn was an herbman, too, who tended the poor folk. He made the dweomer seem a human thing, but there was no doubting that it was dweomer nonetheless, and for some reason that she couldn't put into words, she was terrified by the very thought.

Late in the afternoon the army met the baggage train, a straggling long line of wooden carts, servants, and spearmen, just about three miles from the sea-coast. Since the carts carried ale, the men had a more pleasant camp that night. On the morrow, Cullyn woke Jill early.

"You'd best get ready to ride, my sweet," he said. "Lord Rhodry's going to want that message on its way."

"Well and good, Da, but I still wish you'd—"

When Cullyn raised his hand for a slap, Jill held her tongue.

"Have a good ride," he said. "And I'll see you when I do."

Cullyn walked away so fast that she knew that she wouldn't see him again before she rode. It was better that way; she hated saying farewell to him before a war because speaking the words made them both aware that it might be the last farewell they ever said.

All that morning, as the army made its slow way east, Nevyn and Aderyn rode together at the rear behind the carts and the servants. Although Rhodry had offered them a place of honor at the head of the line, they had a dangerous sort of rear guard to keep. At any moment, they might have to turn their horses out of line and dismount, because not even mighty masters of dweomer like they could assume a full trance on horseback without falling headlong into the road. No matter what the bards claim, the dweomer has its limits.

"I'm cursed grateful you'd come along," Aderyn said. "By rights, this little job should be mine alone."

"Well, you'll have to fight the last battle without me, sure enough, but I haven't spent years brooding over Rhodry like a hen with one egg just to have him killed by a pack of rebels. Here, do you think Loddlaen will try to attack you directly?"

"I don't know what to think. That's why I'm so glad you're here."

When Nevyn turned in the saddle to look at him, he realized that Aderyn was frightened.

"We've never faced each other in combat," Aderyn went on. "For all I know he's stronger than me, and I've never tried to kill a man in my life, while he's already murdered one. Ah by the hells, it's not my life I fear for, but my work. It isn't finished yet. I can't afford to waste all that cursed time being reborn and growing up again. You know as well as I do that without human dweomer on the border, there'll be open war between man and elf."

"So I do. Well, I'm going to do my best to convince your successor that she should take up the dweomer."

"And is that our Jill's Wyrd?"

"I'm not certain, of course, but I'm beginning to think so. First she'll have to be firmly rooted in the ways of her own kind. That's my task. And then? Well, the Lords of Light will give her omens when the time is ripe."

"Just so. But that's a long way away, and the Elcyion Lacar need me there now."

"Well, if worst comes to worst, I'll ride west. There are others in the kingdom who can do my work in Eldidd."

"My thanks. You can't know how much that eases my heart."

"Good. But you're not dead yet, my friend. If we stay on guard, we'll keep you alive, sure enough."

Near noon, one of the carts shattered a wheel—a common occurrence. Irritably Rhodry announced that the army might as well have its midday rest while the carter made repairs. The men spread out along one of those tiny streams so common in the Eldidd meadowlands and unsaddled their horses to let them roll, then clustered around the carts to get their rations. Since neither Nevyn nor Aderyn ever ate more than two spare meals a day, they had time for more important things. They turned their horses over to a servant and walked downstream until the noise and bustle of the army were far behind them.

"I want a look at things," Nevyn said.

"I'll admit that it'll gladden my heart if you can scry him out," Aderyn said with a wry smile. "I haven't done so much flying in years, and my arms ache all day long."

Nevyn shuddered. Even though he'd seen Aderyn fly many a time over the past years, there was just something about a shape-changer that creeped a man's flesh, even if that man had other dweomer himself.

"Then you haven't been scrying him out on the etheric?" Nevyn said.

"I'm quite simply afraid to meet him there until I test his strength some other way."

"That's doubtless wise. Well, I'll see what I can find out for you. I have the feeling the young cub will run like the hells were opening under him if he comes face to face with me."

Nevyn lay down on his back in the grass and crossed his arms over his chest. Aderyn stood nearby, ready to keep anyone from disturbing him. Nevyn slowed his breathing, then closed his eyes. In his mind, he pictured his body of light, a simple manlike form made out of a bluish glow and joined to his solar plexus with a silver cord. He refined the form until it seemed solid, then imagined that he was looking out of its eyes and transferred his consciousness over. He heard a sharp click, like a sword striking a shield, and felt his body drop away. He was indeed looking out of the simulacrum's eyes at his sleeping body lying about ten feet below him. Nearby, Aderyn's aura was a pulsing egg of soft golden light, his body just visible within it.

Rust red with a vegetable aura, the meadowlands spread out under the shimmering blue light of the etheric plane. The stream was a tall veil of elemental force, extending about fifty feet into the air, like a silver waterfall with no river above. Nevyn floated up higher, the silver cord paying out behind him, until he was about a hundred yards away from his body. Upstream the army was a fiery glow of intermingled auras, pulsing and swarming as the men walked around, a mix of many colors, but the predominant one was the blood red of true killers. To Nevyn it was an ugly sight, but he'd be looking for another just like it. He went up higher, then flew, gliding over the landscape below in the cold blue light.

As he headed north, the Wildfolk came to join him. Here on their true plane of existence, they had no bodies at all but were beautiful, shimmering nexuses of lines of colored light. At times they refracted out into a pattern like the glimmer of a bright star; at others, they shrank to a little core of consciousness. As Nevyn's body of light carried his mind along, the Wildfolk wheeled around him like seagulls around a ship. As much as Nevyn loved them, they were also a cursed nuisance. If Loddlaen happened to be up on the etheric, he would see this army of lights coming from miles away. When Nevyn told them firmly to depart, the

Wildfolk fled. He had been accepted by their kings, and they obeyed him like a great lord.

After some time—as much as one can measure time on the etheric, anyway—Nevyn saw a glowing dome of light in a meadow off to one side of his path. He checked his flight and drifted over to examine it. The pale silver dome covered fully an acre, and it was marked at the four cardinal points and the zenith by flaming pentagrams traced in different colors and set round with the sigils of the elements. It was altogether a showy and pretentious job of setting an astral seal. Under it, doubtless, lay Corbyn's army, and its presence told Nevyn just how afraid of Aderyn Loddlaen must be, to exert so much energy to build himself a shelter. Nevyn drifted up until he hovered over the pentagram that shone with the pale purple of the element of Aethyr.

"In the name of the kings," Nevyn thought. "Allow me to pass by."

Like a hatch cover on a ship, the pentagram lifted up to make a door in the dome. So much for Loddlaen's mighty magicks, Nevyn thought sourly, he might well be daft, at that. Slowly and cautiously Nevyn sank down through the door. Loddlaen might well have felt his entry and be coming to meet him, yet he saw nothing but the pulsing swarming red mass of the army below. He dropped down close enough to begin to sort out the shapes of the overlapped auras of men and horses, but it was impossible to count them. Rhodry would have to be content with the information that Corbyn's army was much the same size as his own.

As he drifted this way and that, Nevyn saw a pair of men off by themselves and floated over for a better look. One aura was blood-red shot with darkness, and it spun unevenly around the body within. A thin rope of gauzy light fastened it to the other, a shifting, pulsating mass of color that changed as Nevyn watched from gold to sickly olive green. Nevyn could easily guess that the red aura belonged to Corbyn, ensorceled and bound to Loddlaen. Loddlaen's aura changed again to mottled brown and gold, then swelled only to contract suddenly. Ah ye gods, Nevyn thought, he's so far gone that it's a miracle he can work dweomer at all! He watched for a few minutes more, but never did he see the black lines of stress in the aura, which would have indicated Loddlaen was working the dark dweomer.

Nevyn shot up through the door in the seal and closed it behind him, then flew back as fast as he could, following the silver cord that inexorably led to his body. He was about halfway along when the Wildfolk appeared, a frightened crowd, swelling, shining, and beating about him. He stopped his flight and tried to understand what they were trying to tell him. Since they had no words, only waves of feeling, all he could sort out was that something had frightened them while he was in the dome. He thanked them for the warning—for warning it seemed to be— then went back on his way. At last he saw Aderyn's clear golden aura and his own body, a lump of dead-looking matter. Slowly he slid down the silver cord and hovered just above. All he had to do then was relax and let his mind follow the pull of the flesh. He dropped, heard another sharp click, and then he was looking out of his physical eyes at Aderyn, standing above him. Nevyn absorbed the body of light back into himself, slapped his hand thrice on the ground as a sign that the operation was over, and sat up.

"Did you find him?" Aderyn said.

"I did." Nevyn hesitated, but there was no easy way to break the news. "You are right. Loddlaen is mad, stark raving mad."

Aderyn wept, sobbing aloud like an elf. Nevyn patted him on the shoulder and tried to think of something comforting to say. There wasn't. Loddlaen, after all, was Aderyn's only son.

While he swilled a wooden cup of ale, Lord Corbyn looked at Loddlaen with all the devotion of a well-trained dog. Raven-haired, blue-eyed, Corbyn had once been a good-looking man, but now his eyes were puffy and his cheeks mottled with fine red lines. Loddlaen hated him, but he was a necessary tool, since he had reasons of his own to want Rhodry Maelwaedd dead. The darkness voice had promised Loddlaen that if Rhodry died, soon men and elves would kill each other all down the border. Loddlaen gloated over the promise like a jewel.

"As soon as the men finish the noon meal," Corbyn was saying, "we'll be on our way and after him. They'll be moving slower now that they have their supply train."

Loddlaen started to reply, but the darkness swirled out of

nowhere and enveloped his mind. It was the first time that it had come unbidden, and Loddlaen was terrified.

"Fear not," came the silky voice. "I'm your friend, and I've come to warn you. Someone has been spying on you. Someone breached your astral seal. Beware. Stay on guard."

Then the voice and the darkness were gone, so fast that Corbyn apparently had noticed nothing.

"Does that plan suit you, councillor?" he said.

"It does." Abruptly Loddlaen rose and shoved his hands into his brigga pockets to hide their shaking. "I know I can always trust you in matters of war."

Without another word he stalked off, leaving Corbyn puzzled behind him, and walked to the edge of the area covered by the astral dome. Yet he was too shaken to check his various seals. For the first time, it occurred to him to wonder just who it was who spoke to him in the darkness.

Sitting packed in together, standing along the walls, drinking ale and talking in a sea roar of laughter and jests, a hundred and eighty-seven men were crammed into Dun Cannobaen's great hall. Fifty of them were the fort guard that Sligyn had left behind, but the rest rode for the three lords sitting with Lovyan at the honor table—Edar, Comerr, and Gwryn. Lovyan had never doubted Edar's loyalty for a minute, but she'd been pleasantly surprised when the other two had shown up at her gates. The servants bustled around to clear away the food from the noon meal and serve mead all round. Edar, a blond beaky man in his twenties, finally said aloud what they'd all been thinking.

"If Cenydd isn't here by now, he isn't joining the muster, and that goes for Dromyc and Cinvan, too."

"So it does," Lovyan said. "Well, Cinvan has the smallest warband in the rhan. Let him go over, for all I care."

The lords grinned and saluted her with their goblets. Caradoc ran to the table with a young silver dagger in tow.

"Messages, my lady," Caradoc blurted out. "From Lord Rhodry."

The silver dagger knelt and drew the messages out of his shirt. As she took them, Lovyan noticed his smooth face and wondered how one so young could have earned that cursed dagger.

"Carro, take this lad over to the men and get him some food," she said. "Then fetch the scribe."

Although Lovyan was perfectly capable of reading the message herself, it would have hurt Grotyr's feelings. He snappily shook out the rolled parchment and cleared his throat several times as the lords leaned onto the table to listen. Rhodry described in terse detail the battle at the ruined dun, then ordered the reinforcements to ride northwest to meet him. He was making for a little tributary of the Brog while he tried to circle around Corbyn's army.

With a clatter of chairs being shoved back and the jingle of swords at their sides, the lords rose to do his bidding. Grotyr leaned down to whisper.

"A private note at the end, Your Grace," he said. "From Nevyn."

Lovyan snatched the parchment.

"My dear Lovva," the note ran. "Although the situation is grave, I have cause for hope. Our dweomer enemy is so daft that it's a marvel he presents any threat at all. Aderyn and I will keep Rhodry safe, I'll wager. May I beg you for a boon? The silver dagger who rode this message is not the lad she seems, but a lass, and someone dear to me. Would you give her proper shelter? Your humble servant, Nevyn."

"Oh by the gods!" Lovyan laughed aloud. "Carro, run and fetch that silver dagger to me. Tell her to bring her meal and finish it here."

"Her, Your Grace?" the startled page said.

"Just that. I must be going blind or suchlike."

When Jill brought her trencher of bread and meat to the table, Lovyan could see that indeed, she was female and quite pretty at that. She introduced herself as Gilyan, the daughter of Cullyn of Cerrmor. For all that Lovyan knew little of matters of war, she recognized the silver dagger's name.

"Well, isn't this interesting?" Lovyan said. "Have you known Nevyn long, child?"

"Only a few days, Your Grace, but truly, I never met a man I liked more, for all his dweomer."

"I felt much the same, truly, when first we met. Now, finish your meal. After we see the warbands off, we'll get you a bath and find you a chamber up in the women's quarters."

When they came out to the ward, the riders were already bringing their horses into line, and the carters were hitching their teams to the carts. Every lord in the tierynrhyn owed Lovyan his fully provisioned warband for forty days—and not one day more. Her heart was heavy as she wondered if Corbyn would make the war drag on beyond that just so she would have to pay the lords to serve longer. Sligyn, of course, would fight at his own expense for as long as necessary. She doubted the others, even though they gathered around her with every show of respect.

"Until you join up with Rhodry, my lords," Lovyan said, "Edar will be your cadvridoc."

"My thanks for the honor, Your Grace," Edar said with a bow. "I'll send a man back with a message as soon as we've found them. Let's hope it's quick."

"Indeed. May the gods ride with you."

Lovyan and Jill stood in the doorway of the broch and watched as the army slowly got itself into a line of march and filed out the gates of the dun.

"If you've been riding with your father," Lovyan said idly, "you must have seen this many a time."

"I have, Your Grace, and every time, I'm half sick with fear, wondering if I'll see Da again."

Lovyan was suddenly struck by how terrifying it would be to be out on the roads with no family to turn to if her father were slain. It gave her a sick feeling. No matter what had happened to her husband, she herself would always have been safe, an important member of her vast clan. She caught Jill's filthy hand and squeezed it.

"Well, here, child," Lovyan said. "You've come to a safe place now. For Nevyn's sake alone I'd offer you my shelter, but I'd be a poor excuse for a noble-born woman if I couldn't care for the orphan of a man who was in my service. No matter what happens, you'll have a place in my retinue."

Jill started shaking, a little tremor of her whole body.

"Your Grace is truly the most generous lord I've ever met," Jill said. "If ever you have need of my sword, then it's at your disposal."

It was such a masculine way of thanking someone that

Lovyan nearly laughed, but suddenly an odd coldness down her back stopped her, as if she'd been given an omen.

"Let's pray things never come to that," Lovyan said. "But you have my thanks."

"So Corbyn's taking our bait?" Rhodry said.

"He is," Nevyn said. "I found the army farther east than I expected. They're angling round to follow you, sure enough."

"Splendid." Rhodry glanced up at the sun—about three hours after noon. "What of the men from Cannobaen?"

"They're on the way. Aderyn can tell your messenger exactly where to find them."

"I'll detail a man straightaway. My thanks."

After the messenger rode off, Rhodry led the army a bit farther east, then decided to make camp and wait for the reinforcements, who, according to Aderyn, were riding fast and letting their provisions follow. Rhodry felt profoundly ungrateful, but he thought to himself that all this dweomer aid, as useful as it was, was a cursed unsettling thing to have around you. The rest of the noble-born doubtless agreed. When just at nightfall Edar rode in, he was swearing in amazement at the ease with which the messenger had found the reinforcing army.

"At first I thought it was some trick of Corbyn's," Edar said. "But Comerr recognized your man."

"Well, there's somewhat odd afoot," Rhodry said. "Uh, come have somewhat to eat, and I'll tell you about it."

As the noble-born sat around a campfire together and shared a meal, Rhodry had the unpleasant job of convincing still more of his allies that the rumors of dweomer were true and twice true. With Sligyn on his side, the job was easier, because no one had ever seen Sligyn give in to the slightest touch of whimsy and fancy. For a long time they sat in silence, the noble-born as cowed as their men. Rhodry wondered why none of them—and he included himself in this—were comforted by the knowledge that they had dweomer on their side. Finally he realized that they all felt insignificant, mere playing stones on a game board of the dweomer's choosing. For weeks Rhodry had thought of himself as the focus of the rebellion and his death as its goal. Now he was only a little pebble, set down as one small move in a war between Aderyn and Loddlaen.

That night, long after the other lords had gone to their tents, Rhodry walked down to the banks of the stream. In the light from the stars and the waning moon, he could see quite well, an odd talent that he'd had since childhood but kept strictly to himself. Out in the meadow surrounding the sleeping camp, guards prowled back and forth on watch. The stream itself ran silver, flecked with foam as it chuckled over the rocks. All day Rhodry had been troubled by a premonition, and now it clung to him with cold arms. Something was going to happen to him, something important and irrevocable—and for a warrior, there was only one thing that something could be. He didn't want to die. It seemed cursed unfair that he was going to die, when all his death would mean was that Loddlaen had jumped one of Aderyn's stones and taken it off the board.

When he heard someone moving behind him, he swirled, his sword half drawn, but it was only Cullyn, stumbling a bit in the darkness.

"I just wondered who was out here, my lord," Cullyn said. "It's my turn on watch, you see. Is somewhat wrong?"

"Naught. I was just thinking of Carnoic. Ever play that game, silver dagger?"

"Oh, every now and then, my lord. There's not a cursed lot of challenge in it."

"You think so, do you? Well, then, when this war's over, we'll have to sit down and play, and you can teach me what you know."

Cullyn smiled briefly, as if he was wondering if they'd live to sit down to a board together. Rhodry felt the premonition again as a clench of his stomach. Something irrevocable was about to happen, something that had guided his whole life here, to this moment and to Cullyn of Cerrmor.

"I'd best get back to my post, my lord," Cullyn said.

"So you'd better. Here, Cullyn, tomorrow on the line of march, you come ride beside me."

"What? Here, that's too big an honor for a dishonored man like me."

"By the hells, it's not! Have any of the noble-born made me an offer to stick close to me in the fighting? You ride with me, and you eat with me, too."

It was later that same night that Nevyn felt the dweomer-warning, a cold, clammy prickling down his back that brought him suddenly and completely awake. His first thought was that Corbyn might be riding to make a night strike on the camp, and he crossed his arms over his chest and went into a trance in order to do a little scouting. In the body of light he soared up high over the camp, dimly glowing from the indrawn auras of the sleeping men. Above him in the dark blue light of night on the etheric, the stars blazed, great silver orbs of pure energy. He could see far, but nothing moved in meadow or woodland except a few deer, off on the horizon.

If the danger wasn't from Corbyn, it might well be from Loddlaen. Nevyn turned his attention to the etheric itself and saw, far above him, a tiny figure like a silver flame. From talking with Aderyn, Nevyn knew that Loddlaen had been trained to assume an elven-style body of light—one silver flame as opposed to a human-shaped form. With a grim little smile, Nevyn darted up fast, but the flame shape fled, rushing away through eddying currents of the blue light. Nevyn might have caught him, but he saw a more curious prize. Shadowing Loddlaen at a long distance was one of the Wildfolk, a peculiarly bent nexus of dark lines and dim glow. Nevyn summoned the light and made a silver net, woven of the malleable etheric substance, then swooped to the side after the creature.

In an exhalation of terror it fled from him, but Nevyn called upon his own Wildfolk, who swarmed around it, joustling it, shoving it back, thrusting it finally out of the swarm where he could net it easily. Swelling, flashing, it struggled against the lines of force, but the net held, and he hauled it in like a fish. Now came the trick. With the struggling Wildfolk firmly in hand, Nevyn floated back to his body. He hovered above it, fought the pull of the flesh, stayed fully conscious as he slipped back in. The fight was painful; rather than merely lapsing back into normal consciousness, he felt the melding in every bone and vein as he took up residence in his body again. Yet in spite of the pain he kept the etheric net tight and brought, at last, the captured Wildfolk back with him.

Nevyn sat up and found a very peculiar prize indeed struggling in his hands. On the physical plane it was a gnome of sorts, but even more deformed and ugly than usual—twisted, shrunken shoulders, stubby legs, enormous hands, and a snarling warty face with tiny eyes and long fangs.

"Someone's shaped you, hasn't he?" Nevyn said to it. "Someone's worked some strange magick indeed upon you."

Paralyzed with terror, the gnome went limp in his hands. Nevyn let his feeling flow out to it, a deep pity, a sympathy, in fact, a kind of love for this creature deformed against its will. When he released it, the gnome threw itself against his chest.

"You're safe now," Nevyn said. "You'll never have to go back to your master again. Was your master Loddlaen?"

Terrified again, the gnome looked up and shook its head in a no.

"Indeed?" Nevyn whispered. "How cursed interesting. Come with me, little brother. I'm going to summon your king here, on this plane. I think it might be safer all round."

With the gnome riding on his shoulder, Nevyn left the sleeping camp and went a good ways away, where he could sit down and work in private. In his mind he built up a flaming pentagram of blue light, then pushed the image out until it seemed to stand in front of him, a glowing star some six feet high. The gnome saw it, too, and stood transfixed as Nevyn slowly chanted the secret names of the King of the Element of Earth. The space inside the star changed into a silver swirl of pale light, light of the sort that never shone on land or sea, and in that light appeared a figure, vaguely elven, yet glowing so brightly that its form was hard to discern.

"One of my kind has tormented this little brother," Nevyn said aloud. "Will you take it into your charge?"

The voice came back only within his mind.

"I will, and my thanks, Master of the Fifth of Us, Master of the Aethyr."

When the figure held out pale glowing hands, the gnome ran to it and threw itself into the sanctuary of the King. The silver light disappeared; there was only the blue star, which Nevyn methodically banished. He stood up and stamped thrice on the ground to end the working.

"As our Cullyn would say," Nevyn remarked to the night wind. "Oh horsedung and a pile of it!"

Nevyn hurried back to camp to wake Aderyn. He knew that only a master of dark dweomer could have deformed the gnome in that particular way. This dark master was in for a shock, too, when his little messenger never returned. The question was, Why was the dark dweomer spying on Loddlaen?

On the morrow, Rhodry made sure that Cullyn rode next to him, even though Peredyr and Daumyr both made nasty remarks about silver daggers. They set out, angling toward the northeast, and in a mile or two reached the settled farmlands of Eldidd. The roads and lanes rambled between fenced fields, farmsteads, pastures, and stretches of open meadow and woods, all jumbled together with no true pattern. Since there was no law that made farmers will all their holdings to only their eldest son, the land got cut up into a patchwork that made any kind of straight travel difficult. At noon, they stopped to rest on a strip of unused land between triangular fields of cabbages and turnips.

While Cullyn and Rhodry were sharing a chunk of salt meat to go with their soda bread, Aderyn trotted over, looking grim.

"Corbyn's army is turning south, lord cadvridoc," the dweomerman said. "They've stopped only about three miles away."

"Well and good," Rhodry said. "Then they're as sick of this cursed game of carnoic as I am."

Rhodry tossed the chunk of meat to Cullyn, then rose, painfully aware that all the lords were looking at him for their orders.

"We're leaving the baggage train under the guard of the spearmen," Rhodry said. "The rest of us will arm and ride to meet them. If the bastards want a chance at me so cursed badly, then let's give it to them."

They cheered him and what they saw as his courage, never knowing that Rhodry had the simple desire to get dying over with—unless, perhaps, Cullyn guessed how he felt, because the silver dagger merely looked distracted, as if his thoughts were far away.

Thanks to Aderyn's detailed report, Rhodry knew exactly where to draw up the army. Corbyn was marching his men down the road as straight as he could; it was not the Deverry way to hedge and maneuver for position once a battle was unavoidable. A mile north, the road crossed a big cow pasture. As the army clattered along, frightened farmers stared at them from the fields or ran away from the roadside. When the marchers reached the

pasture, there wasn't a cow in sight. From long experience, the
peasantry knew something about the art of war.

Rhodry drew up his men in a single line, a crescent with the
embrace facing the road. He personally rode down the line and
disposed the various warbands. For all that Rhodry was young,
he'd been riding to battles since he was fourteen, and his father
and uncles had trained him ruthlessly for war. When he came to
the left flank, he found the two Westfolk there, wearing salvaged
mail and carrying short bows that they held crosswise. Their
horses had no bridles.

"So," Rhodry said. "You know how to ride in a fight as well as
stand and shoot, do you?"

"Oh, in truth," Calonderiel said with a grin. "These are just
hunting bows. It'll be interesting to see how they do as weapons
of war."

"What?" Rhodry snapped. "Here, if you've never ridden in
this kind of a scrap before, there's no dishonor in staying out of
it."

"There is. Dishonor and twice dishonor. I want vengeance
for my slaughtered friend."

Jennantar nodded in agreement, his mouth set.

"Then may the gods of your people protect you," Rhodry
said. "And I admire your guts."

Rhodry trotted back and took up his position in the center of
the line, with Cullyn on his left and Caenrydd on his right. By the
honor of the thing, Corbyn would be at the head of the charging
wedge when the attack came, and the two cadvridogion would
close with each other while their men turned into a mob all
round. Except for the occasional stamp of a horse and a jingle of
tack, the waiting line fell silent, each man wrapped in his own
thoughts. Now that his Wyrd was coming to meet him, Rhodry
felt perfectly calm, except that he'd never seen such a beautiful
afternoon. Every blade of grass in the meadow seemed preternaturally green, and the sunlight preternaturally golden. Some
distant trees looked like green velvet against the sapphire sky. It
seemed a pity to leave all that behind for the shadowy Otherlands. Then, far down the road, he saw a plume of dust. He bent
down and drew a javelin from the sheath under his right leg.

"Here they come," Rhodry called out.

All down the line javelin points winked in the sun as the men took on faith what they couldn't yet see. One last time, shields were settled, swords loosened in scabbards, as the horses danced, feeling the coming battle in their riders' moods. The plume of dust came closer, swelled, like smoke from a fire sweeping down the road. Rhodry forgot that he was sure he was going to die. He felt himself smiling as if his face would split from it. As the battle fit took him over, it seemed that his body had turned as light as air.

About five hundred yards away, Corbyn's army broke from the marching line and swirled around to form a wedge for the charge. Rhodry chuckled as he saw the green and tan shields of Corbyn's warband take the head. Soon he and the man who had rebelled against his rule would face off in single combat. As for the rest, there were over three hundred men out there, a nice fair fight. In anticipation, his own army moved forward a pace or two, but it held its formation. Finally silver horns rang out among the enemy. Howling out warcries, Corbyn's men charged.

Closer, closer, with the dust pluming around them they came, slapping into the crescent. Rhodry rose in the stirrups, threw his javelin overhand into the mob, then drew his sword on the follow-through. The line of darts arced up, winking as they fell indiscriminately among Corbyn's men, who answered with a straight fling of their own. Rhodry bounced one off his shield, then kicked his horse to a gallop and charged straight for the rider in the lead. Screaming warcries, his men surged forward, falling from the flanks to close a circle of death.

Rhodry began to laugh, the bubbling choking battle-laugh that he could never control on the field. He heard himself howling like a madman as he closed with the lead rider. He ducked under a clumsy swing, slashed in, getting a nick on his enemy's arm, and then realized that he was facing an ordinary rider, not Corbyn at all. He threw up his sword in a parry and risked glancing around—no sign of Corbyn, and he was trapped. Men were pouring around him, mobbing for him in a tight circle. Rhodry desperately swung his horse around and felt a grazing blow bounce off the mail on his back as he charged straight for a young rider. The lad gave ground; he was almost out—then more men closed the gap. His laugh rose to a howl as he saw how neatly his honor had trapped him; he'd fallen for a false decoy like a waterfowl.

"Rhodry!" It was Cullyn's voice, close at hand.

Rhodry swung his horse around just as Cullyn cut through the closing circle and fell into place beside him, their horses nose to tail so they could guard each other's left.

"Parry!" Cullyn screamed at him. "Forget the kills!"

Twisting in the saddle, ducking, parrying with shield and sword both, Rhodry followed orders and fought for his life. He felt a blow graze his shoulder, twisted, and flung up his shield against another. The wood cracked. A blade flashed in toward his face; he caught it on his sword. For a moment the blades hung locked; then someone else struck him from the back, and Rhodry had to pull free. He flung up his shield just in time; it cracked again, splitting down the middle to the boss. Over his own laughter and the battlecries around him, he heard his men screaming "To Rhodry! To Rhodry!" Suddenly the man straight ahead of him in the crush tried to pull his horse's head around. The Cannobaen warband was beginning to fight through. Rhodry had no time to take the advantage. He parried a slash from the side with his sword, then twisted in the saddle to take another on his shield. The crack ran together with the first one, and half the shield fell away.

Rhodry howled like a banshee and went on parrying with half a shield. All at once, the horse to his right screamed with that ghastly half-human sound that horses make only in agony and reared straight up. As it came down, stumbling, Caenrydd killed its rider from behind. Amyr was right behind him, swinging like a fiend, and Rhodry's two men were through.

"My lord!" Cullyn yelled. "Follow me out!"

Rhodry swung his horse around as Caenrydd and Amyr fell in behind him, but he refused to follow any man. He spurred his horse up beside Cullyn, ducked under a slash, and slashed back at the enemy on his right. The blow missed the fellow's clumsy parry and caught him on the ribs, making him grunt and sway in the saddle. Rhodry slashed back from the other side and knocked the dazed rider off his horse to fall under the feet of a comrade's horse beside him. When that horse reared, disrupting the mob on one side, Rhodry and his men could begin to move forward, cutting their way out of the mob at the same time as the rest of the Cannobaen warband tried to cut its way in.

It was a slow thing, forcing their horses ahead by sheer will, leaning, slashing, dodging, always striking at the nearest enemy while Corbyn's men tried to parry Cullyn and strike for Rhodry. The silver dagger fought silently, looking utterly bored as he struck and parried with a terrifying ease, as if he were some natural force, a storm wind blowing among this screaming cursing mob.

They were almost out when someone pushed in past Caenrydd in the rear and slashed Rhodry's horse hard. With a scream, the gelding reared. Rhodry knew it would never come down alive; he slipped his feet from the stirrups and threw the remains of his shield as it fell. He flung himself over his horse's neck and rolled, but with calm clarity he knew that he was doomed. A hoof kicked him in the middle of the back, and for a moment he couldn't breathe. All around him he heard screams and warcries; all he could see were the legs of horses. Grunting in pain, he pulled himself up to a kneel and twisted out of the way just in time to avoid a kick to his head. He heard Cullyn screaming at someone to pull back, and only then did he realize that he was under the hooves of his own men's horses. Another kick came his way and grazed his shoulder.

All at once hands grabbed him and pulled him to his feet. Rhodry twisted around and landed against Cullyn's shoulder just as a terrified horse bucked up and nearly fell on the pair of them. Cullyn dragged Rhodry back just in time and shoved him against the side of his horse.

"Can you mount?" Cullyn yelled.

Gasping for breath, Rhodry hauled himself into the saddle. Ahead of him he saw his own men cutting hard, driving the enemy back. The horse danced and shuddered, but Rhodry got it under control, then kicked his feet free of the stirrups to let Cullyn mount behind him. Cullyn put one long arm around his waist and took the reins. Over the shouting, a silver horn rang out a retreat. Rhodry's first thought was that his side had lost the battle; then he remembered that this time, he was the cadvridoc and that the horn had to be Corbyn's. The enemies around them fell back and fled as the battle press broke up.

"Caenrydd!" Rhodry howled. "Sound the call to stand!"

Cullyn's arm tightened slightly around his waist.

"My lord?" Cullyn said. "Caenrydd's dead."

For a moment Rhodry's mind simply refused to understand what Cullyn meant.

"Rhodry." Cullyn gave him a shake. "Sound the call."

Rhodry drew the horn from his belt, but he merely held it. Finally Cullyn grabbed it from him and blew the signal to pull back. Rhodry wiped a scatter of tears away on the back of his gauntlet. Only then did he realize that he was doubled up with pain.

"Two cursed inches to the right, and that kick would have broken his spine," Nevyn said. "Two lower, and it would have hit his kidneys. Our cadvridoc here has a silver dagger's luck."

Cullyn nodded his agreement. Stripped to the waist, Rhodry was lying on the tailgate of one of the wagons, Nevyn's improvised surgery. A wedge shape of red and purple had already swollen bigger than an apple on his back.

"I'm just surprised that his ribs aren't broken."

"So am I," Nevyn said.

Rhodry turned his head to look at them. Up by his shoulders and down along his arms were more bruises and small cuts, where sword blows had driven his mail through his shirt and into his skin in a blurry pattern of rings. It was odd, Cullyn always thought, that while bards sang of warriors slicing each other into shreds, you generally killed a man by beating him to death with your sword.

"I don't need to be fussed over like an old woman," Rhodry snapped. "You should be tending the men worse off than me."

"Nonsense," Nevyn snapped. "There are three chirurgeons with this army, and Aderyn as well, who's as good with his herbs as I am. Besides, the battle was only bloody in the fighting around you, my lord."

Cullyn whistled sharply under his breath, because he hadn't realized that. Nevyn rummaged through the packets of herbs laid ready on the wagon bed, dumped one into a mortar, and added some water from the kettle that hung nearby on a tripod over a small fire.

"I'll make a poultice for that bruise," Nevyn said. "You won't be able to ride unless we can get the swelling down. What about you, silver dagger? Do you need my aid?"

"I don't, my thanks. Those young cubs of Corbyn's can't fight worth the fart of a two-copper pig."

"Cursed modest, aren't you?" Rhodry said. "Don't listen to him, Nevyn. Without him, I'd be dead, and I know it."

Nevyn looked up sharply and stared into Cullyn's eyes. Cullyn felt as if the stare were searing his soul like hot iron, making him remember some old guilt or shame, a memory that faded as soon as he tried to capture it.

"Then it's a fine thing you've done today, Cullyn of Cerrmor," Nevyn said softly. "We'll see if Rhodry can repay the debt he owes you."

"I don't want payment," Cullyn snarled. "I know I'm naught but a silver dagger, but I didn't ride into that mob for coin."

"That's not what I meant at all."

With a toss of his head, Cullyn strode away. Whether the old man was dweomer or not, cursed if he'd let him mock him.

The army was settling in around the baggage train. Cullyn was heading toward his horse to rub it down when Lord Sligyn caught up with him. His lordship's mail was spattered with some other man's blood, and his mustaches were limp with sweat.

"I saw you pull Rhodry out of that stampede," Sligyn said. "My thanks, silver dagger."

"None needed, my lord. I promised him I'd guard him."

"Hah! Many an honor-sworn rider forgets his oath when it comes to dismounting in the middle of a mob. By the asses of the gods, man, you've got a cursed sight more honor than that piss-poor Corbyn." Sligyn's voice rose to a bellow. "You saw what happened. The coward! A base-born bastard's trick, decoying Rhodry out there like that! The dishonor of the thing! Thank every god that you saw what was happening in time."

"Not exactly, my lord. I was expecting somewhat like that."

Sligyn's mouth went slack in disbelief.

"A lord who'd slaughter a merchant caravan to trap an enemy is a lord without honor," Cullyn said. "So when Rhodry charged, I was right behind him."

When, at the dinner hour, the lords met for a council of war, Cullyn was invited by Peredyr himself to join them. Although by then Rhodry could walk and sit up, albeit with difficulty, Cullyn knew that he'd be as stiff as a sword on the morrow. Both Cullyn and Rhodry listened with rising fury as the other lords described the battle. None of them had been mobbed or even seriously threatened; they'd merely been blocked from riding to help Rhodry.

"What gripes my very soul," Rhodry said, "is the way I never even saw Corbyn on the field. The little coward!"

"Wasn't cowardice," Peredyr said. "He doesn't want to be the man who personally kills the gwerbret's brother and the tieryn's son. This way, if the time came to sue for peace, he could blame your death on the fortunes of war."

"And that's what he's after, curse him and his balls both," Sligyn broke in. "He'll hammer at us until someone kills the cadvridoc, and then he'll place his suit."

"If I may speak, my lords?" Cullyn said. "Then there's only one thing to do—kill Corbyn before he has a chance to sue for anything."

"Cursed right!" Sligyn snarled. "When you see a dog foaming at the mouth, you don't call the cursed kennelman. You cut its head off."

They drew close together to lay their plan. In the next battle, the lords would ride as a unit, with Rhodry safely in the middle and Cullyn and Sligyn at the head. Their best men would be around them to hold off the enemy while they coursed the field and found Corbyn.

"And I wager we'll find him at the rear," Edar said. "I'm going to tell my men to fight for blood, when it comes to facing Corbyn's allies. No more of this dancing all around us while they parry. It's time they saw what kind of a man they've allied themselves with."

Sligyn stood up with a grim little laugh.

"I'm going to go talk to my captain," he said. "I suggest the rest of you do the same."

When the lords dispersed, Rhodry kept Cullyn at his side and had his manservant bring both of them mead in wooden cups. For a while Rhodry was silent, downing the mead in big gulps as he stared at the fire.

"Lord cadvridoc?" Cullyn said. "It's no dishonor to have a bodyguard when someone's trying to murder you."

"Ah, it's not that that aches my heart." Rhodry paused for another gulp of mead. "I was thinking of Caenrydd. Amyr told me that Caenno ordered him forward and took the rear by himself. He knew what that meant."

"So he did. He pledged to die for you, and he kept his word."

"But by the hells!" Rhodry turned to him, and there were tears glistening in the lad's eyes. "Don't you see that's the worst of it? Here, I've never ridden at the head of a warband before. Oh, I've always been Lord Rhodry, but no more than my father's captain, or Rhys's extra man. In all the battles I ever rode, no one was dying for my cursed sake. I expected to die someday for someone else's."

"I've never met another noble-born man who troubled his heart about such things."

"Then curse them all! By the hells, why did my uncle have to go and get himself killed? I don't want his demesne."

"I've no doubt his lordship will feel a good bit differently about that in the morning."

"Oh, no doubt." Rhodry stared moodily into his cup. "I'd be cursed and twice cursed before I'd let Rhys have it, anyway."

"Here, I've got no right to be asking you this, but is your brother as bad a man as all that?"

"He's not about anything but me. Oh, he's just, generous, and brave—everything a cursed noble-born man is supposed to be, except when it comes to a matter of my affairs. Cursed if I know why he's always hated me so much."

Cullyn heard as much hurt as anger in the lad's voice.

"Well, my lord," Cullyn said. "My elder brother was much the same to me. He'd give me a good cuff whenever he could get away with it, and it didn't sweeten his temper to have Mam take my side all the time."

"By the hells." Rhodry looked up with an oddly embarrassed smile. "Of course you had a clan, didn't you? Here I've been thinking of you as somewhat like the wind and the rain, always there, wandering the kingdom."

"Nothing of the sort." Cullyn had a cautious sip of mead. "My father was a shipwright down in Cerrmor, and a drunken bastard he was, too. I had to dodge him as much as I dodged my brother's fists, truly. And when he finally did us all a favor and drank himself to death, the priests of Bel got my mother a place in the gwerbret's kitchen. I cursed well grew up in that dun."

"And is that where you learned to fight?"

"It is. The captain of the warband took pity on the greasy scullery lad who was always playing with sticks and calling them swords." Cullyn washed away his rising feeling of shame with the mead. "He was a good man, and then I had to break his faith in me."

Rhodry was listening with a fascinated curiosity. Cullyn set the empty cup down and rose.

"It's late, lord cadvridoc. If I may speak so freely, we'd best get ourselves to bed."

He walked away before Rhodry could call him back.

Even for a Deverry man, Lord Nowec was tall, six and a half feet of solid muscle and broad bones. That night, he was an angry man, too, standing with his arms crossed over his chest and glowering as Corbyn and the rest of the allies laid their plan. Loddlaen kept a careful eye on him. Finally the lord stepped forward with an oath that was almost a growl.

"I don't like this," Nowec snarled. "I'm sick to my heart of all this cursed dishonor. That ruse this morning is enough."

All the others turned to look at him with a flash of guilt in their eyes.

"Do we fight like men," Nowec went on, "or do we fight like stinking rabble?"

"Oh now here." Lord Cenydd stepped forward, a paunchy man with thick gray mustaches. "Which is more dishonorable— to use the wits the gods gave us, or to kill noble-born men when we don't even have a feud going with them?"

"True spoken," Corbyn said. "Our quarrel's with Rhodry and no one else."

"Pig's balls!" Nowec spat out. "You're afraid of the gwerbret intervening and naught else. I don't like it, I tell you, sneaking around like a pack of stray dogs creeping up on a townsman's slop heap."

The younger lords were wavering, stung by Nowec's words, and Corbyn and Cenydd were unable to look him in the face. Loddlaen decided that it was time to take a hand in this. He sent out a line of force from his aura and used it to slap Nowec's aura, just as a child uses a whip to spin a top. The lord staggered slightly, and his eyes turned glazed.

"But my lord," Loddlaen said in a soothing sort of voice. "If we drag out the war, we could kill Sligyn or Peredyr by mistake. That would be a grievous thing."

"So it would." His anger quite gone, Nowec spoke slowly. "I agree, councillor. The plan's a good one."

"Then no one has any objections?" Corbyn got in quickly. "Splendid. Go give your captains their orders."

As the council of war broke up, Loddlaen slipped away before Corbyn noticed. He couldn't bear the thought of sitting and drinking with his stinking lordship. As he walked through the camp, he noticed the men glancing sidewise at him and furtively crossing their fingers to ward off witchcraft. They were afraid of him, the mangey dogs, as well they might be—let them cower before Loddlaen the Mighty, Master of the Powers of Air! At the edge of the camp, he paused, debating. As badly as he wanted to get away from the army for a little while, he was quite simply afraid to go out alone with Aderyn so close by. Finally he went to his tent, ordered his manservant out, and lay down fully dressed on his blankets.

Noise filtered in, men laughing and talking as they strolled by, swords clanking at their sides. Once, Loddlaen's trained mind had been capable of shutting such distractions out; now, they drove him to rage. Fists clenched at his side, jaw tight, he lay shaking, trying to close down his senses and let sleep come as he had once known how to do. He did not want to summon the darkness. All at once, he was afraid of it, afraid of the voice that would pour into his mind as smoothly as oil.

Yet, in the end, it came to him. He saw it first as a tiny black point in his mind; then it began to swell. He fought it, tried to fill his mind with light, tried to banish the dark with ritual gesture and curse, but inexorably it grew, billowed, until he seemed to stand in a vast darkness, and the voice spoke to him, gently, patiently.

"Why do you fear me, you of all dweomer-masters, Loddlaen the Mighty? All I want to do is aid you, to be your friend and ally. I came to sorrow with you, that so clever a plan went astray. You almost trapped Rhodry today."

"Who are you?"

"A friend and naught more. I have information for you. That silver dagger is the key to everything. You have to kill him before you can kill Rhodry. I've been meditating and doing deep work-

ings, my friend, and I've seen that the forces of Wyrd are at work
here."

"Well and good, but who are you?"

The voice chuckled once. The blackness was gone. Loddlaen
lay there sweating for a moment and blessed what he had just
cursed—the normal human noise of the army around him. Then
he got up and left the tent to find Corbyn's captain. He wanted to
give him some special orders about this wretched silver dagger.

Cullyn came awake suddenly to find Sligyn hunkering down
next to him. The wheel of the stars showed that it was close to
dawn.

"Old Nevyn just woke me," Sligyn said. "Corbyn's army is
getting ready to ride. Those dishonorable scum are going to
make a dawn strike on us."

"Oh, are they now? Well, then, my lord, we'd best pull a trick
of our own."

When Cullyn explained, Sligyn roared with laughter and
woke up half the camp. The provision carts were already drawn
up in a circle some hundred yards from camp with the horses in
their midst. Half the men readied the horses while the others
arranged saddlebags and gear under blankets to look like sleeping men. Then the armed and ready warband hid in the circle of
carts, each man crouched beside his horse. To the rear huddled
the servants and suchlike; up in front stood the spearmen, ready
to fill the gap in the circle once the horsemen rode out.

Cullyn took his place beside Sligyn just as the sky was light-
ening to a gray like mole's fur. In the chilly dawn, the army
trotted closer and closer across the wide meadow. The news
whispered through Rhodry's men—get ready to mount and ride.

At the far end of the meadow, Corbyn's army drew up,
paused for a moment, then began to sort itself out into a long line
for the charge. Cullyn began to wonder if they would see through
his ruse; if the camp truly was asleep, by now someone would
have been wakened by the noise of the distant jingling of tack.
Walking their horses, the army came on, then broke into a trot,
on and on—and suddenly they were galloping, charging to the
sound of horns and warcries straight for what they thought was
the sleeping camp. Their javelins sped ahead of them into the
fake bodies on the ground.

"Now!" Rhodry screamed.

There was an awkward shoving scramble in the narrow space as the warband swung itself into the saddle. Shrieking at the top of his lungs, Sligyn led out the squad of lords, and their men surged out after them in ranks of four abreast. Out ahead, the startled enemies were cursing as they tried to check the momentum of their charge and wheel to face this unexpected attack. As they galloped, Rhodry's army sent their javelins on ahead of them. Horses reared and men swore as Corbyn's line turned into a disorganized mob.

"For Corbyn!" Cullyn yelled, and he glanced back to make sure that Rhodry was safely in the midst of the squad.

Sligyn wheeled his unit along the battle's edge just as the main armies hit. Horses dodged and reared as the two lines passed through each other like the fingers of one hand woven through those of the other. The riders turned them and swung back to break off into single combats or the occasional clot of fighting. Cullyn stayed close to Sligyn as the lord led his squad around the field. Suddenly Sligyn howled in triumph and kicked his horse to a gallop. Taken by surprise, Cullyn fell a little behind as the lord charged for his prey—a lord with a green and tan blazon on his shield. Cullyn heard Rhodry's crazed berserker laugh sweep by him as the unit charged after Sligyn.

Riding hard, Cullyn galloped after them, but a man on a black cut him off, coming straight for him. As Cullyn wheeled his horse, he got a glimpse of pouchy eyes and a dark-stubbled chin under the enemy's helm. They swung, parried, trading blow for blow while he cursed and yelled and Cullyn stayed dead silent, flicking away the enemy's sword with his own until in frustration the man tried a hard side swing that left his right unguarded. Cullyn caught the strike on his shield and slashed in to catch him solidly on the right arm. Blood welled through his mail as the bone snapped. Grunting in pain, he dropped the sword and tried to turn his horse. Cullyn let him go. He wanted Corbyn.

Ahead, Sligyn's squad was mobbing around Corbyn and some of Corbyn's men, fighting ably to defend their lord. Cullyn urged his horse forward just as a fresh squad of green-and-tans galloped up.

"My lord Sligyn!" Cullyn yelled. "The flank!"

But the enemy was riding for him, not for Sligyn. Cullyn

wrenched his horse around to meet the enemy charge just as they swarmed around and enveloped him from all sides.

"The silver dagger! Get him!"

Cullyn had no time to wonder why they were mobbing a silver dagger as if he were a noble lord. A blow cracked him across the left shoulder from the flank as the man in front of him angled for a stab. Cullyn parried it barely in time and twisted away, slashing out at the man pushing in from his right. They could get four on him at once, and all he could do was twist and duck and slash back and forth. He caught a strike on his shield that cracked the wood; then he felt a stab like fire on his left side. Over the screaming battle noise he heard Rhodry's laugh, coming closer.

Gasping with pain, Cullyn killed the man in front of him with a slash to the throat that collapsed his windpipe and knocked him off his horse, but there was another enemy waiting to take his place. A hard blow made fire run down Cullyn's left arm. He twisted in the saddle and tried to parry, but the shield dragged his broken arm down. With a curse he let it fall and twisted back to fend a blow from the right. Rhodry's laugh sounded louder, but still too far away.

Suddenly the man at Cullyn's left flank screamed, and his horse reared to fall dead. Something sped through the air past Cullyn's face. The arrow pierced the mail on the enemy at his right with a gout of blood. The man tried to turn his horse, but another arrow caught him in the back, and he went down with a cry. The mob peeled off and tried to flee, but they turned straight into Rhodry's men charging to meet them. In the last clear moment left to him, Cullyn saw Jennantar riding up with a curved bow in his hands. Cullyn dropped his sword and tried to hold on to the saddle peak, but his gauntlets were slippery with his own blood. He stared at them in amazement as darkness came out of nowhere, and he fell, sliding over his horse's neck.

It seemed that he was trying to swim to the surface of a deep blue river. Every now and then, he drew close; he could see light ahead and hear what sounded like Nevyn's voice, but every time, a vast eddying billow would sweep him back down where he would choke, drowning in the blue. All at once, he heard a voice, mocking him, a smooth little voice that poured into his mind like oil. It seemed that the voice was coming closer out of the billowing blue stuff around him. Then he saw a glowing silver cord that stretched from his oddly unsubstantial body down to—somewhere. He didn't know where it went. Another wave enveloped him in a shifting sinking blueness. The voice poured over him again, taunting, mocking him for a dead man.

Suddenly he saw Nevyn—or a pale blue image of him—it was hard to tell which, but the old man was striding to meet him, and as he came, he was chanting in some peculiar language. The blue river seemed to slow, to hold steady, and then Nevyn caught his hand.

All at once, Cullyn was awake, and Nevyn was leaning over him in the sunlight. In spite of his warrior's will, he moaned aloud from his pain. When he tried to move, the splints on his left arm clattered on the wagon bed.

"Easy, my friend," Nevyn said. "Lie still."

"Water?"

Someone slipped an arm under his head and raised it, then held a cup of water to his lips. He gulped it down.

"Want more?" Rhodry said.

"I do."

Rhodry helped him drink another cupful, then wiped his face with a wet rag.

"I tried to reach you in time," the lad said. "Please believe me—I tried to reach you."

"I know." Cullyn was puzzled by his urgency. "What of Corbyn?"

"Escaped. Don't let that trouble you now."

The sunny sky circled and swooped around him. He fell back into the darkness, but this time, it was only a sleep.

While servants carried Cullyn away and laid another wounded man on the wagon bed, Nevyn washed his bloody hands in a bucket of water. Only he knew how hard he'd had to fight to save Cullyn's life; he was rather amazed at himself, that he'd actually been able to go into a trance and stay standing up. A little green sprite crouched on the ground and solemnly watched as he dried his hands on a clean strip of cloth. Nevyn risked whispering to her.

"You were right to warn me. My thanks to you and your friends."

The sprite grinned, showing blue pointed teeth, then vanished. If the Wildfolk hadn't warned him, Nevyn might never have realized that someone was up on the higher planes, trying to drive Cullyn's etheric double away from his body and then snap the silver cord that bound him to life. Someone. Not Loddlaen, but someone who stank of dark things, someone who was standing behind him or perhaps even hiding behind him.

"You overreached yourself badly, my nasty little friend," Nevyn said. "Now I know you're there, and I'll recognize you when we meet again."

Just before dawn Jill woke, tossed irritably in bed for a while, then got up and dressed. When she came down to the great hall, the servants were yawning as they took the sods off the fire and fanned the coals to life. Lady Lovyan was already seated at the head of the honor table. When Jill made her a bow, Lovyan waved her over to sit beside her.

"So, child," Lovyan said. "You had trouble sleeping, too?"

"I did, Your Grace. I usually do when Da's off to war."

A servant hurried over with bowls of steaming barley porridge and butter. While Jill and Lovyan ate, the men on fortguard began trickling in in twos and threes, yawning and chivying the servant lasses. One of them must have tripped or suchlike, because from behind her Jill heard the clatter and ring of a scabbard striking against a table. She started to turn around to look, but the noise rang out again and again, like a bell tolling, louder, ever louder until she heard a battle raging, the clash and clang of sword on shield, the whinneying of horses, men screaming and cursing. She heard her own voice, too, babbling of what she saw

as indeed she did see it, spread out below her in the meadow, as if she hovered over the battle like a gull on the wind. Rhodry was trying to force his way into a mob around one rider, and he was howling with laughter, utterly berserk as he swung and parried with a blood-running sword. The man inside the mob could barely swing; he turned desperately in the saddle. Cullyn. Jill heard her voice rise to a shriek and sob as Jennantar's arrows sped past her father and one by one, began to bring his enemies down. At last Rhodry was through, leaping off his horse in time to catch Cullyn as he fell

and the battle noise faded away into the sound of her own

sobs and Lovyan's frightened voice, barking orders to the servants. Jill looked up straight into Lovyan's face and realized that her ladyship had her arms tightly around her. Leaning over was Dwgyn, captain of the fortguard.

"Your Grace," he burst out. "What—"

"Dweomer, you dolt!" Lovyan said. "What else could it be, and her a friend of Nevyn's and all?"

Jill's tears stopped, wiped away by the icy realization that Lovyan was speaking the truth. She felt herself shaking like an aspen in the wind as a servant ran over with a bit of elderberry wine. Lovyan forced her to drink it.

"Jill," she said gently. "Is your father dead?"

"He's not, but he's as close to it as he can be. Your Grace, please, I beg you, I've got to ride to him. What if he dies, and I've never gotten to say farewell?"

"Well, here, my heart aches for you, but you'll never be able to find the army."

"Won't I, Your Grace?"

Lovyan shuddered.

"Besides," Jill went on, "that battle was cursed hard-fought. Lord Rhodry's going to need as many men of the fortguard as you can send him. I know I can lead them straight there, I truly do know it. They're only some twenty miles away. Please, Your Grace."

Lovyan sighed and stood up from the bench, then ran shaking hands through her hair.

"Done, then," she said at last. "Dwgyn, get thirty men ready to ride straightaway."

As Jill ran up to her chamber to get her gear, she was cursing her Wyrd, hating herself and hating the dweomer for taking her over. But for her beloved father's sake, she would use any weapon that came her way.

There were times when the depth of his pride surprised even Rhodry himself. His back hurt so badly from the kicks and bruises of the day before that he could barely stand, and now that the berserker fit had left him, he was feeling every new blow that he'd gotten, but he drove himself to accompany Sligyn on a tour through the somber camp. The men were still bringing in the dead from the battlefield. Everywhere Rhodry heard men curs-

ing or keening as they recognized dead friends. They needed to
see their cadvridoc on his feet.

"Do we call this a victory or not?" Rhodry said.

"Corbyn's the one who fled, eh?"

Down near the supply wagons, Jennantar and Calonderiel
were standing guard over the prisoners, who slouched on the
ground in twos or threes, clinging together for comfort. Most
were wounded, but they'd have to wait for the chirurgeons to
finish with Rhodry's men.

"Any news of Cullyn?" Jennantar asked.

"Still the same." Rhodry wearily rubbed the side of his face.
"I came to thank you."

"No thanks needed. He did his best to save the life of a friend
of mine. I would have loosed more shafts, but I was afraid of
hitting you and your men. I came close enough to killing Cullyn
as it was."

"Better you than one of those scum."

"Well, you pulled him out in the end, eh?" Sligyn laid a
fatherly hand on Rhodry's arm. "All that matters, eh? In the laps
of the gods, now."

Rhodry nodded. He could never explain, not even to himself
in any clear way, just why it was so important that he be the man
who saved Cullyn. He should have pulled him out of the mob just
so they would have been even on that favor. It was cursed important that each owe the other nothing—and yet he couldn't say
why.

His tunic red with gore, Aderyn trotted up with a couple of
servants laden with medical supplies.

"Your men are all tended, lord cadvridoc," Aderyn said. "But
Nevyn said to tell you that Lord Daumyr just died."

Rhodry tossed back his head and keened. Now a noble-born
man had died for his sake. Sligyn tightened his grip on Rhodry's
arm and swore under his breath.

"I'll be working on the prisoners," Aderyn said.

Beckoning to the servants, he walked away, looking for those
who were the worst off.

"Ah by the hells," Jennantar said. "I still don't see how Corbyn got away. I was sure you and Daumyr had him trapped."

"So was I." Sligyn shook his head in furious bafflement. "It
was cursed luck, that's all. Lot of little things, like Daumyr's

sword breaking. And then that horse went down in front of mine, and I couldn't reach him. Luck, cursed ill luck."

One of the prisoners laughed, an hysterical mutter under his breath. When Rhodry swung around to look at him, he flung up one arm and cringed back. His blond hair was crusted with blood.

"I'm not going to strike a wounded man," Rhodry said. "But what are you laughing about?"

"My apologies, I didn't even mean to," the prisoner said, and his voice was full of panic. "But it wasn't luck that let our lord escape. By the gods, you'll never kill Corbyn! It's the cursed sorcerer. He made a prophecy, you see."

"A what?"

"Loddlaen made this prophecy. He got it from his scrying stone." He paused to lick dry lips. "It says that Lord Corbyn can never be slain in battle except by a sword, but he'll never be slain by any man's hand. It's true, my lord. You saw what happened on the field today. It must be true."

Sligyn's florid face turned pale. Aderyn turned to listen.

"Aderyn?" Rhodry said. "Is there any truth in this?"

"The lad's not lying to you, my lord," Aderyn said. "So Loddlaen must have made a prophecy."

"That's not what I meant."

"Does the cadvridoc really want me to tell him if the prophecy's a true one?"

"It must be, or you'd be assuring me that it's false."

Aderyn gave a sigh that was more like a groan.

"I'm sworn never to lie," he said. "And at times, I wish I'd never made that vow."

Rhodry turned and blindly walked away. He felt his death lay a heavy arm around his shoulder and walk with him. Puffing a little, Sligyn caught up with him near the edge of the camp.

"Now here," Sligyn said. "I don't believe a word of it, eh? Doesn't matter if it is true. Lot of horsedung."

"Is it now? If Aderyn can turn himself into an owl, why can't he know the true or false of a prophecy?"

Sligyn started to reply, then looked away and chewed furiously on his mustaches.

"It's a cursed strange feeling, being doomed by dweomer," Rhodry went on. "And doomed I am. When Corbyn chooses to cut his way to me, no one's going to be able to stop him. When we face off, I won't be able to kill him."

"Only one thing to do, eh? Send you back to Cannobaen."

"Never! And what good would my life do me, if I spent it as a shamed man?"

All at once Rhodry felt his berserker's laugh, welling out of his mouth. He tossed back his head and howled until Sligyn grabbed him and shook him into silence.

By late afternoon, the news was all over the camp. Rhodry had never had the experience before of seeing an army's morale crumble like a bit of dried mud rubbed between a man's fingers. It wasn't a pretty sight. Although the noble-born blustered and swore like Sligyn, they looked at Rhodry with a horrified pity. Rhodry walked through the camp and tried speaking personally to the men in the hopes of wiping away a fear so strong that he could smell it. At first, some of the men tried to jest with him, but as the afternoon wore on, they drew back as if he were a leper, this man whom the gods had cursed, lest his ill luck rub off on them.

To spare them the sight of him, Rhodry walked to the edge of the camp with Amyr, the only man in his warband who seemed glad of his company. Blond and bland-looking, Amyr at sixteen was new to the warband, but he had more honor than most.

"My lord, when we face Corbyn again, I'll fight right next to you," Amyr said. "I swore I'd follow you to the Otherlands, and I will."

"I honor you for it, but there's no need. I'm going to challenge Corbyn to single combat and let him put an end to it."

"What?"

"Just what I said. Why by the hells should the rest of you die in a hopeless cause? We'll never kill Corbyn, and so well and good, once he kills me, the rebellion's over."

Amyr turned to him with tears in his eyes.

"Speak well of me after I'm dead, will you?" Rhodry said.

His mouth working, Amyr walked a few steps away. As Rhodry looked down the road, he saw a small troop of horsemen coming up from the south. He waited until he was reasonably sure that Amyr could see them, then pointed them out. As the troop came closer, Rhodry could pick out the colors on their shields, a mixed lot from his various allies, and Jill at their head.

"By the hells, it's the Cannobaen fortguard!" Rhodry said. "What are they doing here?"

As soon as she dismounted, Jill enlightened him on the point.

"Reinforcements, my lord," Jill said matter-of-factly. "I saw the battle in a vision, and you know I'm not daft because there was one, wasn't there? So, by the Goddess herself, where's my father?"

Amyr started to giggle, so loudly and so high that Rhodry grabbed and shook him.

"Pull yourself together!" Rhodry snapped. "We've seen enough dweomer to take a little more."

"It's not that," Amyr said. "It's Jill."

"What? Of course it's Jill. I can see her."

"Not that, my lord. Look—look at Jill. So Corbyn won't die by any *man's* hand, will he?"

Her thumbs hooked into her sword belt, Jill frowned at them as if she was thinking they'd both gone daft. Her stance, her gesture were so much those of a fighting man that suddenly Rhodry saw Amyr's meaning. He threw back his head and howled with laughter until Jill could stand it no longer.

"By the gods!" she snapped. "Have I ridden into a camp filled with madmen?"

"My apologies," Rhodry said. "I'll take you to your father straightaway, but Jill, oh Jill, I should fall to the ground and kiss your feet."

"Has my lord cadvridoc been hit on the head? What is all this?"

"I'll explain after you've seen Cullyn. Silver dagger, I've got a hire for you."

Rather than let Cullyn lie outside with the rest of the wounded, Rhodry had turned his tent over to the man who saved his life. When Jill came in, Cullyn was asleep in Rhodry's blankets with his bound and splinted left arm out of the covers. His hair was streaked with dried blood. As she knelt down beside him, Jill wept in a scatter of tears. When she ran her hand through his hair, he sighed in his sleep and turned his head toward her.

"Jill?" Nevyn said, ducking under the tent flap. "I heard you were here."

"Of course I am. Did you think I wouldn't know when Da was hurt?"

Nevyn smiled briefly and knelt beside her. She thought of telling him about her vision, but it was too frightening to face.

"Answer me truly," Jill said. "Is he going to die?"

Nevyn considered for so long that her heart pounded.

"I doubt it," Nevyn said at last. "That's as honest as I can be. He nearly did die under my hands, but that was the shock, and it's passed off now. Your Da's a cursed strong man, but there's a deep cut on his side. If it goes septic—"

He let the words hang there. Jill sat back on her heels and wondered why she felt so numb, as if she had no body at all.

"He won't wake for some time now," Nevyn said. "Rhodry wants to speak with you. I—well, I'd best let you hear it from him. I'll stay with Cullyn until you return."

Jill ducked out of the tent into a crowd. In quiet ranks the entire army stood around the tent, and every man looked at her in a peculiar way—worshipful, really, as if she were the goddess Epona come to visit them as in the old tales—yet not one man said a word to her. When Amyr escorted her to Rhodry, the men silently followed. Out in front of Sligyn's tent stood the noble-born, staring at her so intently that Jill wished she could just run away. Rhodry made her a bow.

"I've no doubt you can swing that sword you wear," he said. "Have you ever thought of swinging it in battle?"

"Many a time, my lord, but Da's always said me nay."

"He's not going to get a chance this time," Edar muttered.

"Oh here, my lords," Jill said. "Are you as badly outnumbered as all that?"

"Not in the least." Rhodry paused, chewing on his lower lip. "I've got a cursed strange thing to tell you."

"Now here!" Sligyn stepped forward. "How well does the lass know how to fight? I won't have a helpless woman slaughtered. Don't care how desperate we are. Honor of the thing, eh?"

Jill glanced around and saw the servants off to one side, standing ready with dinner for the noble-born.

"My lord Sligyn is the very soul of honor," she said. "But if he'd be so kind as to fetch me one of those apples?"

With a puzzled shrug, Sligyn did as she asked.

"If you'll stand behind me, my lord," Jill went on. "And throw that apple up into the air on the count of three?"

Jill drew her sword and held it point down while she waited for the count. On "three" she spun around, the sword flashing up as the sight of the falling apple filled her vision. Without any conscious aim she hit it perfectly. Two nearly equal halves of the apple fell at Sligyn's feet. The warbands surged forward, cheering, yelling out her name until Rhodry screamed them into silence.

"By the hells!" Sligyn sputtered. "Couldn't do that myself, eh? Well!"

"My thanks, my lord," Jill said. "But don't let me give myself airs. My father can cut one into quarters like that."

Rhodry laughed, but it was a mad sort of delight brimming in his eyes.

"And why do you want me to ride with you?" Jill said.

"Because of dweomer, silver dagger," Rhodry said. "Loddlaen's made a prophecy about Corbyn, and Aderyn's had to admit that it's true. It runs this wise: Corbyn will never die in battle but by a sword, and yet he'll never die by any man's hand."

"Oho! They always say that every dweomer prophecy's like a sword blade." Jill held hers up flat in illustration. "It's sharp on both sides."

The cheers of the army went to Jill's head like mead. When Sligyn yelled at them, the men dispersed, laughing and jesting as they headed back to their campfires. Jill sheathed her sword, then turned to Rhodry, who was holding a silver piece to pledge her the hire.

"If you take my coin," he said, "you're pledging yourself to die for me if need be. Do you truly want to do it, Jill? Never would I wheedle and plead."

"And because you won't, I'll take it." Jill held out her hand. "But if I kill Corbyn for you, you're giving me one of those western hunters I saw in your herd."

With a laugh, Rhodry dropped the coin into her palm.

"Done, and you're a true silver dagger, sure enough."

As Jill pocketed the coin, she glanced at Rhodry's face, and their eyes met. Suddenly she realized that she knew him to the very core of her soul, that somehow, in some strange way, she'd seen that crazed berserker's smile on his face a thousand times before. It seemed that he must have recognized her, too, because suddenly his smile faded, and he stared deep into her eyes as if he was trying to read some secret hidden there. Abruptly he turned away and beckoned to the servants.

"Bring mead!" he said. "So we can pledge my avenger."

"Your what?" Sligyn snapped.

"Well, by every god and his horse," Rhodry said, and that daft grin was back. "Do you think I can ask a lass to save my life? I'll cut Jill's way to Corbyn, who'll kill me, no doubt, and then she can end the rebellion by killing him."

Swearing, yelling at the top of their lungs, the noble-born tried to argue Rhodry down, but he stood firm, his eyes half mad with honor. Jill grabbed his manservant by the arm.

"Run get Nevyn," she said. "He's in your lord's tent."

As he followed the servant back, Nevyn was cursing Rhodry in his mind. Although his heart ached at the thought of Jill riding to war, he knew that he could never stop her. He had, however, expected that Rhodry would have the sense to let her keep him alive. When he reached the arguing crowd, he found Jill standing off to one side. Her eyes pleaded with him for help.

"Now what's all this, you stupid dolt!" Nevyn said to Rhodry. "Use the wits you were born with!"

"Wit has naught to do with it." Rhodry tossed his head. "It's a matter of honor. I can ask a woman to kill the rebel I'll never be able to kill myself, but I'll live shamed if I ask her to save my life. I'd rather die."

"Methinks, lord cadvridoc, that you're cutting the point of honor far too fine."

"Am I now? A Maelwaedd I am, blood and bone, and the honor of my clan is known to every lord in Deverry. Cursed if I'll put the slightest smear on that name."

When Rhodry set his hands on his hips and glared at him, Nevyn growled in utter frustration.

"You put me in mind of the old saying," Nevyn said. "When a Maelwaedd lord starts splitting fine points of honor, it takes three gods to make him hold his tongue."

"Then maybe you'd best start calling on them."

Nevyn grabbed him by the shirt and hauled him close.

"Now you listen to me, Rhodry Maelwaedd!" He gave him a

little shake. "There's more at stake here than your cursed honor! Have you forgotten the dweomer?"

Rhodry turned a little pale.

"I see you had," Nevyn went on. "Your Wyrd is Eldidd's Wyrd. You've been marked by dweomer from the moment you were born, you little dolt! Why do you think I was always hanging around your court? I'm not letting you throw your life away now, if I cursed well have to ensorcel you!"

"Oh by the gods," Rhodry whispered, and he was shaking.

"Think!" Nevyn snapped. "Which is the worse dishonor, letting Jill do what the dweomer drew her here to do, or heaping some strange ruin upon Eldidd because you were too stubborn to fulfill your Wyrd?"

Rhodry turned his head and glanced this way and that, as if appealing for help from the frightened lords around them. When Nevyn let him go, he stepped back sharply.

"Either you swear to me on the honor of the Maelwaedds that you'll fight to save your life, not lose it," Nevyn said levelly, "or I'll take steps here and now."

"Then I'll swear it to you."

"On the honor of the Maelwaedds?"

"On the honor of the Maelwaedds."

"Good. Then I'll leave you to your dinner, my lord. Jill, come with me."

As Nevyn strode away, Jill hurried to catch up, too frightened to disobey, judging from the look on her face.

"So much for Rhodry," Nevyn said. "I'm cursed glad you had the wit to send for me."

"I thought you'd know what to say, but truly, I never dreamt that Rhodry had such a splendid Wyrd. Here, was it really dweomer that drew me here at just the right time?"

"It was. Did you truly doubt it?"

Jill stopped walking, and her mouth went a little slack.

"I know all these strange things must ache your heart, child," Nevyn said. "But Aderyn and I are here to deal with them. Go tend your father. I'll come look in on him in a bit."

Jill ran off so fast that he knew she was terrified. Although he would have liked to have comforted her, he had a crucial piece of work on hand.

By then, twilight had faded into night, and the astral tides, which influence the flux of forces in the etheric plane, had settled down after their change from the dominance of Fire to the dominance of Water, a change that marks the coming of night. Nevyn found Aderyn, and together they left the camp. About half a mile away was a stretch of woodland that would give them the privacy they needed.

"Do you think our enemy will truly try to scout us out?" Aderyn said. "After all, he got a taste of your power this afternoon."

"But he never truly got a chance to look me over. He fled as soon as I started the banishings. Well, I can't know, of course, but I intend to stand guard anyway."

"It's doubtless for the best." Aderyn sounded profoundly weary. "So you were right, and there is dark dweomer mixed up in this."

"I don't know how deeply it's mixed. My guess now is that this fellow is trying to work on the edges of things. Or he was. He betrayed himself nicely this afternoon."

"And why was he trying to kill a silver dagger, anyway? I should think our Cullyn would be beneath his notice."

"So would I." Nevyn hesitated, considering. "I can only think it was because Cullyn's the best guard Rhodry could have. Here, it's been obvious from the first that killing Rhodry is the true point of this rebellion. The rebel lords may think that they're getting him out of the way to lower their cursed dues, but they're only so many tools in the paws of this dark master. I'm fairly certain that Loddlaen is only a tool as well. Here, you trained the lad. Does he have the power to make a true-seen prophecy about Corbyn's death?"

"He doesn't."

"Well, then, where did he get it from? I'll wager someone told him. And another thing. Loddlaen has no way of knowing that Rhodry is crucial to Eldidd's Wyrd, and no reason to kill him, either. I think our real enemy's been subtly influencing Loddlaen for months, using him like a stick to stir up a stench in a fetid pond."

"And why does the dark master want Rhodry dead?"

"I don't know." Nevyn allowed himself a grim smile. "There he has the advantage of us. It's the dark dweomer that's always brooding about Wyrd and the future, not men like us who have the Light to trust in. I've been content to wait for more omens from the Great Ones about Rhodry's Wyrd and let them reveal it to me in their own good time. I'll wager our enemy's been brooding and prying into closed things, and that he has a cursed good reason to want Rhodry out of the way. Whatever it is, it bodes ill for Eldidd."

Aderyn nodded slowly. In the darkness, it was impossible to see his face, but the whole slumped set of his body showed his grief.

When they reached the woodland, they found a clearing near the edge. Nevyn lay down, went into his trance, and transferred into the body of light. He flew up slowly, circling the woods, a tangled reddish glow of vegetable auras, until Aderyn's pure gold aura was a mere spark, far below. This far from the earth, the etheric was an eerie place. Unanchored by any living beings, the blue light shifted and swirled; at times it seemed to grow as thick as sea fog, then suddenly thinned again to reveal the silver glare of the stars above.

At last, after an untellable length of time, Nevyn saw what he was expecting. Far away to the east, a cluster of Wildfolk appeared, circling around a central point as if they were curiously watching a visitor to their plane. All at once they vanished— either out of terror, or because they'd been banished by someone who knew how to dispel them. Nevyn summoned the Wildfolk who knew him and sent them off to distract the possible enemy, but with a warning to keep their distance, then followed along behind them. The ruse worked; he was quite close before the enemy saw him coming.

And an enemy he was. No one but a dark dweomerman would have fashioned such a showy and pretentious body of light: a figure cloaked in a black, hooded robe, hung about with sigils and signs, and belted with a strip of darkness from which hung two severed heads. The figure retreated a few paces, then hovered uncertainly. Nevyn could make out a face inside the hood, two eyes that glowed with the life of the soul inside the simulacrum, and a mouth that worked constantly, forming soundless words. Wherever his body was, it was talking automatically and relaying information to a listener.

"An apprentice, are you?" Nevyn sent out the thought to his

consciousness. "Was your master too much of a coward to risk facing me?"

The figure flew away from him, but as Nevyn started after, it held steady. From the terror in the apprentice's eyes, Nevyn could guess that his master was forcing him to stay and face the enemy.

"Who are you?" The apprentice sent out a tremulous thought.

Nevyn debated, then decided that the truth might be the best stick he had for driving these hounds away.

"Tell your master that in this plane I'm known as the Master of Aethyr, but on the physical, I'm no one at all."

Nevyn saw the mouth working; then the apprentice sent out a thought wave of sheer terror. The simulacrum swooped to one side, tumbled back, then began to break up, the black robe shredding and dissolving as the hood fell away. Thrashing desperately before him was the simple etheric double of a young man, and the silver cord that should have bound him to his body was broken, dangling from his navel. The master had killed his apprentice rather than risk letting Nevyn follow him back to their hiding place.

"You poor little fool!" Nevyn thought to him. "Do you see now what kind of master you trusted? You have one last chance to repent. I beg you, call on the Light and forswear the Dark Path now!"

In a thought sending of pure rage, the apprentice raced away, swooping, tumbling, but rising ever higher into the billows of the blue light. Nevyn let him go, but sorrowfully. He would have liked to have redeemed that soul, but soon enough, the Lords of Wyrd would catch the apprentice and drag him, kicking and screaming, to the hall of light. How they called judgment upon him was no longer Nevyn's concern.

Nevyn followed the silver cord back to his body and slipped in, slapping his hand thrice on the ground to close the working. When he sat up, Aderyn leaned close, listening carefully as he told the story.

"I think me that our enemy is someone who knows you well," Aderyn said.

"So it seems. Well, that apprentice of his is better off dead. He won't be getting himself in deeper in that black muck."

"True spoken. Huh—if the master is that terrified of you, I doubt if he'll come sniffing around here again tonight."

"He won't be able to. Losing an apprentice is a hard blow for one of the dark ones. The masters feed off their vitality, you see, with an etheric link. I'll wager he's sick and shaking right now. Good."

Aderyn shuddered. Like most dweomerfolk in the kingdom, he'd had little contact with the masters of the dark art. But Nevyn was Master of the Aethyr, set like a guard on the border of the kingdom's soul, on constant watch against unclean things that few of those he guarded knew existed. He stood up and began brushing the leaves and dirt off his clothes.

"Let's get back to camp," he said. "I want to set a special seal over our Rhodry's aura."

Some miles away, Loddlaen lay in his tent and tried to sleep. He twisted this way and that, silently cursed the men making noise outside, and even considered drinking himself blind with mead. He was so exhausted that his body felt like a sack of stones, but every time he drifted off, some thought or image would jerk his mind awake. Finally, he surrendered and tried to summon the darkness. He imagined the point of black in his mind, then willed it to swell and spread. It merely vanished. Although he tried for hours, the blackness never came to him.

"We're going to have to let the men spend a day in camp," Sligyn said. "All there is to it, eh? Yesterday's scrap almost tore the heart out of this army."

"You're right enough," Rhodry said. "But it aches my heart to just sit here when Corbyn's so close, and we've got Jill."

"The morrow will see the end to it," Peredyr broke in. "Corbyn can't move any more than we can. His losses were worse than ours."

In the cool gray dawn, the noble-born were having a council of war over their breakfast. Aderyn had told them Corbyn's dispirited troops were camped some five miles to the north, just an easy ride away, but Rhodry knew that Sligyn was right.

When the council broke up, Rhodry had the grim job of composing a letter to go home with Lord Daumyr's body. His men, and all the others, were already buried out on the field where they'd fallen. When he took the letter over to Daumyr's manservant, who would accompany the body, he found the men from Daumyr's warband waiting for him. Their captain, Maer, knelt before him.

"A boon, lord cadvridoc," Maer said. "By rights, we should go home with our lord. Let us stay. We want vengeance, my lord."

Rhodry hesitated, debating. Technically these men now rode for Daumyr's nine-year-old son, who should have been consulted over such a breach of custom.

"Please, my lord," Maer said. "Dweomer killed our lord, and we want to help the dweomer put an end to Corbyn. I know you're thinking about our lord's lad, but what son wouldn't want his father avenged?"

"True spoken. Granted then. Ride with me and my men, and you'll be riding straight for Corbyn."

The men spontaneously cheered him.

After he saw Daumyr's body with its spare honor guard of two wounded men on its way, Rhodry headed for his tent to look in on Cullyn. On the way, he met Nevyn, whose arms were full of medical supplies.

"I'm just going to change the dressings on Cullyn's wounds," Nevyn said. "You'll have to wait if you want a word with him. Here, lad. I don't want you telling him what Jill's up to. He's too weak to hear it."

"Well and good, then. By the gods, I hadn't truly thought of what he might think about all this."

"Indeed? His lordship might spend a moment or two thinking every now and then."

"But here, what's Cullyn going to say when he asks for her on the day of the battle and finds her gone?"

"Oh, he's taken care of that himself. The man's as stubborn as a bear, I swear it. When he woke this morning, he was as grateful as ever a man could be to see her, and in the next breath he's ordering her to go straight back to Cannobaen so she wouldn't be in danger."

"Well, that's honorable of him. After all, he loves his daughter."

"So he does." And Nevyn, oddly enough, looked troubled. "Oh truly, so he does."

Rhodry followed Nevyn over to the tent in the hopes that Jill would take the chance to get herself some breakfast, and indeed, she came out a few minutes after Nevyn went in. They went first to the supply wagons, where Rhodry drew rations for her, then walked away from camp to an open spot in the sunny meadow. When they sat down together, Rhodry was thinking that he'd never wanted a woman as much as he wanted Jill. Every now and then, she smiled at him in a way that gave him hope.

"You know, Jill," Rhodry said at last. "You truly are a falcon, and my heart's just like a little bird, caught in your claws."

"Oh here, my lord, you hardly know me."

"And how long does it take a falcon to stoop and capture?"

Jill stared at him as if she couldn't believe her ears. Rhodry smiled and moved a little closer.

"Well, come now," he said. "You must know how beautiful you are. I'll wager that all along the long road men sighed when you wandered on your way."

"If they did, they wouldn't have dared tell me about it. Da made cursed sure of that. Besides, if I've had men sighing over me, which I doubt from the bottom of my heart, you've had a few lasses do the same over you. What about the soapmaker's daughter?"

"Oh by the hells, how do you know about her?"

"Your lady mother made a point of telling me when I was at Cannobaen."

"Curse her! What—why—"

"She told me I was beautiful, too, and I think me that she knows his lordship very well. I may be a silver dagger, my lord, but there's only one way I earn my hire."

Rhodry felt himself blush.

"Oh ye gods," he said at last. "You must despise me."

"I don't, but I don't want one of your bastards."

Rhodry flopped onto his stomach and studied the grass, which had suddenly become profoundly interesting.

"When we ride out," Jill said. "Nevyn told me to camp with Aderyn, and I'm following his orders."

"You've made your cursed point. Don't pour vinegar into my wounds, will you?"

Rhodry heard her get up and walk away. For a long time he

lay in the grass and wondered at himself, that he would be so close to tears over a lass he barely knew.

Nevyn was walking back to the wagons after tending the wounded when he heard Jill hail him. As he waited for her to catch up, he noticed that all the men in camp looked up when she passed by. Some rose to bow to her; others called out her name like a prayer. They saw her as a dweomer talisman, he realized, and one that at last, after so many terrifying things, they could understand. He also realized that if he did try to keep her out of the battle, as he was sorely tempted to do, Rhodry would have a mutiny on his hands. If only Calonderiel or Jennantar had trained with a sword, he thought bitterly. But he knew that neither of those two archers had a chance against a warrior lord like Corbyn, for all that a sword in an elven hand would have slashed Loddlaen's prophecy to shreds, and there was no time to send west for an elven swordsman.

"Did you want to speak with me, child?" Nevyn said to Jill when she came up. "Is somewhat wrong with your father?"

"Naught, truly, or well, naught's changed for the worse. I just wanted a private word with you."

They strolled past the wagons and out into the meadowland, where there was no one around to overhear. Jill looked badly troubled, and she stood in silence, staring at the ground, for a long time before she finally blurted out what she had to say.

"Do you remember how I knew that Da had been wounded? Well, I saw the whole cursed thing in a vision, and it came on me from nowhere."

Nevyn caught his breath in surprise; he'd been assuming that she'd just had a sudden intuitive knowledge of his danger.

"Will I keep doing things like that?" she went on, and her voice was shaking. "I don't want to. I don't want the dweomer. It's haunted me all my cursed life, but I never asked for it. It's all very well for such as you, but I don't want it."

"No one can force you to take the dweomer." Nevyn hated every bitter truth he spoke, but his vows forced him to tell them. "You have raw talent, certainly, but if you don't train it, it'll simply fade away, much as your legs would wither if you never walked."

She smiled in an evident relief that wrung his heart, then let the smile fade.

"But what about the Wildfolk?" she said. "Will I stop seeing them, too?"

"Oh, no doubt. You know, many children can see the Wildfolk, but they lose the talent by the time they're ten or so. It's odd that you still can, truly, without having been trained."

"I don't want to lose them. They were the only friends I had on the long road."

Her voice ached with remembered loneliness, and at that moment, she looked as much a lass as a woman, caught on the edge of her childhood.

"Well, Jill, it's your choice. No one can make it for you, not your da, not me."

She nodded, scuffing at the grass with the toe of her riding boot, then suddenly turned and raced back to camp. As he watched her go, Nevyn cursed her and his Wyrd both. Sharply he reminded himself that she was just a young lass, overwhelmed by the strangeness of this irruption of dweomer into her life. Although his vows forbade him to argue or plead, he could become her friend, and in time, she would see that the dweomer was in its own way perfectly natural—or he could hope she would. He felt profoundly weary as he walked back to camp, wondering if he'd ever pay back the debt he owed her by bringing her to the dweomer and her true Wyrd. And for her sake more than his own, he wished that he could make her see that she would never be truly happy unless she used the talents that were her birthright.

Then, as he reached the camp, he saw her sitting with Jennantar and Calonderiel. If she would turn instinctively for comfort to a pair of elves, he had no reason to despair so soon. Half laughing at himself, he went to look for Aderyn.

Determined to put her talk with Nevyn out of her mind, Jill watched as Jennantar and Calonderiel played a complicated game, something like dice. The pieces were tiny wooden pyramids, painted a different color on each side, which they shook by the handful, then strewed out in a rough line. The order in which the colors appeared and how many there were of each determined who won the round. Finally Jennantar swept them up into a leather pouch.

"We're being cursed rude to Jill," he remarked.

"Hah!" Calonderiel said. "You're losing and you know it, but truly, Jill, it's good to have a word with you. How's your father this morn?"

"As well as he can be. Nevyn says he's doing better than he'd expected."

"Then that's splendid news," Jennantar said. "I only wish I could have gotten within bowshot faster than I did."

Jill nodded miserably, wondering how she could bear to lie to her father when he lay wounded. Yet she'd never wanted anything more in her life than this chance to ride to war.

"Huh," Calonderiel said. "Here comes our round-eared cad-vridoc. I'll wager it's not us he wants a word with."

Jill looked up as Rhodry strolled up to them—in truth, it was her that he was watching with one of his soft smiles on his handsome face. At times Jill hated him for being so handsome; here was a man that she couldn't simply dismiss. Although she and Jennantar got to their feet, Calonderiel lounged insolently on the grass. Rhodry turned to him with the smile gone.

"When the cadvridoc speaks to you," he snapped, "you stand."

"Oh, do I now?" Calonderiel said. "What makes you think I ride at your orders?"

"You ride at my orders, or you leave the army."

Slowly and deliberately Calonderiel rose, but he set his hands on his hips in a gesture far from respectful.

"Listen, lad," he said. "Save your Eldidd arrogance for others of your stinking kind. I came here with the Wise One of the West, and for no other reason than he asked me to."

"I don't give a pig's fart why you came. You're here now, and you follow my orders or leave."

Jennantar sighed in irritation, then muttered something in Elvish, which Calonderiel ignored. Rhodry and the elf were staring each other down, both of them unblinking and tense. Jill thought of trying to say something conciliatory, but she suddenly knew, in a wordless way that ached with dweomer, that it was crucial for Rhodry to have Calonderiel's respect, and for more reasons than simple army discipline.

"If you have a bone to pick with me, round ear," Calonderiel said at last, "then let's pick it clean between us—and now."

"Now here!" Jennantar stepped forward. "He doesn't know how men duel in our lands."

"Oh, don't I now?" Rhodry said, and he had a twisted little grin. "My uncle made Westfolk welcome at his court, and I've seen your folk before. You're on, then, Calo."

In the middle of a growing crowd they stripped off their shirts and faced off, Calonderiel with his knife, and Rhodry with Jennantar's, since his dagger blade was unfairly short. Jill's heart was pounding; she could see the livid bruises up and down Rhodry's back, and she knew that they would slow him down. Yet it was too late to run and fetch Nevyn, and again the warning came to her—let him do it.

Calonderiel began to circle, and Rhodry moved with him, both of them dropped to a crouch, circling in dead silence. Rhodry feinted in; Calonderiel sprang and slashed; Rhodry twisted out of the way barely in time. Again they circled, slowly, eyes locked, until Calonderiel feinted in. Rhodry stepped back smoothly, then sprang from the side. Calonderiel struck up from below, but Rhodry's left hand moved so fast that Jill could barely see it and caught the elf's dagger hand under the wrist, forcing it up, while the knife in his right flashed in the sun—then darkened with blood. Calonderiel leapt back with a thin red cut dripping along his ribs.

"Do you ride at my orders?" Rhodry snarled.

"I do." Calonderiel lowered his knife. "Lord cadvridoc."

To the cheers of his men, Rhodry wiped the knife off on his brigga leg, handed it to Jennantar, then grabbed his shirt from the ground and strode off. As she watched him go, Jill realized that for all she liked Calonderiel, she was glad that he'd won, that seeing him defeated would have ached her heart. She felt strangely guilty when she turned back to the elf, who was staunching the wound with his shirt while Jennantar watched sourly.

"Our young lord's quick for a round ear," Calonderiel remarked. "Cursed quick."

"So he is," Jennantar snapped. "And now maybe you'll hold your ugly tongue. Aderyn warned us that he wanted no trouble, or have you forgotten that?"

"I hadn't, but I can't ride under a man who can't best me in a fight."

"No doubt you see it that way." Jennantar turned to Jill. "Our Calo here's somewhat of a cadvridoc himself, back in our lands. I suppose when you're used to ordering hundreds of archers around, you find it hard to take another man's orders."

"Only a round-ear's," Calonderiel put in. "Don't I put up with your stinking arrogance all the time?"

Jennantar laughed easily.

"Cadvridoc or not," Jill said. "You'd best see Aderyn about that cut."

"Oh, it's but a nick. Rhodry held his hand a bit. He's not a bad man, truly, for a round-ear. Besides, the owl's off flying, scouting out our enemy. It makes the old man nervous, having our rebels so near at hand."

A river of blood flowed over Corbyn's camp, ran slowly and thickly around the tents, eddied around the men, and lapped at the horses. Even though he knew it was only an out-of-control vision, it took Loddlaen a long time to banish it, and even when the river was gone, it seemed that a rusty stain remained on everything it had touched. He pressed his hands between his thighs to hide how badly they shook, while he tried to listen to the council of war. The noble-born were arguing about something, but their words seemed torn by a wind from nowhere. Finally he got up and strode away without a word to them. As he walked through the camp, he could feel the hatred of the men like daggers in his back.

Inside his tent, it was cool and mercifully quiet. The army was too dispirited and battle weary to make much noise. Loddlaen lay down on his blankets and breathed deeply and slowly until his hands stopped shaking. He was going to have to summon the darkness. Even though they were out of control, his visions showed him that everything was falling apart, and he knew that somewhere in the darkness was a power that could help him. He shut his eyes, let himself go limp, then pictured the darkness in his mind and called to it. The image was only a picture; no power flowed, no darkness came. He tried again, and again, but he could summon not even the tiny point of black that was the starting of the true dark.

All at once he knew: he had been deserted. His strange ally who had come unbidden was gone, utterly gone beyond calling. He opened his eyes and felt himself shaking, sweating. For a moment he was as confused as a child who goes to sleep in its mother's arms only to wake in a strange bed. What had he done, involving himself in this petty rebellion when he should have been running, traveling east as fast as he could to get beyond Aderyn's reach? Suddenly he remembered the murder, the elf he had slain over a scrying stone. Aderyn was only a few bare miles away, and he would want retribution. How could he have forgotten? Only then did he realize just how deeply he'd been ensorceled—and for months. He wept, throwing himself facedown and sobbing into the blankets.

Gradually he became aware of the noise outside. It built on the edge of his mind for a long time before it became insistent enough to take his attention. Men were shouting in anger, running back and forth outside, and horses nickered as they trotted past. It had to be an attack. Loddlaen got to his feet just as Corbyn threw back the tent flap.

"There you are!" Corbyn snapped. "Help me, by the hells! Don't lurk in here like a sick hound!"

"Watch your tongue when you speak to me! What's so wrong?"

"Cenydd and Cinvan are trying to pull their men out. They want to desert the rebellion."

With an oath, Loddlaen followed him out. He was terrified, wondering if there were anything he could do, now that the darkness had deserted him.

Nevyn sat on the ground in the shade of the wagon. Since his eyes were closed and his shoulders slumped, the servants apparently thought that the old man was having a little nap, because they spoke in whispers whenever they came near him. They could have shouted aloud for all that it would have disturbed his trained concentration, and rather than sleeping, he was meditating. He held the image of a six-pointed star, a red triangle and a blue intertwined, in his mind and used it the way a clumsier dweomerman would have used a scrying stone. In the center of the star images came and went, mental reflections from the astral plane, which embraces the etheric the way the etheric embraces

the physical. There, thought-forms and images have a life of their
own, and it holds memories of every event that has ever happened on the planes below.

Through this vast treasure house Nevyn searched, looking
for traces of the dark master who had become an immediate and
pressing enemy. Since the event was so recent, it was easy for
Nevyn to bring up the images of the last battle, a confusing,
flickering, overlapping mob of pictures. At last he sorted through
and found Cullyn, fighting desperately with the squad around
him. Nevyn froze the picture in his mind, then used it as a seed to
let other images gather round it, just as a bit of dust in the air is
the seed for a drop of rain. Finally he saw what he was looking
for. Flickering into the center of the star came a presence, a
certain blackness, hovering far on the etheric over the battle.
When Nevyn tried to bring it closer, it vanished. The dark master
had hidden his tracks well.

Nevyn broke off the meditation in something like irritation.
He hadn't expected to discover much, but he'd had hopes that
way. He got up and stretched, wondering what tack to try next,
when he saw Aderyn, running full tilt back to camp and heading
for the tents of the noble-born. Obviously Aderyn had important
news, and Nevyn hurried after him.

Rhodry was sitting with Sligyn and Peredyr in front of Sligyn's tent when Aderyn ran over to them. He could see that the
dweomerman was troubled, and he rose to greet him.

"My lords," Aderyn said, panting a little to catch his breath.
"Corbyn's broken camp, and he's marching north. I found him a
good ten miles away."

"Ah curse his very balls! What's he doing, running for his
dun?"

"It looks that way, and here, there's only about a hundred
sound men with him. I saw only two blazons—Corbyn's green
and tan, and a red shield with a black arrow."

"Nowec's men," Sligyn joined in. "So his other allies have
deserted, eh? That's the best news I've had in many a day."

"Then he's bolting for his dun sure enough," Rhodry said.
"We've got to catch him. Cursed if I'll have him suing for peace
now, and we'll never take Dun Bruddlyn. Here, if we leave the
baggage train behind, we can overtake him late today."

"Normally I'd agree with that," Peredyr said. "But Loddlaen will know what we're up to. Corbyn will have the time to pick a strong position, and there we'll be, charging with exhausted horses."

Rhodry felt like cursing him, but it was true.

"Well and good, then," he said. "We'll follow him along today, and try to catch him on the morrow." Then he noticed Nevyn, standing nearby and listening. "Here, good sir, you and Aderyn truly should ride near me at the head of the line when we ride."

"Oh, Aderyn can ride where he likes," Nevyn said, "but I'm going to accompany the wounded back to Dun Gwerbyn."

"What?" Rhodry snapped, feeling deserted.

"Here, lad, I haven't told you before, but you've got a worse enemy than Loddlaen at your back. I intend to do a rear-guard action, shall we say? Aderyn can deal with Loddlaen, and indeed, he has to settle this matter by himself."

Nevyn walked off before Rhodry could argue further, and for all that he was cadvridoc, he didn't feel like trying to order the old man around.

Getting the army fed, packed, and moving took well over an hour, which Rhodry spent in a fury of impatience. To free his servant for other things, he saddled his own horse and got his gear together, then sent for Jill. He took her over to a cart carrying the mail salvaged from the slain men. Much to his horror, she'd never worn mail before.

"Ah ye gods," Rhodry snapped. "How are you going to fight if you're not used to the weight?"

"I'll have to get used to it cursed fast, then, my lord."

"Let's pray you can, but this troubles my heart. Ah by the black hairy ass of the Lord of Hell, I wish you weren't riding with us."

"It's your Wyrd, and because of that, I'll kill Corbyn, sure enough, even if I die with him."

Jill spoke so quietly that he wanted to weep for the shame of it, that his Wyrd would put her in danger. He left her to find a mail shirt and helm and went out to the horse herd. Among the extra horses he had a particularly fine western hunter, named Sunrise, with a coat of the palest gold. He'd been keeping this horse out of the battles just because it was so valuable, but he was

determined that Jill would have him. He saddled Sunrise up with
a proper war saddle, then led it back to her. Seeing her wearing
mail, with the hood pushed back around her shoulders and her
golden hair gleaming in the sunlight, made his heart ache all over
again. She was so beautiful, and for all he knew, his Wyrd had
doomed her. Jill greeted him with a wry smile.

"You're right about the weight," she said. "Ye gods, I never
realized that mail was so heavy."

"It's a good two stone, sure enough." He handed her the
reins. "Here, silver dagger. Here's the horse I promised you."

"Oh by the hells! His lordship is far too generous."

"He's not. If I have to ask a lass to guard me, then she'll
cursed well get the best horse in the whole army."

Jill laid her hand softly on his cheek.

"Rhodry," she said. "If you didn't feel dishonored by this, I'd
scorn you, but if you don't let me fight for you, then you're a
dolt."

He turned his face against her hand and kissed her fingers.

"Then I do as my lady commands," he said. "And live."

He walked off, leaving her speechless behind him, and his
mind was torn this way and that, like leaves driven by the autumn wind, between wanting her and fearing for her life.

At last the army was ready to ride. Alone at the head, Rhodry
led his allies and his men north, following the road that zigzagged
through fields and woodlands, curved maddeningly around farmsteads, and rambled through villages that Rhodry in his impatience felt were placed there just to slow him down. His one
comfort was that Corbyn was traveling with wounded and thus
would have to travel more slowly than he could. Late in the
afternoon, he saw lying by the side of the road two corpses—
some of Corbyn's men who'd died from their wounds as they
tried to keep up with the forced retreat. Rhodry halted the army,
and Sligyn rode up beside him.

"Poor bastards," Sligyn remarked.

"Just that. I wonder how many more we'll find. Corbyn's
cursed desperate."

"He's got every right to be, eh? We're riding to kill him."

For all that he wanted to make speed, Rhodry had some of
his men wrap the bodies in blankets and put them into one of the

carts. That night, when they made camp, they buried them properly.

It was well after sunset when a messenger from Rhodry came to Dun Cannobaen. The men on fortguard, just as anxious as Lovyan was for news, crowded round while the scribe read out the dispatches. When she heard of Daumyr's death, Lovyan groaned aloud.

"I'm heartsick at this news," she remarked to all and sundry. "He was a good man and a true one." She paused, thinking things out. "On the morrow, we'll all ride out. If Corbyn's running like a fox to his earth, there's no danger he'll besiege me here. Men, you'll escort me and my womenfolk to Dun Gwerbyn, then ride after the army."

The fortguard cheered her. Dannyan turned her way with a quizzical lift of an eyebrow.

"I want to be nearer the war," Lovyan said. "If Corbyn's allies have deserted him, then they'll all have to sue for a separate peace. I want to be at Dun Gwerbyn to receive them. What if Rhys takes it into his mind to be at Dun Gwerbyn in case they want to sue directly to him?"

"He might, at that. I'd forgotten about Rhys."

"I can't, not for one cursed minute of one cursed day."

Once the army had pulled out to chase Corbyn, Nevyn went to his blankets and slept all afternoon, waking just in time to tend the wounded at the dinner hour. As soon as it was dark, he left the camp and walked to the woodland. He'd been telling Rhodry the simple truth when he talked of standing a rear guard, and to do it he had no need of being physically close to Rhodry, any more than the dark master needed to be physically close to attack him. Nevyn was sure that the dark master was very far away, at least far enough to flee in plenty of time should Nevyn send armed men after him.

Safely hidden in the woods, Nevyn went into his trance and up to the etheric plane. Flying faster than any bird, he sped north until he saw the tangled mass of auras that marked Rhodry's army below him. Like a sentry, he hovered above it and circled this way and that as the hours slipped by, unmarked and untellable until midnight, when the astral tide changed from Water to

Earth, and the etheric began to billow and churn. Nevyn fought and held his place, like a swimmer treading water in a choppy sea.

Now, if the dark master was desperate enough, was the perfect time for him to make an attack. Nevyn kept low, close to earth where the billows were less severe, and he tried to keep his guard. Every now and then, he rose up higher, fighting the waves, to get the distant view before he was forced to sink down again. Slowly the waves grew slower, smoother; slowly the billows and churning died away. Just when the tide had finally turned, he saw someone coming to meet him—but it was Aderyn, floating along in a simple blue body of light much like his own.

"How goes it?" Aderyn thought to him.

"Dull, so far. Not a sign of our enemy."

"I've seen naught, either. I risked going in this form to Corbyn's camp. Loddlaen never challenged me."

Aderyn's grief swept out like a wave, almost tangible there on the etheric.

"Think of him as dead, my friend." Nevyn put as much gentle sympathy into the thought as he could. "Mourn him and let him go."

"There's naught else I can do."

Abruptly Aderyn turned away and, following the silver cord, floated down fast to his body.

Nevyn kept his watch all that night, until the Aethyr tide began rolling in a little before dawn. Since no dark master could work magic under the tides of Aethyr or Air, Nevyn returned to his body. As he walked back to camp, he was mulling over his long, boring night. It was possible that the dark master was merely holding his hand, waiting until Nevyn dropped his guard, possible, but highly unlikely. Nevyn dwelt on the dark master, thought of every grim thing he might do, but no dweomer-warning came to him, not the slightest twinge. From its lack, he knew that the master had fled the field entirely.

"I should have done that last night and saved myself the boredom," he remarked aloud. "But truly, I never thought he'd give up so easily."

All at once, he had to laugh at himself. He took his powers so much for granted that he'd forgotten how terrifying they would be to someone with good cause to fear him.

The night before, Rhodry's army had camped in a common pasture about half a mile from a farming village. Although Rhodry woke everyone before dawn and yelled orders to hurry and get ready to ride, they had to linger for at least an hour, simply to allow the horses to graze. Jill supposed that Corbyn was already on the march; he could risk harming his horses because he was headed for his dun.

As Jill was drawing her rations, Aderyn came up to her and asked her to walk with him aways. Nearby was a copse of willows around a duck pond, and they went there for a bit of privacy. With a sigh, Aderyn sat down on a fallen tree trunk. The brightening light picked out the wrinkles around his eyes and made him look very weary, indeed.

"I hope I don't offend you, Jill," Aderyn said. "But do you truly think you can best Corbyn? I won't have you killed in a hopeless cause. If nothing else, Nevyn would never forgive me, and his wrath is nothing to invoke lightly."

"Oh, I can well believe that. But as long as its in single combat, I think I can get him sure enough. From what Rhodry says, he's old, slowing down, and he's got a good paunch on him. If I can keep him moving, I'll wear him down."

"Old? I thought he was but eight and thirty."

"Well, no offense on my part, but that's old for a fighting man."

"I suppose so. I—"

Suddenly the light in the copse dimmed around them. Aderyn jumped to his feet and swore as a mass of thick gray rain clouds swept down out of an otherwise clear sky. With a slap, wind hit the copse in a welter of falling leaves. In the distance, thunder cracked and rumbled.

"Is Loddlaen behind this?" Jill said.

"Who else? I'll deal with it. Run, child—the horses!"

Under the shadows of clouds, scudding in fast with the cold scent of rain, Jill raced back to the camp and found it in confusion: men swearing, captains and lords running, yelling orders, the horses dancing at their tether ropes. Just as Jill reached the herd, the first lightning struck, a crackling blue bolt ominously near. Neighing and plunging, the horses pulled at their tethers. The lightning hammered down again; big drops of rain fell in a scatter. Jill grabbed the halter of the nearest horse and pulled it down just in time to keep it from breaking free. Swearing, the rest of the army was among the herd and doing the same. Rhodry came running and grabbed the horse next to her.

"Get ready to run," he yelled. "If they stampede, save yourself and let them go!"

With a slap of wind the rain poured down, drenching them in two minutes. The horses danced and tossed their heads as the men pulled them down and talked endless nonsense to soothe them. But that was the end of the lightning, as if the god Tarn had snatched his weapons back from Loddlaen. In a few minutes more, the rain stopped with an eerie suddenness. When Jill looked up, she saw the clouds breaking up and swirling in a troubled, gusty wind. For a moment it seemed that they would mass again and more would follow them in, as a real storm would have done, but the stretch of blue sky overhead stayed stubbornly clear, then widened, as if the clouds were spilled flour and a giant with a broom were sweeping them away.

"Oh ye gods." Rhodry whispered. "Dweomer."

The last of the clouds dissolved. They did not blow away; they did not thin out and slowly dissipate; they dissolved, suddenly and completely gone. Jill shuddered convulsively.

Yet even though Aderyn had dispelled the storm, it still slowed the army down. Soggy provisions had to be repacked; wet blankets, wrung out; mail, rubbed dry; nervous horses, soothed. They set out a good hour later than they might have—an hour that meant three more miles between them and Corbyn.

"We're leaving the carts behind," Rhodry snapped. "Jill, ride next to me. We're going all out to catch the bastard."

When Jill rode into line, her heart was pounding in fear. For all that she'd bragged to Aderyn, wearing unfamiliar mail was going to slow her down, and speed was her greatest weapon in any fight. Her shoulders ached like fire from the weight, too. But when Rhodry gave her one of his berserker grins, she smiled back at him with a little toss of her head. Cursed if she'd let him see that she was afraid.

The army went at a walk-trot pace, which meant they could do five miles an hour compared to Corbyn's three. As they rode,

Jill looked up constantly, and after a few miles she saw a hawk, circling high above them. Her stomach clenched. When the hawk flew away, it headed straight north. They rode on, past farms shut up tight against the doings of warring lords, through fields and woodlands. Jill decided that dying in battle would be easy, compared to this clammy fear that clung to her.

And yet, in the end, Corbyn escaped them. They came to a stubbled field, where they saw provision carts, some ten wounded horses, and fourteen wounded men, dumped there by their lord to live or die with no help from him. Corbyn had left everything behind that might slow him down and was making a run for Dun Bruddlyn.

"Ah horsedung and a pile of it!" Rhodry snarled. "We'll never catch them now." For a long moment he sat slumped in the saddle, then looked up with a sigh. "Well, no help for it, huh? Let's go see what we can do for these poor bastards. The baggage train and the chirurgeons will catch up to us soon enough."

As she dismounted, Jill was thinking that she'd never met a lord so honorable as he. Together they walked over to the improvised camp, where wounded men lay shivering in wet blankets on the ground. Loddlaen's storm had swept over them, too. One man stood, leaning against a cart, his head wrapped in a bloody bandage and his right arm splintered. When he saw Rhodry, two thin trails of tears ran down his face.

"What's your name, lad?" Rhodry said. "And how long have you been here?"

"Lanyc, my lord, and since last night. We all camped here last night, and then they left us."

"And did your lord give you any choice in the matter?"

"None, my lord, or well, none to the others. I said I'd stay with them. At least I can stand, and I've been trying to feed everybody." Lanyc paused, looking at Rhodry with eyes half drunk with pain. "It was the sorcerer, my lord. Lord Corbyn never would have deserted us, but Loddlaen made him. I saw it. He ensorceled him. Ah ye gods, I'd rather be your prisoner than shut up with that stinking sorcerer."

"By the hells," Jill said. "I don't blame you a bit."

At the sound of her voice, Lanyc sobbed under his breath. "A lass," he whispered. "Oh ye gods, a lass with a sword." Then he burst out sobbing.

The baggage train creaked up about an hour later. Rhodry set the two remaining chirurgeons to doing what they could for Corbyn's men, but Aderyn joined in the council of war. The lords stood despondently in a circle and looked at the muddy ground.

"Well, that's torn it," Sligyn said. "Might as well ride on and invest him anyway, eh? The honor of the thing."

"True enough," Rhodry said. "Ah by the hells, he's probably got messengers on their way to Rhys right now, begging him to intervene. It's going to hurt when my ugly brother calls me off like a hound from the kill."

"Indeed, my lord?" Aderyn broke in. "What if the messengers never reach him?"

All the lords turned to look at this frail old man who held power beyond what they could even dream of.

"Loddlaen has to be stopped and now," he went on. "Do you think Gwerbret Rhys is going to believe us if we tell him that Loddlaen incited this rebellion with dweomer? Of course not. And then Loddlaen will get off lightly in the malover by paying a blood price for the man he killed back in our lands, and he'll be free to work more mischief."

"That's all well and good," Rhodry said. "But even if we catch the messengers, they'll testify against us to Rhys unless we kill them. Cursed if I'll kill a pair of helpless men."

"Never would I want you to," Aderyn said with a small smile. "Leave them to me, lord cadvridoc. I won't harm a hair on their heads, but Rhys will never get Corbyn's message. I promise you that."

The line of carts carrying the wounded moved slowly and stopped often to let the men rest. At noon, they lingered for a long time while Nevyn and the chirurgeon did what they could. Nevyn had just found time to get himself something to eat when he felt Aderyn's mind calling to him. He walked a little ways to a tiny brook and used the sun dancing on the water as a focus. Aderyn's image built up quickly.

"Did you catch Corbyn?" Nevyn thought to him.

"We didn't, curse him. He's going to stand a siege in his dun. Quick—tell me somewhat. You know the politics of Eldidd a cursed sight better than I do. Suppose Corbyn were going to send a desperate message to some ally, asking him to relieve the siege. Who would it be?"

"Oh come now, do you really think he'd be that stupid? He should be sending a messenger to Rhys to sue for peace."

Aderyn's eyes were unusually sly.

"No doubt he is," he thought. "But answer my question anyway. I'll explain later when there's more time."

"Well and good, then. Let me think. Huh—Talidd of Belglaedd, no doubt."

"My thanks."

And then the image was gone, leaving Nevyn to wonder just what scheme his old pupil had afoot.

Because Lord Corbyn received coin in taxes from his bridge over the Delonderiel, Dun Bruddlyn was a solid fort, ringed by stone walls and large enough to house a warband of over a hundred men. Although Loddlaen usually hated being penned up there, he was glad to reach it that night. As what was left of the army crawled in the gates, Loddlaen turned his horse over to a servant and hurried up to his chambers on the top floor of the broch. He threw back the shutters from the window in his bedchamber and leaned out into the clean evening air. He was so exhausted that he was close to tears.

It was all Aderyn's fault, he told himself, all his fault because he wouldn't let me send the storm like I wanted. Well, maybe the old man won the first skirmish, but there'll be other battles.

"I'm not defeated yet!" Loddlaen snarled in Elvish. "No, not I, Loddlaen the Mighty, Master of the Powers of Air!"

But when he turned from the window, he saw Aderyn, standing in the middle of the chamber. The image was so clear and solid that Loddlaen cried out, thinking that he was there in the body. Only when the vision wavered slightly did he realize that it was a projection and that he had forgotten to set his astral seals over the dun.

"Lad, lad, listen to me," Aderyn said. "You still have one last chance. I know that someone was working on you, using you. Surrender now and make restitution. If any more men die because of you, you'll be beyond forgiveness. Surrender now while you can still be helped."

Aderyn looked so heartsick that Loddlaen sobbed once

aloud. His father was standing there, offering to forgive him; his father had known all along what he'd only just discovered, that he'd been ensorceled—that he'd been weak and stupid enough to let himself be ensorceled by an enemy that he didn't even know.

"Lad," Aderyn said. "I beg you."

Shame, embarrassment, a kind of self-loathing—they rose, choking him, turning suddenly to dirty smoke that filled the room and obscured Aderyn's image. Loddlaen wanted to cry out, to reach out his hand to his father, but the smoke was making him gag, and all at once, he was furious, trembling and screaming with rage.

"Get out! Get out! I don't need your help!"

Loddlaen called up power and threw a stream of pure force, a barrage of fiery light, but long before it could hit, the image was gone. Loddlaen fell to his knees and wept in the midst of the churning, filthy smoke, which slowly, a wisp at a time, cleared of its own accord.

It was a long time before he could get himself under control. He rose and staggered to a small table, where a pitcher of mead and a goblet stood ready, poured himself a full goblet, and drank it straight down. All at once, he could no longer bear to be alone. Goblet still in hand, he ran out of the chamber and hurried down the spiral staircase.

Lord Corbyn's great hall was a hot smokey confusion of men, sitting at tables, standing in the curve of the wall, talking in low voices or merely drinking ale down as fast as the servants could pour it. Loddlaen took his usual place at Corbyn's right. Across from him was Nowec, his eyes dazed as he looked around him. Even though Loddlaen had lost the others, he'd been able to ensorcel this lord. Corbyn was eating a slice of roast pork, biting into it, then cutting off the bite with a greasy dagger.

"Glad you came down, councillor," Nowec said. "Your lord and I have just been discussing sending messengers to the gwerbret to sue for peace."

"He'll grant decent terms," Corbyn said, his voice too loud with a false cheer. "But we've got to get the men on their way tonight. I'll wager Rhodry invests us tomorrow."

Both men looked expectantly at Loddlaen.

"Of course," Loddlaen snapped. "You don't need dweomer to tell you the obvious."

Both lords nodded sheepishly. Corbyn fanged his pork and sawed off another mouth-filling bite.

"We need to know exactly where Rhodry is," Nowec said. "Can't have the messengers blundering right into them."

Corbyn nodded his agreement, then belched. Loddlaen could stand them no longer.

"I'll attend to it straightaway," Loddlaen said.

As he hurried up to his chamber, he was sweating with fear. He was too afraid of Aderyn to scry on the etheric plane, and that meant he would have to fly. Trying to shape-change when exhausted was dangerous. Upon entering his chamber, he lit the candle lantern with a snap of his fingers. Seeing the flame spring to his call soothed him. He still had power, more power than those round-ear dogs even knew, him, Loddlaen the Mighty! He stripped off his clothes and threw them onto the bed. Not even the mightiest masters of the dweomer could transform dead matter like cloth.

Loddlaen laid his hands far apart on the windowsill and stared up at the starry sky until he was perfectly calm. Slowly he felt power gather, carefully he invoked more, until it flowed through his mind like a mighty river. In his mind, he formulated the image of the red hawk, many times life size, proud and cruel, then sent the picture forward until it perched on the windowsill between his hands. At this point the hawk image existed only in Loddlaen's imagination, and it was only in imagination that he transferred his consciousness over to the bird. He had spent years on tedious mental exercises that allowed him to imagine that he stood on the windowsill and saw the view below with the hawk's eyes. Keeping his consciousness firmly focused in the hawk, he chanted the power word, a simple hypnotic device, that opened the door to the etheric for him. When he saw the view through the cold blue light, he knew that he'd transferred his consciousness up a level.

At this point, things had gone beyond simple imagination. When he glanced back, he saw his body slumped on the floor and joined to the hawk with a silver cord. He could have scried on the etheric with the hawk as a body of light, but he had a more dangerous plan. In his mind he chanted a second set of words,

one that only the Elcyion Lacar knew, and saw the lips of his
body twitch in rhythm. When he flexed the hawk's wings, the
arms below him raised. Now came the true difficulty. The etheric
double of every person is like a matrix that holds and forms flesh;
if the double is strong enough, the flesh will follow its lead. Loddlaen chanted, struggled, bent all his will into the imagining that is
more than imagination until at last, with one final wail of chant,
the etheric drew the physical into its new mould.

Loddlaen the man was gone from the chamber. Only the
hawk stood on the windowsill and stretched proud wings. With a
harsh cry of triumph, Loddlaen sprang into the night and flew
out over the dun. He loved flying, the perfect freedom of drifting
on the wind, the view from on high, where every fort and house
seemed just a tiny toy, scattered by a child's careless hand. Even
in the hawk form, Loddlaen retained the etheric sight that was so
important a part of the transformation. The countryside below
glowed in the bluey night with the reddish auras of the living
vegetation. Here and there were daubs of yellow glow where
horses or cows huddled together. The road was a cold black strip.
Following the road, Loddlaen flew south until he saw the gleaming mass of auras that had to be the men and horses of Rhodry's
army.

Loddlaen flew upward to gain height, then circled in a long
sweep about the camp. His mind was alert, feeling out the
etheric plane for the traces of Aderyn's dweomer working. When
he found none, he assumed that the old man was asleep or busy
wasting his time by tending wounds. Then he heard a cry, the
soft mournful note of the owl. With a start and a flap of terror,
Loddlaen beat hard against the wind and gained more height. He
saw a trace of silvery motion below him as the great silver owl
sprang out of the trees. In stark terror, Loddlaen turned on the
wind current and raced for the dun, beating his wings hard and
steadily until he was sure that he'd left the clumsier owl behind.
Yet even though he reached the dun safely, as he settled onto the
windowsill he heard or thought he heard a call, one soft note of
mourning drifting in the night.

Toward noon of the next day, Rhodry's army reached
Corbyn's demesne. Everywhere the farmhouses were shut up
tight, with not so much as a chicken out in the farmyard. From

bitter experience the farmers knew that the army of even a lord like Rhodry would steal any fresh food that came its way. Corbyn's dun stood at the top of a low artificial hill in the middle of a big stretch of open pasture, but none of his lordship's cows were to be seen when the army reached it. Leaving the carts behind, they trotted over, fully armed and ready in case Corbyn stupidly tried to sally, but they found the heavy iron-bound gates shut. Up on the catwalks men stood half hidden by the merlons. Defiant at the top of the broch flew Corbyn's green banner. Rhodry ordered his men to fan out and surround the dun. The investment had officially begun.

Just as the carts arrived, Corbyn sent out a herald, his aged chamberlain Graemyn, trembling even though he carried the beribboned staff that would have kept him safe from even the most murderous lord in all Deverry. When he saw the portly old man puffing down the hill, Rhodry dismounted and honorably walked a few steps to meet him—but he made sure he stayed out of bowshot of the dun.

"Greetings, Lord Rhodry," Graemyn said. "My lord requests that you withdraw from his lands."

"Tell your lord that I respectfully decline to fulfill his request. He is a rebel and under my proscription."

"Indeed?" Graemyn licked nervous lips. "Even now messengers are riding to Gwerbret Rhys to sue for his intervention in this affair of war."

"Then I'll wait here with my army until his grace arrives. You may consider yourselves under full siege until the gwerbret personally orders me to withdraw. Tell your lord also that he's harboring a murderer, Loddlaen his councillor, and that I demand he be turned over to me speedily for trial."

Graemyn blinked twice, then trembled a little harder.

"I have sworn witnesses to Loddlaen's crimes," Rhodry said. "If Loddlaen is not delivered to me by nightfall, then your lord is twice in rebellion. There's one more thing, good herald. Although I'm determined to prosecute this war against Corbyn, I'm extending pardon to Nowec and his men. All they have to do is ride out and ask for it."

Graemyn turned and fled, going as fast as his short breath would allow. Rhodry laughed, then walked back, shouting out orders to the army to settle in and start digging earthworks.

Needless to say, nightfall came without Loddlaen being handed over, but by then the army was firmly entrenched. The carts were drawn up in a circle and guarded by a narrow ditch and bank; the tents were raised and surrounded by a broader one. Armed patrols trotted endlessly around the hill in case Corbyn tried to escape. As the men settled down to their well-earned dinner, Rhodry and Sligyn walked through the camp for an inspection.

"I wonder if any of this will do us the least bit of good," Sligyn said gloomily. "It's all very well for Aderyn to ramble on about stopping the messengers, but what could he have done? Can't see one old man murdering them on the road, eh?"

"After all the cursed dweomer I've seen, I'm ready to believe anything. We'll just have to wait and see."

As it turned out, the wait was a short one. Around noon the next day, a guard ran up to Rhodry with the news that a noble lord, come with an escort of twelve men, was waiting just outside the camp. The lord turned out to be Talidd of Belglaedd, who owed direct fealty to the gwerbret. Since Rhodry could only assume that he was there with a message from Rhys, he was cursing inwardly as he bowed. A man of close to forty, Talidd looked shrewdly on the world out of narrow green eyes.

"And what brings you to me, my lord?" Rhodry said.

"A cursed strange business." Talidd turned to gesture to his men. "Bring those prisoners here."

When they were led up, Rhodry recognized them as two of Corbyn's men. They knelt at Rhodry's feet and stared at the ground in a humiliated shock.

"Did you know that my sister is Corbyn's wife?" Talidd said.

"I didn't," Rhodry said. "She has my sympathy."

Talidd allowed himself a twitch of a smile.

"I should say she was Corbyn's wife," Talidd went on. "When she and her women came to me at the beginning of this cursed war, I made a vow that she'd never go back to her piss-poor excuse of a husband even if you didn't hang him. He's driven her mad, stark raving mad! She's been babbling about evil dweomermen and evil spirits taking Corbyn over until I can't stand it anymore."

"By the hells!" Rhodry did his best to look shocked and horrified. "What a terrible thing!"

"So I thought. Well, then, yesternight these two ride in with a message from Corbyn, asking me ever so sweetly to raise an army and ride to lift the siege."

Rhodry whistled under his breath at the gall of it.

"Cursed right!" Talidd snapped. "As if I'd break the gwerbret's peace and meddle in somewhat that's none of my affair, especially after the way he's treated one of my blood kin! If your lordship agrees, I'm going to take these riders down to Rhys and present the matter. Corbyn didn't send a letter, you see, so I need their testimony."

"Nothing would gladden my heart more. All I ask is that you let me show them off in front of the dun before you go, so Corbyn knows that my herald is speaking the truth when he says I've got them."

They went into Corbyn's chambers to discuss the news in private. Nowec perched on the windowsill, Corbyn paced back and forth, and Loddlaen sat in a chair and tried to project a calm contempt for this turn of events. Grunting like a pig, Nowec repeatedly rubbed his mustaches with the back of his hand.

"It was cursed stupid of you to approach Talidd," Nowec snarled.

"I didn't!" Corbyn snapped. "Can't you get that through your thick skull? I never sent any message to Talidd. I sent those two men to Aberwyn to sue for peace, just like we'd decided."

Loddlaen swore in Elvish.

"A traitor," Corbyn went on. "There has to be a traitor in the dun, and he judged Talidd's mind to a nicety, too."

"And just who would this traitor be?" Nowec said. "There's no one here but us and our men, and I can't see your two lads thinking that up on their own."

"Just so." Corbyn stopped pacing to turn on him. "I was wondering about that myself. I'm not the one who received the offer of pardon."

When Nowec's hand drifted toward his sword hilt, Loddlaen jumped up and got in between them.

"Don't be fools," Loddlaen snapped. "It would have been cursed easy for Rhodry's men to take the messengers on the road and bribe them then and there."

Corbyn sighed and held out his hand to Nowec.

"My apologies," Corbyn said. "I'm all to pieces over this."

"And so am I." Nowec shook his hand firmly. "Well and good, then. Well, can't drink spilled ale, can you? The question is, what do we do now?"

"I haven't given up hope yet," Corbyn said with a flattering smile at Loddlaen. "Maybe there are other ways to send messages, ones that don't require horses."

Loddlaen felt sweat spring up on his back. Aderyn was right outside, waiting and watching for him to try to escape.

"Perhaps." Loddlaen forced out a smile. "His lordship has been pleased with my subterfuges in the past."

Corbyn smiled. Nowec began running his fingers through his mustaches as if he meant to tear it out.

"If my lords allow," Loddlaen went on, "I'll retire to my chamber and consider the problem."

Loddlaen ran up the staircase to his chamber, barred the door behind him, then flung himself down on his bed. All his talk of Rhodry's bribing messengers was just so much chatter to keep up the two lords' morale. He knew that Aderyn had to be the one behind the ruse. It would have been easy for the old man to ensorcel them and inject an image into their minds, to plant a clear and vivid memory of Corbyn telling them the message to Talidd. They would have no way of discovering that the memory was as false as a dream.

He got up and paced restlessly to the window. Maybe he could reach the gwerbret with the message. He could put Corbyn's letter and some clothes into a sack that the hawk could carry in its talons, then somehow evade Aderyn and fly to Aberwyn. Somehow. He laughed, an hysterical giggle, knowing that no matter how fast he flew, Aderyn would be following behind. Unless, of course, he killed Aderyn first. He clutched the windowsill hard with both hands. To kill your own father—oh ye gods, had he come this low?

Loddlaen flung himself down on the bed again. All afternoon he lay there, and his mind was as choppy as the sea when the tide runs one way and the wind, another.

Since there was a chance that Corbyn would make a desperate sally now that his messengers had been apprehended, everyone in Rhodry's camp went armed that afternoon. Jill joined

Calonderiel and Jennantar, who were standing guard over the horses with their longbows ready. As the hours dragged by, even the two elves were hard-pressed to find jests.

"You know, Jill," Jennantar said. "I've been thinking about our Lord Rhodry ever since that little scrap he had with Calo here. There's something about the way he moved, and how quick he was, that's suspicious. Would you do somewhat for me? See if you can get him to touch your silver dagger. I wager it glows."

"What's the old saying?" Jill said. "Elven blood in Eldidd veins?"

"Oho!" Calonderiel joined in. "You think, lass, unlike the rest of the cursed round-ears."

"Would you not use that word?" Jennantar snapped. "It's cursed discourteous, especially in front of Jill."

"Now, Jill may have round ears." Calonderiel pointed at one of them with his bow. "But she's not a round-ear. There's a big difference."

Jennantar growled like a dog.

"Oh well and good then." He gave him a grin. "I won't sully your pointed ears with the word again." He ducked back as the other elf swung a fake punch at him. "But truly, Jill, see what happens when Rhodry gets that blade in his hands."

"I'll do my best," Jill said, honestly intrigued. "And as soon as I can, too."

By then it was nearing sunset, and the fading light made a sally impossible. When Rhodry called off the guard, Jill and the two elves went back to camp. Since everyone was expecting a long siege, the elves had raised the tent they'd brought on their travois. It was a beautiful thing, about ten feet across and eight high, made of purple-dyed leather and painted with pictures of running deer in the forest, so realistically done that Jill could have sworn that the deer would turn their heads and look at her. While Jennantar went to draw rations for the three of them, Calonderiel helped Jill off with her chain mail. She felt as if she were floating just by contrast.

"I pray to every god in the sky that Corbyn doesn't sally before I get used to this cursed stuff," she said.

"So do I." Calonderiel looked sincerely worried. "You might ask Aderyn for some ointment if your shoulders are sore."

"You know, I think I will."

Aderyn did indeed have a rubifacient mixture in sweet lard that took some of the ache away. Jill went into the comfortable privacy of the tent and rubbed the minty-smelling stuff into her shoulders and upper arms, then merely sat there for a while to rest. Now that she was faced with the hard reality of the coming battle, she was frightened, thinking that her father was right enough. She knew nothing of the screaming shoving confusion of a real battle.

"It's too late now to get out of it," Jill remarked to the gray gnome. "And better dead than a coward."

The gnome yawned in unconcern. She supposed that he could have no idea of what death meant.

"Jill?" It was Rhodry's voice. "Are you in there?"

"I am, my lord. I'll come out."

But Rhodry slipped in just as she put on her shirt, and he was grinning in triumph at catching her alone. The gnome opened its mouth in a soundless snarl as he sat down beside her.

"This tent is splendid," Rhodry said. "I wanted a look at the inside."

"I never knew that the lord cadvridoc had an interest in leather cushions and tent poles."

"A very great interest." Rhodry inched a little closer. "Why, I don't think I've ever seen finer cushions than these."

The gnome leaped up and slapped his face. Rhodry swore and looked around for the source of the blow, but the gnome jumped onto his back and grabbed handfuls of his hair. With a yelp, Rhodry batted at the enemy he couldn't see.

"Stop that!" Jill snapped.

With an audible hiss the gnome disappeared. Rhodry gingerly rubbed his scalp.

"In the name of every god," Rhodry said, "what was all that?"

"I don't know, I'm sure. Are you having spasms? Maybe you should consult with Aderyn."

"Don't tell me that." Rhodry grabbed her wrists. "You know cursed well what happened. Why else did you yell 'stop that'?"

Jill twisted against his thumbs, broke his grip, then started to scramble up, but he caught her by the shoulders and dragged her back. For a moment they wrestled, but Jill began to giggle and let him win.

"Answer me," Rhodry said, and he was smiling. "What was it?"

"Oh, well and good, then. It was one of the Wildfolk, and he was jealous of you."

Rhodry let her go and sat back.

"Are you daft?" he snapped.

"You felt it pull your hair, didn't you?"

Rhodry looked at her with such revulsion on his handsome face that she suddenly hated him. She pulled her silver dagger and held it close to him. The light ran like water down the blade.

"Oho!" Jill said. "Elven blood in Eldidd veins, indeed! Don't you look so snot-faced about me. I may see the Wildfolk, but you're half an elf."

When Rhodry grabbed the dagger from her, it flared as brightly as a sconce full of candles. Swearing, he turned it this way and that while Jill laughed at him.

"It's got an enchantment on it," Jill said smugly. "It glows around the Elcyion Lacar, and that's who the Westfolk really are. You're half one of them, I swear it."

"Hold your tongue." Rhodry flung the dagger down. "And don't you laugh at me."

The order, of course, only made her laugh the more. Rhodry grabbed her by the shoulders and shook her, so hard that she slapped him across the face.

"You little hellcat!" Rhodry snarled.

Shoving and swearing, they wrestled like a pair of wild things, but he was the strong one when her fighting tricks were of no use. Finally he pinned her on her back, lay half across her, and smiled, his face only a few inches from her own.

"Cry surrender," Rhodry said.

"Shan't."

He bent his head and kissed her. It was the first kiss a man had ever given her, and it seemed to burn on her mouth, as if she were aflame with thirst and only Rhodry's kisses could slake it. She slipped her arms around his neck and kissed him again, open-mouthed and greedy.

"My pardons, lord cadvridoc," Aderyn said. "But is this truly wise?"

With a yelp Jill shoved Rhodry away and sat up. His arms crossed over his chest, Aderyn stood over them, and he wasn't smiling. Rhodry turned scarlet and sat up, too, smoothing his shirt down.

"From the noise in here," Aderyn said with great asperity. "I thought I'd have to break up a fight. What are you two, cats squawling with love in a barnyard? By the hells, Jill, I've got to answer to both Nevyn and your father about you. I don't care to face either of them in a rage."

Neither did Jill. She wanted to melt like spring snow and sink into the earth with shame. Rhodry forced out a sheepish smile and picked up the silver dagger, which promptly glowed in his hands.

"I know what you're going to say, good Aderyn," Rhodry said, fiddling nervously with the dagger hilt. "And you'll be right, too. It would be a shameful thing of me to dishonor the woman I love in the middle of an army camp. I had no intentions of doing anything of the sort."

"There are times," Aderyn said, "when I truly wish I could turn men into frogs! It's cursed hard to believe those fine words. I—"

All at once Aderyn stopped and stared at the dagger. Jill supposed that he was so used to dweomer that he'd only just noticed the enchantment on the blade.

"So," Aderyn said at last. "It's a cursed strange thing about elven blood in a clan. It skips generation after generation, and then all at once, out it comes in someone."

"What?" Rhodry squeaked. "What cursed nonsense—"

"No nonsense at all. Jill, take that dagger back. You're coming with me. As for you, my lord, think about this. I know it's a bit of a shock, but you're as much kin to the Elcyion Lacar as you are to the Maelwaedd clan."

Just that evening, the wagon train with the wounded and the prisoners reached Dun Gwerbyn. Standing on the crest of a hill, the dun towered over the little town that had grown up around the tieryn's principal residence. Inside the dun walls were a triple broch and enough huts and houses for a village. Although Nevyn was pleased to learn that Lovyan had already arrived, he had no time to talk with her for some hours. Together with the official chirurgeon, he oversaw getting the wounded bunked down in the barracks, changed the dressings on everyone's wounds, then bathed before he went to the great hall. At the door he met Lord Gwynvedd, the chamberlain, a highly efficient man despite having lost his right arm in battle years before.

"I followed Rhodry's orders about the silver dagger," Gwynvedd said. "He's in a chamber in the broch, and the chirurgeon's already seen him."

"Splendid. I'll look in on him myself in a bit. Where have you seated me for meals?"

"At the table of honor, of course. Her grace is there now, and she wants a word with you."

Lovyan's great hall was easily a hundred feet across. In between the windows tapestries hung on the wall, and the floor was covered with neatly braided rushes. Lovyan rose to greet Nevyn and seated him at her right hand. Since everyone else had long finished eating, a servant brought him a trencher of roast pork and cabbage and a tankard of dark ale.

"Nevyn," Lovyan said. "Where's Jill? Several people now have told me she's with the army, but that can't be true!"

"I'm afraid it is, curse her. Have you heard of the dweomer prophecy? That's true, too."

"Oh ye gods! I thought everyone had gone daft." Lovyan took his tankard and helped herself to a sip of ale. "Truly, I'm as worried about Jill as I am about Rhodry. It was odd, considering how short a time she sheltered with me, but I've never met a lass I liked more."

Nevyn merely smiled, thinking that it was hardly odd at all, considering how deeply Lovyan's Wyrd had been entwined with Jill's in lives past.

After he finished eating, he went to his chamber up in one of the joined towers. A page had already brought him a pitcher of water and started a charcoal fire in the brazier to take the damp off the stone walls. Nevyn opened the shutters over the window for a bit of air, then stood over the glowing coals and thought of Aderyn. In a few minutes Aderyn's image appeared, floating over the fire.

"I was going to get in contact with you later," Aderyn thought to him. "I've just found out somewhat that's cursed interesting. I saw young Rhodry holding Jill's silver dagger, and it was glowing like fire. All the elven blood in the Maelwaedd clan's come out in him."

"By the gods! Of course! I should have seen that years ago. It explains many an odd thing about the lad."

"It's a hard thing to spot about a man sometimes. I suppose that's why the dwarves developed that dweomer for their silver. I'm more concerned with keeping the lad alive than ever. When the time comes for the meeting of elves and men, it would be useful to have him tieryn on the western border."

"Useful and twice useful. I've always had strange omens about the lad, and I wonder if this lies at the core of them."

"It might, at that, and truly, I wonder if Rhodry's elven blood is what made him so interesting to our dark enemy."

"Indeed? Why?"

Aderyn hesitated, looking puzzled.

"I don't know," he said at last. "The thought just seemed to come to me."

"Then it's an idea worth pondering. You may have been given a message."

After Aderyn broke the link, Nevyn paced back and forth and wondered if indeed Rhodry was the man meant to mediate the ancient feud between elf and man. It's difficult in the extreme for the Great Ones—the Lords of Wyrd and the Lords of Light—to communicate with their servants on earth, simply because those disincarnate beings inhabit a plane far removed from the physical, far more deeply within the heart of the universe than even the astral plane. If one of the Great Ones has to send a message, he has to work a dweomer of his own, first building a thought form that's roughly the equivalent of a dweomer-master's body of light, then using that form to travel down the planes to the lowest level such a being can reach. From that plane, he can then either direct the elemental spirits to produce certain effects, such as thunder from a clear sky, or else send images, emotions, and with great difficulty, short thoughts into the mind of a person trained in dweomer. If one of the Great Ones had gone to such effort to send Aderyn a message about Rhodry's elven heritage, then something very important indeed was at stake.

As Nevyn thought about it, he could see that the dark dweomer might have some interest in ensuring that peace never came to the elven border, simply because those who follow the dark arts are safer in troubled times, when lords can't be bothered with tales of peculiar people who do strange things in out-of-the-way places. And yet, the reason wasn't quite adequate. Unlike the evil magicians in the bard songs, who love to cause misery and suffering for its own sake, the men of the dark dweomer never act directly in the world without some very good reason. If a dark master wanted Rhodry dead, it had to be because Rhodry presented some specific threat to him or to his kind. It was puzzling, all of it, and Nevyn knew that he had many hard hours of meditation ahead of him if he was going to begin to sort the puzzle out. He was sure that he had more clues than he could easily see, and that the roots probably lay deep in his own past and in the past lives of those in his care.

"I grow so cursed old," Nevyn remarked to the brazier. "And so cursed weary."

Whenever Nevyn looked over his life, the memories were crowded and tangled, as if he were looking at the wrong side of a tapestry and trying to figure out the pattern on the front. Quite simply, he'd never had the chance to sort things out in the state called death, where the experiences of a lifetime are sorted and condensed to hard, clear seeds of experience. Everything ran together and blurred until at times, he could barely remember the names of people who had been important to him, much less why they had been important, simply because the information was sunk in a sea of meaningless details. At other times, when he was trying to make a decision, the memories crowded so thickly that he could barely act. Every possible course of action would immediately suggest three or four possible different results that had happened or might have happened in the past. Every fact became qualified a hundred times over, like some passage from a Bardek poet when adjective after adjective clusters round and overwhelms one poor little noun. In truth, as he considered the problem that night, Nevyn realized that he thought very much like an elf.

"So be it," he said with a laugh. "It's not my will, anyway, but the will of the Light."

Fortunately he had too much work on his hands. to sit and brood. He gathered up his supplies and went for a look at Cullyn. Cullyn was awake, lying propped up on pillows, and a servant had lit the candles in the silver sconce on the wall.

"Nevyn," Cullyn snapped. "I just heard—ye gods, how could you lie to me that way?"

There was only one thing he could mean.

"Who told you she's with the army?" Nevyn said.

"The cursed chirurgeon. By the hells, he's cursed lucky I'm too sick to stand, or I'd have taken his head for this. How could you lie to me?"

"There wasn't anything else I could do. She was determined to go, and I didn't want you upsetting yourself."

Cullyn growled under his breath. He was close to tears.

"Did our fat-mouthed chirurgeon tell you of the prophecy, too?" Nevyn said.

Cullyn nodded a yes.

"She's most likely going to kill Corbyn," Nevyn went on. "The whole thing has the ring of Wyrd to me, and she's your daughter, after all."

"She's never been in a battle. How could Rhodry—I save his cursed life, and this is how he repays me. I swear it, if she dies, I'll kill him. I don't care what his ugly clan does to me for it. I'll kill him."

What might have been a boast from another man was the simple truth coming from Cullyn of Cerrmor. Nevyn felt trouble coming, sweeping over them all like a breaking wave.

"I thought I liked the lad," Cullyn went on. "I was fool enough to think I honored him."

"Hush! You can't do anything about it now, and you're just upsetting yourself."

"Hold your tongue, old man! I don't give a pig's fart if you're dweomer or not. Just hold your tongue."

At that moment he sounded so much like Gerraent that Nevyn nearly slapped him. Sharply he reminded himself that Cullyn was no more Gerraent than he was still Prince Galrion.

"I'm going to look at that wound whether you like it or not," Nevyn said.

"Go ahead. Just hold your tongue."

Cullyn closed his eyes and pressed the side of his face down hard into the pillow. As Nevyn opened his sack of supplies, he was thinking about the coming trouble. Sooner or later, Cullyn would realize that Rhodry and Jill were besotted with each other. Would he fly into a rage and kill the most important man in

Eldidd? And what of Jill? Would he keep her from the dweomer? Would his honor fail someday the way Gerraent's had?

"Well," Cullyn snapped. "Get on with it, will you?"

"I will. Just getting out a clean bandage."

It was then that Nevyn was faced with severest temptation, the bitterest test of his entire dweomer-touched life, which had tested him so many times before. When he took the chirurgeon's clumsy bandage off the wound on Cullyn's side, he saw immediately that infection was setting in. The signs were so very small— just the slightest swelling at the edges of the torn flesh, just the slightest unnatural redness—that only he would have noticed. Obviously the chirurgeon hadn't. He could ignore it if he chose. He could ignore it for just this one night, and by the morrow, when the chirurgeon came round again, the infection would have spread so far that not even Nevyn would be able to check it. He could stand there and let Gerraent die. His desire was like a burning in his whole body.

"By the hells," Cullyn snarled. "Get on with it!"

"Hold your tongue! You're in a bit of danger. I don't like the look of this wound. Did that chirurgeon remember to wash his cursed hands?"

And the moment was over, but Nevyn would remember it for years, the time when he had nearly broken every solemn vow he had ever sworn.

"He didn't," Cullyn said. "Not that I saw, anyway."

"Those cursed dolts! Why won't they believe me when I tell them that foul humors linger on their filthy paws! I'm sorry, lad, but I'm going to have to take the stitches out and wash the whole thing with mead."

Cullyn turned his head to look at him and did the last thing Nevyn would ever have expected—he smiled.

"Go ahead," Cullyn said. "The pain will take my cursed mind off Jill."

"Wonder how long they're going to stew in there, eh?" Sligyn said. "They should just surrender or sally, curse them."

"Corbyn will never surrender," Rhodry said. "He knows I'm going to hang him from his own gates."

Sligyn nodded and stroked his mustaches. They were sitting

on horseback at the edge of the camp, looking up at the dun, where the green pennant flew in a stiff morning breeze.

"I hope to every god that Nowec takes my offer of pardon," Rhodry said.

"If the cursed sorcerer will let him, eh? Here, Aderyn tells me he's keeping some kind of watch on the dun. Says he'll know the minute that Corbyn's men start preparing for a sally." Sligyn shook his head in angry bafflement. "And then he had a jest on me, too. I say to him, how will you know, a scrying stone or suchlike? Oh, not that, says he, the Wildfolk will tell me. Eh! That's what you get for asking questions of sorcerers, I suppose."

Rhodry forced out a brief smile. He didn't care to tell Sligyn that the Wildfolk were real enough. He wanted to believe that Aderyn and Jill had been only having a jest on him, but he'd felt something pull his hair. As he thought it over, it also occurred to him that Aderyn had sworn a vow never to lie, which meant that it was the simple truth that the Westfolk were the Elcyion Lacar of legend, and that he himself was half-kin to them. Elven blood in Eldidd veins. At that moment, Rhodry hated the old proverb.

The slow, hot day passed without Corbyn making a sally. At dinner the noble-born ate together and wondered why Corbyn kept postponing the inevitable. There was only one answer, that he hoped his sorcerer would eventually pull him out of this particular fire. For all they knew, Loddlaen might be able to send Rhys a message by magic.

"Aderyn would stop him," Rhodry said.

"One hopes," Edar said gloomily. "Who knows what the dweomer can do or not?"

Somehow no one volunteered simply to ask Aderyn, and in an uneasy silence, the council of war broke up. Rhodry got a clean shirt and went downstream from the camp to bathe. In the starlight he walked surefooted, then stripped off his clothes and plunged into the cool water. Getting reasonably clean soothed his nerves somewhat, but as he was dressing, he saw the two men of the Westfolk coming, as surefooted in the dark as he was. Calonderiel hailed him with a laugh.

"As clean as an elf, too, aren't you?" he said.

"Oh by the hells!" Rhodry snarled. "What did Jill do? Open her big mouth and spill the tale?"

"Of course," Jennantar joined in. "We're the ones who put

her up to it. I've noticed a thing here and there, and I've been wondering about you, lad."

Rhodry looked him over carefully. In the starlight Rhodry was color-blind like any ordinary man, and small details were blurred and lost, but he could see enough to find a certain kinship in the narrow build and long fingers he shared with Jennantar. Although both of them were heavily muscled, they were built straight from shoulder to hip, just as he was.

"Does it ache your heart," Jennantar said, "finding out there's wild blood in your clan?"

"I can't lie and say it doesn't," Rhodry said. "But I mean no insult to you."

"None taken," Calonderiel said. "Here, I've been searching my memory, and if I've got the tale right, one of our womenfolk ran off with a Maelwaedd lord named Pertyc."

"That was the first Maelwaedd to be Gwerbret Aberwyn," Rhodry said. "And it was a cursed long time ago, too. I wish now I'd listened better when the bard was reciting all those tales and genealogies about my ancestors. It doesn't seem so tedious, all of a sudden."

They both laughed, and Calonderiel gave him a friendly cuff on the shoulder.

"Come back to our fire with us," Jennantar said. "We've been hoarding a skin of our mead, but this seems like a good time to break it out."

"And I'll wager you've always been able to drink any other man under the table," Calonderiel said.

"I have at that," Rhodry said. "And is that another thing I share with you?"

"It is, and one of the best traits of the Elcyion Lacar, too," Calonderiel said. "If you ask me, anyway."

Elven mead turned out to be twice as strong as the human variety, and cleaner-tasting, too, so that a man could drink more of it. The three of them sat by the campfire and passed the skin around silently while Rhodry decided that he liked his newfound kin. All his life he'd known that he was somewhat different from the men around him, and now at last he knew the reason. It was comforting to find out that there was a reason.

"Where's Jill?" Rhodry said at last.

"Standing a turn on the night watch," Calonderiel said.

"Oh by the hells, she doesn't have to do that!"

"She insisted," Jennantar said. "It's not a silver dagger's place to lounge around like a lord, she tells me."

"And soon, no doubt," Calonderiel said. "The lord cadvridoc will be inspecting the night watch, just to make sure none of them have fallen asleep on duty."

"Hold your tongue," Rhodry said. "Unless you want another knife fight."

"After all the mead we've drunk, we'd doubtless trip right into the fire," Calonderiel said. "Just a jest, and my apologies."

The meadskin went round again in a companionable silence. And what of Jill? Rhodry asked himself. What if he did manage to seduce her, what then? He could never marry her; she would end up pregnant like Olwen, and there would be another woman whose life he'd ruined. This time, the woman would be someone who was risking her life in his service. Perhaps the mead helped, but he saw it quite clearly, that he loved her too much to dishonor her that way, that he loved her enough to let her go. He would have to treat her like a sworn priestess of the Moon, so far beyond a man's lust that it meant death to touch her.

Yet, when Rhodry was walking back to his tent, he saw Jill coming in from the watch. For a moment his lust was so strong that he couldn't breathe. Although he'd always scorned those bard songs that told of men dying for a woman's love, that night he almost believed them. He made himself turn away and walk into the darkness before she saw him. He was afraid of what he might do if she gave him one word of encouragement.

There comes a point in any illness when the sufferer realizes not that he's mending, but that at some point, he will mend, if not soon, then eventually. Cullyn reached that point that evening, when he woke to find his mind clear for the first time since he'd been wounded. The pain had receded, as if his slashed side stood a little ways away from the rest of him, and his broken arm was merely sore under the splints. For the first time, too, he truly noticed the luxury that surrounded him—a private chamber, a bed with embroidered hangings, a carved chest where someone had laid out his sword and silver dagger as if he were a lord. It was all because he'd saved Rhodry's life, he supposed. He lay very still and tried to decide if he were sorry now that he'd done so.

Eventually Nevyn appeared with his sack of medical supplies.

"Will you have to wash that cut again?" Cullyn said.

"I hope not." Nevyn gave him a thin smile. "I'm beginning to understand why you have so much glory. You're the first man I've ever tended who didn't scream when I poured mead on his open wound."

Cullyn sighed at the memory. Keeping silent had cost him every scrap of will he possessed. Nevyn poured him water from the silver flagon by the bedside.

"Do you remember cursing me last night?" Nevyn said.

"I do, and you have my apologies for that. It's not your fault Jill went off to the cursed war. Here, I can hold that goblet myself."

"Good. You need to start moving to get your strength back."

"So I do."

Cullyn heard the venom in his own voice. When Nevyn gave him the goblet, he raised one bushy white eyebrow in a questioning sort of way.

"I meant what I said about Rhodry," Cullyn said. "That wasn't just a sick man's temper."

"I never doubted it for a minute. May I humbly suggest that you wait to see if she's killed before you start brooding your revenge? She might very well kill Corbyn. I wouldn't have let her go if I didn't think she could."

Ignoring him, Cullyn took a couple of greedy gulps of water. "How long before I can fight again?"

"Months. You'll have to get your shield arm back in shape after it mends."

"Ah horsedung. And how long before I can get out of this bed and fend for myself?"

"Oh, much much sooner. Tomorrow I'll have you walk a few steps just to see what that does."

"Good. As soon as I can, I'm leaving Rhodry's hospitality. I don't want another cursed favor from him. I wish by every god that they'd dumped me in the barracks with the other men."

"Oh ye gods, Gerro! I swear you're the most stubborn man alive."

"What did you call me?"

There was a certain grim pleasure in seeing a dweomerman look utterly flustered. Nevyn's cheeks even turned a bit pink.

"My apologies," Nevyn said. "I've tended so many men today that I can't seem to tell one from the other."

"No doubt. It's not like I took any insult, mind."

Much to Cullyn's relief, Nevyn pronounced the wound free of infection when he changed the dressing. The old man sent a page to fetch bread and milk, then stood by while Cullyn ate it.

"Answer me somewhat," Cullyn said. "I'm cursed surprised that Rhodry's honor would let Jill do his fighting for him. Why did he take her along?"

"The dweomer of the thing," Nevyn said. "And Jill herself. Once she heard that prophecy, it would have taken the Lord of Hell himself to have kept her out of the army. She wants battle glory as much as any lad, my friend. You might think about that before you take Rhodry's head off his shoulders."

"There are times when Jill can be a little dolt. Ah ye gods, what did I expect, dragging her along with me? Oh well and good, then. I'll think about it, but if she's killed—" He let the words hang there.

Nevyn raised his eyes to the heavens as if calling the gods to witness Cullyn's stubbornness, then packed his supplies and left without another word. Cullyn lay awake for a long time, hoping that the siege would be a good long one. Maybe he would heal enough to ride there and pull Jill out before it came to battle. For all his rage, it would ache his heart to kill young Rhodry, he decided. Cullyn winced when he remembered how hard Rhodry had tried to pull him out of the mob—him, a cursed lousy silver dagger. Many a lord saw a silver dagger's death as a convenient way out of paying him his hire and nothing more. And yet if Jill were killed—the thought made him weep, just a quick scatter of tears that he saw as shameful.

The letter from Rhys was brief and maddening.

"My lady," it ran. "I understand that your cadvridoc still holds the siege of Dun Bruddlyn. Since Lord Talidd has brought me proof of Lord Corbyn's continuing treachery, I will let you settle the matter by the sword if you prefer. Let me warn you that even your eventual victory may not quiet all the grumbling against you as long as Rhodry is your heir."

Lovyan crumpled the parchment into a little ball. She was tempted to throw it into the messenger's face, but after all, it wasn't the young rider's fault that his lord was an arrogant pig-headed fool.

"I take it my lady is displeased?" Nevyn said.

With a little snort Lovyan smoothed the parchment out and handed it over.

"You may go," she said to the messenger. "Have some ale with my men. I'll have an answer for you soon."

The lad scrambled up and made his escape from her wrath. Nevyn sighed over the message, then handed it back.

"Rhys is dead wrong about the grumbling," Nevyn said. "Rhodry's proven himself in this war."

"Of course. He just wanted to infuriate me to salvage some of his cursed pride, and he's done it quite successfully, too."

They were sitting in the great hall, which was peculiarly silent. Only ten men, some of the recovering wounded, were with them in a room fit for two hundred.

"Do you think I should ask Rhys to intervene?" Lovyan said. "It aches my heart to think of more men dying over this."

"Mine, too, but if Rhys does disinherit Rhodry somehow, then all the men who've come to admire him will start grumbling. It might lead to another rebellion, and even more men will die in that."

"True spoken." Lovyan folded the parchment up neatly and slipped it into the kirtle of her dress. "I'll calm myself, then send Rhys an answer, saying his intervention will not be required."

Up at Dun Bruddlyn, the besiegers slipped into a routine that was tense and tedious at the same time. Since Corbyn might have sallied at any moment, everyone went armed and ready, yet there was nothing to do but polish weapons that were already spotless, ride aimless patrols to exercise the horses, and wager endlessly on one dice game or another. Although Jill tried to leave Rhodry strictly alone, it was impossible to avoid him in so small a camp. At times she would go to draw rations only to find him among the carts or come face to face with him as she walked back to camp after tending Sunrise. At those chance meetings he said very little and made no effort to keep her at his side, but every now and then, when they looked at each other, she would feel that she was drowning in the blue of his eyes.

By the seventh day of the siege, Jill felt that she just might go mad from this endless waiting for battle. As she admitted to Aderyn that night, she was quite simply afraid.

"Da says that anyone with any sense is always afraid before a battle," she said. "So I suppose I can take comfort in that. At least I've gotten used to the cursed mail. I was sparring with Amyr today, and it doesn't slow me down anymore."

"Well and good then. I've been waiting for that."

Jill felt a cold shiver run down her back.

"Loddlaen is the key to everything," Aderyn went on. "Corbyn's been ensorceled so long that without Loddlaen, his nerve will break, and he'll either surrender or sally. I've already asked Jennantar and Calonderiel to help me kill Loddlaen. Will you come with us when we go hunting the hawk?"

"I will, truly, but how are we going to get at him?"

"I'm going to make him fly. I wager I can lure him out, because I know him very well indeed." He got up slowly. "It may take some time, mind, but I'll just wager he comes to us in the end."

After Aderyn left her, Jill sat by the campfire and wondered what strange dweomer Aderyn would use to lure his enemy out. She was still musing over it when Rhodry stepped out of the shadows as silently as one of the elves and sat down next to her. Jill's heart pounded to have him so close to her.

"Tell me somewhat," Rhodry said. "Are you sure that Nevyn spoke the truth about my Wyrd being Eldidd's Wyrd?"

"I am. Rhodry, are you aching your heart again over having a lass fight for you?"

"Well, what man's heart wouldn't ache? But it's not just the honor of the thing. I can't bear to think of you being harmed. I think I'd rather have bards mock my name than to risk you getting one little scratch."

"Has his lordship been drinking mead?"

"Oh, don't be all My Lady Haughty with me! You know I love you, and you love me too."

Jill got up, threw a branch on the fire, then watched the Wildfolk dancing along the dry bark in a long flare. After a long moment she heard Rhodry get up behind her.

"Jill?" he said. "I know I can bring you nothing but harm. You're right enough to be cold to me."

Jill refused to answer.

"Please?" Rhodry went on. "All I want is to hear you say you love me. Say it just once, and I'll be content with that."

Rhodry slipped his arms around her from behind and pulled her back to rest against him. The simple human comfort of his touch went to her head like mead.

"I do love you," Jill said. "I love you with all my heart."

His arms tightened around her; then he let her go. She stared into the fire while he walked away, because she knew that she would weep if she watched him go.

"We've got one last hope, the way I see it," Nowec said. "Rhys hates his cursed brother so much that he might intervene just to shame him."

"He might, truly," Corbyn said.

When they both looked at him, Loddlaen merely shrugged. They had been besieged for eight days now, eight stinking days in the hot dry autumn weather, eight days of living behind stone walls—a torment for a man used to riding with the Elcyion Lacar. He wanted to make them share his torment by telling them the bitter truth, but he wanted to have a plan of escape laid by before he did. If he could find a plan of escape.

"I've been working on the gwerbret's mind, of course," Loddlaen lied smoothly. "But the situation's vexed for him. He has councillors who argue against intervention."

"Ah ye gods!" Nowec said. "We've got to think of morale. Can't you do somewhat faster?"

"The dweomer has its own times of working."

"Oh indeed, you piss-proud beggar? You were quick enough to get us into this mess."

Loddlaen stared straight at him. From his own aura he sent a line of light and struck at Nowec, spinning the lord's aura. Nowec's eyes went glazed.

"I do not care to be cursed," Loddlaen said.

"Of course," Nowec whispered. "My apologies."

Loddlaen spun the aura once more, then released him.

"Besides," Loddlaen went on. "I assure you that the question of morale is very much on my mind. No doubt I can keep the men confident of our eventual victory."

Loddlaen rose, bowed, and swept out of the chamber. He had to be alone to think. All he wanted to do was to call forth fire and burn that stinking dun to the ground. He would escape; he'd pack his clothes and a few coins in a sack, then fly away alone and free. Somewhere he'd find another lord to ensorcel, somewhere far to the east where Aderyn would never find him.

"I'll follow you, lad," Aderyn said. "Even to the ends of the earth."

With a yelp, Loddlaen spun around, but the corridor was empty. Aderyn's presence lingered like the scent of smoke in an empty hearth.

"Sooner or later," Aderyn's voice went on. "I'll come in after you, or you'll have to come out. Sooner or later, you'll look me in the face."

Then the presence was gone. Loddlaen hurried to his chamber and slammed the door behind him. He couldn't escape; Aderyn wasn't going to let him escape, as somewhere in his heart he'd been sure his father would do.

"Then I'll have to win," Loddlaen said softly.

If only Aderyn were dead, Loddlaen could do much more than merely carry messages to the gwerbret. He could send fire into Rhodry's tents, rot into his provisions, disease to his men and horses, and stir Rhodry's army to such a panic that the men would desert like snow melting in the sun. If only Aderyn were dead. If.

Toward the middle of the afternoon, Loddlaen went to the window and tried to call up a storm. If nothing else, it would soak Rhodry and his cursed army and give Loddlaen something to brag about to Corbyn and Nowec. He called upon the elemental spirits of Air and Water, invoked them with mighty names, and saw clouds begin to swell and thicken in the sky. Wave after wave, the storm rushed in at his command as the wind picked up strong. All at once, the wind died, and the clouds began to dissipate. Loddlaen swore and struggled and cursed the spirits, until at last he saw one of the elemental kings striding across the sky. Huge and storm-tossed, the King was a vaguely elven shape of silver light surrounded by a pillar of golden light as fine as gossamer. The King waved one hand, and the spirits fled, far beyond Loddlaen's power to call them back.

Loddlaen leaned onto the windowsill and wept, knowing that Aderyn had summoned the King. Once he had stood at Aderyn's side and been presented to those mighty beings as Aderyn's successor. Now he was an outcast and beneath their contempt.

It was over an hour before Loddlaen felt strong enough to leave his chamber and go down to dinner. As he was going down the staircase, he saw Aderyn walking up. Loddlaen stood riveted, his hand tight on the rail, as his father came closer and closer. Aderyn gave him a faint smile of contempt, as if he were showing Loddlaen that he could break Loddlaen's seals anytime he wanted and enter anywhere he wished. Then the Vision vanished.

Loddlaen hurried to the noise and company of the great hall. While he ate his dinner, he was brooding murder.

Late that evening, Jill and the two elves were swearing over a game of dice by their campfire when Aderyn came to them. He was carrying two long arrows, and Jill's heart pounded in excitement.

"It's time," Aderyn said quietly. "Which of you archers wants these arrows?"

"I do," Jennantar said.

"The revenge belongs to you, sure enough," Calonderiel said. "I'll have steel arrows ready to back you if need be."

Only then did Jill realize that the two arrows had silver tips.

"Jill," Aderyn said. "If Jennantar can bring the bird down, you might have to finish it off on the ground. Use your silver dagger and only your silver dagger."

"I will," Jill said. "So, the old tale's true, is it? Only silver can harm dweomerfolk?"

"Oh, steel can cut a dweomerman as easily as it can other flesh, and steel would harm the hawk, too. But if the silver kills him, his body will come back to man-shape when he's dead."

Aderyn led them about a mile from the camp down a road dimly lit by the first quarter moon. They passed two farmhouses, tightly shuttered against Rhodry's army, and came to a meadow bordered by a line of oaks.

"Hide under the trees," Aderyn said. "I'm going to go throw the challenge. Be ready, will you? He could always outfly me."

Aderyn climbed the lowest tree and steadied himself against the branches to take off his clothes. Jill could just dimly see him, a dark shape among the leaves, as he crouched there. She thought she saw the indistinct, shimmering image of an owl beside him; then suddenly a glow of blue light enveloped both the shape and Aderyn. The old dweomerman was gone. In his place was the silver owl, spreading its wings for flight. With one soft cry, the owl leaped and flapped off steadily in the darkness. Jill caught her breath.

"It always creeps your flesh," Calonderiel remarked. "No matter how many times you see him do it."

Jennantar nocked the first silver arrow in his bow. Slowly the moon rose higher. Jill kept a watch on the starry sky in the direction of the dun, but Calonderiel saw them first.

"Look!" he hissed.

Jennantar raised the bow and drew, but it was another good minute before Jill saw a dark speck moving against the stars—the owl, flapping and gliding as fast as it could. All at once she saw another bird, dropping down from high above, plunging, stooping, nearly catching the owl. Flying straight and steadily, the owl and the hawk raced for the trees, and the hawk was gaining. Muttering under his breath, Jennantar stood tense, waiting for the hawk to come in range. Nearer and nearer they flew, and the hawk was getting far too close to the owl. Jennantar swore and loosed, but the arrow fell short. The hawk plunged down and caught the owl, grappling with him in the air.

They fought exactly like real birds of prey—closing with each other high in the air, grappling and clawing as they fell, then breaking apart to fly up, circling each other to gain height again. Jill heard the hawk shriek with rage every time the weary owl twisted free. Every now and then, one great feather would fall to earth, flashing silver in the moonlight. Jill and Jennantar ran out into the meadow under the fight, but Jennantar didn't dare shoot for fear of hitting the owl.

As they wearied in this unnatural battle, the two birds dropped, swooping closer to the ground, rising less high when they broke to grapple again. Shrieking and clawing at each other, they came down low, only to break apart and flap up again. The owl was tiring badly and rose slowly.

"Aderyn!" Jill screamed. "Drop low! Cursed low!"

Indifferent to her voice, the hawk stooped, plunged, and caught the owl. Down and down they dropped, and this time the owl made little effort to break free, and merely slashed with its beak as they fell. Jill ran off to get a start, and waited tensely with the dagger in her hand—she would have only one chance at this —then raced across the meadow and leapt up, stabbing at the hawk. Its shriek of agony told her she'd made her strike as she dropped to her knees in the grass. She felt the rush of wings as the owl broke free and flew just in time to save itself from plunging into the ground. Jill staggered up just as Jennantar's bowstring sang out.

Pierced to the heart, the hawk shrieked once and began to fall. In a flash of blue light it changed, so that for one hideous moment Jill saw something that was half hawk, half man, feather and flesh oozing into one another. Then it fell to earth with a sickening, perfectly ordinary thud. The owl called out a long cry of mourning and settled into the grass. It vanished cleanly, leaving Aderyn sitting there, bleeding from long claw slashes all over his body. Jill ran to him.

"We've got to staunch those wounds!" she cried.

Aderyn shook his head no and staggered up to lean on Jill's shoulder. She half carried him over to join the two elves beside Loddlaen's corpse. He lay twisted on his back, his face clawed, his thigh slashed open from the silver dagger, his chest pierced with the silver arrow. Aderyn raised his hands heavenward.

"It is over," he called out. "Let him go to the Halls of Light for his judging. It is finished."

Rolling across the meadow came three great knocks, like thunder from a clear sky. Jill cried out, her blood running cold at the sound. Slowly Aderyn lowered his hands and glanced at the corpse. Even in the gauzy moonlight Jill could see that he was fighting with all his will to keep himself under control. Jennantar laid his arm around the old man's shoulders and, whispering gently in Elvish, led him into the trees.

"Let's get this lump of meat back to camp." Calonderiel idly kicked Loddlaen in the head. "The sight should gladden our cadvridoc's heart."

As they stooped to pick up the body, Jill heard Aderyn wail, a long high keening from among the trees. On and on it went in a frantic rhythm so painful that she was glad when they were

finally out of earshot. Although she was stunned that Aderyn
would mourn his enemy, all she could assume was that the old
tales were true, and that working dweomer together made
strong bonds between men.

When they staggered into camp with their burden, one of
the guards recognized Loddlaen and howled his name. The rest
of the army came running. Laughing and slapping each other on
the back, the noble-born and the commoners alike crowded
round when they dumped the body at Rhodry's feet.

"So the bastard bleeds like any other man, does he?" Rhodry
called out. "Here, men, how do you feel about his cursed dweomer now?"

The army answered with catcalls and obscenities. Rhodry
held up his hands for silence.

"It would only be honorable of me to return the councillor to
his lord, wouldn't it?" he said, grinning. "I wonder what the piss-
poor little weasel will think when he sees this?"

The men laughed and cheered him roundly. Jill looked up at
the silent dun and wondered if Corbyn and his men could hear
the noise. With a touch of dweomer-cold, she knew that tomorrow would bring the battle. The only way that Corbyn and
Nowec could salvage one scrap of their lost honor was to sally and
die.

Later that night, Nevyn attempted to contact Aderyn. He
could feel his old pupil's mind, grief-struck, torn, filled with a
pain so palpable that a few tears came to Nevyn's eyes. He broke
off the attempt and left Aderyn alone with his mourning. Later
there would be time to talk and learn the details, but Nevyn
knew the most important thing: Loddlaen was dead. He left the
brazier and flung open the shutters over the window in his chamber.

Far below him the tiny town of Dun Gwerbyn lay wrapped
in darkness and silence. Once a dog barked; once a lantern
bloomed briefly in a yard, then went out. The sleeping house-
holders would never have to know what strange dangers had
been threatening them and their overlords, and Nevyn was profoundly grateful for it. Over the past week, he had been contact-
ing the other dweomer-masters in the kingdom, who were scattered like a wide-meshed net across the land. A few had picked

up traces of the dark dweomer close at hand, and now all were alerted. Soon Nevyn might have news of his fleeing enemy. He hoped so, because he would have to take steps against him as soon as he could.

"And tomorrow will see the end of this little tangle," he remarked to the starry sky. "O dear gods, keep my Jill safe."

The camp was struck, the baggage train sent farther down the meadow. In the brightening sunlight Rhodry's army sat on their horses outside Dun Bruddlyn and waited. In a last honorable gesture to the enemy, Rhodry had positioned his men far enough back so that Corbyn would be able to get his entire force outside before the fighting started. Off to one side, Jill rode between Sligyn and Rhodry himself. Ready behind them was a squad of picked men to guard their dweomer warrior.

"Remember your orders," Rhodry said to Jill. "You hang back and let the rest of us cut your path to Corbyn. Then he's yours."

Jill smiled at him; now that the time had come, her fear was far away, a little coldness in the pit of her stomach. Under her, Sunrise stamped, battle-eager and ready. Suddenly the wind carried the sound of silver horns, ringing in the dun. Jill pulled her mail hood over her padded cap, settled her helm on top of it, then got her shield into position as javelin points winked up and down Rhodry's line. As the distant horns sang out again, she drew her sword.

The gates to Dun Bruddlyn creaked open. With Lord Peredyr at its head, the main body of Rhodry's army surged forward, held steady for a moment, then charged as the enemy poured out the gates in waves, turning and wheeling into a ragged line to meet the charge. Javelins arched through the air and fell as the field exploded with warcries.

"Get into position!" Rhodry yelled at the squad.

The men surrounded Jill, but they kept several yards away to give her room to maneuver once the fighting started. She rose in the stirrups and looked out over the field, where dust swirled in thick clouds. Nowec and Corbyn's men fought gamely, riding in pairs with their horses nose to tail as they fended off the mobs around them. Jill saw a thick clot of fighting around Nowec with Peredyr in the middle of it. The noise was horrible; somehow she hadn't expected that battle would be such a deafening, shrieking thing.

"There!" Sligyn screamed. "Just coming out the gates!"

His green shield trimmed with silver, Corbyn galloped out on a black horse with a squad of men behind him. With a yell, Rhodry waved his squad forward at the trot. All at once Rhodry started to laugh, a cold, fiendish delight straight out of the Dawntime. The squad leapt forward at the gallop and burst into the midst of the fighting. Jill felt like a leaf caught in a torrent as they wheeled, screaming and slashing, to face off with Corbyn's men.

Up ahead, Rhodry was howling with berserk laughter, and Jill saw his sword swing up bloody in the sunlight. Through the dodging, shifting mass of men and horses, she could just see him, hard-pressed by two of Corbyn's men while Sligyn tried to come in at his flank. All around men slashed and swore; horses reared as they tried to shove forward. All at once Rhodry's laugh changed to a bubbling mirth that Jill instinctively knew meant he was in grave danger. She risked rising in the stirrups and saw Corbyn's men parting ranks—and letting their lord through. Corbyn was going to make one last try on Rhodry's life, and she was the only one who could stop him.

At that moment, Jill went berserk. A blood-red haze flared up to tint the world; laughter welled out of her mouth; she could no longer think. She swung Sunrise free of her startled squad and kicked him straight for Rhodry while she slashed and swung and went on laughing. When a man on a chestnut wheeled to face her, Jill charged him, a battle of nerves that she won when he pulled aside out of her way. When Sunrise turned perfectly to follow, Jill got a good strike on the rider's exposed side that drove him around in the saddle. Before he could parry, she slashed him across the face backhand. Screaming he fell forward under the hooves of his own horse.

As the chestnut stumbled and went down, Sunrise dodged without a word or touch from Jill, and she was through, falling into place at Rhodry's left. Just ahead in the mob was Corbyn's silver-trimmed shield. As she parried a blow from the side, Jill got a glimpse of Corbyn's face, sweat-streaked and snarling as he slashed at Sligyn. Sligyn dropped his sword and clung wounded to the saddle, an easy mark for Corbyn's next strike. Jill howled and slapped Sligyn's horse to make it dance back—out of the way barely in time. One of Sligyn's men grabbed its reins and fled with his lord.

"Corbyn!" Jill screamed. "Your Wyrd's riding for you!"

He heard her—she knew it from the way he tossed his head and turned her way. For all that she was covered with dust and sweat, he must have realized that she was a lass, too, because for the briefest of moments, he froze. Howling with laughter, Jill fended strikes from the side and pressed straight toward him. Suddenly he wrenched his horse's head around and fled, shoving through his men. One of them wheeled directly in front of Jill to cover his retreat.

"Coward!" Jill screamed.

Then her laughter stole her voice. Hitting hard, slashing, barely remembering to parry, she drove for the rider ahead. All at once he broke and wrenched his horse around to gallop off as shamelessly as his lord. Sunrise leaped over a dead horse, and they were free of the mob. Under a pall of dust the battle swirled across the meadow. Here and there were clots of fighting around one lord or another; single combats were scattered across the meadow; men rode aimlessly, nursing wounds. Far away the black horse carried Corbyn off at a comfortable trot.

"Bastard," Jill whispered. "Sunrise, catch him."

The western hunter flung himself forward at a dead run, as if he, too, had sighted their prey. Leaping over dead bodies, dodging around combats, they charged across the field, risking their lives on the rough ground. In the screaming battle noise, Corbyn never heard them coming until it was almost too late, but as Sunrise put on one last burst of speed, some evil god or other made Corbyn glance round. He smacked his horse with the flat of his blade and made the black dart forward.

"Stand!" Jill screamed. "Coward!"

Sunrise stretched low and tried to keep up, but he was sweating in acrid gouts of gray foam as the fresh black pulled inexorably ahead. In tears of rage, Jill pulled him to a jog. Corbyn was going to get away, and all because he was a cursed coward. Then the black reared up, pawing madly, and came down hard—with an elven arrow in its throat. Corbyn rolled free barely in time and staggered up, groping for his sword. With a howl of laughter, Jill swung down and ran for him. Dimly she was aware of Calonderiel, riding to join her.

His sword in hand, his shield at the ready, Corbyn dropped to a fighting crouch. Under the sweaty dust, his face was dead white. With a shout, Jill thrust forward in a feint, then swung up. Barely in time, he caught the blow on his shield.

"Oh, I can fight, can't I?" Jill said. "You're going to die, Corbyn. How do you like dweomer prophecies now?"

When he slashed at her, she parried easily, the faster by far, and stabbed in from the side. Blood welled up through the mail on his left arm. She pulled free and parried his clumsy answering strike. With the last of the strength in his left arm, he threw the shield at her head. Jill ducked easily and dodged in from the side. She feinted, dodged, feinted again until he had no choice but to turn and step back, again and again, until he was trapped between her and his dead horse. Shouting a warcry, he flung himself sideways and stumbled. Jill got an easy cut on his face. Blood welled on his cheeks.

"For Rhodry!" Jill thrust forward on his name.

She struck Corbyn full in the chest, and his mail shattered. The sword bit deep just below his breastbone. When she pulled it free, Corbyn fell forward onto his knees and looked up at her with bubbles of blood breaking on his lips. Then he folded over himself and died at her feet.

"Well played!" Calonderiel called.

The berserker fit still upon her, Jill swung around to see him dismounting. He was watching her warily, his violet cat eyes wide with a touch of fear, and he kept his distance.

"Jill, do you know me?"

"I do. You can come up."

She turned back to the corpse and saw Corbyn's shade. A pale bluish form, a naked body with Corbyn's face, it hovered over the corpse while it stared at her, its lips working soundlessly, its eyes filled with bewildered terror. Jill screamed aloud.

"What's wrong?" Calonderiel grabbed her arm.

"His shade. Can't you see it?"

"What? There's nothing there."

Corbyn watched her in an anguish of reproach and fear. From the way his mouth moved, it seemed that he was trying to ask her something. Calonderiel threw his arms around her and hauled her bodily away.

"We've got to get to Aderyn," he said.

As suddenly as a blown candle, the berserker fit left her. Jill clung to him and sobbed in his arms.

The battle was over. Sword in hand, Rhodry rode back and forth across the field and shouted orders to his men. They began to dismount, some collecting the horses and leading them away, others looking for the wounded among the dead and dying. Peredyr and Edar fell in at Rhodry's side.

"Have you seen Jill?" Rhodry yelled at them.

"I have," Peredyr said. "Corbyn's dead, sure enough. I saw that Calonderiel fellow taking Jill to the chirurgeons. She was weeping, but she could walk."

"Oh by the gods, she's been hurt!" Rhodry felt tears rising in his throat. "And a fine man you must think me, letting a lass take a cut meant for me."

"Hold your tongue!" Edar snapped. "You had no choice in the matter, none."

"Here, lord cadvridoc," Peredyr said. "Come look at Corbyn, and then see how shamed you feel about letting a poor weak little lass ride in your battle."

As soon as he dismounted by Corbyn's body, Rhodry saw what Peredyr meant. Jill's blow had shattered a well-made mail shirt and spitted Corbyn like a chicken.

"By the hells!" Rhodry whispered. "Did she truly do that?"

"I saw her with my own eyes, or I wouldn't believe it," Peredyr said. "She laughed while she did it, too."

Rhodry found Jill near Aderyn's wagon, where the old man was working over one of the wounded. Jill sat on the ground and leaned back against the wagon wheel while she stared blindly out at nothing. When Rhodry knelt in front of her, she said nothing.

"Where are you hurt?"

"I'm not," Jill said slowly. "No one ever got so much as a nick on me."

"Then what's so wrong?"

"I don't know. I truly don't know."

That was all the answer Rhodry got, too, until Aderyn was done tending what wounds he could. Still exhausted from his battle of the night before, Aderyn stood stiffly to one side and watched as a servant sluiced blood off the tailgate with buckets of water. He caught Jill's hand and squeezed it.

"Are you cut?" Aderyn said.

"I'm not." All at once Jill broke, turning pale, speaking much too fast. "I saw his shade, Corbyn's I mean. I killed him, and then I saw him, standing on his body. He was all blue, and ah ye gods, the look in his eyes!"

Rhodry felt himself turn cold, but Aderyn merely nodded.

"The battle fit was on you," Aderyn said. "I heard how you shattered Corbyn's mail. Could you do that now, child, in cold blood?"

"Never," Jill said. "It's hard to believe I did it then."

"Just so. It was the battle fit. I don't truly understand it, but it must disrupt the humors somehow—probably it's an excess of fiery humor in the blood. But it gave you strength far beyond yourself, and you saw things that are normally hidden."

"So his shade was truly there?" Jill said. "I thought I was going mad."

"You weren't." Aderyn chose every word carefully. "What you call a man's shade is his real self, the part that indwells his body and keeps it alive and that holds his mind and consciousness. When the body's injured beyond repair, this etheric double, as the dweomer terms it, withdraws. What you saw was Corbyn himself, utterly bewildered at being dead."

Jill seemed to be about to speak, then bolted like a terrified horse, dodging through the wagons. When Rhodry started to follow, Aderyn grabbed his arm.

"Let her go," Aderyn said. "She needs to be alone with this."

"No doubt. Just hearing you talk creeped my flesh. Here, Aderyn, I'm a berserker myself, and I've never seen anyone's shade."

"You aren't marked for the dweomer like Jill is. Remember that, Rhodry Maelwaedd. Jill is marked for the dweomer."

All at once Rhodry was frightened of this slender, weary, old man. He made a muttered excuse and hurried away.

Laden with chain mail, exhausted from the battle, Jill couldn't run far. She got free of the baggage train, jogged downstream for a bit, then tripped in the long grass and fell to her knees, gasping for breath. She flung herself facedown and stretched out her arms, as if she could hold the sun-warmed earth like a mother. Wildfolk clustered around her; the gray gnome appeared and ran his twisted fingers gently through her hair. At last Jill sat up and looked across the meadow to Corbyn's dun, where the green pennant was coming down. Jill had the uncanny feeling that Corbyn's shade was wandering through the halls, trying to come home. She nearly vomited.

"So much for glory," Jill said to the Wildfolk. "May I never ride to war again!"

Later she would realize that the gesture was a mad one, but at the time, all she could think was that she had to have a bath. She stripped off her mail and clothes, then plunged into the shallow stream. While she scoured herself with handfuls of sand from the bottom, the gray gnome perched in the grass and watched her.

"I want my spare shirt," Jill said. "It's in my saddlebags."

The gnome nodded and disappeared. By the time he returned, dragging the shirt behind him, it was no longer strictly clean, but at least it didn't stink of sweat and another man's blood. Jill dressed, then rolled the mail up in a bundle. Although she'd already cleaned her sword once, she did it again until she could be sure that not one speck of Corbyn's blood remained. Then she merely sat unthinking in the grass with her gnome until Jennantar came to fetch her.

"You've been out here for hours," he said.

With a start Jill realized that the sun was low in the sky, and the shadow of the dun lay long and dark on the meadow.

"Here, Jill," Jennantar said. "Don't ache your heart over killing Corbyn. He deserved to die if ever a man did."

"It isn't that. It's having seen him. Ah by the black ass of the Lord of Hell, I don't even know what I mean."

Jill dumped her mail into a supply wagon, then went with Jennantar up to the dun, where, he told her, the wounded were already settled in Corbyn's barracks and the victors were drinking his mead in his great hall. Walking into the ward gave her a peculiar feeling. For days this place had been as unattainable as the moon; now here she was, striding across it as a conqueror. The great hall was crowded and deafening. Although Jill tried to slip in, half-a-dozen men saw her and turned to stare, pointing her out to their fellows. Slowly the noise dropped to silence as man after man turned to look at their dweomer-warrior. At the head of the honor table, Rhodry rose to his feet.

"Come sit in my place," Rhodry called. "The god-touched deserve every honor I can give them."

Every man in the hall cheered as Jill made her way to him. God-touched—she supposed that was how they had to see her, a favorite of some god or other, rather than admitting that she was merely a woman who could fight as well as a man. Yet no matter the reason, the honor they were paying her was real enough, and all at once the glory of it made her laugh aloud. The noble-born rose and bowed to her; Rhodry filled a goblet of mead and handed it to her like a page.

"So much for rebels," Rhodry said. "You've earned your hire, silver dagger."

With a laugh, Jill pledged him with the goblet.

"You have my thanks, my lord," Jill said. "For letting me earn it. I wasn't looking forward to facing Nevyn if I rode back alive and you didn't."

Frightened and pale, Corbyn's servants crept in to set out a feast from their dead lord's stores. While they ate, the noble-born discussed the disposition Lovyan might make of Corbyn and Nowec's lands. Apparently there were plenty of land-hungry minor lords among the Clw Coc. As the mead flowed, Jill had little mind to listen to the merits of this cousin or that. All she could think about was Rhodry, so close to her. Every now and then, he would glance her way with hungry eyes. Jill wanted him so badly that she felt shamed, that she would turn into a slut with nothing more on her mind than having a man's arms around her.

Resolutely Jill rehearsed every bitter truth: he was too far above her; he would only get her with child and then desert her; worst of all, her father would beat her black and blue. Yet all at once, something snapped in her mind. She was the victor at this feast. She'd risked her life for all of these noble lords. A horse was all very well, but why by every god shouldn't she have the prize she truly wanted? In a berserker fit of its own, she turned to Rhodry and smiled at him, kept smiling until he grew quiet, bound to her every gesture and glance.

Finally the warbands drank themselves into a staggering silence. Jill begged the lords to excuse her and left the hall with Aderyn. She took him down to the elven tent and made sure he was comfortably settled in, then went to her own blankets. For a long time she lay awake, listening as a few at a time, the men stumbled back to their bedrolls. When the camp was utterly silent, she got up and slipped out of the tent without waking Aderyn. At Rhodry's tent she hesitated, but only for a moment, before she lifted the flap and ducked in. In the darkness she heard Rhodry sit up with a sleepy grunt. She made her way over and sat down beside him.

"Jill!" he whispered. "What are you doing here?"

"What do you think?"

"You're daft. Get out before I shame us both."

When she stroked the side of his face, he went stone still.

"Stop it," Rhodry said. "I'm only made of flesh and blood, not cold steel."

"And so am I. Can't we have just this one night?"

When he refused to answer, Jill pulled her shirt over her head and threw it on the ground. Rhodry turned and caught her by the shoulders, pulled her close, and kissed her so hungrily that for a moment she was terrified, simply because he was so much stronger than she. His hands ran down her bare back, then turned her in his arms while he kissed her over and over again. She felt as limp and weak as a rag doll, utterly in his control, but when he caressed her, his hand trembling on her breast, she felt her lust rising to match his. She threw her arms around his neck and took a kiss from him as he laid her down on the blankets. The last of her fear vanished like a leaf burning to ash in a fire.

And far away in Dun Gwerbyn, Nevyn sat straight up out of a sound sleep and knew what had happened.

"Those young dolts!" he said to the darkness. "Well, I hope they have the sense to hide it from Cullyn, that's all."

Eldidd, 1062

Can a carpenter make a house stand without nails? Can a tailor make a shirt without thread? In just this way, honor holds the kingdom together, by making a man obey those above him and treat those below generously. Without honor, the kingdom would crumble, until none obeyed even the King himself, and none gave a starving child even a scrap of bread. Every noble-born man, therefore, should honor his overlord in all respects, scrupulously observing every law and pomp of his court. . . .

Prince Mael y Gwaedd, On Nobility, *802*

And so Jill's slain Corbyn," Lovyan said. "By the Goddess herself, I never would have thought it."

"Oh, I had faith in her," Nevyn said. "She has resources, you might call them, beyond what she even knows herself."

"That's a most cryptic remark."

"It will have to stay that way. My apologies."

Lovyan smiled at him in fond exasperation. They were sitting in the little garden behind the joined brochs of Dun Gwerbyn, where the last red roses drooped against gray stone.

"Will your friend from the west be coming here?" Lovyan said.

"He won't. I'd hoped he would, just in case Rhys wanted to hear that Loddlaen was a murderer, but both he and the Westfolk with him are eager to get back to their people."

"They're a strange lot, the Westfolk. It's odd, so many people abhor them, but I've always found them congenial—not enough to ride off with them, but congenial."

Although she spoke casually, Nevyn felt an odd doubt nag at his mind.

"Lovva," he said. "Can I ask you somewhat that might be cursed insulting?"

"You may, but I might not answer."

"Fair enough. Was Tingyr truly Rhodry's father?"

Lovyan tilted her head to one side and considered him with mischief in her eyes. In spite of her gray hair and the marks of age upon her face, he could clearly see how beautiful she must have been twenty years past.

"He wasn't, at that," Lovyan said. "Not even Medylla and Dannyan know, but he wasn't."

"Your secret will be safe with me, I assure you. Here, where did you meet a man of the Westfolk?"

"Oho! You have cursed sharp eyes, my friend. It was right here in Dun Gwerbyn, when my brother was tieryn." Lovyan looked away, her smile fading into bitterness. "It was the summer that Tingyr made Linedd his mistress. I was still young then, and I didn't understand things the way I do now. Just thinking that in the Dawntime he would have had a whole stableful of concubines was very cold comfort indeed, so I rode off in a huff and came to visit Gwaryc. I remember sitting in this very garden and weeping for my hurt pride. Then, as they do every now and then, some of the Westfolk rode in to pay the tieryn a tribute of horses, and with them was a bard who was the most beautiful man I've ever seen, for all his peculiar eyes." She paused, the smile returning. "I wanted somewhat of my own back, and I took it. Do you despise me?"

"Not in the least, and you don't sound like a woman who feels herself shamed."

"Well, if anything, I still feel rather smug." Lovyan tossed her head like a young lass. "And somehow my bard made me realize that it wasn't Tingyr I loved, but the power of being his wife. When I went home, I made sure that little Linedd knew who ruled in Aberwyn's court. But I'll admit to being quite nervous when the time came for my childbed. When they laid Rhodry on my breast, the first thing I looked at was his ears."

"Oh, no doubt." Nevyn allowed himself a chuckle. "Are you ever going to tell Rhodry the truth?"

"Never, and not for the sake of my rather besmirched honor. It's simply that every man in Eldidd has to believe that Rhodry's a true-born Maelwaedd or he can never rule in Dun Gwerbyn. I doubt me if my poor honest son could keep the secret."

"So do I. The lad's got a fine honor indeed. My thanks for telling me the truth. It clears up a great puzzle. Aderyn's been rambling about Westfolk blood in the Maelwaedd clan, and how it skips generations to all come out in someone, but that seemed cursed farfetched to me."

"And quite unnecessary," Lovyan said with a small firm nod, then proceeded to change the subject in a way that made it clear she never wanted it raised again. "I wonder when Rhys will ride our way? He'll have to give his agreement on the way I settle this rebellion. I suppose he's already polishing a few nasty remarks to spoil his brother's victory. You can't know how hard it is for a woman to have two of her sons wrangling like this. Nevyn, do you know why Rhys hates Rhodry so much?"

"I don't. I wish I did—I'd put a stop to it."

This time, Nevyn wasn't merely putting Lovyan off with cryptic remarks. Over the years, he'd done many meditations to discover if Rhys's hatred was part of the tangled chain of Wyrd that Nevyn and Rhodry shared. It was no such thing, merely one of those irrational tempers that spring up between blood kin. At some point Rhys and Rhodry would have to resolve it, if not in this life, then in the next, but that, mercifully, would be no concern of his.

There were other souls, of course, who were his concern, and that afternoon Nevyn went to Cullyn's chamber. He found Cullyn dressed and out of bed, sitting on the carved chest by the window with his left arm in a sling. Cullyn was pale and so gaunt that the dark circles under his eyes looked like pools of shadow, but he was mending nicely.

"How well will this cursed arm heal, do you think?" Cullyn said.

"I truly don't know. We'll have to wait until we get the splints off. It was a clean break, and you were too sick at first to move it much, so there's hope."

"At least it wasn't my sword arm."

"Now here, are you still brooding about Rhodry?"

"Don't be a dolt, herbman. Jill's safe and that's an end to it." Cullyn looked idly out the window. "But I've still got to eat along the long road."

So he did, and Nevyn felt an odd pang of sympathy for his old enemy, whose very life depended on how well he could use sword and shield. A broken bone was a very hard thing to mend, even for someone with his lore, simply because splints and strips of cloth and rabbit-skin glue never really held the break perfectly immobile.

"Well," Nevyn said at last. "At least you'll have all winter to recover. Rhodry will certainly give you his shelter till spring."

"True spoken. Our young lord's got more honor than most. Will you be sheltering here, too?"

"I will."

Nevyn felt like adding "Cursed right I will!" He was going to be needed. Soon they would all be shut up together in a stormy Eldidd winter, and he doubted if Jill and Rhodry would be able to hide their love affair. After all, they were remembering a passion that they'd shared life after life, the memory close to the surface of their minds, where they'd merely found it but thought it new. Even without a shield, Cullyn would be a cursed hard man for Rhodry to best, especially when Eldidd law gave a father every right to kill the man who dishonored his daughter.

The army stayed in Dun Bruddlyn for some days to bury the dead and let the wounded rest before the long journey home. Jill was pleased when out of respect for the dweomer, Rhodry had his men put Loddlaen in a proper grave rather than throwing him in the trench with the other rebels . . . but then, everything that Rhodry did pleased her, as if in her eyes he were a god come to walk among mortals. The memory of her night in his arms haunted her. Rather than ending her hunger for him, it had made it worse, like trying to douse a fire with oil. Yet she kept her bargain and did her best to avoid him. Another thought haunted her constantly, too: What if Da ever found out?

Finally the morning came when they would return to Dun Gwerbyn. After she saddled her horse, Jill went to say farewell to Aderyn and the two elves, who were grinning at the prospect of leaving the lands of men for home.

"Here, Jill," Calonderiel said. "If ever you weary of Eldidd, then ride west and find us. The Wildfolk will show you the way."

"My thanks," Jill said. "Truly, that would gladden my heart, to see you all again."

"Maybe someday you will," Aderyn said. "And if not, think of me every now and then, and I'll do the same for you."

As they mounted their horses, Jill suddenly felt like weeping. She'd never known men she'd liked so well so fast. Someday I will ride west, she thought, someday. Yet she felt a little coldness around her heart from somehow knowing that that "someday" was a cursed long time away, if it ever came at all. She waited at the edge of the camp until they'd ridden out of sight, then went back to her own people and to Rhodry, waiting for her at the head of the army.

On the day that the victorious army returned to Dun Gwerbyn, Cullyn sat by the window, where he had a good view of the gates and the ward below. The day was wet, with a fine drizzle of rain that turned the cobbles below as clean and slick as metal, and the draft through the window was cold, but he kept his watch until at last he saw them filing in, the men wrapped in wool cloaks. At the head was Jill, riding a golden western hunter. Grinning in a gape of relief, Cullyn leaned on the windowsill and watched as she dismounted, threw her reins to a servant, then ran for the broch. Cullyn closed and barred the wooden shutters without a doubt that she was running to see him. In just a few minutes, Jill flung the door open and stepped in, pausing out of breath in the doorway.

"What did you do?" Cullyn said. "Run all the way up?"

"I did. If you're going to beat me, I want it over with."

Cullyn laughed and held out his good arm to her.

"I'm still too weak to beat you," he said. "And I don't even want to, I'm so cursed glad to see you alive."

When she flung herself down next to him, he hugged her gingerly, aware of the ache down his side from the healing wound, then kissed her on the forehead. She gave him a smile as beautiful as the sun rising.

"Your old Da's head is swollen these days, my sweet," Cullyn said. "So my lass gained the honor of the day, did she? I saw that horse you rode in. Was it a gift from the cadvridoc?"

"It was." Jill grinned at him. "And after the battle, I ate at the head of the honor table."

"Listen to you, you little hellcat." Cullyn gave her an affectionate squeeze. "But I warn you, if I ever hear you talking about riding to another battle, I'll beat you so hard that you won't be able to sit on a horse."

"Don't trouble your heart, Da." Her smile was abruptly gone. "Oh, it's splendid to sit here with you and share my glory, but I don't ever want to ride to war again."

"Well and good, then. I suppose you had to see for yourself

and learn the hard way. You're too much like me to learn any other way."

When she laughed, he bent his head to kiss her, then realized that Nevyn was standing in the open doorway and watching them with an oddly frightened expression, quickly stifled. Cullyn let go of Jill and moved away. The old man's stare was like a mirror, making him see an ugly twisted thing that he'd hidden from himself until that moment.

"How do you fare?" Nevyn said. "The cadvridoc wants to see you, but I wanted to make sure you weren't overtired."

"I'm fine."

"Indeed?" Nevyn raised one eyebrow. "You look pale."

"I'm fine!" Cullyn snarled. "Jill, leave us alone."

"Da! I want to hear what his lordship says."

"I said go."

Like a kicked dog she got up and slunk out of the room. Letting her go, knowing how much he'd hurt her, made his heart ache. He was afraid to look at Nevyn.

"You know," Nevyn said. "There's more than one kind of battle that a man has to fight."

Cullyn felt shame flood him like cold water, but mercifully Nevyn left without another word. Cullyn leaned back against the shutters and felt himself shaking. As soon as he was well, he told himself, he was going to ride out and leave Jill behind under Lovyan's protection. It was going to hurt like poison, but it was best that way. He knew he could do it when the time came, because he'd be doing it for her sake, and if he died in his next battle, somewhere far from Eldidd, she'd never even have to know he was dead.

"Cullyn?" Rhodry said.

Cullyn looked up with a start; he'd never even noticed the lord come in.

"How do you fare?" Rhodry said. "I can leave."

"I'm fine, my lord."

Rhodry had never looked more like a lord than he did that morning, in his soft shirt embroidered with red lions, his plaid thrown back from his shoulders and pinned at one side with a jeweled ring brooch, his hand on the hilt of his finely worked sword, but Cullyn found himself thinking of him as a boy, and one

he might have loved like a son. It was going to hurt to leave
Rhodry behind, too.

"Will you forgive me for taking Jill off to war?" Rhodry said.
"It ached my heart to let a lass do my fighting for me."

"And who were you to argue with the dweomer? You know,
my lord, ever since Jill was a little lass, all she ever talked about
was getting a chance at battle glory. I'm not surprised she
grabbed her chance when it came. She always could lie like a
little weasel when she wanted somewhat."

"Well, true enough." Rhodry looked sharply away. "But you
truly do forgive me? It's been aching my heart, wondering what
you thought of me."

"Here, lad. It doesn't become the noble-born to care one
way or another what a dishonored man like me thinks of them."

"Oh horsedung! You must have been dishonored once, or
you wouldn't be carrying that dagger, but what do I care what
you did all those years ago? I came to offer you a place in my
warband, and not just any place. I want you for my captain. It's
not just me—Amyr and the lads have been dropping hints, like,
about how honored they'd be to ride behind you."

"Oh ye gods, I can't take that."

"What? Why not?"

"I—uh—it's just not fitting."

"Nonsense!" Rhodry tossed his head. "I even asked Sligyn
what he thought of the idea, and he said it was a cursed good one.
You don't need to worry about my vassals looking down their
noses at you or suchlike."

Cullyn opened his mouth, but no words came. He could
never tell Rhodry the real reason he wanted to ride away from
the most generous lord he'd ever met.

"Oh by the hells, Cullyn!" Rhodry said. "Are you truly going
to say me nay?"

"I'm not, my lord."

"Well and good then. We can leave all the kneeling and fine
words for when you're better. Here, your face is white as snow.
Let me help you up, captain. You'd better lie down."

Cullyn took the offered aid and made it safely back to his
bed. After Rhodry left, he lay there and stared at the ceiling.
Rhodry had handed him back the honor and decency he thought
he'd lost forever, but he would know that he was unworthy, that

everything was poisoned at the heart. Jill, Jill, he thought, how
could I—my own daughter! He turned his face to the pillow and
wept for the first time since he'd lain on Seryan's grave, and this
time, too, he was weeping for her and for their daughter.

After Cullyn ordered her out of his chamber, Jill went down
to the great hall in a sulk, but soon she realized that it was
probably best that she be gone when Rhodry and Cullyn were
together. Since the warbands were off tending their horses, and
the noble-born in conference with the tieryn up in Sligyn's
sickroom, the hall was deserted except for a serving lass, desulto-
rily wiping the tables with a wet rag. Jill dipped herself a tankard
of ale, then stood by the warband's hearth, where a peat fire
smouldered against the chill. In a few minutes Rhodry came
down the staircase and strode over to her. She loved watching
the way he moved, with the graceful strength of a young pan-
ther. He made her a bow, then looked at her with eyes so hungry
that she knew he was remembering their night together.

"I've just spoken with Cullyn," Rhodry said. "I made him the
captain of my warband."

"Did you do it for his sake or to keep me here?"

"For his sake."

"Then I thank you from the bottom of my heart, my lord."

"It hurts to hear you call me my lord." Rhodry looked down
and scuffed at the floor with the toe of his boot. "But I'm mindful
of our bargain, one night and no more."

"Well and good, then."

Yet when they looked at each other, all she wanted was to
throw her arms around him and kiss him, no matter who might
see.

"Mother's going to offer you a place in her retinue," Rhodry
said at last. "Cursed if I'd have you waiting on table or chopping
turnips out in the kitchen."

"Would you offer me a place in your warband?"

"Do you want one? I will."

"I don't. I just wanted to see what you'd say."

"I'd give you anything you wanted, if only I could. Ah Jill, I'd
marry you if they'd let me. I mean that. It's not just some weasel-
ing words from a dishonorable man."

"I know. And I'd marry you if I could."

Rhodry's eyes filled with tears. He's like an elf indeed, Jill thought, but she felt like weeping herself. Irritably he rubbed his eyes on his shirt sleeve and looked away.

"Ah ye gods, I respect your father so cursed much!" Rhodry said. "I think that hurts worst of all."

Rhodry strode off, slamming out the door of the hall. For a moment Jill thought of riding off alone as a silver dagger herself, but rationally she knew that she had to take Lovyan's offer. The long road had come to an end, here in Dun Gwerbyn, where she would live close to Rhodry—but far far away. All at once, she wanted to be with her father. She refilled the tankard, then took it upstairs for him. When she came in, he was lying on his bed, and something about his eyes told her that he'd been weeping. She thought she understood—of course the honor would mean that much to him.

"Is that ale for your old father?" Cullyn sat up and hastily arranged a smile. "My thanks."

"Lord Rhodry told me how he honored you." Jill handed him the tankard. "It's so splendid. It's about time someone recognized what kind of a man you are."

Cullyn winced.

"Does that wound ache?"

"A bit. The ale will help."

Jill perched on the end of the bed and watched him drink. She felt that she'd never loved him more than she did that afternoon, her wonderful father who now had his pride back to match his glory.

Later in the afternoon, Lovyan summoned Jill to the women's hall. The second floor of one of the secondary brochs, it was more a large suite than a hall, a sign that the tieryns of Dun Gwerbyn could support their womenfolk in luxury. There were bedchambers for Lovyan's serving women, and a large half-round of a room with Bardek carpets, little tables, and carved and cushioned chairs in profusion. Lovyan greeted her warmly and led her to a chair, while Medylla offered her a plate of honeyed apricots and Dannyan poured her a goblet of pale Bardek wine.

"I must say I never thought I'd have to thank a lass for saving my son's life," Lovyan said. "But I do thank you, and from the bottom of my heart."

"Her Grace is more than welcome, and truly, you've offered me more repayment than I deserve."

"Nonsense," Lovyan said with a comfortable smile. "You have much to learn about life in a court, of course, but I'm sure you'll do splendidly. The first thing we have to do is sew you some proper dresses."

Jill's dismay must have shown on her face, because the three of them laughed gently at her.

"Oh come now," Dannyan said. "You can't go around dressed like a lad."

"Besides," Medylla broke in. "You're so pretty, child. Once your hair grows, and we've gotten you all turned out, why, you'll have lads clustering around you like bees around a rose bush."

Jill stared blankly at her.

"Child?" Lovyan said. "Is somewhat wrong?"

"Well, Your Grace, I mean no disrespect, but don't you all remember that I've killed two men?"

They went as still as if they'd been turned to stone by dweomer. Only then did Jill realize just how completely her one victorious battle had set her apart from other women. Not even the powerful Lovyan would ever know what she knew, the bitter tangled glory of wagering your life against another's and winning.

"So you have," Lovyan said at last. "I was assuming that you'd want to put all that behind you."

"I do, Your Grace, but I can't—not so easily, anyway." Jill began to feel like a horse in a bedchamber. "I mean no insult, truly I don't."

"Of course not, child, and none's taken," Lovyan said. "But true enough, chatter about lads and pretty clothes isn't going to amuse you the way it used to amuse the three of us. This is very interesting, Jill. Have you ever thought of marrying, by the way?"

"I haven't, Your Grace. Who would I have married without a dowry? Some tavernman?"

"True spoken, but all that's changed now." Lovyan gave her a good-humored smile. "Your beauty and my favor are dowry enough for any lass. There's many a rising young merchant who'd admire a wife with your spirit, and for that matter, many a landless noble lord who needs my good will. You wouldn't be the first woman to win a title with her looks."

"I see."

"But if you don't want to marry," Dannyan broke in, "no one will force you into it, either. It's just that most lasses do."

"My thanks, but this is all so sudden, I don't know what to think."

"Of course," Lovyan said. "There's no hurry."

Although all of them smiled at her, Jill realized that they were looking on her as a strange kind of invalid, a victim who needed nursing back to health. She began to feel like a falcon, used to soaring at the edge of the wilderness, but now caught and brought back to hunt at a lord's command.

Since Lovyan practically ordered her to, Jill agreed to wear women's clothes down to dinner that night. As pleased as if they had a new daughter, Medylla and Dannyan fussed over Jill. She had a bath with perfumed soap, dried herself off on thick Bardek towels, then submitted to having Medylla comb her hair before she dressed. First came the narrow white underdress with tight sleeves, then a blue overdress, hanging full from gathered shoulders. Around her waist a kirtle of Lovyan's plaid tucked the dress in and made pockets of a sort with its folds, enough to carry a table dagger and a handkerchief. Although Medylla offered her a tiny jeweled dagger, Jill insisted on carrying her own. In spite of all the honor of being treated this way, there were limits to what she'd put up with. She took a few steps and nearly tripped. The underdress was far too narrow for her usual stride.

"Poor Jill," Dannyan said with honest sympathy. "Well, you'll get used to it in a bit."

Alternately mincing and stumbling, Jill followed them down to the great hall, where Lovyan was already seated at the head of the honor table. Since they would have to await Rhys's final judgment on the war, all of Rhodry's noble-born allies were there, except, of course, for the wounded Sligyn. The lords rose and bowed rather absently to Her Grace's women; then Edar laughed aloud.

"Jill!" he said. "I swear I didn't recognize you."

"I hardly recognize myself, my lord."

Jill took a place at the foot of the table between Medylla and Dannyan. Although everyone was waiting for Rhodry, he never came in, and eventually a somewhat annoyed Lovyan had the meal served without him. Jill had to pay strict attention to her manners and constantly remind herself that she couldn't wipe her hands on her borrowed dresses. She aped Medylla and Dannyan and ate using only her fingertips, which she could dabble clean on the handkerchief hanging from her kirtle.

The meal was nearly finished when a page hurried to the table to announce Lord Cinvan, the first of Corbyn's allies come to sue for peace. As befitted the ritual of the thing, he came alone and completely unarmed, with not so much as a table dagger in his belt, and he knelt before Lovyan like a common rider. The entire hall fell silent as Lovyan coolly considered him. The noble-born leaned forward, Edar with a tight twist of contempt to his mouth, the rest expressionless.

"I've come to beg for your forgiveness and your pardon," Cinvan said, his voice choking on his shame. "For raising my sword in rebellion against you."

"This is a grave thing you ask of me," Lovyan said. "What restitution do you offer?"

"Twenty horses, coin for my share of lwdd for Daumyr and all men dead, and my little son to live in your dun as hostage."

Although Jill was thinking that this sounded like cursed little to her, Lovyan nodded.

"If the gwerbret approves those terms," Lovyan said, "I shall take them. No doubt you're hungry after your long ride. You may sit with my men, and a servant will feed you."

Cinvan winced, but as a sign of submission, he did it, taking a place at the end of one of the riders' tables. They all ignored him, looking through him as if he were made of glass. As the general chatter picked up again, Jill turned to whisper to Dannyan.

"Why did our lady let him off so lightly?" Jill said.

"He's a poor lord as it is," Dannyan said. "He'll have to borrow from every cousin he has just to pay the lwdd, and if our lady made his clan destitute, they'd rise in rebellion some fine day."

"Besides," Medylla put in, "by being so generous, she's shamed him good and proper. That'll sting worse than the coin."

The two nodded sagely at each other. Jill realized that they were going to be her guides and teachers in this new world, where intrigue was as dangerous as a thousand swords.

As soon as possible Jill left the table and went to look in on her father. As she made her way down the corridor, she heard laughter coming from his chamber, and when she opened the door, she saw Rhodry, sharing a meal with Cullyn. The sight of them together made her freeze, her hand on the open door, as they both turned to look at her. The lantern light seemed to swell into the glow of a fire, picking out the glitter of the silver dagger in Cullyn's hand.

"Well, by the gods!" Cullyn said. "This fine lady can't be my scruffy little silver dagger's brat."

"Da, don't tease," Jill said. "I'm miserable enough as it is." She allowed herself one glance at Rhodry. "I'll leave you to your talk with your captain, my lord."

"My thanks," Rhodry said.

Jill stepped out and shut the door behind her. Only then did she realize that she was terrified, just from seeing Cullyn and Rhodry together, as if in some mad way, she thought they were plotting about her behind her back.

Seven days passed without a word from Gwerbret Rhys, who would have to oversee the judgments Lovyan made upon her rebel lords. Rhodry was furious, seeing the delay as a slap at him, a perception no one bothered to deny. Jill's presence in the dun was another constant torment to him, too; he simply couldn't keep his mind off her, and seeing her was worse, making him remember their night together, the first time he'd ever had a woman who could match him in bed. He took to spending as much time as possible alone, going for long rides or merely walking out in the ward.

During one of these aimless rambles he ran across Cullyn, down by the back wall of the dun. Although his left arm was still in a sling, Cullyn was working out with one of the light wooden swords used to train young boys. Moving so slowly that it was a kind of dance, Cullyn was lunging and falling back while he described a figure eight with the point of the blade in a perfect concentration that was more like dweomer than swordplay. Even sore and weak, Cullyn was a marvel when he moved with a weapon in his hand. Finally he noticed that Rhodry was watching him and stopped to make him a bow.

"How does your arm fare?" Rhodry said.

"Not too badly, my lord. Maybe tomorrow we'll get the splints off for a look, the herbman tells me." Cullyn glanced around, then pointed at a second wooden sword that was leaning against the wall. "Ever tried to spar this slowly?"

"I haven't." Rhodry took the sword. "Looks like a good game."

To keep things fair, Rhodry tucked his left arm behind his back. The sparring seemed like a humorous parody of real combat at first, with both of them moving like men in a trance. It was a matter of moving in slowly, catching the other's blade in a parry, then ever so slowly breaking free to glide in again from another direction. Yet it was difficult, too. Rhodry had never been so aware of every subtle move he made when he was fighting and of every move his opponent was making as well. Keeping his concentration so finely honed was a struggle. Finally his mind wandered a little too far, and Cullyn slipped slowly under his guard and flicked his shirt with the blunt point of his sword.

"By the hells!" Rhodry said. "A touch, sure enough."

Cullyn smiled and saluted him with the wooden sword, but all at once Rhodry felt that he was in danger, that wooden or not, that blade could kill him in Cullyn of Cerrmor's hands, and that Cullyn was thinking just that.

"Somewhat wrong, my lord?" Cullyn said.

"Naught. Here, you've done enough for one day."

"So I have. It gripes my heart to admit it, but I'm tired. Ah well, I'll get my strength back soon enough."

Again Rhodry felt a shudder of danger, as if Cullyn were giving him a warning. Had he noticed the way Rhodry'd been looking at Jill? If he'd been obvious, Cullyn might well have. Rhodry wanted to say something reassuring, some good plausible lie to put Cullyn at ease, but he was just sensible enough to realize that he'd best not speak Jill's name where her father could hear it.

"It looks remarkably good," Nevyn said. "I'm pleased."

Cullyn was glad that the herbman was pleased, because to him his once-broken arm looked cursed bad—white flesh, puckered and wrinkled, and far thinner than his other arm after the long weeks in the splints.

"The break mended fairly straight," the old man went on.

"It should be good enough for shield work if you're cursed careful about building it up. Favor it for some time."

"My thanks, truly, for all your work on me."

"You're most welcome." Nevyn paused, considering. "Truly, you are."

Now that his wounds were fully healed, it was time for Cullyn to formally take Rhodry's service. That very night, before everyone in the dun, assembled in the great hall, he knelt at Rhodry's feet. Rhodry leaned forward in his chair and took both of Cullyn's hands in his. By the flaring torchlight, Cullyn could see how solemn the young lord looked. It was a grave thing they were doing.

"And will you serve me truly all your life?" Rhodry said.

"I will. I'll fight for you and die with you if need be."

"Then may every bard in the kingdom mock and shame me if ever I treat you unjustly, or if ever I'm miserly to you."

Rhodry took a comb from a waiting page and made the ritual strokes through Cullyn's hair to seal the bargain. As Cullyn rose to the cheering of the warband, he felt strangely light and free, even though he'd just pledged his life away. The thought was puzzling, but he somehow knew that he had just repaid a debt.

Now that he was officially the captain of the tieryn's warband, Cullyn was back in the barracks, but he had a chamber of his own over the tack room, not over the horses, with a proper bed, a chest for his clothes, and the biggest luxury of all, a hearth of its own. When he moved in, Amyr carried up his saddlebags and bedroll, and Praedd brought an armload of firewood—two prudent moves to curry favor with the man who had the power to discipline them with a whip if need be. Cullyn hung his new shield, blazoned with the red lion, up on the wall and decided that he'd unpacked.

"Well and good, lads," Cullyn said. "We'll be taking the horses out soon. I want to see how well you all sit on a horse, now that I'm not distracted by little things like dweomer."

The two riders allowed themselves small smiles.

"Captain?" Amyr said. "Are you and Lord Rhodry going to start finding new men soon?"

"Cursed right. We're badly understrength."

They were, truly, because out of the fifty men Rhodry had at Dun Cannobaen, only seventeen were left, and out of the fifty from Dun Gwerbyn, only thirty-two. Yet Cullyn knew that soon enough, young men would show up at the gates to beg for a place in the warband. Not for them to worry that places were open because of so many bloody deaths; they would want the honor enough to ignore such an inconvenient fact—the honor, the chance at glory, and at root, the freedom from the drudgery of their father's farm or craft shop. That very afternoon, when Cullyn went down to the ward to exercise, three of the spearmen from Cannobaen asked him if they could join.

"At least you know what a war's like," Cullyn said. "I'll speak to Lord Rhodry for you."

And they were grateful, sincerely and deeply grateful, that such an important man as he would do them a favor.

Rhodry was gone from the great hall, and the pages had no idea of where he was. Cullyn searched the ward, and finally, as he passed by a storage shed, he heard Rhodry's voice and a woman's giggle—Jill. Cullyn felt that he'd been turned into a tree and taken root on the spot. He'd been a fool to take Rhodry's offer; Jill was very beautiful, and Rhodry already had sired one bastard, hadn't he? Since he couldn't quite hear what they were saying, he cautiously edged around the shed until he could just see them, standing between a stack of firewood and the dun wall. They were a decent space apart, but they were smiling at each other with such absorption that they never looked up and saw him.

Cullyn's hand sought his sword hilt of its own will, but he forced it away. He'd sworn a solemn oath to Rhodry, and later he'd have a talk with Jill. As he walked away, he saw Nevyn coming toward him.

"Looking for me?" Cullyn said.

"For Jill, actually. Her Grace wants her."

"She's back there." Cullyn jerked his thumb in her general direction. "Talking with Rhodry."

Nevyn's eyes narrowed as he studied Cullyn's face. Cullyn stared right back, a battle of wills that Nevyn eventually won when Cullyn could no longer bear to look at the man who knew full well the cause of his jealousy.

"Tell my lord I need a word with him, will you?" Cullyn said. Then he walked off, leaving Nevyn to think what he would.

Amid piles of chain mail and racked swords in the shed that

did Dun Gwerbyn for an armory, Cullyn was just taking down a practice sword when Rhodry caught up with him.

"My lord?" Cullyn said. "Three of the Cannobaen spearmen want to ride for you. They claim to know somewhat about sword-craft."

"Try them out. If you think they'll do, I'll take them on. You can make that a general principle, truly. I trust your judgment of a man."

"My thanks."

For a long painful moment they merely looked at each other. Since Cullyn had never been given to pondering his feelings and considering subtleties, he began to feel like he was drowning. How could he both admire Rhodry and hate him this way? It was because of Jill, but it was more than Jill. He simply couldn't understand. His enraged bafflement must have been obvious, because Rhodry grew more and more uneasy. Yet he, too, couldn't seem to break away, and the silence grew so thick it was painful.

"Cullyn?" Rhodry said at last. "You know I honor you."

"I do, my lord, and you have my thanks."

"Well, then." Rhodry turned idly away and seemed to be examining a nearby sword rack. "Would I do somewhat that would cause you grief?"

Somewhat—as palpably as if she'd walked in the door, Cullyn felt Jill's presence between them.

"Well?" Rhodry said. "Do you hold me in such low esteem as all that?"

"I don't, my lord. If I did, I wouldn't be riding for you."

"Well and good, then." Rhodry turned back with a faint smile. "Here, do you remember when I asked you to play Carnoic with me?"

"I do, and truly, I never thought we'd live to do it."

"But we have. Tonight I'll bring a board over to your table, and we'll have a game."

After Rhodry left, Cullyn stood in the shed for a long time, the wooden sword in his hands, and wished that he were better at thinking. On the long road he'd seen more courts from the underside than any man in the kingdom, and never had he met a lord like Rhodry, so much what every lord was supposed to be but few were. If only it weren't for Jill. If only. He swore aloud and went out to the practice ground to work his frustrations away.

Cullyn worked a little too hard. By the time he realized that he had to stop, his head was swimming. By walking slowly and concentrating on every step, he reached his chamber without having to ask for help and flopped onto the bed, boots, sword belt, and all. When he woke, Jill was standing beside his bed, and the slanting light through the window told him it was close to sunset.

"What are you doing here?" Cullyn snapped. "You shouldn't be anywhere near the barracks."

"Oh, I know, and I hate it. Da, I miss you. We hardly get a chance to talk these days."

When Cullyn sat up, rubbing his face and yawning, Jill sat down next to him. In her new dresses she looked so much like her mother that he wanted to weep.

"Well, my sweet, I miss you, too, but you're a fine lady now."

"Oh horseshit! Lovyan can heap honors on me all she wants, but I'll always be common-born and a bastard."

She spoke so bitterly that even Cullyn could catch this subtle point.

"Rhodry will never marry you, truly," Cullyn said. "And you'd best keep that in mind, when you're giggling and flirting with him."

Jill went pale and still, clutching a handful of blanket.

"I've seen the pair of you looking at each other like hounds at a joint of meat," Cullyn went on. "You stay away from him. He's an honorable man, but you wouldn't be the first beautiful woman that made a man break his own honor."

Jill nodded, her mouth working in honest pain. Cullyn felt torn in pieces. He was sincerely sorry for her, that she'd never have the man she loved, and at the same time, he wanted to slap her just because she loved another man.

"Come along." Cullyn stood up. "You're not a barracks brat anymore, and you can't be hanging around here."

Cullyn strode out, leaving Jill to follow. Yet her words haunted him that evening, that she loved him, that she missed him. He wondered how he would feel if she married some man the tieryn picked out for her, and she went off to live with her new husband. He would probably never see her but once or twice a year. He even had the thought of simply leaving Rhodry's service and going back on the long road, where he would neither know nor care where Jill was sleeping, but as he sat in the captain's place at the head table of the warband, he knew that he could never give up his newfound position. For the first time in his life, he had too much to lose.

Later, after the warbands drifted back to the barracks and the noble lords up to their chambers, Rhodry brought over a game of Carnoic, the finest set Cullyn had ever seen. The playing pieces were flat polished stones, white and black. The thin ebony board was inlaid with mother-of-pearl to mark the starting stations and the track, sixteen interwoven triangles, so that even in firelight it was easy to follow.

"I'll wager you beat me soundly," Rhodry said.

Cullyn did, too, for the first three games, sweeping Rhodry's men off the board as fast as the young lord put them on. Swearing under his breath, Rhodry began pondering every move he made and gave Cullyn a harder run for it, but still he lost the next three. By then, only one drowsy servant remained in the hall to refill their tankards. Rhodry sent the man to bed, stopped drinking, and finally after four more games, ran Cullyn to a draw.

"I won't press my luck anymore tonight," Rhodry said.

"It wasn't luck. You're learning."

Cullyn felt the simple comfort of it as overwhelming. Here they were, two men who'd given themselves up for dead, safe at home by a fire, with plenty of ale and each other's company. While Rhodry put the game back in its lacquered box, Cullyn got up and fetched more ale. They drank silently at first, and slowly, making the moment last as the fire died down and the shadows filled the hall. Cullyn suddenly realized that he was happy, a word that had never had much meaning for him before. Or he would be happy, if it weren't for Jill, whom he loved too much but loved truly enough to want her to be happy, too. Maybe it was the ale, maybe it was the late hour, but he suddenly thought of the clear and simple way to solve the whole tangled mess—if he could do it. If he could bear to do it.

All unconsciously, Rhodry gave him the opening he needed, the chance to think about what had seemed so unthinkable before.

"By the hells, I wish Rhys would get himself here," Rhodry

said. "Oh well, in a way he's doing me somewhat of a favor. As soon as the rebellion's settled, my esteemed mother's going to put all her boundless energies into marrying me off."

"It's about time you did, my lord."

"I know—the cursed rhan needs its cursed heirs. Ye gods, captain, think how I must feel. How would you like to be put to stud like a prize horse?"

Cullyn laughed aloud.

"Aches a man's heart, doesn't it?" Rhodry said, grinning. "And for all I know, she'll have a face and a temper to match the Lord of Hell's. It's her cursed kin that count, not what I might think of her."

"Huh. I see why the cursed priests are always telling a man never to envy the noble-born."

"And right they are, truly. Men like me marry to please our clans, not ourselves."

The old proverb struck an odd place in Cullyn's mind, some long-buried memory that he couldn't quite get clear. He had a long swallow of ale and considered his peculiar idea. He could think of no way to broach it subtlely.

"Tell me somewhat, my lord," Cullyn said. "Would you marry my Jill if you could?"

Rhodry went so tense that Cullyn realized that the lad was as afraid of him as Jill was. It was gratifying. Common-born or not, he was still Jill's father, still the man who'd decide what she would or wouldn't do.

"I would," Rhodry said at last. "I'll swear that to you on the honor of the Maelwaedds. I've never wanted anything as much as I want to marry her, but I can't."

"I know that."

They drank for a few minutes more, and Rhodry never looked away from his face.

"You know, my lord," Cullyn said. "The mistress of a great lord has a cursed lot of power in his rhan and court."

Rhodry jerked his head as if Cullyn had slapped him.

"So she does," Rhodry whispered. "And no one would dare mock her, either."

"Provided she was never cast off to her shame."

"There're some women who would never have to fear such a thing."

"Good." Absently Cullyn laid his hand on his sword hilt. "Good."

They sat together drinking, never saying another word, until the fire was so low that they could barely see each other's face.

Perhaps the thing that Jill hated most about being in a lady's retinue was that she had to learn to sew. For all that Lovyan was a rich tieryn, most of the clothing worn in the dun was made there, and she owed every rider in her warband and every servant in her hall two pairs of shirts and brigga or two dresses a year as part of their maintenance. Every woman in the dun, from the lowliest kitchen wench to Dannyan and Medylla, spent part of her time producing this mountain of clothes. Even Lovyan took a hand and sewed Rhodry's shirts for him, as well as embroidering the blazons on the shirts for her skilled servitors such as the bard. Since there was a definite honor among women about the fineness of their sewing, Jill dutifully practiced, but she hated every clumsy stitch she made.

That morning Nevyn came to the women's hall, which was open to him because of his great age and, while she worked, entertained her with tales of Bardek, that mysterious country far across the Southern Sea. From the wealth of details, it was plain that he'd spent much time there.

"Studying physick, truly," Nevyn admitted when she asked him. "They have much curious lore in Bardek, and most of it's worth knowing. It's a cursed strange place."

"So it sounds. I wish I could see it someday, but it's not likely now."

"Here, child, you sound very unhappy."

"I am, and I feel like the most ungrateful wretch in the world, too. Here her grace has been so generous to me, and I'm living in more luxury than I ever dreamt of, but I feel like a falcon in a cage."

"Well, in a way, you are trapped."

It was such a relief to hear someone agree with her that Jill nearly wept. Irritably she threw the sewing into her wicker workbasket.

"Well, if you truly hate this kind of life," Nevyn went on, "perhaps you should leave it."

"What can I do? Ride the roads as a silver dagger?"

"I should think not, but many a woman has a craft. If I spoke
to the tieryn, she'd pay the prentice-fee for you."

"Oh, and what sort of thing would I do? I'd hate to spin or
sew or suchlike, and no armorer or weaponmaster would take a
woman as an apprentice, not even if the tieryn asked them."

"There are all sorts of crafts."

All at once, Jill remembered that he was dweomer. He was
so kind to her, so bent on winning her friendship, that at times
she forgot this frightening truth. The gray gnome looked up from
the floor, where he'd been amusing himself by tangling her embroidery threads, and gave her a gaping grin.

"My lord," Jill said, her voice shaking. "You honor me too
highly if you think I could take up your craft."

"Maybe I do, maybe I don't, but it's a closed issue if you don't
want it. I was merely thinking about herbcraft, the plain and
simple medicine I know. I've learned a lot in my long years, and
it would be a pity to let the knowledge die with me."

"Well, so it would." Suddenly Jill felt her first real hope in
days. "And you travel everywhere and live the way you want."

"Just that, and you're bright enough to learn the lore.
Lovyan will understand, truly, if you want to leave. She'll know
you'll be safe with me."

"But what about Da? I doubt me if he'd let me go with you,
and truly, we've been through so much together, him and me,
that I'd hate to leave him, too."

"No doubt, but at some time you have to leave him."

Although Nevyn spoke quietly, his words cut like a knife.

"Well, why?" Jill snapped. "If I stay here—"

"And aren't you the one who was just telling me you were so
wretched here?"

"Oh so I was."

"Just think about it. You don't have to decide straightaway."

Nevyn left her to the tedious task of untangling the skeins
that the gnome had ruined. As she worked, Jill thought over his
offer. Oddly enough, she could see herself wandering the roads
with a mule and dispensing herbs to farmers much more easily
than marrying some minor lord and living in comfort. While it
would hurt to leave Cullyn, she could always come back and see
him whenever she felt like it. It would hurt much less than being
shut up in the dun with Rhodry and his new wife, seeing him

every day and knowing that another woman had what was beyond her reach.

Or so Jill thought of him that morning, as beyond her reach. Toward evening, she went out in the ward just for some fresh air, and Rhodry followed her, catching her out by the wall among the storage sheds.

"My lord should be more careful about chasing after me," Jill said. "What if someone saw you?"

"I don't give a pig's fart if they did or not. I've got to talk with you. Let's find a place where we can be alone."

"Oh indeed? It's not talk that's on your mind."

"It is, and it isn't. What of it?"

Rhodry smiled at her so softly that Jill followed him when he went round a shed to a private place in the curve of the wall.

"This will do for now," Rhodry said. "I uh—"

The words seemed to stick in his throat.

"Uh well," he started again. "You see, I had a—I mean, that sounds so cursed cold."

"You haven't said much yet that sounded like anything."

"I know. Well, it's about that bargain we made, truly."

"I thought as much. I meant what I said, curse you."

"Things have changed somewhat. I—"

And he was stuck there again, looking at her with a feeble, foolish smile. In sheer irritation Jill started to walk away, but he grabbed her by the shoulders. When she swung round to break his hold, she tripped over the hem of her dress and nearly fell into his arms. He laughed and kissed her, held her tight when she tried to squirm away, and kissed her again so sweetly that she threw her arms around his neck and kissed him, clung to him, while she remembered all the pleasure his kisses promised.

"Leave your chamber door unbarred tonight," Rhodry said.

"You dolt! If someone catches you, the news will be all over the dun."

"Who's going to be up in the middle of the night but me?" He kissed her softly, letting his mouth linger on hers. "Just leave the door unbarred."

When Jill shoved him away, he grinned at her.

"I know you'll do it," Rhodry said. "Till tonight, my lady."

In a fury of lust and rage both, Jill hiked up her skirts and ran, turning round the shed and nearly running straight into Cullyn.

She yelped aloud in terror. He must have heard, must have seen. He set his hands on his hips and looked at her so mildly that she was sure she was in for the worst beating of her life.

"Da, I'm sorry!" Jill stammered.

"And so you might be, carrying on like a serving wench where anyone might see you."

"I won't do it again. Promise."

"Good. You've got a chamber for that sort of thing, don't you?"

Jill's head reeled as badly as if he had slapped her. Cullyn gave her the barest sort of smile and walked past, calling out to Rhodry to wait for him. The two of them went off together, discussing some new men for the warband.

"So that's what Rhodry wanted to tell me," Jill whispered. "Oh by the Goddess herself!"

She felt betrayed. Jill stood there for a long time and considered it, that where she might have been pleased, she felt betrayed. Cullyn had handed her over to Rhodry to be his mistress, just handed her over like a horse, and she wanted Rhodry too much to protest. At that moment, she saw clearly what her life would become, caught between the two of them, loving them both, yet kept away from both. Rhodry would have his wife, and Cullyn, the warband. She would be important to them, in her way, rather like a valuable sword that they would never use in battle, only hang on a chamber wall to be taken down and admired once in a while. I can't do that, she told herself, I won't! Yet she knew that she could, and that she would. The bars of her cage were made out of love, and they would keep her in for all her gnawing at them.

All evening, Jill debated the question of whether Rhodry would find her door open or barred. She decided that she should hold out and make him realize that he would have to court her, that she wasn't a bit of battle loot to be distributed by her father. When she went to bed that night, she barred the door, but she couldn't sleep, and slowly, a bit at a time, her resolve wore away like sand under a storm tide. She cursed herself for a slut or worse, then got up and lifted the wooden bar free of the staples. She stood there for a moment, barred it again, then lifted it off and left it off. She stripped off her nightdress, lay down, and felt her heart pounding in the darkness. Not more than a few moments later, he came to her, as surefooted and silent as a thief.

"Just once, my love," he whispered. "I'd like to have you in the light. I want to see what your face looks like when we've done."

Jill giggled and threw the blankets back. He took off his clothes and slipped in next to her. At the touch of his naked body on hers, she forgot every worry she'd ever had about honor and betrayal, but she pretended to shove him away. He grabbed her wrists and kissed her until she struggled free, then he caught her again. They wrestled with each other as much as they caressed each other, until at last she could wait no longer and let him win, pressing her down, catching her, filling her with an aching fiery pleasure that made her sob in his arms.

Since Nevyn never slept more than four hours a night, he was up late that evening, brooding over the dark master and his peculiar plot. For all his scrying on the etheric, he'd found no further traces of the enemy, and neither had any other dweomer-master in the kingdom. He was just thinking that it was late enough for even him to be in bed when Jill's gray gnome popped into manifestation on the table. The little creature was furious, making soundless snarls and pulling at its hair as it danced up and down.

"Now, now," Nevyn said. "What's all this?"

The gnome grabbed his hand and pulled, as if it were trying to haul him to his feet.

"What? You want me to come with you?"

The gnome nodded a vigorous yes and pulled on him again.

"Is somewhat wrong with Jill?"

At that, the gnome leapt into its little dance of fury. Nevyn lit a lantern and followed the gnome as it led him toward the women's quarters. As soon as the gnome realized that he was going to go to Jill's chamber, it disappeared. Holding the lantern low, Nevyn turned down the main corridor and met Rhodry, barefoot, touseled, and obviously very tired. Rhodry squeaked like a caught burglar, and Nevyn collared him like one.

"You little dolt!" Nevyn hissed.

"I just couldn't sleep. Just taking a bit of air."

"Hah! Come along, lad."

Nevyn marched Rhodry back to his chamber, which was some ways away on the floor above the women's quarters, and shoved him through the door. Rhodry sank into a chair and looked up bleary-eyed. His lips were swollen.

"How by every god did you know I was in Jill's bed?"

"How do you think I knew, dolt?"

Rhodry squeaked and flinched back.

"I'm not going to blast you with dweomer-fires or suchlike," Nevyn said with some asperity. "Tempted though I may be. All I want you to do is think. You won't be able to keep this midnight trysting a secret forever. As the saying goes, fine dresses can't hide a big belly. What will Cullyn do then, pray tell?"

"Nothing. We've had words about it, and he let me know that Jill's mine as long as I treat her as well as a great lord's mistress deserves."

Nevyn felt like a man who's drawn his sword with a flourish only to find it broken off at the hilt.

"Truly, I couldn't believe my ears either." Rhodry did look sincerely amazed. "But he did. I swear to you that I'll always treat her well. Ah ye gods, Nevyn, can't you understand how much I love her? You must have been young once. Didn't you ever love a woman this much?"

Nevyn was caught speechless by the irony of the thing—so he had, the same one. Unceremoniously Nevyn kicked the heir to the tierynrhyn out of his chamber and barred the door behind him. He sat down in the chair and ran his fingers idly over the rough wood of the table edge. Jill's gnome appeared, all smiles and bows.

"I'm sorry, my friend," Nevyn said. "You'll have to put up with this, just like I will."

The gnome hissed and disappeared. Nevyn was just as heartsick. She was gone from him in this life as she'd gone in so many others, he was sure of it. All the amusements and crises of a great court would fill her mind and her time until her latent dweomer talents faded away. He could see it all: although Rhodry's wife would have to accept his mistress, she would come to hate Jill when the various vassals paid their court to Jill, not to her. The fight would come to the surface when Jill had a couple of Rhodry's bastards and was trying to get them settled in good positions. No doubt Rhodry would favor Jill's children, too, making his wife hate her more than ever. None of this would leave any place for the dweomer.

Nevyn's first impulse was to leave the dun that very night and ride far away, but Jill would need him. For all the pain of seeing his vow go unfulfilled for yet another long stretch of years, he would stay, simply because she needed him. For a moment Nevyn felt so odd that he didn't know what was wrong with him. Then he realized that for the first time in a hundred years, he was weeping.

When the tenth day passed with no word from Rhys, Lovyan was furious enough to dispense with formalities and send a message to him. Although she carefully phrased the letter in humble and courtly terms, at root she told him that the entire tierynrhyn would be in upheaval until he cursed well did something about it. When the scribe read it to her impatient vassals, they cheered.

"You have my sympathy, my lords," Lovyan said to them. "We'll see if a mother's words can prod the gwerbret to action."

Lovyan left them to discuss her letter and went up to the women's hall. As a child she had played there at her mother's side, and the familiar room was still a comfortable refuge, even though she was the lord of the dun now, not its lady. When she came in, she found Dannyan trying to help Jill with her sewing.

"Shall I fetch Her Grace some wine?" Jill said.

"Anything to get out of the cursed sewing?" Lovyan said with a smile. "You may lay that aside if you wish, Jill, but truly, I don't want anything at the moment."

Jill threw her practice piece into the workbasket with such fury that Lovyan and Dannyan both laughed at her.

"Here, Dann," Lovyan said. "It's truly time we put some thought into getting Rhodry married."

"True enough," Dannyan said. "I've been thinking about the gwerbret of Caminwaen's younger daughter. With Rhys and Rhodry always feuding, it would be wise to give the tieryn some connections with another gwerbretrhyn."

"Now that's an excellent point, and she's a levelheaded lass."

Jill went as still as a hunted animal. A number of things that Lovyan had noticed all came together in her mind.

"Oh Jill, my sweet," Lovyan said. "You're not in love with my wretched son, are you?"

For an answer Jill blushed scarlet.

"You poor child," Lovyan said. "You have all my sympathy, but Jill, I can never let you marry Rhodry."

"I'm more than aware of that, Your Grace," Jill said, and she was in perfect control of every word. "Besides, I have no doubt at all that Lord Rhodry is going to make his wife a very bad husband."

It was so perfectly done that Lovyan was impressed.

"I see." Lovyan gave her a pleasant little nod. "I'm glad that you're such a sensible lass."

Lovyan and Dannyan exchanged a glance, then changed the subject. Later, they sent Jill off on an errand and discussed the matter, agreeing that whether she could sew or not, Jill was going to fit very well into the court. Without an open word being said, they now knew who Rhodry's mistress was, and they could pick his wife accordingly.

Since Lovyan knew that Nevyn had an interest in Jill, she made a point of discussing the matter with him privately. As she expected, Nevyn was disappointed, but he seemed resigned.

"After all," Nevyn said. "I'll see her often in your dun."

"Of course, as long as things sit well with you."

"Oh here, Lovva! What have you been thinking, that I was an old ram about to make a fool of myself over a young ewe?"

Lovyan felt her cheeks coloring, but Nevyn was far more amused than insulted.

"I assure you," he went on, "that I'm more aware than most of the years I carry. I'm fond of Jill, but truly, my main interest in her is her raw dweomer talent."

"Of course! It's very odd, but it's so hard to keep in mind that you're dweomer—that anyone can be dweomer, truly—and here I saw Jill have that vision of hers."

"Well, the mind shrinks from what it can't understand. I heard your bard practicing his praise song about the war. He's reporting very faithfully what happened. Do you think anyone will believe a word of it in say, fifty years?"

"They won't. A typical bard song, they'll say, full of lies and fancies. And you know, maybe it's just as well."

Three days later, the message finally came from Rhys. Lovyan had an odd premonition about it and decided to read it privately rather than having it read aloud in the open hall. She'd made the right decision.

"My Lady Mother," it ran. "Forgive me for the delay in attending to your important affairs. I have been investigating the matter of this war in order to ascertain whether Lord Rhodry's report was in the least accurate. I am summoning him and his allies to Aberwyn to give me an account of their conduct. You, of course, are also most welcome to my meat and mead, and we shall settle the other matters then. Your humble son, Rhys, Gwerbret Aberwyn."

"You little beast!" Lovyan said aloud. "*You're* certainly Tingyr's son, aren't you?"

Nevyn was more than pleased when Lovyan asked him to join her entourage for the trip to Aberwyn. He even allowed her to provide him with a new shirt and decent brigga, so that he could pass inconspicuously as one of her councillors. Lovyan was taking Jill, Dannyan, her scribe, several servants, and then Cullyn as the captain of an honor guard of twenty-five men, fifteen for her, ten for Rhodry, as their ranks allowed. As she sourly remarked, Rhys could cursed well feed part of her household for a while after letting her vassals feed off her for so long.

"I'm rather surprised you're taking Jill," Nevyn remarked. "She's unused to large courts and their ways."

"Well, she really does have to start getting used to them. Besides, having her there will keep Rhodry calm."

Nevyn was about to make some remark about trouble with Cullyn if Jill were blatantly displayed as Rhodry's mistress, but he stopped himself, simply because the captain seemed to have no objections to his daughter's position. Ruefully, Nevyn had to admit that he was disappointed. He'd been hoping that her fear of her father's wrath would keep Jill away from Rhodry and free for the dweomer.

The night before they left for Aberwyn, Nevyn decided to seek Cullyn out and found him in his chamber in the barracks. Dressed in a new shirt blazoned with red lions, Cullyn sat on the side of his bed and polished his sword by lantern light. He greeted Nevyn hospitably and offered him the only chair.

"I just wanted a few words with you," Nevyn said. "About a somewhat delicate matter."

"I'll wager you mean Jill."

"Just that. I'll admit to being surprised that you'd let her do what she's doing."

Cullyn sighted down the sword blade, found some near-invisible fleck of rust, and began working on it with a rag.

"I think you'd be the least surprised of any man," Cullyn said at last. "You're the one who knows why I had to let her go."

When he looked up, straight into Nevyn's eyes, Nevyn had to admire him for the first time in four hundred years. All the arrogance that Gerraent had flaunted, life after life, was gone, leaving only a certain proud humility that came from facing the bitter realities of his life.

"There's more kinds of honor than battle glory," Nevyn said. "You deserve yours."

With a shrug, Cullyn tossed the sword onto the bed.

"Besides," he said. "Jill's going to do cursed well out of this, isn't she? She'll have a better life than any that I thought I could ever give her. Even if I had a lord's ransom for her dowry, what kind of husband could I have found her? A craftsman of some kind, a tavern owner, maybe, and there she'd be, working hard all her life. For a silver dagger's bastard, she's risen cursed high."

"So she has, truly. I'd never thought of things quite in that way."

"Doubtless you've never had to. What's that old saying? It's better for a woman to keep her poverty than lose her virtue? I'd have slit Jill's throat rather than let her turn into a whore, but when you ride the long road, you learn not to be too fussy about fine shades of virtue. Ye gods, I sold my own honor a thousand times over. Who am I to look down my nose at her?"

"Well, true spoken, but most men wouldn't be so reasonable about their only daughter."

Cullyn shrugged and picked up the sword again to run cal-loused fingertips down the gutter of the blade.

"I'll tell you somewhat," Cullyn said. "I haven't told a soul this tale in nineteen years, but have you ever wondered why I ended up with the cursed silver dagger?"

"Often. I was afraid to ask."

"As well you might have been." Cullyn gave him a thin smile. "I was a rider in the Gwerbret of Cerrmor's warband. There was a lass I fancied there, waiting on table in the great hall

—Seryan, Jill's mother. And another lad fancied her, too. We fought over her like dogs over a bone until she made it clear enough that she favored me. So this other lad—ah by the hells, I've forgotten the poor bastard's name—anyway, he wouldn't take her at her word and kept hanging around her. So, one night I said somewhat to him about it, and he drew on me. So I drew and killed him." Cullyn's voice dropped, and he looked down at the sword across his knees. "Right there in the gwerbret's barracks. His grace was all for hanging me, but the captain stepped in, saying the other lad drew first. So his grace kicked me out instead, and my poor Seryan insisted on riding with me when I went." Cullyn looked up again. "So, you see, I swore then that I'd never kill another man over a woman. It doesn't do you or her one cursed bit of good."

Nevyn was speechless for a moment, simply because Cullyn had no idea of just how much of his Wyrd he was laying aside with that simple truth.

"You learn," Cullyn said. "I was a stubborn young dog, but you learn."

"Truly. I was as stubborn myself, when I was that young."

"No doubt. You know, herbman, why we rub each other so raw? We're too cursed much alike."

Nevyn laughed, seeing what his grudge had hidden for so many years.

"Oh by the hells," Nevyn said. "So we are."

At that time, Aberwyn was the biggest city in Eldidd, with over seventy thousand people living in its warren of curving streets and closely packed houses. Unwalled, it spread along the Aver Gwyn up from the harbor, where the gwerbret's fleet of war galleys shared piers with merchantmen from Deverry and Bardek both. Right in the middle of town stood the enormous dun of the gwerbret, a towering symbol of justice. Inside the thirty-foot stone wall was a ward covering some thirty acres, cluttered with the usual huts, barracks, and sheds. In the middle rose a broch complex, a round central tower of six stories, three secondary towers of three, but the most amazing thing of all was that the broch stood in the middle of a garden: lawns, beds of roses, a fountain, all set off from the ward by a low brick wall.

Everywhere writhed the open-jawed dragon of Aberwyn,

carved onto the outer gates, displayed on the blue and silver
banners hanging from the brochs, sculpted in marble in the center of the fountain, carved again on the doors into the broch,
inlaid in blue slate on the floor of the great hall, blazoned on the
shirts of every rider and servant, embroidered into the bed hangings and cushions of the luxurious chamber that Jill was going to
share with Dannyan. On the mantel over their hearth there was
even a small silver statuette of the dragon. Jill picked it up and
studied it.

"It's lovely, isn't it?" Dannyan said. "The Maelwaedds have
always collected fine silver."

"It is." Jill set it back down. "It must have been quite a
wrench for you to leave all this splendor when her grace retired
to Cannobaen."

"It was. I'll admit to being just the least bit glad when Lovyan's brother got himself killed. Terrible of me, but there you are."
Dannyan dismissed the subject with a little shrug. "Now, Jill,
you'll have to be very careful while we're here."

"Oh, I'm sure of that. Dann, I'm terrified."

"Now, people will make some allowances, but follow what I
do. Stick as close to me as possible, and please, don't say horsedung and suchlike. You're not in the barracks anymore. Now let's
have a bit of a wash, and then get you out of those nasty brigga
and into a proper dress."

Since Jill had never ridden sidesaddle in her life—and an
untrained woman was in real danger of falling—she'd been allowed to wear her old clothes on the ride to Aberwyn. She was
surprised at how good they felt and how much she hated to take
them off again. Once she was dressed to Dannyan's satisfaction,
Dannyan took her to the women's hall to present her to the
gwerbret's wife. Donilla was a lovely woman, with fine dark eyes,
a wealth of chestnut hair, and a figure as slender as a lass's. She
seated them graciously, and had a servant bring wine in real glass
goblets, but she was distracted as she and Dannyan chatted, and
all the time, she twisted and untwisted a silk handkerchief between her fingers. Jill was glad when they left.

"Dann," Jill said as soon as they were back in the privacy of
their chamber. "Is Her Grace ill or suchlike?"

"She's not. Rhys is about to put her aside for being barren.
My heart truly aches for her."

"And what will happen to her?"

"Our lady's going to make her a marriage with a widowed cousin of hers. He has two heirs already, and he'll be glad of a beautiful new wife. If it weren't for that, she'd have to go back shamed to her brother. I doubt me if he'd receive her well."

Jill felt honestly sick. She had never realized before just how dependent on their men noble-born women were. There was no chance for them to work a farm with the help of their sons, or to marry their dead husband's apprentice and keep his shop, much less open a shop of their own. Suddenly she wondered what was going to become of her. Would she someday be reduced to cringing and fawning around Rhodry to make sure she still had his favor?

"Donilla will ride back with us when we leave," Dannyan went on. "We'll all have to be very kind to her. The worst thing of all is that she has to be there when Rhys publicly denounces her."

"Oh by the black ass of the Lord of Hell! Is his grace as hard-hearted as that?"

"Jill, lamb, do watch your tongue, but it's not Rhys, it's the laws. Rhys would spare her the shame if he could, truly he would, but he can't."

When they went down to the great hall for dinner, Jill was relieved to find that they wouldn't be eating at Rhys's table. Where an ordinary dun only had one honor table, Aberwyn's hall had six, one for the gwerbret and his family, the others for guests and the noble-born officials of his court. Jill and Dannyan sat with the seneschal, the equerry, the bard, and their wives. From where she was seated, Jill could just see Rhodry, seated at his brother's left. Although they had the same coloring and a certain shared look to their jaw that they'd inherited from Lovyan, they were so different that Jill found it hard to believe they were brothers. Doubtless it was Rhodry's elven blood that made his face so chiseled and delicate that in comparison, Rhys looked coarse. Yet the gwerbret was still a good-looking man in his way, not the fiend that Jill had been picturing.

The meal was elaborate, with a course of pickled vegetables arranged in patterns on little plates, a course of lark pies and one of fruit preceding the roast pork. Jill paid strict attention to her manners and spoke to no one until at last the bard's wife, a round-faced little blonde named Camma, turned to her with cool, appraising eyes.

"This must be your first time at court," Camma said.

"It is, truly," Jill said. "It's rather splendid."

"Indeed. Was your father one of our country lords?"

Jill was taken utterly aback. Dannyan leaned over with a limpid smile for Camma that seemed to be masking the word "bitch."

"Jill is a very important member of Tieryn Lovyan's retinue," Dannyan said. She allowed herself a glance at Rhodry. "Very important."

"I see." Camma gave Jill a warm smile. "Well, you must allow me to entertain you in my chambers sometime."

"My thanks," Jill said. "I shall have to see how much leisure my duties to Her Grace allow."

Dannyan gave Jill a small nod of approval. Jill picked at her food and decided that she was no longer hungry. Although she thought of herself as a falcon, she felt as if she were dining with eagles, who might turn on her at any moment. She found herself watching Rhodry, who was eating fast and silently. Finally he rose, looked her way with a toss of his head, and strode out of the hall. Flustered, Jill turned to Dannyan.

"You can follow in a little bit," Dannyan whispered.

Jill dutifully sipped her wine and made small talk for some minutes, then excused herself and hurried away from table. She found a page who knew where Rhodry was quartered and followed him up the spiral staircase and through the confused corridors of the joined brochs for what seemed an embarrassingly long way before he pointed out Rhodry's door with a sly and knowing smile. Jill hurried in and frankly slammed the door behind her. The tiny chamber was sparsely furnished with what looked like castoffs from grander chambers elsewhere. Its one window looked directly down on the kitchen hut, and the smell of grease hung in the air. His boots and belt already off, Rhodry was lounging on the lumpy bed.

"Has Rhys said anything about the rebellion?" Jill said.

"Naught. Not one cursed word. We'll have the formal discussion tomorrow morn, says he, the piss-proud little bastard, as if I was a criminal, hauled up before him for stealing horses. I don't

want to talk about it, my love. I want to get you into this bed and
keep you here until you beg for mercy."

"Indeed?" Jill began to untie her kirtle. "Then you'll have a
cursed long night of it."

It was just at dawn that Nevyn finally had concrete news of
the dark dweomer-master. Down in Cerrmor lived a woman
named Nesta. Although her neighbors thought of her only as the
somewhat eccentric widow of a rich merchant, she had studied
the dweomer for over forty years—and other things as well. Her
husband's long years of trading in Bardek spices had given her a
great deal of information about other, less savory kinds of trade
with that far-off land. When she contacted him that morning, her
round little face was troubled under her neat black headscarf.

"Now I can't be as sure as sure," Nesta thought to him. "But I
think me the man you're looking for has just taken ship for
Bardek."

"Indeed?" Nevyn thought back. "I trust you haven't put
yourself in danger by trying to scry him out."

"Oh, I followed your orders, sure enough, and kept well
away from him. Here, see what you think of this tale. Yestermorn,
the Wildfolk came to me, quite troubled they were, too, about
some dark thing that was scaring them. It made me think that
your enemy might be in Cerrmor, and so I did a bit of scrying and
picked up some odd traces in the etheric. I drew back, then, as
you told me to do." She paused, and her image pursed wrinkled
lips. "But you know that I know half the people in Cerrmor, and
my connections with the guilds give me ways of finding things
out without using the body of light. I asked around here and
there about peculiar strangers in town, and finally I talked with
one of the young lads at the Customs House. He'd seen a strange
old fellow boarding one of the last Bardek merchantmen in harbor, and here, that ship's suspected of being involved in the
poison trade."

Nevyn whistled under his breath. Nesta's image gave him a
grim little smile.

"And the ship sailed with the tide not two hours ago," she
went on. "And now the Wildfolk are as calm as you please, and
there's not a trace of anything to be found on the etheric."

"Then if it wasn't him, it was another of his foul kind, but I'll

wager it was my enemy. He'd know I couldn't follow him to
Bardek with the winter coming on."

"He was cursed lucky to get a ship himself. It was like the
boat was waiting for him, wasn't it now?"

"It was indeed. I'll wager you tracked our rat to his hole, sure
enough. My humble thanks, Nesta, and my thanks to that sharp-
eyed customs officer, too."

"Oh, he's a good lad." She chuckled briefly. "He prenticed
with my man and me, and I taught him how to use his two eyes."

After Nesta said farewell, Nevyn spent some time pacing in
his chamber and considering this news. Since neither he nor
anyone else had picked up any other traces of dark dweomer, he
was quite sure that Nesta had spotted the enemy. It made him
curse aloud, because with a winter's head start, the enemy would
be impossible to find in Bardek, a land of many small states and
constant political turmoil that made local authorities very lax on
matters of civil law. Since not even the greatest dweomer-master
in the world could scry or send a projection over a large body of
water, Nevyn would even have to wait until spring to send letters
to those who studied the true dweomer in Bardek and warn them
of this enemy's coming. As much as it ached his heart, he was
going to have to let the enemy escape. For now, he told himself—
just for now. Then he put the matter aside forcibly and went to
distract himself by dressing for the gwerbret's inquiry into the
rebellion.

The formal hearing was held in the gwerbret's chamber of
justice, an enormous half-round of a room on the second floor of
the main broch. In the exact middle of the curve were two
windows with the dragon banner of Aberwyn hanging between
them. Under it was a long table, where Rhys sat in the center
with the golden ceremonial sword of Aberwyn in front of him. To
either side of him sat priests of Bel, his councillors in the laws. A
scribe had a little table to the right, and the various witnesses
stood to the left, Rhodry himself, his various allies, and Lovyan,
who as a mark of respect had a chair. The rest of the room was
crowded with the merely curious, including Nevyn, who stood by
the door and watched sourly as the proceedings dragged on.

One at a time, Rhodry's allies knelt in front of the table and
answered Rhys's questions about every detail of the war, day by
day until Nevyn wondered if the cursed thing would take longer

to discuss than it did to fight. Over and over again, the allies testified that Rhodry had comported himself mercifully and abided by every law of honor. Yet Rhys sent for Cullyn, too, and questioned him while Rhodry turned dangerously sullen and Sligyn's face turned redder and redder with rage. Finally Rhys summoned Rhodry one last time.

"There's only one small point left, Lord Rhodry," Rhys said. "How do you expect me to believe all this talk of dweomer?"

Nevyn sighed; he should have expected that.

"Because it's true, Your Grace," Rhodry said. "As all my witnesses have attested."

"Indeed? It makes me wonder if you're all spinning a wild tale to cover a worse one."

When Sligyn, his face scarlet, lunged forward, Peredyr grabbed his arm and pulled him back. Lovyan rose from her chair and stalked over to the table.

"If I may have leave to speak, Your Grace," Lovyan said. "Will you sit there and say that your own mother is lying to you?"

"Of course not," Rhys said. "But you may have been lied to."

Sligyn made a noise as if he were choking, and Edar muttered something under his breath.

"I take it, then, Your Grace," Lovyan said. "That the reports of dweomer are the whole point of this malover."

"They are," Rhys said flatly. "I want the truth."

"Then you shall have it." Lovyan turned, her eyes searching the crowd. "Nevyn, will you assist me in this matter?"

Nevyn hesitated, wondering if displaying the dweomer before a crowd were contrary to his vows. Then it occurred to him that perhaps it was time for more men to know that the dweomer existed; after all, one reason that the dark dweomer could thrive was that most people laughed at the very idea of dweomer. He worked his way through the crowd and made the gwerbret a bow, but he stayed standing.

"Your Grace," Nevyn said. "I understand your skepticism in the face of such peculiar events, but I assure you that men such as me have all the strange powers of which Lord Rhodry has spoken."

The crowd gasped and eased forward. Rhys leaned back insolently in his chair.

"Indeed?" he said. "And do you expect me to believe that on your word alone?"

Nevyn raised his hands and called upon the Wildfolk of Air and Aethyr in his mind, where he gave them his commands. Suddenly a blast of wind stormed through the chamber and set the banner flapping and the parchments of priests and scribes flying through the air. Thunder boomed, and bolts of blue fire crackled and gleamed like miniature lightning. Nevyn himself glowed with an intense golden light. Screaming, shoving each other, the crowd of onlookers fled the chamber. Rhys leapt to his feet with an oath, his face dead white, and the priests clung together like frightened women as the wind raged around them with strange, half-heard laughter rippling in it. Nevyn raised his arm slowly and snapped his fingers. The wind, fire, and light all vanished.

"Not on my word alone, Your Grace," Nevyn said.

Sligyn was laughing so hard that he was nearly choking, but Peredyr dug his elbow into the lord's ribs and made him hold his tongue. Rhys looked this way and that, his mouth working as he tried to speak. Rhodry got to his feet and bowed to him.

"Does my brother still disbelieve me?" Rhodry said.

Rhys turned to Rhodry's allies and made them the bow.

"My lords, you have my sincere and humble apologies for ever doubting one word you spoke," Rhys said. "I beg you to find it in your hearts to forgive me for slighting your honor, because I was ignorant and had never seen the things you have seen."

Sligyn growled, but Peredyr got in before him.

"No need to grovel, Your Grace," Peredyr said. "We all had a cursed hard time believing it ourselves at first."

"My humble thanks, my lord." Rhys picked up the ceremonial sword without even glancing Rhodry's way and rapped the pommel three times on the table. "The malover is closed. The gwerbret has spoken."

Since he had no desire to be mobbed by the curious, Nevyn lingered just long enough to grab Rhodry's arm and haul him away. They went out to the gardens, where the leafless aspens shivered in a cold wind, and the marble dragon in the fountain looked as if it should have goose bumps as the water rose and fell over it.

"My thanks, Nevyn," Rhodry said. "I've never liked any

sight more than the sight of Rhys's pig face when the fires went
crackling around him. Do you want Corbyn's demesne? I'll get
Mother to bestow it upon you."

"Spare yourself the effort, but I appreciate the thought. I
think I'm going to have to hide in my chamber for the rest of this
cursed visit."

"Then come with me. I'm going to leave tomorrow with Jill
and some of the men. Cursed if I'll sit around here and let Rhys
insult me. You saw him turn and speak to Peredyr, not me."

"I did, and you've got every right to be furious, but please,
lad, try to contain yourself. You're right; by all means, let's leave
on the morrow—and early."

"At the crack of dawn. I can stand it for one more night."

Rhodry spoke so calmly, and his plan of leaving was so sensible, that Nevyn never felt the trouble coming. Later, of course,
he would curse himself for a fool.

In Lovyan's enormous suite, the noble lords who'd fought
with Rhodry were having a conference of sorts. For all that
Peredyr tried to calm them, they were furious at the insult.
Sligyn in particular limped around and swore that if he weren't
such a law-abiding man, he'd lead another rebellion then and
there. Rhodry perched on the windowsill and rather wished that
he would. Finally, when Dannyan and Jill came to serve the men
ale, Sligyn stopped his puffing and sank wearily into a chair.

"My lord?" Jill said, offering Sligyn a tankard.

"My thanks." Sligyn took one from the tray. "I'm cursed glad
you weren't there to listen to His Grace's little farce, Jill. Would
have ached your heart, eh?"

"That's an odd thing," Lovyan broke in. "I wonder why he
didn't have Jill summoned. He certainly had everyone else up
before him. I wouldn't have been surprised if he'd hauled in the
carters and spearmen."

"I admit I wondered about that, Your Grace," Jill said. "But
I'm glad he didn't."

"No one likes being called a liar to your face, eh?" Sligyn
paused for a soothing gulp of ale. "Cursed good thing old Nevyn
was there."

Jill came over to Rhodry and offered him the tray. When he

took one, she smiled at him in a way that soothed him considerably. The lords went on with their wrangling.

"We're leaving for home on the morrow," Rhodry said softly. "Nevyn's going to come with us, too. I've had all I can stand of my cursed brother for now."

"So have I, truly."

"What do you mean by that?"

"Naught. The way he treats you aches my heart, that's all."

With his free hand Rhodry caught her arm so hard that she nearly dropped the tray.

"What has Rhys been saying to you?" he hissed.

"I just happened to meet him in the corridor, that's all."

"Tell me the truth."

"Well, he bowed and said I was beautiful. Just a courtly sort of compliment."

All at once Rhodry realized that every person in the room had turned their way. He let Jill go and stood up to face his mother's level gaze.

"Rhodry," Lovyan said wearily. "Your brother was doubtless speaking to Jill only to annoy you. He's so torn to pieces about his wife that he's not going to prowl around some other woman."

"You'd best speak the truth, Mother."

"I do. I swear it to you."

"Then I believe you."

Much later, when it was time to go down to the great hall for dinner, Rhodry had a chance for a private word with Lovyan. She agreed wholeheartedly that he should leave on the morrow.

"The rest of the settlement lies between me and Rhys, anyway," she said. "You'll only have one more meal at his table, so please, Rhoddo, watch what you say tonight?"

"I will, Mother. I promise."

When he took his place at Rhys's left, Rhodry did his best to keep that promise by attending strictly to his food and speaking only when spoken to. Rhys never said one word to him since he was discussing the land settlements with Lovyan. Finally, when the mead was being served, Rhodry got up and bowed to his brother.

"If his grace will excuse me?" Rhodry said.

"By all means." Rhys paused, smiling. "By the way, brother,

you've found yourself quite a little mistress, haven't you? She seems to be as skilled with a sword as she is in other matters."

Through a red berserker's haze Rhodry heard Lovyan gasp.

"I'd rather His Grace left Jill out of this," Rhodry said.

"Indeed?" Rhys rose to face him. "You seem to have kept her quite in the middle of it. How does it feel to have a lass fight your battles for you?"

Rhodry's sword was half out of its scabbard before he realized what he was doing. The screams of the women brought him to his senses, and he froze, his hand still on the hilt, the blade still exposed, about sixteen inches of cold steel that was going to hang him. Rhys stepped back, and he was smiling in the fierce joy of victory.

"So," Rhys said levelly. "You'd draw on a gwerbret in his own hall, would you?"

Rhodry had the brief thought of killing him, but Lovyan threw herself in between them. The entire great hall was silent, staring. When Rhodry sheathed his sword, the slap of metal into leather seemed to ring to the ceiling.

"Rhys," Lovyan hissed. "You provoked that!"

"It's no affair of yours, Mother." Rhys caught her arm and shoved her aside. "Call your women to you and leave the hall. Go!"

Her head held high, Lovyan turned away just as the shouting broke out on the rider's side of the hall. Rhodry dodged Rhys and ran for his warband, who were rushing to meet him. Cursing and shoving, Rhys's men were on their feet and trying to surround the Clw Coc men, but there were only two men between Rhodry and Cullyn. The way the silver dagger looked at those two made them back off, and Rhodry was through to the solid comfort of his twenty-five loyal riders. Cullyn gave him a grim smile.

"Do we make a fight of it, my lord?" he said.

All around them the two hundred men of Rhys's warband went dead silent, hands on sword hilts as they waited for Rhodry's answer. Rhodry glanced around and saw that his men were as ready, that they were willing to die there with him in one last hopeless fight. All he had to do was say the word, and Rhys's great hall would run with blood. He could die clean, not hang like a horse thief. He wanted it so badly that it was like a fever, burning him, troubling his mind as slowly he let his hand drift to his sword hilt. But some of that blood would belong to Jill's beloved father, and to men who had no graver fault than the ill luck to be serving the Clw Coc. He wrenched his hand away.

"We don't," Rhodry said. "Stand aside and let them take me. Cullyn, serve my mother faithfully, will you?"

"I will, my lord, and I'll see you again."

The meaning hung there as clear as a noose—again, before they drag you out and hang you. Rhodry had one last thought of drawing and fighting, but he forced himself to stand still as his men drew back and the gwerbret's men grabbed him by the arms, hauled him forward, and disarmed him.

Nevyn was eating in the privacy of his chamber when Cullyn burst in to give him the news. Cullyn spoke briefly, quietly, his eyes so bland that Nevyn feared he would murder Rhys if all else failed. As he followed the captain back to Lovyan's suite, Nevyn was remembering Gweran the bard, who so long ago had played a similar trick himself. I tried to warn him, Nevyn thought, I told him that it would come round on him someday. Only then did Cullyn's news come real to him, that the man who carried Eldidd's Wyrd in his hands was going to hang on the morrow morn.

Lovyan's reception chamber was packed with angry lords, cursing Rhys and his provocations. Lovyan herself half reclined in a chair with Jill and Dannyan hovering behind her. When Nevyn came in, Lovyan looked his way with hopeless, tear-filled eyes. Jill ran to her father and buried her face in his chest.

"If Rhys hangs Rhodry," Sligyn announced, "he'll have a rebellion on his hands that will make the Delonderiel run red. I heard what he said to the lad. We all did, eh?"

"Just so," Peredyr said. "We'd best get the men and ride out tonight, before he traps us here."

"Hold your tongues!" Nevyn snapped. "Until we have just cause, let us not discuss rebellion, my lords. I intend to speak to the gwerbret myself, and I'm going to do it now."

They cheered him as if he were the captain and they the warband. When Nevyn left, Cullyn came along with him. Once they were in the privacy of the corridor, Cullyn turned to him.

"I've ridden outside the laws for so long that I don't remember them much," Cullyn said. "But doesn't a lord's captain have the right to beg for his lord's life?"

"He does." Nevyn was surprised that he hadn't remembered that himself, but then he realized that he'd been assuming that Cullyn would have been unwilling to do any such thing. "Here, would you truly go down on your knees for Rhodry?"

"I would, and I will, if you let me come with you."

Cullyn was looking at him in a weary grief. Only then did Nevyn realize that Cullyn loved Rhodry as much as Gerraent had loved Blaen before Brangwen came in between them. He realized another thing, too, that he respected this hard-bitten silver dagger who was willing to humble himself for those he loved. As palpably as if he'd thrown down a heavy-laden sack, Nevyn felt the chains of Wyrd break and set him free. Cullyn would never be Gerraent to him again, but merely himself—not even a man whom he'd forgiven for a fault, but a friend. For a moment, he wept. Cullyn laid a well-meant if misunderstanding hand on his shoulder.

"I feel like weeping over it, too," Cullyn said. "But we can pull him out of this rope if ever two men can."

And together, truly together like a pair of blood-sworn warriors, Nevyn and Cullyn went straight to Rhys's private chambers. When Nevyn pounded on the door, a page opened it with the news that his grace was receiving no visitors.

"Then tell him that no one is here," Nevyn said. "Or I'll send a dweomer-storm in ahead of me."

With a yelp the page flung the door wide and let them in. Rhys was seated in a heavy carved chair with the lady Donilla crouched on a footstool at his side. He rose to meet his uninvited guests, hooked his thumbs in his belt, and tossed his head back. Nevyn had to admire him for refusing to be intimidated by the best swordsman in all Deverry and a man who could burn his broch to the ground with a snap of his fingers.

"I suppose you've come to beg for Rhodry's life," Rhys said.

"We have, Your Grace," Nevyn said. "And both of us will go down on our knees if we have to."

Rhys considered them for a moment, then smiled, a cold twitch of his mouth.

"I have no intention of hanging my own brother," Rhys said. "I just want to make sure that the cursed young cub knows his place. All he has to do is beg my forgiveness in open malover, and that's an end to it."

Nevyn let out his breath in a long sigh of relief.

"Here, both of you," Rhys went on. "Did you truly think I'd break my mother's heart and see half of western Eldidd go into rebellion by hanging him?" When they hesitated, Rhys smiled again. "You did, didn't you?"

"Well, Your Grace," Nevyn said. "You've made your feelings about your kin quite clear in the past."

"Ah by the gods!" All at once, Rhys exploded, talking so fast that it was hard to understand him. "And why shouldn't I hate him? All my life all I've ever heard is Rhodry this and Rhodry that, Rhodry's the one with the honor, what a cursed shame that Rhodry wasn't born first so he could have the rhan." Rhys's face was a dangerous shade of scarlet. "To hear them talk you'd think I'd cheated the little turd out of his inheritance when all the time it was rightfully mine!"

With a fluid grace, Donilla rose and caught her husband's arm.

"My lord distresses himself," she said softly.

"So I do." Rhys paused to force himself under control. "My apologies, good sorcerer, and to you too, captain. Rest assured that your lord's life is safe from me."

"Your Grace, meaning no insult and all," Cullyn said, "but do I have your sworn word on that?"

"You do," Rhys said graciously. "No doubt you need it to reassure your men."

"I do, and my thanks, Your Grace, from the bottom of my heart."

Yet Cullyn looked so bored and bland that Nevyn wondered just what the captain was up to.

Since all matters of criminal justice in Aberwyn were under Rhys's jurisdiction, out in his ward stood a proper jail, a long stone building with a common room for local drunks and beggars, and a few tiny cells for more important prisoners. It was some comfort, Rhodry supposed, that he qualified for one of those, even though it was only about six feet square and reeked of urine and garbage. Under the tiny barred window was a heap of somewhat cleaner straw. Rhodry sat down there, wrapped his arms around his knees, and laid his head on them, too. He was shaking, he could not stop shaking, and it was from fear, not rage. He could face dying easily, but the shame of it ate at him, that he would be strung up in Rhys's ward like a common horse thief where every man could watch and mock him.

All his honor, all his hard-won glory in the recent war, all the respect of the men who were once his vassals—it was gone, stripped away from him by one thoughtless act. No bards would ever sing about Rhodry Maelwaedd without reminding their audience that here was a lord who'd died on the end of a rope. He wouldn't even have a proper grave among his ancestors. He was nothing without his honor, just a bit of mud on a road, not even a man at all. He bent all his will to the task, but he could not stop shaking. And what of Jill? At the thought of losing her this way, he wept, sobbing like a frightened child in the dark, until he realized that his tears were shaming him all the more. He unwrapped himself from his cramped position, wiped his face on his sleeve, then curled up again and went on shaking.

Rhodry had no idea of how long he'd sat there before he heard Cullyn's voice at the window, a soft "my lord?" Hurriedly he stood up and peered out. He could see Cullyn's face, looking in.

"Here I am," Rhodry said.

"Good. I've been whispering at every one of these cursed things. The guards won't let me in to talk with you."

"No doubt they're afraid you'll murder them."

"I was cursed tempted, my lord. Here, Rhys has no intentions of hanging you. Nevyn and I went to plead for your life, and he said ever so sweetly that he'd never break your mother's heart that way. He's staged all this to humiliate you and nothing more. All you have to do is beg his pardon in the malover, and he'll forgive you."

Rhodry felt a wave of hatred that burned in him worse than lust. He grabbed the bars over the window so hard that his hands hurt.

"Don't do anything stupid," Cullyn snapped. "Give the bastard what he wants, and we'll be on our way home."

Clinging to the bars, Rhodry rocked back and forth, throwing his weight against them as if he would pull them out.

"Rhodry!" Cullyn said. "Answer me!"

Rhodry went on rocking, shaking, tossing his head back and forth. He wanted to answer Cullyn, but he seemed to have forgotten how to speak. He heard other voices, then, guards yelling insults and orders. When he could at last make himself stand still, Cullyn was gone.

Rhodry sat down, but this time he sprawled out and leaned against the wall. Rhys's little trick had broken something in him, he realized, made him see a part of himself that he'd never wanted to see but that now he would never forget. It would haunt him his whole life, the night he trembled like a terrified child instead of facing his death like a man. All at once he fell asleep where he sat, and all night, he dreamt about Jill.

The guards woke him early and tossed him half a loaf of stale bread that he threw back in their faces. For over an hour he paced back and forth, barely thinking at all. At last the guards returned. They bound his hands behind his back with a leather thong and marched him out of the cell.

"Can't I have some clean clothes?" Rhodry said. "I stink from that straw."

"His Grace said to bring you along straightaway."

Of course, Rhodry thought to himself, of course—it was part of the humiliation, that he would have to kneel filthy and stinking at Rhys's feet. As they crossed the great hall, men looked his way with a pity that hurt worse than scorn. Up and around the staircase, through the last door, and there was Rhys, sitting across the room with the priests beside him and the scribes in attendance. The crowd of onlookers moved aside to let the guards shove him through. When they reached the table, one of the guards kicked Rhodry in the back of the knee and forced him to kneel.

"We have before us a grave charge," Rhys said. "This man drew cold steel upon a gwerbret in his own hall."

"That offense is punishable by hanging," said a priest.

The proceedings stopped to let a scribe scratch out the words. When Rhodry glanced around, he saw Jill standing off to one side, her arms folded across her chest. That she would see him humiliated this way was the last bitter thing he could bear. The scribe stopped writing.

"Well and good," Rhys said. "But I'm minded to show you mercy. I'll admit, brother, that I said hot and insulting words to you, admit it publicly and freely. Yet, the offense is a grave one."

The priest rose and began quoting from the laws.

"No man may draw upon the gwerbret," he intoned. "Why? Because the gwerbret is the very flesh of the law itself, and there must be no bloodshed in his hall. Why? Because no lord would sit in justice if he thought the condemned would revenge himself with steel." The priest sat down again.

"So some redress must I have," Rhys said. "If you kneel there and beg my pardon, pardon is what you'll have."

With a wrench of his body, Rhodry got to his feet.

"I won't," Rhodry said. "I'd rather hang."

Gasps, murmurs from the crowd—Rhodry even heard Jill yell at him to kneel—but Rhodry stared straight at Rhys.

"I'll give you another chance," Rhys said. "Kneel and beg."

"I won't."

"One last chance. Kneel and beg."

"I won't."

Rhys's mouth twitched in a smile of bloodlust. Rhodry refused to break. This time, by every god, he'd face his hanging like a man and redeem himself.

"You leave me no choice but to hang you," Rhys said.

Cullyn stepped out of the crowd and flung himself down to kneel before the gwerbret.

"Your Grace," Cullyn said. "Last night you gave me your sworn word that my lord's life was safe from you."

Rhys caught his breath with a little explosive puff. Cullyn's face was so impassive that anyone who knew him could see that he'd realized what was bound to happen and had laid up a weapon against it. Rhys knew it, too, judging from the way he swung his head to look at Cullyn with a remote, impersonal hatred.

"So I did," Rhys said. "And no Maelwaedd ever breaks his sworn word. Well and good, captain. I hereby commute your lord's sentence of hanging to exile." He turned back to Rhodry. "Henceforth you will be banished from all my lands, from the lands of all men loyal to me, and you will be stripped of all rank and position, all lands and properties, except for one horse, one dagger, two pieces of silver, and the clothes such as any man wears. Never use the name of Maelwaedd again, for the head of your clan has cast you out of it."

While the guards cut Rhodry's hands free, the chamber of

justice was utterly silent; then Lovyan sobbed in a gasping gulp of mourning that broke the silence like dweomer. The onlookers began whispering, then talking in a rising tide of noise that brought Rhys to his feet to yell them into silence.

"And do you have anything to say about your sentence?" Rhys said, but only because the laws required it, no doubt.

"I do," Rhodry said. "You've finally gotten what you wanted all along, haven't you? You'll have the taxes from the tierynrhyn when Mother dies. I hope you spend every cursed copper well, brother. May you choke on the food you buy with it."

Rhys's face turned scarlet. If it weren't for the table between them, he would have lunged forward, but Rhodry threw back his head and laughed.

"Someday the bards will sing about this," Rhodry said. "The gwerbret who was so hungry for silver that he threw his brother's life away."

The priests leapt up, grabbed Rhys by the arms, and hauled him back.

"Well and good, then," Rhys snarled. "You have till sunset to get off my lands. You'd best ride east cursed fast."

Cullyn left the sobbing Lovyan to her womenfolk and ran after Rhodry as the guards marched him away. He caught up with them down by the gates of the dun, just as the guards slammed Rhodry back against the stone wall and snarled at him to stay where he was while they fetched his horse. His berserk fit gone, Rhodry turned to Cullyn with numb eyes.

"My thanks and my apologies, captain," Rhodry said. "But cursed if I'd kneel."

"I wouldn't have either, my lord."

"Never call me my lord again."

"Well and good then, Rhodry."

Rhodry gave him a faint smile. Cullyn wondered if Rhodry were going to break and weep; he wouldn't have held it to his shame if he did.

"Now listen, lad," Cullyn said. "About ten miles this side of Abernaudd is a village and a tavern called the Gray Goat. Ride there, tell the owner you know me, and hole up there for a while. I'll send one of the lads to you with blankets and suchlike, and some more coin if I can get it."

"If Rhys finds out, he'll kill you for it."

"He won't find out. I've bested him once already, haven't I now?"

Rhodry tried to smile, a ghost of his old good humor that was painful to see.

"Try to think, lad," Cullyn said. "We don't have much time. What are you going to do? Ride to one of Rhys's rivals and beg for shelter?"

"I'd rather starve."

"So I thought. Then I'll give you my silver dagger. If anyone asks you why you have my device, just tell them I pledged you to the band."

Rhodry stared at him, tried to speak, then shook his head in a no, back and forth, over and over, wider and wider swings, as if he were desperately trying to deny everything that was happening to him. Cullyn grabbed him by the shoulders and shook him to make him stop.

"If you won't beg, what choice do you have?" Cullyn said. "Or are you going to do what I was too proud to do—beg for work in a tavern or stables?"

"I couldn't do that either, but—"

"Ah by the hells, don't you think I know how hard it is to take the cursed dagger? Don't you think I wept when I saw that it was all that was left to me, to sell my sword and have decent men spit when I walked into a room? But it's a way for a man to fight and gain a little glory while he survives, and you'll survive like I did. You're the first man I've ever met who's my match with a sword."

"Do you truly think I'm your match?"

"I do. Now do you want this dagger or not?"

Rhodry hesitated, then grinned and tossed his head with some of his old spirit kindling in his eyes.

"I do," Rhodry said, "and I'll wear it as proudly as I can."

"Good. We'll all be here working for your recall. Remember that when the long road turns harsh."

Since Jill's first duty was to Lovyan, she helped Dannyan get their lady up to her chambers, then worked her way free of the crowd of cursing lords. By the time she got down to the ward, there was no one by the gates but the pair of guards. When she approached them, they looked at her with a certain pity.

"Has Rhodry already ridden out?" Jill said.

"He has," said one guard. "You'd best get back to your people, my lady, and forget him as best you can."

As Jill walked back through the gardens, she stopped at the dragon fountain. She watched the endless rise and fall of the water and wondered what was so wrong with her, that she couldn't weep, even though Rhodry had ridden out without giving her one last kiss. There Cullyn found her, but even when he pulled her into his arms, her eyes stayed stubbornly dry.

"He left because he didn't want you to see him shamed," Cullyn said. "But he begged me to tell you that he'll love you forever."

"He's not shamed in my eyes, and he never will be."

Together they went back to the broch. In the great hall, servants and noble-born officials alike gossiped furiously; the men of Rhys's warband stood around and cursed Rhodry for daring to draw on their lord. Yet in all the bluster, there was a doubtful undertone, a wondering, hastily denied the moment it appeared, if maybe just maybe Rhodry had been right when he claimed that Rhys was greedy for the coin that the tierynrhyn would bring him. In time, Jill realized, that little doubt would grow until men all over Eldidd accepted it as the solemn truth. Thinking that, she smiled. Rhodry had won a victory that Rhys would never be able to forget.

The reception chamber of Lovyan's suite was empty. Jill could hear Nevyn and Dannyan talking with Lovyan in the bedchamber. Rhodry's noble allies, Cullyn told her, were packing up in a fury and planning on leaving court as fast as they could. Somewhat to Jill's surprise, Cullyn stayed with her. While she slouched miserably in a chair, he paced back and forth, stopping often to listen at the door that led to the corridor. Finally he smiled and opened it. His arms full of gear, Amyr slipped in like a thief.

"I got it all, even his sword," Amyr said. "You were right enough about silver making men see reason. I got his lordship's clothes and suchlike from the servants for only a few coppers, but it took all the coin Lord Sligyn gave me to bribe those cursed guards for the sword."

"I figured that," Cullyn said.

"Do we ride today, captain?"

"It depends on her grace." Cullyn shot an anxious glance at the closed door to the bedchamber. "If we do stay, I don't want brawling and suchlike tonight at table. Remember that."

"Then, captain, we'd best eat in the barracks."

Amyr dumped Rhodry's gear on a table, then hurried off before a servant wandered in and found him there. Cullyn picked up Rhodry's sword and drew it half out of the scabbard so that Jill could see the double device, the dragon of Aberwyn and the lion of his adopted clan, both engraved on the blade.

"Cursed if I'll let Rhys hang it up in his chamber of justice as a mark of Rhodry's shame," Cullyn said. "The thing is, how are we going to smuggle it out?"

"Easily, Da. I'll wear it out."

"What?"

"If I put on my old clothes, and Dann trims my hair short, and I ride with the warband with a sword in an old scabbard, who's going to notice?"

Cullyn laughed, his soft mutter of a chuckle.

"No one," he said. "And I don't mean the herbman, either. Well and good, my sweet. You're my daughter, sure enough."

Eventually Nevyn came out with the news that Lovyan was too exhausted to ride that day. When Cullyn pointed out that it would be best to get Rhodry's warband away from Rhys's men, Nevyn hastily agreed.

"I've got to get out of here myself," Nevyn said. "Soon enough everyone will remember that little show I put on in the malover. I'll have a word with Dannyan, and you get the men ready to ride before we have a brawl on our hands."

"I will," Cullyn said. "And Jill, change your clothes."

Since everyone in the dun had known Jill only as Rhodry's beautiful mistress, no one noticed the scruffy young silver dagger who rode out with the Clw Coc men. As they clattered along the north-running road out of Aberwyn, Jill turned in the saddle for a last glimpse of the silver and blue dragon pennant, flying high over the broch.

"And may I never see Rhys's ugly face again," she said.

"Once more," Amyr said. "When he has to stand there in full malover and announce Lord Rhodry's recall."

It was a beautiful fall day, as warm as summer, with a bluish haze hanging over the distant fields of ripe gold wheat. As they rode north, the River Gwyn sparkled as white as its name as it ran fast beside the road. Jill felt like singing. She wondered what was wrong with her, that she'd feel nothing but joy; then she realized what she should have known all along, from that first horrible moment when Rhodry got to his feet in the chamber of justice. The door to her cage was standing open—if she had the courage to fly.

As soon as he was outside the city, Rhodry kicked his horse to a canter for the first couple of miles, then let it slow to a brisk walk. As they headed east, he kept up a walk-trot pace, making all the speed he could while the horse was fresh. By law, an exile was under the gwerbret's special protection until he left the rhan, but that law had been broken more than once. Some of Rhys's men were likely to decide to curry favor from their lord by following and murdering the man who'd mocked him in his very chamber of justice. Every now and then, Rhodry turned in the saddle to look back. The only weapon he had was his half-elven eyesight, which could pick out from a long distance away the telltale plume of dust that his pursuers would raise on the road.

The road there ran straight while the sea coast curved in and out, sometimes close to the road, sometimes a good mile away. As he jogged along, Rhodry kept an eye out for places to hide if he had to, but mostly he saw small farms, whose owners would doubtless refuse shelter to a man pursued by the gwerbret's riders. Here and there, though, were stands of woodland. If he hid in one of them, his murderers would have to dismount to find him, and he'd have a chance to kill one with his dagger before the others cut him to shreds. His one hope was that no one would bother to follow, because letting him live in shame would be harsher than giving him a quick death on the road.

At times, he considered merely stopping and letting Rhys's men catch him, or perhaps turning his horse loose and then walking into the sea to drown. His shame rode with him, like a rider behind him, clutching at him with heavy arms. Occasionally he would glance at his brigga—old, shabby, and plain blue, spare clothes from Rhys's warband, as was his cloak. As a final humiliation, they'd stripped him of his plaid right there in the ward. Death seemed better than dragging out a miserable life in exile, a life that would end in a few years in some lord's petty feud or in a cheap tavern brawl. The only thing that kept him riding was knowing that Rhys would gloat over his death.

Toward noon, as the road climbed a small rise, Rhodry looked back and saw a small cloud of dust, far behind him. It was coming too fast to be ordinary travelers. He kicked his horse and galloped down the rise, then turned into a small lane that ran north between wheat fields. Puzzled farmers shouted as he raced past, riding aimlessly, turning down lanes and jogging across meadows. Whenever he looked back, he saw the plume of dust behind him. He was an easy mark to follow; his own horse was raising dust, and the farmers were no doubt telling the gwerbret's men exactly what they'd seen ride by. Alternately trotting and galloping, he kept riding until at last he saw a woodland that was more than just a stand of firewood. It seemed to stretch unbroken for miles, and he kicked a last burst of speed out of his tiring horse and galloped hard for it.

When he reached the edge, he could see that the forest was old, thick with brush and enormous oaks. He swung down and led his sweating horse in, crashing along through the underbrush. They were about a mile in when he heard distant yells behind him, at the edge of the forest as far as he could tell. He found a little dell, coaxed the frightened horse down and into tall shrubs, then left it there and slipped through the trees. He moved as silently as a deer, for the first time thankful for that elven blood that had driven him to spend long hours alone in the forest hunting. After some minutes, he heard men calling out behind him, and he froze between two low-growing trees.

"Must be his horse," came the distant voice.

"Leave it for now. He can't have gone far."

The voices were vaguely familiar—his brother's men, sure enough. He could hear them coming, fanning out, and there must have been at least four, judging from the jingle of scabbards and spurs. Suddenly Rhodry was sick to his heart of running like a hunted hare; he decided that it would be better to let them find him quick and get his dying over with. He started to step forward from cover—and tripped.

Or something tripped him; he was sure of it, because it was so sudden. As he went down, he felt hands grab him, a myriad tiny hands that lowered him to the ground without a sound. He was too frightened to shout or even think as a rain of leaves and twigs pattered down over him. The men were coming closer, clumsy and loud in the forest.

As Rhodry lay stone still, he heard another set of noises far past and to the right of where he was, noises that sounded exactly like a man running through the underbrush. With shouts and hunting calls, the gwerbret's men took off after them. A little hand patted Rhodry's cheek, and it seemed that he heard a giggle, just a little whisper of sound. He could hear the false hunt driving on, turning this way and that, the noises fading slowly as the men were led in circles, back and forth, but always farther away. At last the sound died away. A hundred little hands plucked and picked the leaves off him, then one grabbed his hand and pulled.

"You want me to get up?" Rhodry whispered.

The pull came again. Rhodry got to his feet and looked around. Here and there a branch bobbed or a cluster of leaves shivered in the perfectly windless air.

"You must be Wildfolk. Well, by every god, you have my heartfelt thanks."

Suddenly they were gone; he could somehow feel that he was alone. As he made his careful, silent way back to his horse, it occurred to him to wonder if Nevyn had sent the Wildfolk to protect him. He got his horse and led him out as fast as he could, because no horse could move quietly in the underbrush. Apparently his hunters were far away, because he reached the edge of the forest without hearing anyone coming after him.

Out in the meadow were four horses, tethered to a shrubby bush and carrying saddles marked with the silver dragon of Aberwyn. One of them suddenly stamped; another tossed its head in irritation; then all four of them were nickering, stamping, throwing up their heads in panic. As Rhodry mounted, he saw the knots that held their reins slip loose, untied by invisible fingers. The horses pranced, whinnied—and all at once they bolted, racing north in blind panic. Rhodry laughed aloud and called out a last thanks as he turned his horse and galloped south, back to the main road.

Nevyn was riding alone at the rear of the warband when two Wildfolk came back, popping into manifestation on his horse's neck and on his saddle peak. The obese yellow gnome was particularly pleased with himself, grinning from ear to ear and rubbing his fat little stomach. Nevyn slowed his horse and dropped even farther back, out of earshot of the men.

"Did you do what I told you to?" Nevyn said.

The yellow gnome nodded a yes and stretched its mouth in a soundless peal of laughter.

"And Rhodry's safe?"

This time the blue sprite nodded vigorously. She shaded her eyes with one hand and did a pantomime of someone peering and searching while her face registered sheer frustration.

"And you got the horses?"

They both nodded.

"Splendid, splendid. You have my thanks, and you come tell me if Rhodry's in danger again."

They disappeared in a swirl of breeze. As Nevyn rode back up to join the others, he allowed himself a smile for the thought of Rhys's men, walking the whole fifteen miles back to Aberwyn in soft riding boots. It's a good thing I decided to scry Rhodry out, he thought to himself, curse Rhys and his murdering bastards all!

"The warband must have reached your cousin's dun by now," Dannyan remarked.

"Just so," Lovyan said. "It was sensible of Cullyn to think of taking the men away. At least Rhodry's left me a good man to captain the band."

With a sigh, Lovyan sat up on the bed and ran her hands through her tangled hair. She had wept enough for one day; in spite of the pain she felt over Rhodry's exile, she had to go on, pick up the broken pieces of her plans, and make new ones.

"Dann, would you get a servant to fetch me hot water?" Lovyan said. "I'll have a wash and dress now. I must have a word with the gwerbret."

"So soon? Is my lady sure that's wise?"

"Not wise at all, but necessary."

Yet in the end, Rhys came to her. Lovyan had just finished dressing when a page appeared to ask if she would receive the gwerbret. Lovyan took a place by the window and drew herself up to full height as Rhys came in. He looked so timid that Lovyan suddenly remembered that there was something he very badly wanted from her.

"Mother, my apologies," Rhys said. "Truly, I never meant to send Rhodry away, or to hang him either. I was cursed glad when his captain reminded me of my promise. Don't you see? After he stood there and defied me in open malover, what could I do? Knuckle under and be shamed in every man's eyes?"

Lovyan wished that she could believe him. In time, perhaps, she would be able to make herself believe him.

"Mother, please," Rhys said. "I'd already shamed myself once by admitting my fault there in the malover."

"I have no doubt that His Grace perceived his choice that way. I have hopes that he will see a better choice at some future time."

"I suppose you want me to recall him."

"Does His Grace truly have to ask me that?"

With a toss of his head, Rhys began pacing back and forth. Lovyan considered refusing to make the marriage for Donilla unless Rhys recalled his brother, but she knew him too well. In angry pride, he would refuse the bargain, and then Donilla would suffer for her husband's fault.

"I wish to leave your court on the morrow," Lovyan said. "If Donilla's going to ride with us, you'll have to drink the bitter ale tomorrow and put her aside. It's only hurting both of you by delaying it, anyway."

"My thanks." Rhys turned to her in honest relief. "I was afraid that you'd—"

He could not quite bring himself to finish. She let the silence build until he looked down, shamed by her generosity.

"Mother, please?" he said. "Won't you accept my apology?"

"Mother? Never call me that again."

Rhys flinched as if she'd slapped him. She paused just long enough for him to feel the sting.

"Not, at least, until Rhodry's back home."

Rhys started to speak, then turned and strode out, slamming the door so hard that the silver oddments on the mantel rattled. Lovyan allowed herself a small smile.

"I'm a warrior's wife and a warrior's daughter," she said aloud. "And the war, Your Grace, has just begun."

The sun was low in the sky when Rhodry came to the stone marker slab on the border between the gwerbretrhynnau of

Aberwyn and Abernaudd. He paused his horse and looked at the dragon carved on the west side and the hippogriff rampant carved on the east, then rode the last few feet across. For all the good it was going to do him, he was safe. Rhys's men would never risk starting a war by pursuing him into another gwerbret's rhan and thus usurping that gwerbret's jurisdiction.

As the evening wind picked up from the sea, he shivered and pulled his plain blue cloak around his shoulders. His stomach was growling and knotting; he hadn't eaten since the ill-fated feast of the night before. But a few more miles brought him to a big farming village and the Gray Goat tavern, a thatched roundhouse with a stable out in back. As he dismounted, the taverner came out, a bulky blob of a man who reeked of garlic. He looked Rhodry over with a shrewd eye for the blazons on his shirt and the worn spot on his belt where a scabbard should have hung.

"I'll wager you got into a bit of trouble with the captain of your warband," the taverner said.

"What's it to you?"

"Naught. And a silver dagger in your belt, is there? Who pledged you to that?"

"Cullyn of Cerrmor."

"Oho!" The taverner gave him a wide grin, revealing stubs of front teeth. "Then come in and welcome. You can work around the place, like, to earn your keep while you figure out what you're going to do next. Here, lad, have you been flogged? My wife can give you a poultice or somewhat for your back."

"I haven't, but my thanks."

"Good, good. At least your lord was a merciful man, eh? Well, put your horse in the stables. My name's Gadd."

"And mine's Rhodry."

Just in time, he stopped himself from calling himself Lord Rhodry Maelwaedd. That he only had part of his name left gave him a cold feeling, but at the same time, he was relieved at Gadd's easy assumption that he was a disgraced rider. Outside of Rhys's gwerbretrhyn, no one but the noble lords would know who he was, and once he left Eldidd, few of them would recognize him either. Without his name and his plaid, he would only be another cursed silver dagger.

Apparently Gadd had a higher opinion of horses than he did of humans, because while the stable was clean and well tended,

in the tavern room the battered tables were slick with grease and
the straw on the floor smelled like kennel bedding. The stew
however, that Gadd put in front of Rhodry, was thick with meat
and turnips, and the bread that went with it was fresh-baked.
Rhodry gobbled it down while Gadd brought him a tankard of
dark ale and pointed out where the open barrel stood.

"Dip out what you want," Gadd said. "No doubt you'll be
drinking yourself blind tonight. Just do your puking out in the
stableyard."

Yet Rhodry stayed reasonably sober that night. As the place
filled up with local farmers and their wives, he saw them watching him with the hungry curiosity of those to whom a fallen tree
is a village event. Even though Gadd told everyone to leave him
alone, Rhodry felt as vulnerable as if he were walking naked
through city streets. He nursed a couple of tankards and huddled
by the warmth of the hearth while he wondered if Cullyn truly
would be able to get him some coin and a sword. Without a
weapon, he couldn't fight, silver dagger or no. The irony struck
him hard. Before, he'd been the great lord, able to load Cullyn
with honors; now, if he stayed alive, it would be only because
Cullyn had befriended him. Out on the long road, Cullyn's name
meant as much as Maelwaedd did in the world he'd irrevocably
left behind.

Rhodry had no hope at all that Rhys would ever recall him.
The more their mother pressured him, the more stubborn Rhys
would become—Rhodry was sure of it, and with good reason. If
he'd been the gwerbret and Rhys the exile, he never would have
relented. Locked in their hatred, he and Rhys shared a core
where they were twins, not merely brothers, and when they
reached that core, they understood each other better than anyone else in the world. No matter how much his kin schemed and
begged, Rhodry would live and die a silver dagger. He knew it
there, in that core.

Idly he pulled the dagger from his belt to look at Cullyn's
device. At his touch the blade ran with silvery light. He sheathed
it fast and glanced around, but fortunately no one had noticed.
You're worse than just an exile, Rhodry told himself, you're half
an elf, too. All at once he felt dizzy, just from seeing that he no
longer fit anywhere in his world, not among the Westfolk, not
among men, a half-breed with no clan, no rank, no place to call

home, nothing but the silver dagger to give him the identity he'd always taken for granted. He laid his hand on the dagger's hilt and understood why, scum of the kingdom that they were, silver daggers clung to their name and their band. Then he dipped himself out another tankard, drank it fast, and went out to the hayloft over the stable. He had never wanted anything as much as he wanted simply to go to sleep and wipe the world away.

Yet he had a restless night of it, because he was cold. He had no blankets, he was too proud to ask Gadd for some, and the chill autumn night had driven away the false summer warmth of the day. He wrapped himself in his cloak, burrowed into the straw like a dog in a kennel, but every time he drowsed off, he would wake cold and shivering. Finally he sat up to ease the cramps in his back and wondered if he could stand the stink of his saddle blanket. It was small, but it would be something.

Then he heard a horse trotting into the stableyard. It was cursed strange for anyone to travel at night, and he hoped that this traveler was Cullyn's messenger, sent to him as fast as possible to make sure that Rhys never knew. His mind mostly on warm blankets, Rhodry climbed down the ladder and hurried out into the moonlight. He recognized the horse before he did the rider, who was just dismounting. Sunrise tossed a weary head and nickered in greeting.

"There you are, my love," Jill said. "I've got your sword. Da and Lord Sligyn bribed the guards, and we nipped it out right under your stinking brother's nose."

In sheer disbelief, Rhodry stood stock-still. He was sure that he was having a desperate dream and nothing more until Jill walked over and laid her hands on his chest. They were solid and warm.

"Oh here," she said with a laugh. "Did you think I'd let you go into exile and not follow?"

"I did. Forgive me. You'd even leave your father for me?"

"I would." She went tense, and he could hear tears under her words. "But it's hard. I won't lie and say otherwise. But I had to go, and oh ye gods, Rhoddo, I love you so much."

Rhodry threw his arms around her and kissed her. Tight in each other's arms, they laughed and wept by turns until a grumbling Gadd ran out to see who was making all that noise in his stableyard.

Since Lord Petyn, the cousin who was sheltering Lovyan's men, paid direct fealty to Gwerbret Rhys, there was no doubt that it was awkward for him to have the Clw Coc warband under his roof. Just at dawn, Cullyn woke the men, got them fed, and told them to start saddling their horses so that they could meet their lady on the road and spare Petyn the further sight of them. He was just finishing with his own horse when a worried looking Nevyn jogged over to him.

"Cullyn, where's Jill? I can't find her anywhere."

"No doubt. She rode out last night to follow her Rhodry."

Nevyn froze, staring at him open-mouthed.

"You let her go?" the old man said at last.

"And what choice did I have? She could have sneaked off like a thief, but she paid me the honor of coming to me and telling me the truth." Afraid that he would weep, he busied himself with adjusting the bridle, which needed no adjustment. "Besides, the lad needs her. He's never ridden anywhere without a pack of servants. Do you think he could even tell green wood from dry if he wanted a fire?"

"Doubtless not, truly. You know, my friend, you're a cursed strong man."

"I'm not, just one who knows enough to send his weakness far away from him."

When he risked a look, he found the old man smiling in a friendly kind of disbelief. He was surprised at how much having Nevyn's honor meant to him.

"I've had one of the lads ready your horse," Cullyn said. "We'll be riding soon."

"My thanks, but would you mind if I rode after Jill? I want to say farewell to her."

"Mind? Not in the least, and besides, it's not for me to say anymore what she does or doesn't do."

Cullyn escorted Nevyn down to the gates and held the bridle of his horse while the old man swung into the saddle.

"Tell Lady Lovyan that I'll return to Dun Gwerbyn soon," Nevyn said. "If naught else, I have to claim my mule and my herbs."

"Done, then. I'll look forward to seeing you there."

"Will you now?" Nevyn shot him another smile. "And I'll

look forward to seeing you. Do you have any message for your silver dagger of a daughter?"

"Naught. I told her I love her last night. There's naught else to be said."

Cullyn leaned back against the wall and watched him ride off into the brightening dawn. He felt himself trembling like a beggar in the snow.

"Jill," he whispered. "Oh ye gods, Jill, Jill."

Yet now she would never learn of his shame, never have to know that he'd been tempted to dishonor them both. Cullyn was smiling as he walked back into the ward, where his men were waiting for him.

Since Nevyn often stayed in the Gray Goat when he was doctoring the local farmers, Gadd knew him well. When Nevyn rode up that evening, Gadd waddled out, all smiles and bows, to take his horse for him.

"What? No mule?" Gadd said. "You haven't given up herbcraft, have you?"

"I haven't, but I'm just here to look for someone—a young silver dagger and Cullyn of Cerrmor's lass. Which way did they ride when they left you?"

"Left me? Hah! They've been up in my hayloft all day, they have. Ah young lads! A man just doesn't have that kind of stamina when he gets on in years." Gadd shook his head mournfully. "It's a cursed good thing that custom's slow this time of year."

"I see your point, truly. Well, I'll wait in the tavern until they get hungry enough to come down."

Nevyn was just settling down to a bowl of Gadd's good stew when Jill walked into the smokey firelight of the tavern. As tense as a hunted deer, she paused just inside the door and watched him warily. Nevyn got up and went over to her.

"Have you come to fetch me back?" she said. "You'll have to ensorcel me or suchlike to do it. Maybe Rhodry's an exile and a dishonored man, but I'd follow him anywhere."

It stabbed like fire, remember the time when she'd said those same words about Prince Galrion. But she's no longer Brangwen, Nevyn reminded himself, and cursed if you're going to play Gerraent.

"I know you would, child," he said. "And it's your choice. I only wanted to bid you farewell, but would it ache your heart if our roads crossed again? I might find myself wandering the same way you wander at times."

"Ache my heart? What? Never! Here, what would ache my heart would be never seeing you again."

And she turned to him and hugged him. For a moment, he was as stiff as a swordblade with surprise; then he gave her a grandfatherly pat on the head.

"Then we'll meet again," he said. "I'll promise you that."

"Splendid."

Jill spoke so sincerely that Nevyn felt his hope flare. She liked him, she trusted him, and someday he would make her see where her true Wyrd lay. After all, by following Rhodry, she'd set herself free for the dweomer. No longer would she be caught and buried by the intrigues of a powerful court, and the dangers of an unsettled life would keep her latent talents alive. He thought of broaching the subject of her dweomer talent then and there, but the time was still unripe. She would only react with panic this soon after having seen dweomer gone mad and turned to evil ends. He would have to wait, but by letting her go, he was not losing but keeping her.

As they were sitting back down at Nevyn's table, Rhodry came in. With his sword at his side, he strode over as if he were still a lord, but Nevyn could see the change in his eyes, so haunted and weary that he seemed to have aged several years.

"I think I owe you my life," Rhodry said.

"Because of Rhys's men yesterday, you mean?" Nevyn said. "Well, truly, I had a hand in that. Huh. No doubt your brother would have cursed and wrung his hands when your body was found—at least in public."

"No doubt, the piss-proud drunken sot." Rhodry sat down next to Jill. "Well, good sir, it looks like Eldidd will have to work out her Wyrd with no help from me."

"Perhaps so. We'll have to see what the gods have in store."

While they ate, mostly in silence, Nevyn pondered over what the Great Ones might want done, now that the lad had been sent away from the province he was born to serve. He also wondered whether Rhodry were in danger. Now that he no longer held political power, he might well be of no further interest to the dark dweomer, but the hope seemed an idle one. Yet as he considered the problem, not one single dweomer warning came to him, only the generalized and normal fear that silver daggers, after all, often died young in battle. The lack of warnings made it plain that at least for now, Rhodry was in no danger from the masters of the black craft. It would be safe, then, for Nevyn to let them go on their way and to keep watch from a distance while he tried to influence Rhys to recall the exile.

"You know, Nevyn," Rhodry said finally, "I'm cursed lucky that Jill loves me so much, or I'd have died soon enough on the long road."

"Oh pig-bristles!" Jill broke in. "You're not a half-wit. You would have learned how to fend for yourself."

"That's not what I meant." Rhodry's voice went cold and flat. "In every battle I rode, I would have been volunteering for the point of the charge, or riding into the worst mob. There's more than one way for a man to end his exile."

It was a confession, quietly said. Jill grabbed his arm.

"But not now," he went on. "Not when I've got you to live for."

Jill flung her arms around his neck and kissed him. Nevyn sighed aloud at the irony of it, that by keeping Rhodry alive, Jill was already serving the dweomer, though she knew it not.

The next morning, Jill woke just at dawn and found Rhodry's arms tightly around her. Gray light filtered in through the cracks in the stable walls, and the sound of rain drummed on the roof. She rested her head on Rhodry's chest and listened to the rain song mingling with his steady breathing, while she smiled at herself for finding Gadd's hayloft more to her taste than her feather bed back in Dun Gwerbyn. Then she thought of Cullyn, and she had to close her eyes tight to force back her tears. Da, Da, I'm sorry, she thought, but you knew I had to go. At least she'd left him in a safe place, where he'd never have to sleep in the rain again, no matter what happened to her. Bitterly she wondered if she would ever see him again, but she had made her choice, and she would follow Rhodry forever if the gods allowed.

And the gods could do what they wanted, she decided. She'd always lived a single day at a time, simply because she'd never had any choice but to live that way. The long road stretches into mist, Cullyn always said, and no one can see the end of it. She had Rhodry and her freedom to ride. As she fell back to sleep, she decided that they would do splendidly for now.

Far across the Southern Sea, deep in the hill country of Bardek, stood an isolated villa. There, in an upstairs room with dark and perverted sigils upon the walls, a man sat working at a table littered with scrolls and parchments. He was grossly fat, as saggy and wrinkled as a torn leather ball, and only a few wisps of white hair clung to his dark-skinned skull. Whenever he glanced up, his eyelids drooped uncontrollably, half-covering his brown eyes. He had immersed himself so thoroughly and so long in the foul craft of the dark dweomer that he no longer had a name. He was simply the Old One.

He leaned back in his chair and held up a parchment. Scribed upon it was the horoscope of the High King of Deverry, and what the Old One saw there boded His Highness ill.

"If we succeed in this," he said, and his voice was like a pair of dead twigs rubbed together, "the whole cursed barbarian kingdom will be plunged into chaos."

And he laughed aloud at the very thought . . .

Watch for Katharine Kerr's next novel, *Darkspell*, coming from Grafton Books.